CHILLING ADVENTURES OF SABRINA®

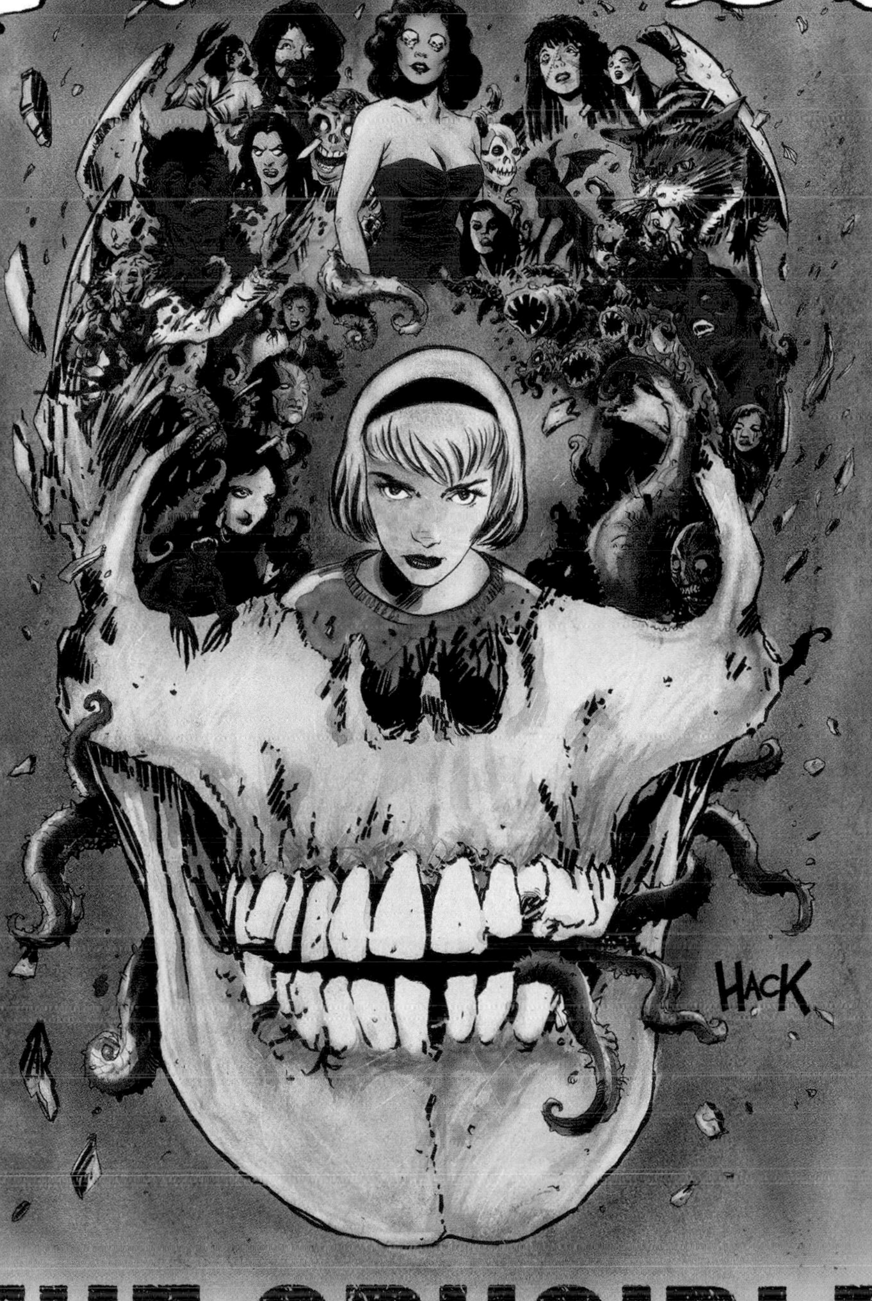
HACK

"THE CRUCIBLE"

STORY BY
ROBERTO AGUIRRE-SACASA

ARTWORK BY
ROBERT HACK

LETTERING BY
JACK MORELLI

PUBLISHER
JON GOLDWATER

INTRODUCTION

BY ROBERTO AGUIRRE-SACASA

Once again, it seems a mad fantasy that this book in your hands exists at all.

After the surprise success of *Afterlife with Archie*, I pitched Archie Comics' CEO and Publisher (and, by now, good friend) Jon Goldwater a companion horror series about Sabrina, the teenage witch. "If *Afterlife* was my love letter to Alan Moore's *Swamp Thing*," I said, "Sabrina would be a love letter to *Sandman*." Jon greenlit it immediately.

If *Afterlife* was about Lovecraft and zombies and body-horror, *Sabrina* would be more psychological, a bit more subtle (but only a bit), a bit more sexual (as stories about witches often are). There would be less humor than *Afterlife*, which strives for a Sam Raimi-vibe; this would be more like *Rosemary's Baby* and *The Exorcist* and *The Omen* and Arthur Miller's *The Crucible* (hence this volume's subtitle). A dark, occult coming of age story. To further set the book apart from *Afterlife* (which featured Sabrina in a minor role), *Chilling Adventures of Sabrina* (which takes its title from an old Archie horror anthology book, *Chilling Adventures of Sorcery*), would be a period piece, set in the 1960s. Not just when all those great satanic movies started to come out, but also, approximately, when the original Sabrina stories were first published.

With all but one of the pieces in place, we were *almost* ready to go. We just needed to find an artist as good as Francesco Francavilla (who draws *Afterlife with Archie*) to draw *Sabrina*. Easy, right? Robert Hack had drawn a variant cover for the first issue of *Afterlife*. And some retro-looking variants for Archie's magazine series, *Life with Archie*. I reached out to Robert and asked if he'd ever done interiors on a comic book. He hadn't, so this was a leap of faith. At first, Robert was only supposed to draw and ink *Sabrina*, not color it. But we went out to many wonderful colorists...and none of them seemed right. We even flirted, for a few days, with publishing the book in black-and-white. Then I went back to Robert and asked if he ever colored his own work. "Yes," he said, "but only single images, nothing on this scale." Another leap of faith. Just as Francesco handles all of the art chores on *Afterlife*, Robert Hack does on *Chilling Adventures*. Their styles couldn't be more different, but they are—in my humble opinion—the two most gorgeous books being published today.

Now let's talk lettering. Jack Morelli letters both *Afterlife* and *Sabrina*. He is the secret ingredient that links these two books across space and time. He is, now and forever, Archie Horror's letterer—an invaluable part of the team. I want Jack to letter everything I write—whattya say, Jack?

What else? Oh, yes, we *love* this book. It isn't easy to make—they never are—but we want it to go on and on and on. All Hail, Sabrina Spellman, Queen of the Church of Night!

Roberto Aguirre-Sacasa

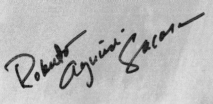

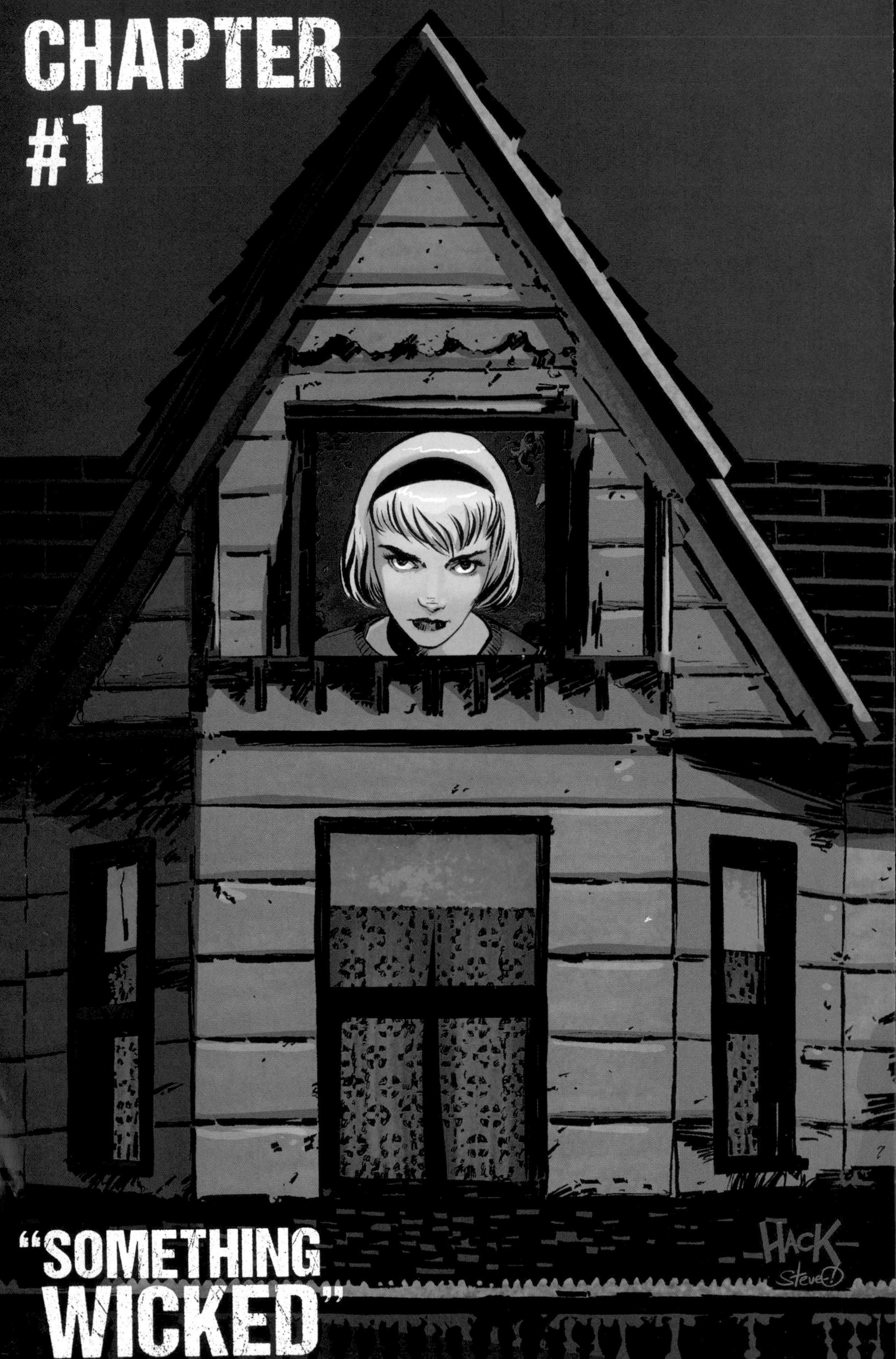
CHAPTER
#1
"SOMETHING
WICKED"
HACK

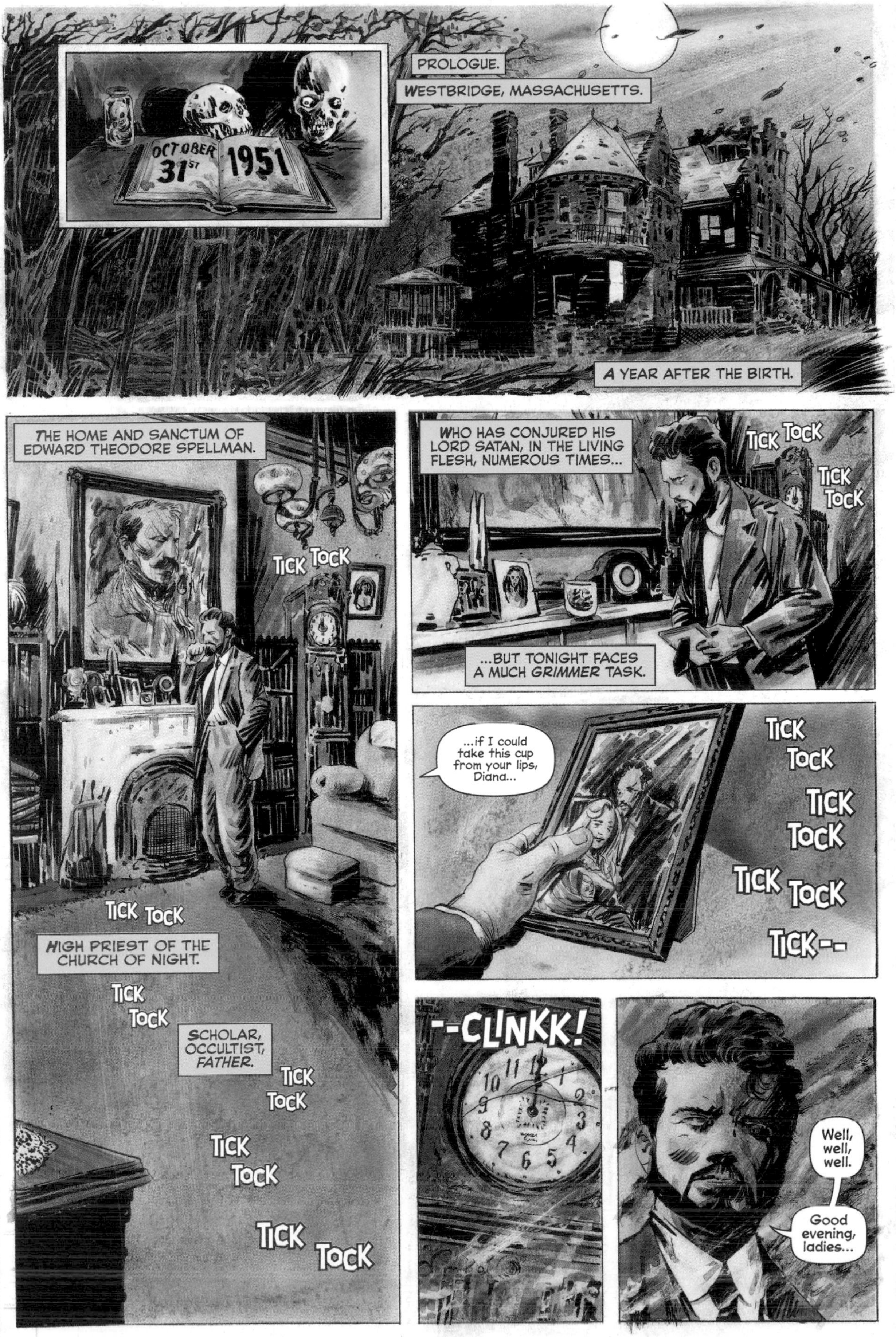

OCTOBER 31ST 1951
PROLOGUE.
WESTBRIDGE, MASSACHUSETTS.
A YEAR AFTER THE BIRTH.
THE HOME AND SANCTUM OF EDWARD THEODORE SPELLMAN.
TICK TOCK
TICK TOCK
HIGH PRIEST OF THE CHURCH OF NIGHT.
TICK TOCK
SCHOLAR, OCCULTIST, FATHER.
TICK TOCK
TICK TOCK
TICK TOCK
WHO HAS CONJURED HIS LORD SATAN, IN THE LIVING FLESH, NUMEROUS TIMES...
TICK TOCK
TICK TOCK
...BUT TONIGHT FACES A MUCH GRIMMER TASK.
...if I could take this cup from your lips, Diana...
TICK TOCK
TICK TOCK
TICK TOCK
TICK--
--CLINKK!
Well, well, well.
Good evening, ladies...

...you do know how to make an entrance.

Welcome, Sisters, and remember: *We stand in His shadow.*

Happy Halloween, Edward--

--yes, Edward, *hallowed* Samhain.

Is our little one ready to go?

She's upstairs, in the nursery. Her mother's saying goodbye.

You stay *right* where you are, Zelda...

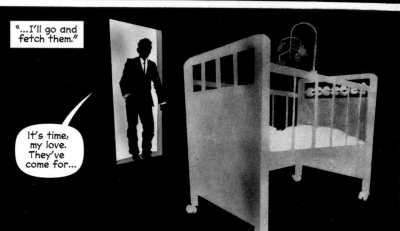

"...I'll go and fetch them."

It's time, my love. They've come for...

EDWARD SPELLMAN MARRIED A WILLFUL, *MORTAL* WOMAN...

HIS SISTERS, EVEN HILDA, WARNED HIM AGAINST BREAKING WITCH-LAW...

OF COURSE, HE'S ALWAYS BEEN WILLFUL HIMSELF.

Oh, Diana...

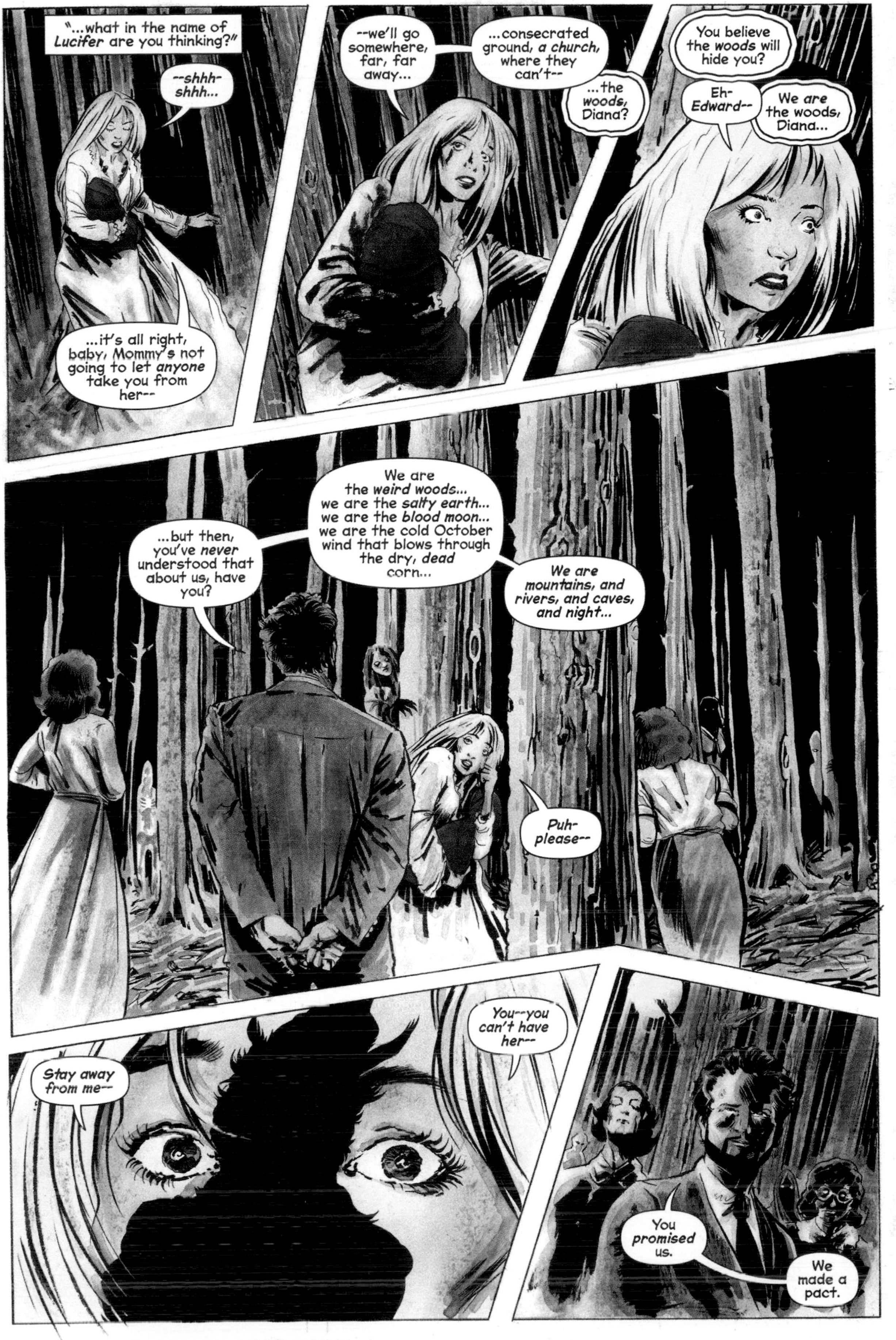
"...what in the name of *Lucifer* are you thinking?"
--shhh-shhh...
...it's all right, baby, Mommy's not going to let *anyone* take you from her--
--we'll go somewhere, far, far away...
...consecrated ground, *a church*, where they can't--
...the woods, Diana?
You believe the *woods* will hide you?
Eh-*Edward*--
We *are* the woods, Diana...
...but then, you've *never* understood that about us, have you?
We are the *weird woods*... we are the *salty earth*... we are the *blood moon*... we are the cold October wind that blows through the dry, *dead* corn...
We are mountains, and rivers, and caves, and night...
Puh-please--
Stay away from me--
You--you can't have her--
You promised us.
We made a pact.

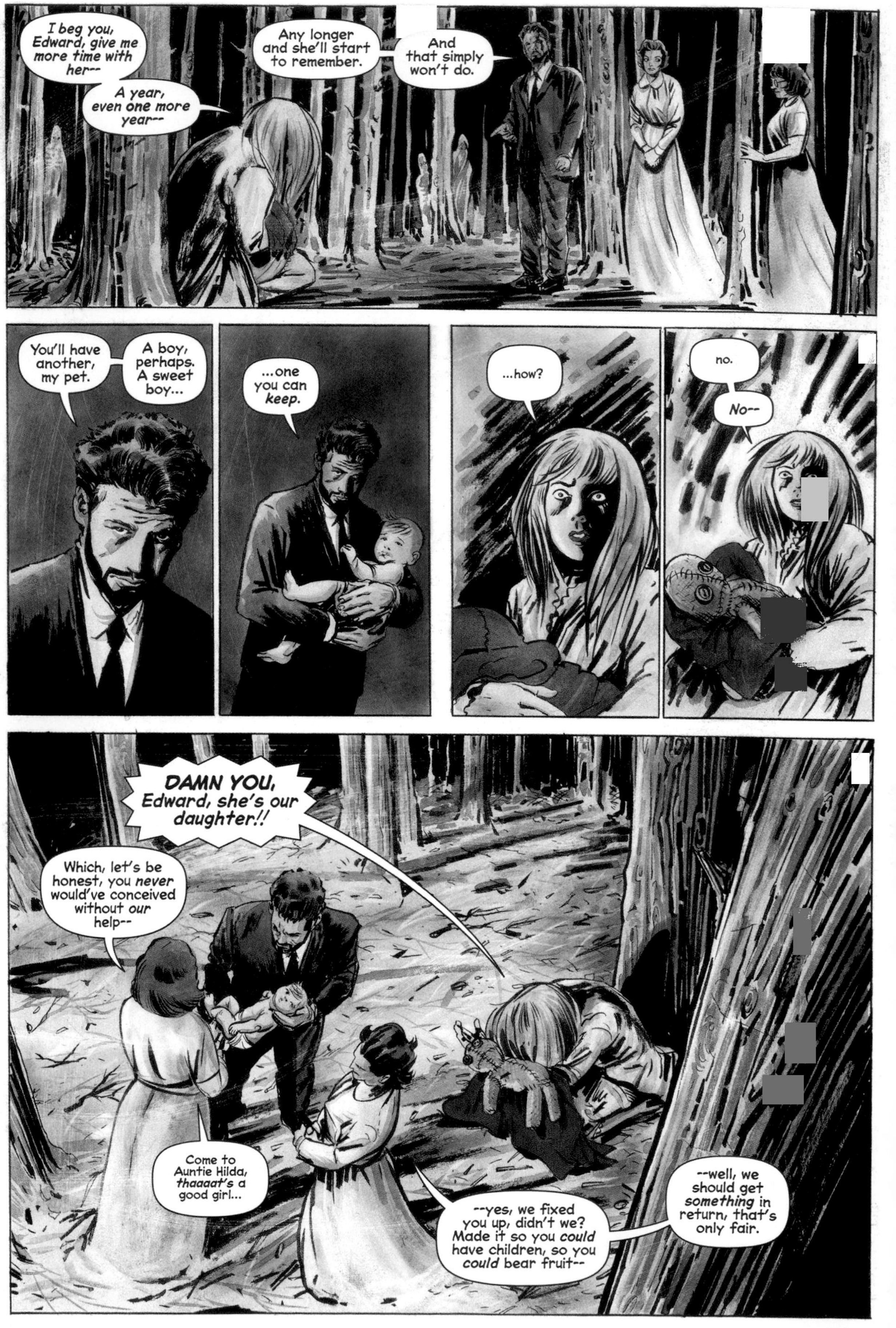
I beg you, Edward, give me more time with her--
A year, even one more year--
Any longer and she'll start to remember.
And that simply won't do.
You'll have another, my pet.
A boy, perhaps. A sweet boy...
...one you can *keep.*
...how?
no.
No--
DAMN YOU, Edward, she's our daughter!!
Which, let's be honest, you *never* would've conceived without *our* help--
Come to Auntie Hilda, *thaaaat's* a good girl...
--yes, we fixed you up, didn't we? Made it so you *could* have children, so you *could* bear fruit--
--well, we should get *something* in return, that's only fair.

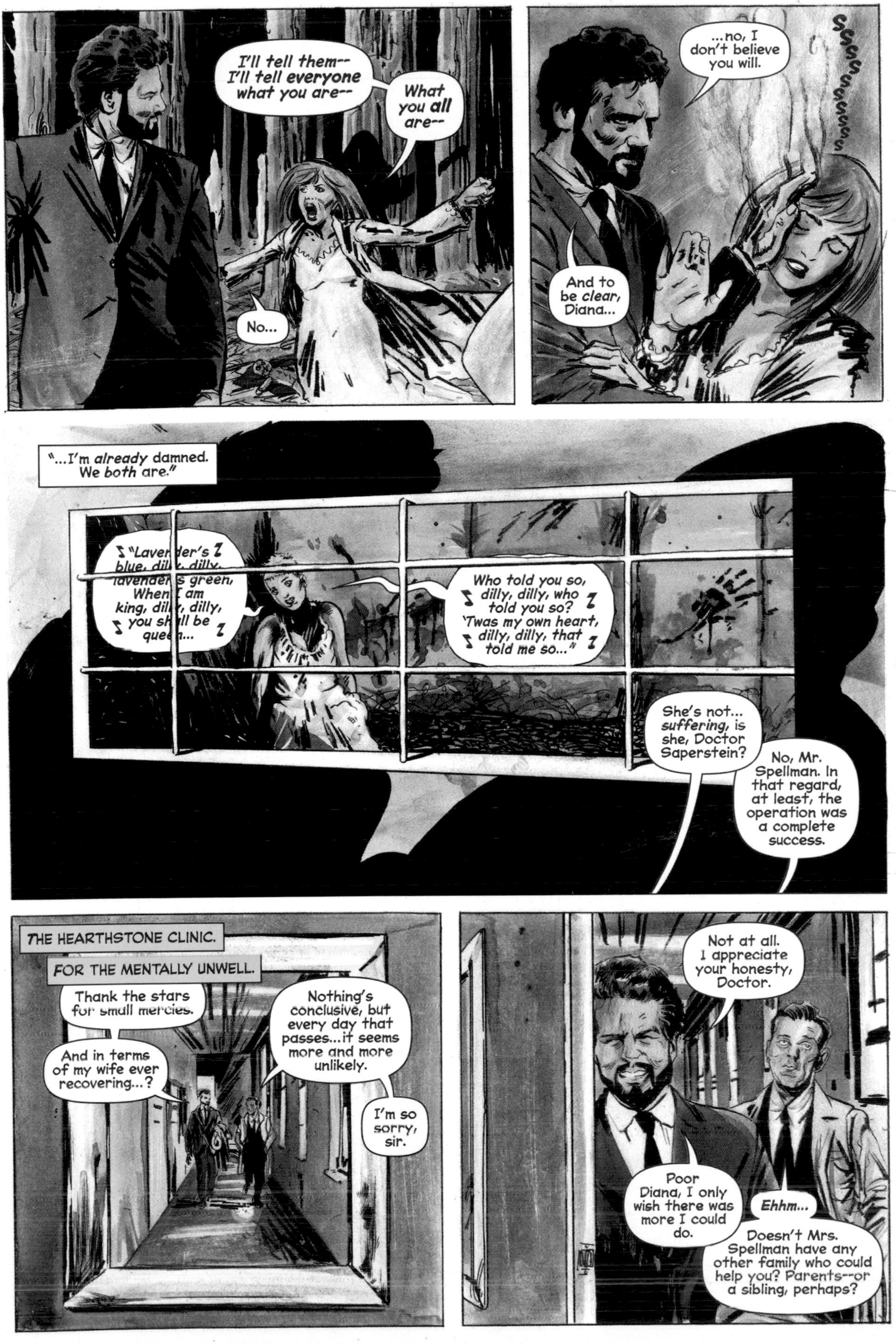
I'll tell them--
I'll tell everyone what you are--
What you all are--
No...
...no, I don't believe you will.
SSSSSSSSSSSS
And to be clear, Diana...
"...I'm already damned. We both are."
"Lavender's blue, dilly, dilly, lavender's green, When I am king, dilly, dilly, you shall be queen...
Who told you so, dilly, dilly, who told you so? 'Twas my own heart, dilly, dilly, that told me so..."
She's not... suffering, is she, Doctor Saperstein?
No, Mr. Spellman. In that regard, at least, the operation was a complete success.
THE HEARTHSTONE CLINIC.
FOR THE MENTALLY UNWELL.
Thank the stars for small mercies.
And in terms of my wife ever recovering...?
Nothing's conclusive, but every day that passes...it seems more and more unlikely.
I'm so sorry, sir.
Not at all. I appreciate your honesty, Doctor.
Poor Diana, I only wish there was more I could do.
Ehhm...
Doesn't Mrs. Spellman have any other family who could help you? Parents--or a sibling, perhaps?

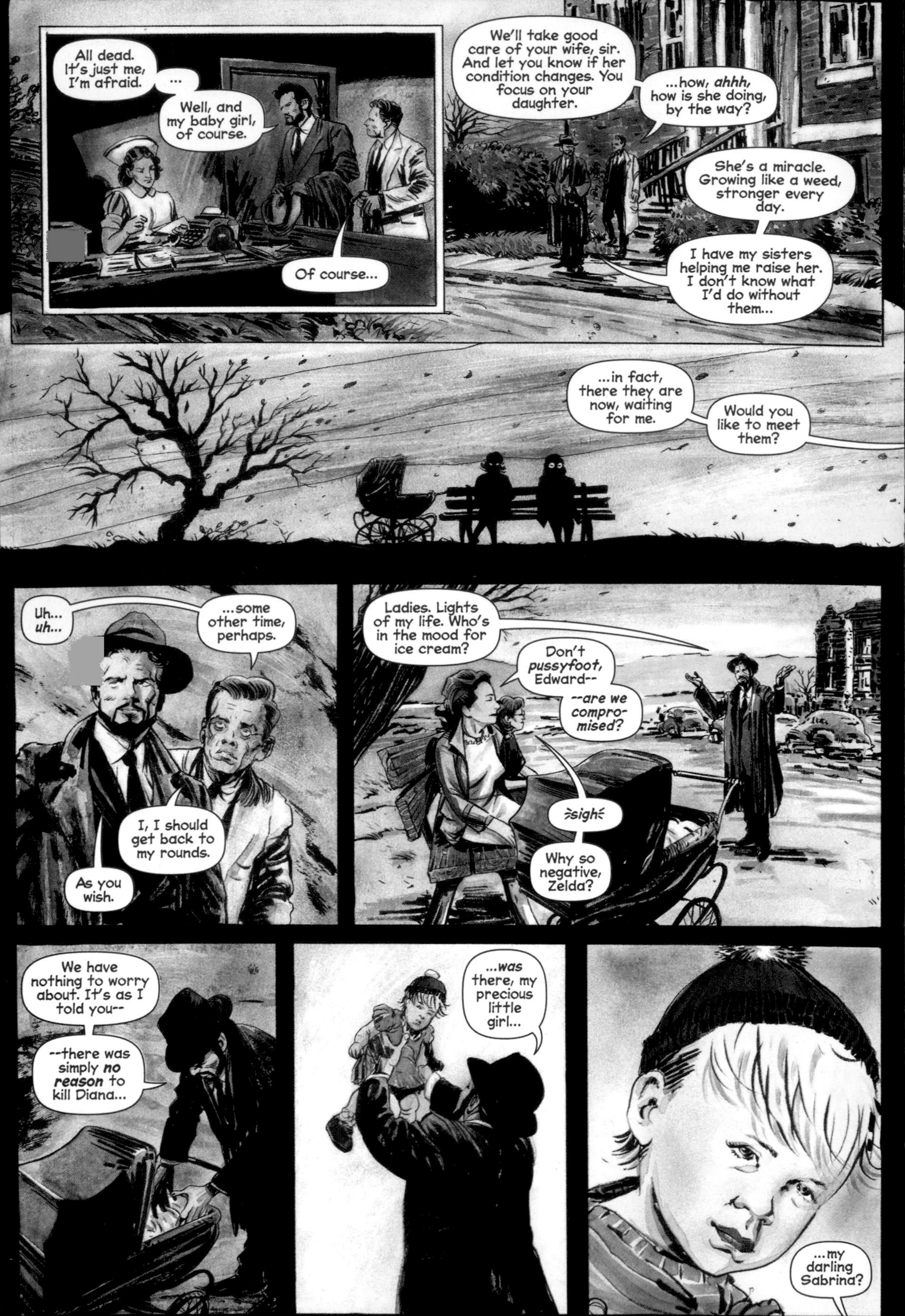
All dead. It's just me, I'm afraid.
...
Well, and my baby girl, of course.
Of course...
We'll take good care of your wife, sir. And let you know if her condition changes. You focus on your daughter.
...how, *ahhh*, how is she doing, by the way?
She's a miracle. Growing like a weed, stronger every day.
I have my sisters helping me raise her. I don't know what I'd do without them...
...in fact, there they are now, waiting for me.
Would you like to meet them?
Uh... *uh*...
...some other time, perhaps.
I, I should get back to my rounds.
As you wish.
Ladies. Lights of my life. Who's in the mood for ice cream?
Don't *pussyfoot*, Edward--
--*are we compromised*?
sigh
Why so negative, Zelda?
We have nothing to worry about. It's as I told you--
--there was simply ***no reason*** to kill Diana...
...*was* there, my precious little girl...
...my darling Sabrina?

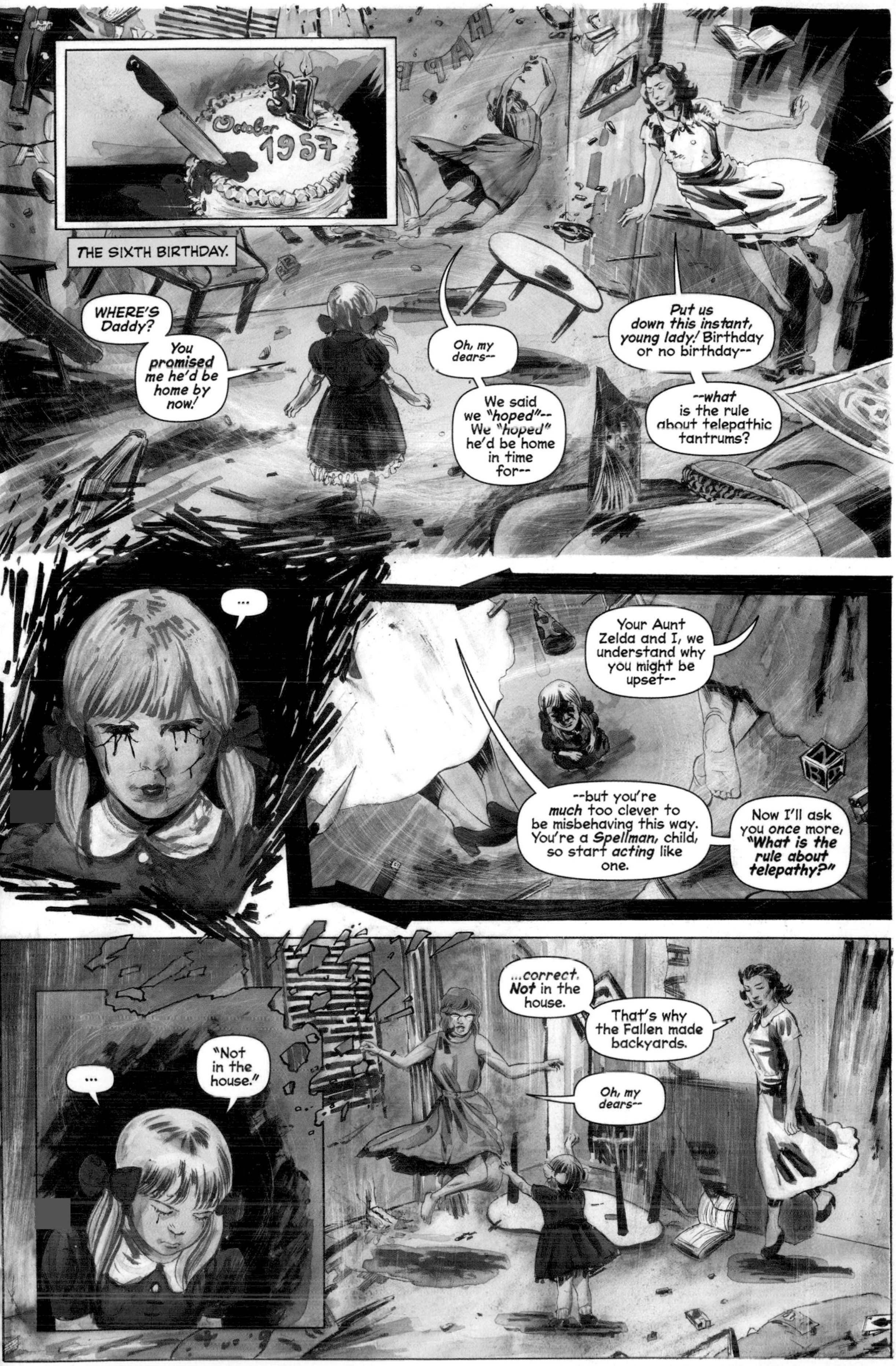

October
1957
31
THE SIXTH BIRTHDAY.
WHERE'S Daddy?
You promised me he'd be home by now!
Oh, my dears--
We said we "hoped"-- We "hoped" he'd be home in time for--
Put us down this instant, young lady! Birthday or no birthday--
--what is the rule about telepathic tantrums?
...
Your Aunt Zelda and I, we understand why you might be upset--
--but you're much too clever to be misbehaving this way. You're a Spellman, child, so start acting like one.
Now I'll ask you once more, "What is the rule about telepathy?"
...
"Not in the house."
...correct. Not in the house.
That's why the Fallen made backyards.
Oh, my dears--

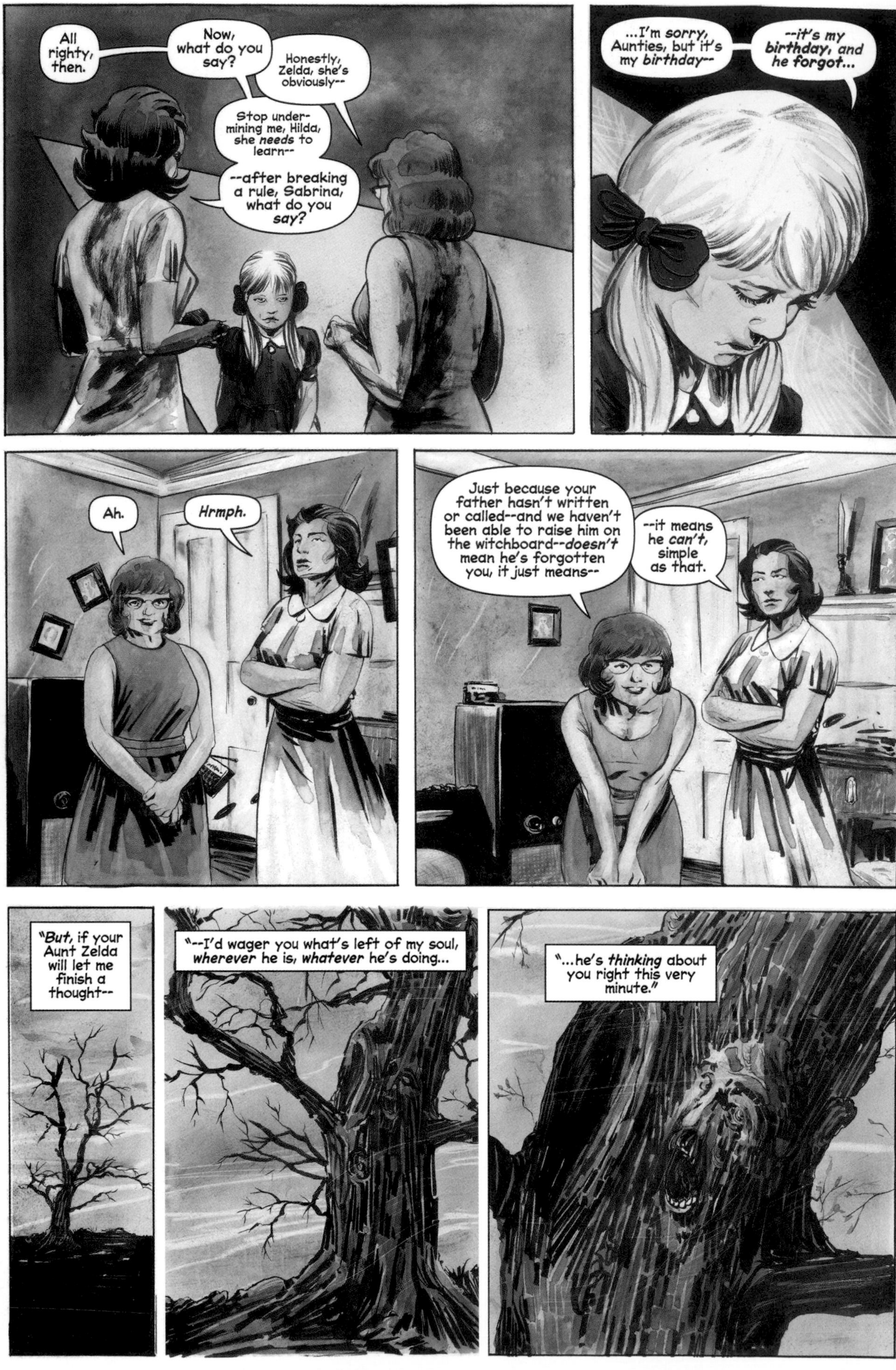
All righty, then.
Now, what do you say?
Honestly, Zelda, she's obviously--
Stop under-mining me, Hilda, she *needs* to learn--
--after breaking a rule, Sabrina, what do you *say?*
...I'm *sorry,* Aunties, but it's my *birthday*--
--*it's my birthday, and he forgot...*
Ah.
Hrmph.
Just because your father hasn't written or called--and we haven't been able to raise him on the witchboard--*doesn't* mean he's forgotten you, it just means--
--it means he *can't,* simple as that.
"*But,* if your Aunt Zelda will let me finish a thought--
"--I'd wager you what's left of my soul, *wherever* he is, *whatever* he's doing...
"...he's *thinking* about you right this very minute."

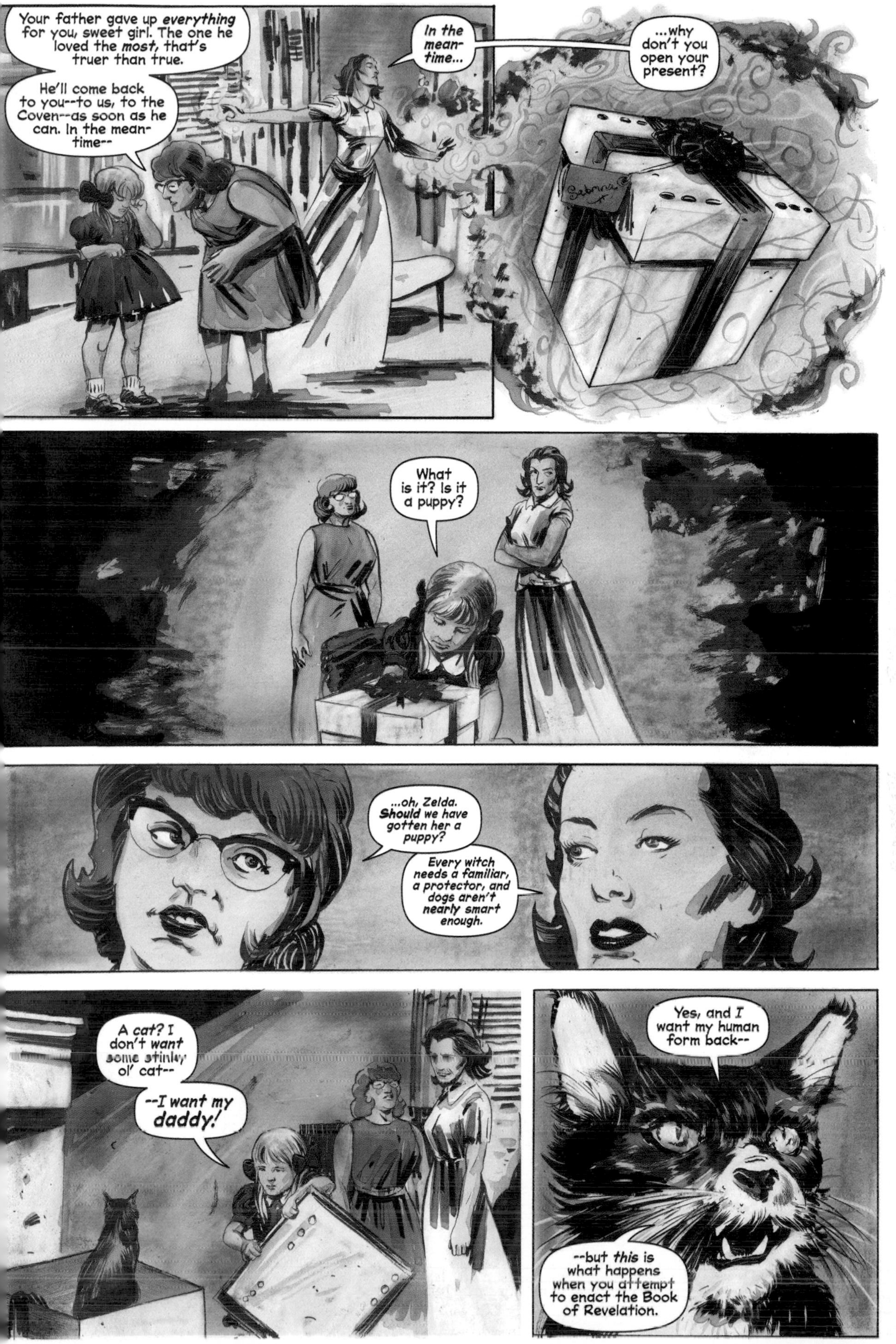

Your father gave up *everything* for you, sweet girl. The one he loved the *most*, that's truer than true.
He'll come back to you--to us, to the Coven--as soon as he can. In the mean-time--
In the mean-time...
...why don't you open your present?
Sabrina
What is it? Is it a puppy?
...oh, Zelda. ***Should*** *we have gotten her a puppy?*
Every witch needs a familiar, a protector, and dogs aren't nearly smart enough.
A *cat?* I don't *want* some stinky ol' cat--
--*I want my* ***daddy!***
Yes, and *I* want my human form back--
--but *this* is what happens when you attempt to enact the Book of Revelation.

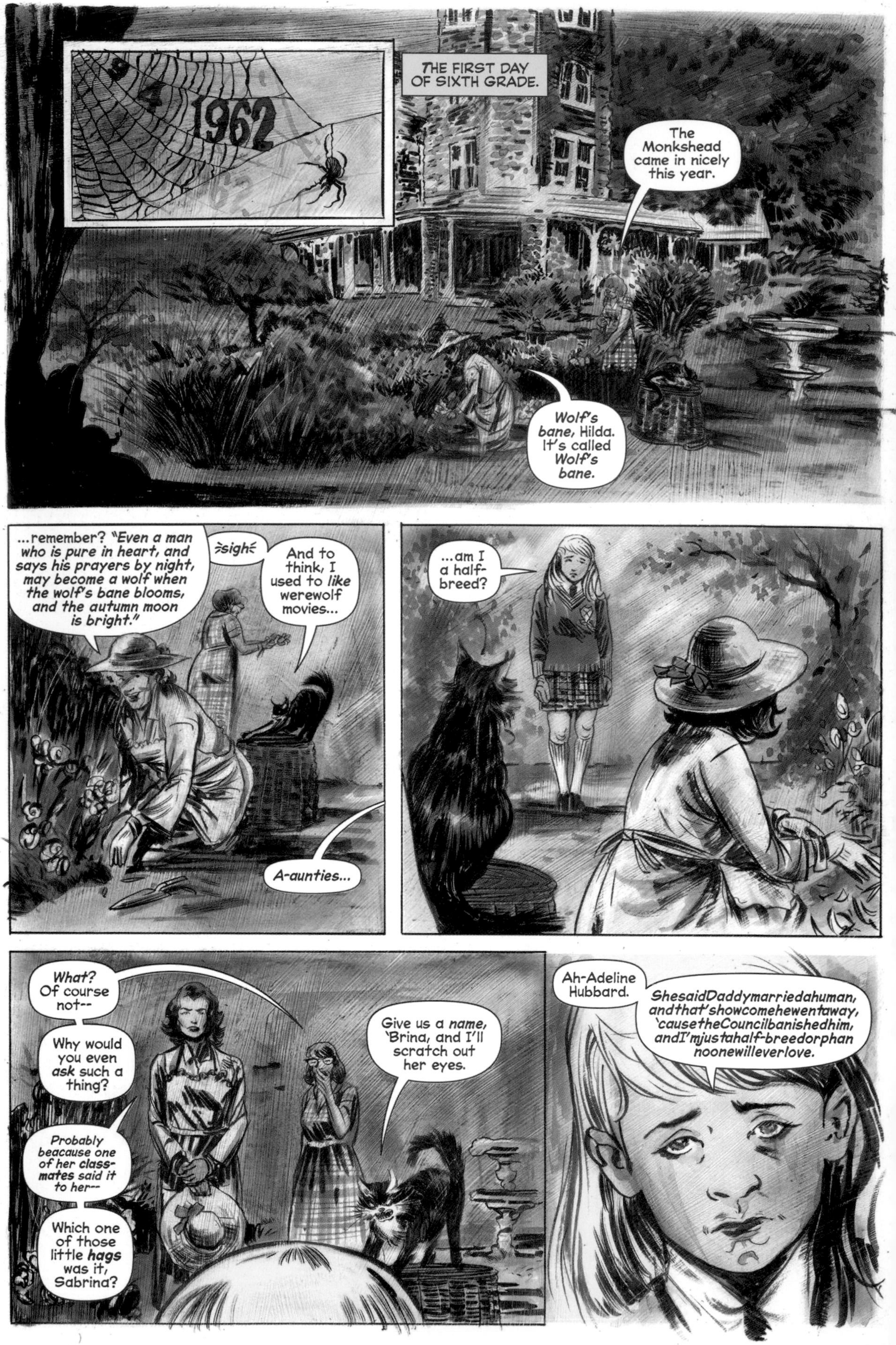
9 4 1962
THE FIRST DAY OF SIXTH GRADE.
The Monkshead came in nicely this year.
Wolf's bane, Hilda. It's called Wolf's bane.
...remember? "Even a man who is pure in heart, and says his prayers by night, may become a wolf when the wolf's bane blooms, and the autumn moon is bright."
sigh
And to think, I used to like werewolf movies...
A-aunties...
...am I a half-breed?
What? Of course not--
Why would you even ask such a thing?
Probably beacause one of her classmates said it to her--
Which one of those little hags was it, Sabrina?
Give us a name, 'Brina, and I'll scratch out her eyes.
Ah-Adeline Hubbard.
ShesaidDaddymarriedahuman, andthat'showcomehewentaway, 'causetheCouncilbanishedhim, andI'mjustahalf-breedorphan noonewilleverlove.

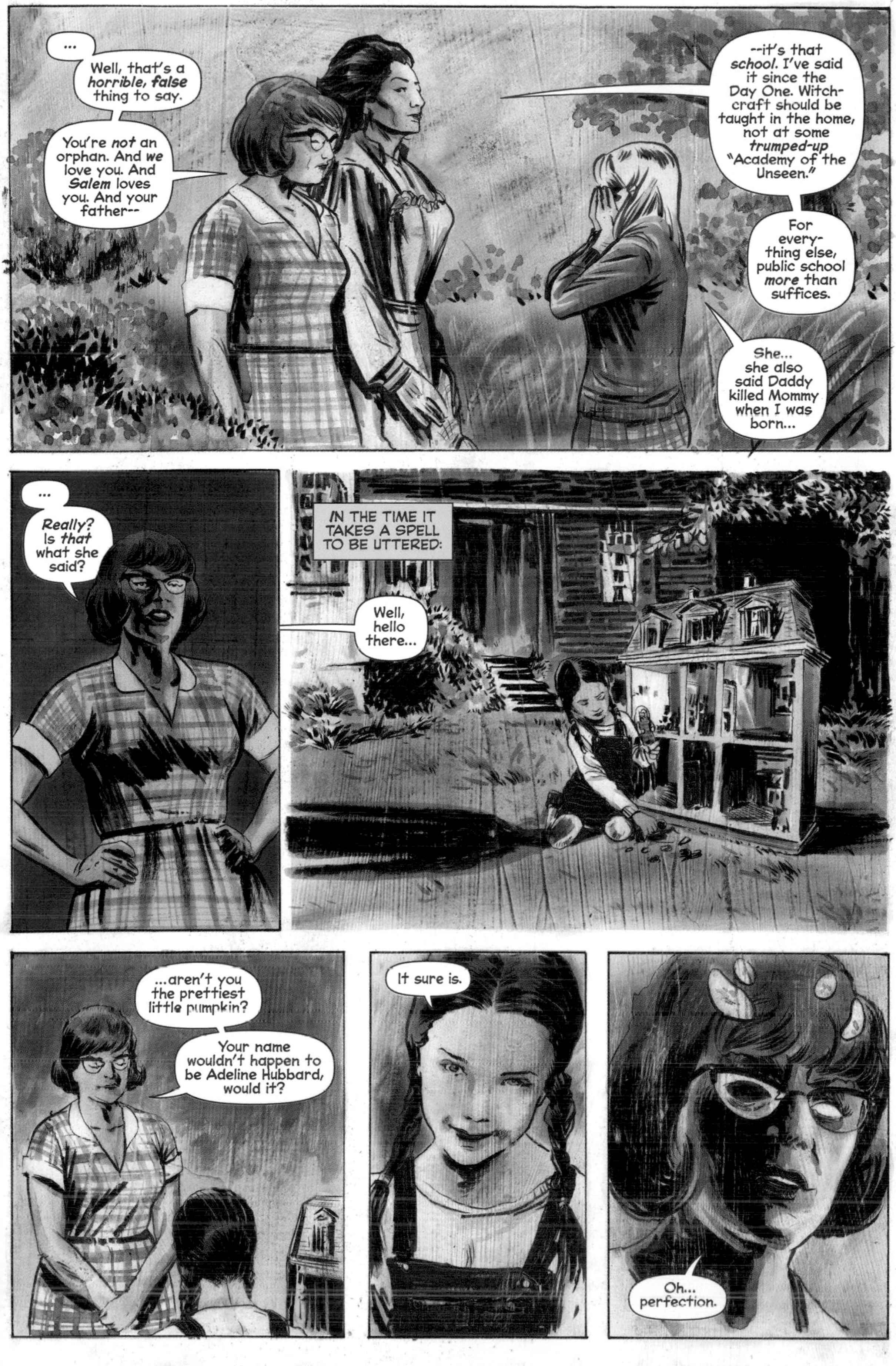
...
Well, that's a *horrible, false* thing to say.
You're *not* an orphan. And *we* love you. And *Salem* loves you. And your father--
--it's that *school*. I've said it since the Day One. Witch-craft should be taught in the home, not at some *trumped-up* "Academy of the Unseen."
For every-thing else, public school *more* than suffices.
She... she also said Daddy killed Mommy when I was born...
...
Really? Is *that* what she said?
IN THE TIME IT TAKES A SPELL TO BE UTTERED:
Well, hello there...
...aren't you the prettiest little pumpkin?
Your name wouldn't happen to be Adeline Hubbard, would it?
It sure is.
Oh... perfection.

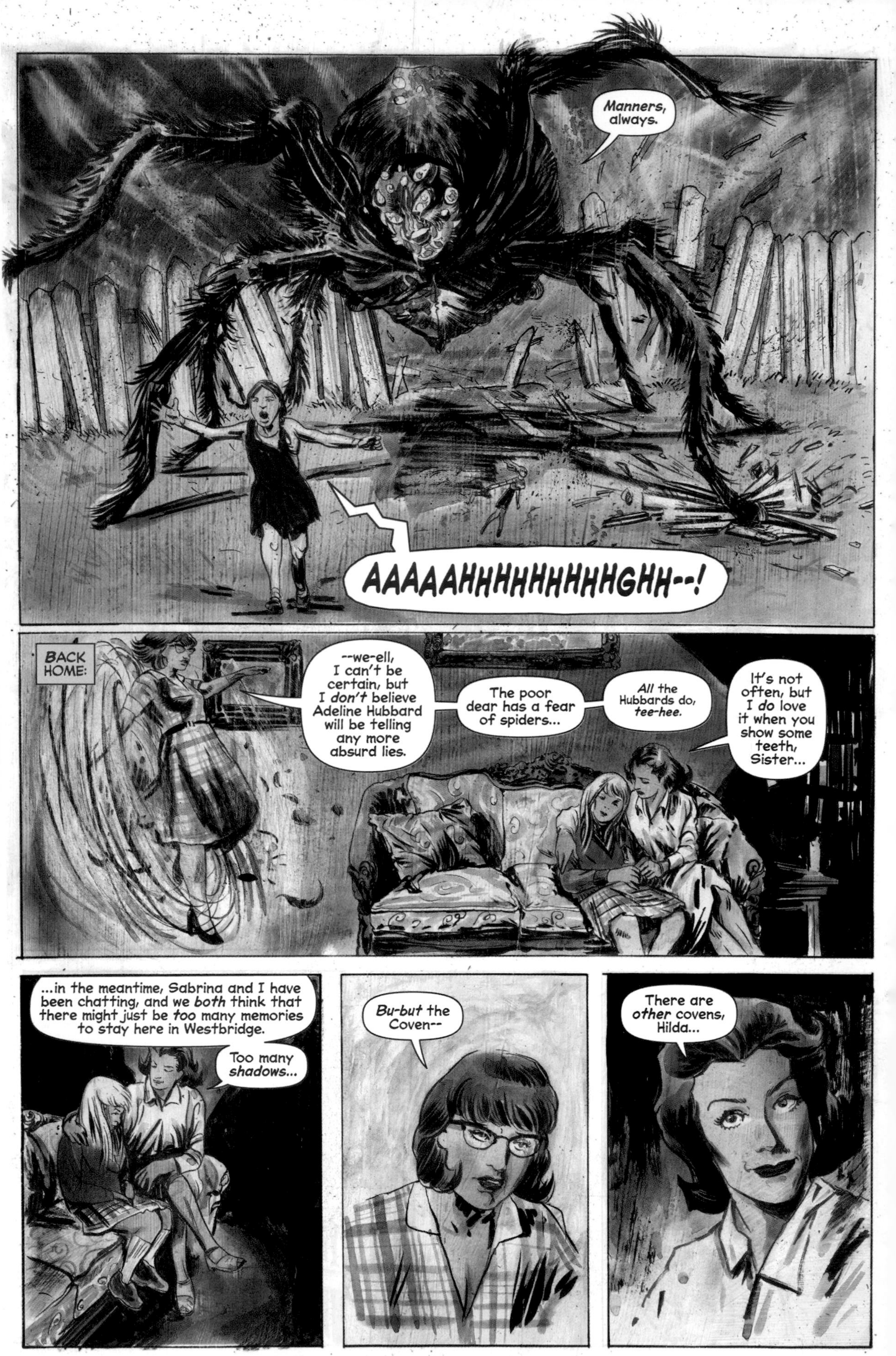
Manners, always.
AAAAAHHHHHHHHHGHH--!
BACK HOME:
--we-ell, I can't be certain, but I don't believe Adeline Hubbard will be telling any more absurd lies.
The poor dear has a fear of spiders...
All the Hubbards do, tee-hee.
It's not often, but I do love it when you show some teeth, Sister...
...in the meantime, Sabrina and I have been chatting, and we both think that there might just be too many memories to stay here in Westbridge.
Too many shadows...
Bu-but the Coven--
There are other covens, Hilda...

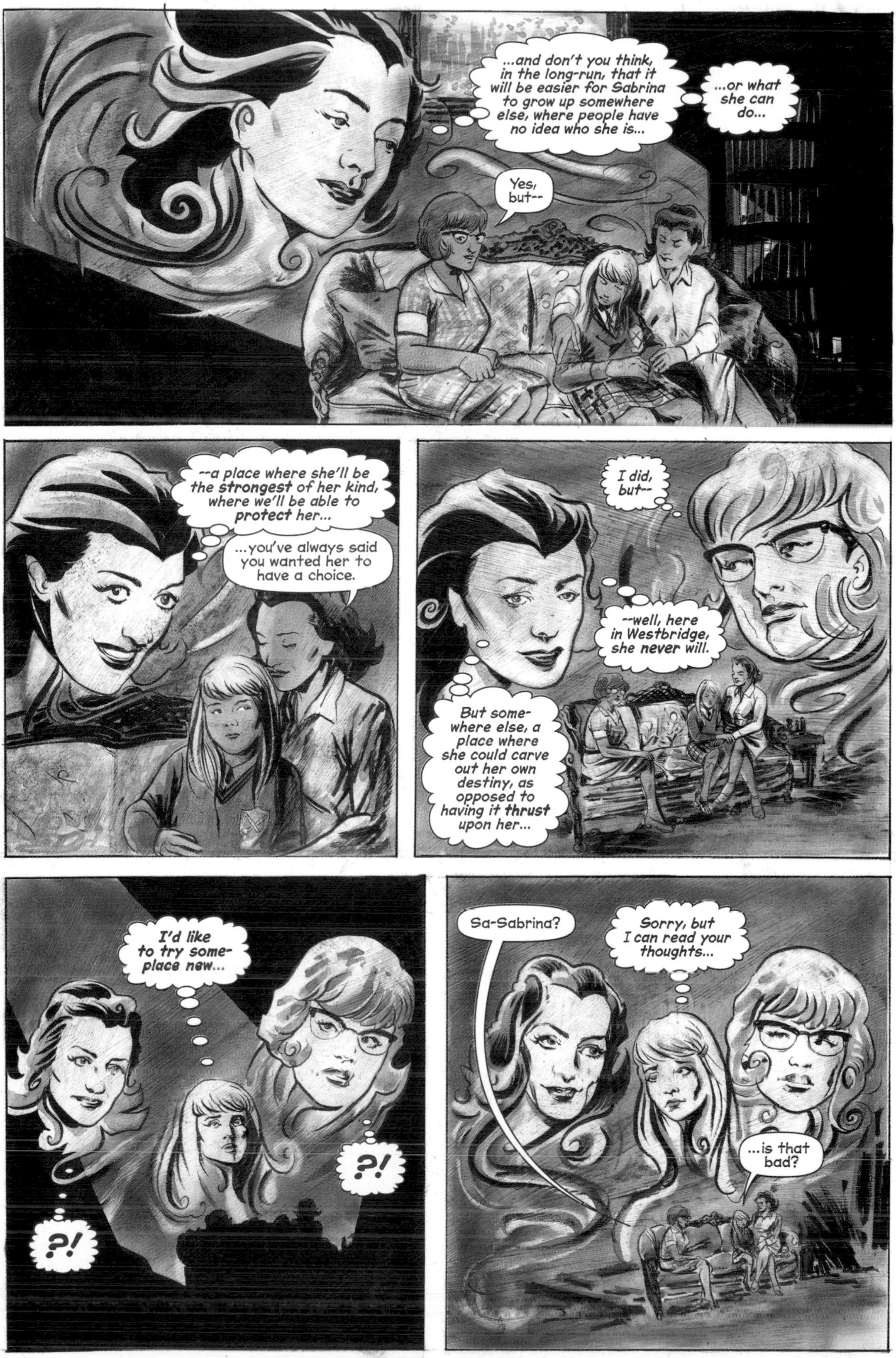
...and don't you think, in the long-run, that it will be easier for Sabrina to grow up somewhere else, where people have no idea who she is...
...or what she can do...
Yes, but--
--a place where she'll be the **strongest** of her kind, where we'll be able to **protect** her...
...you've always said you wanted her to have a choice.
I did, but--
--well, here in Westbridge, she **never** will.
But some-where else, a place where she could carve out her own destiny, as opposed to having it **thrust** upon her...
I'd like to try some-place new...
?!
?!
Sa-Sabrina?
Sorry, but I can read your thoughts...
...is that bad?

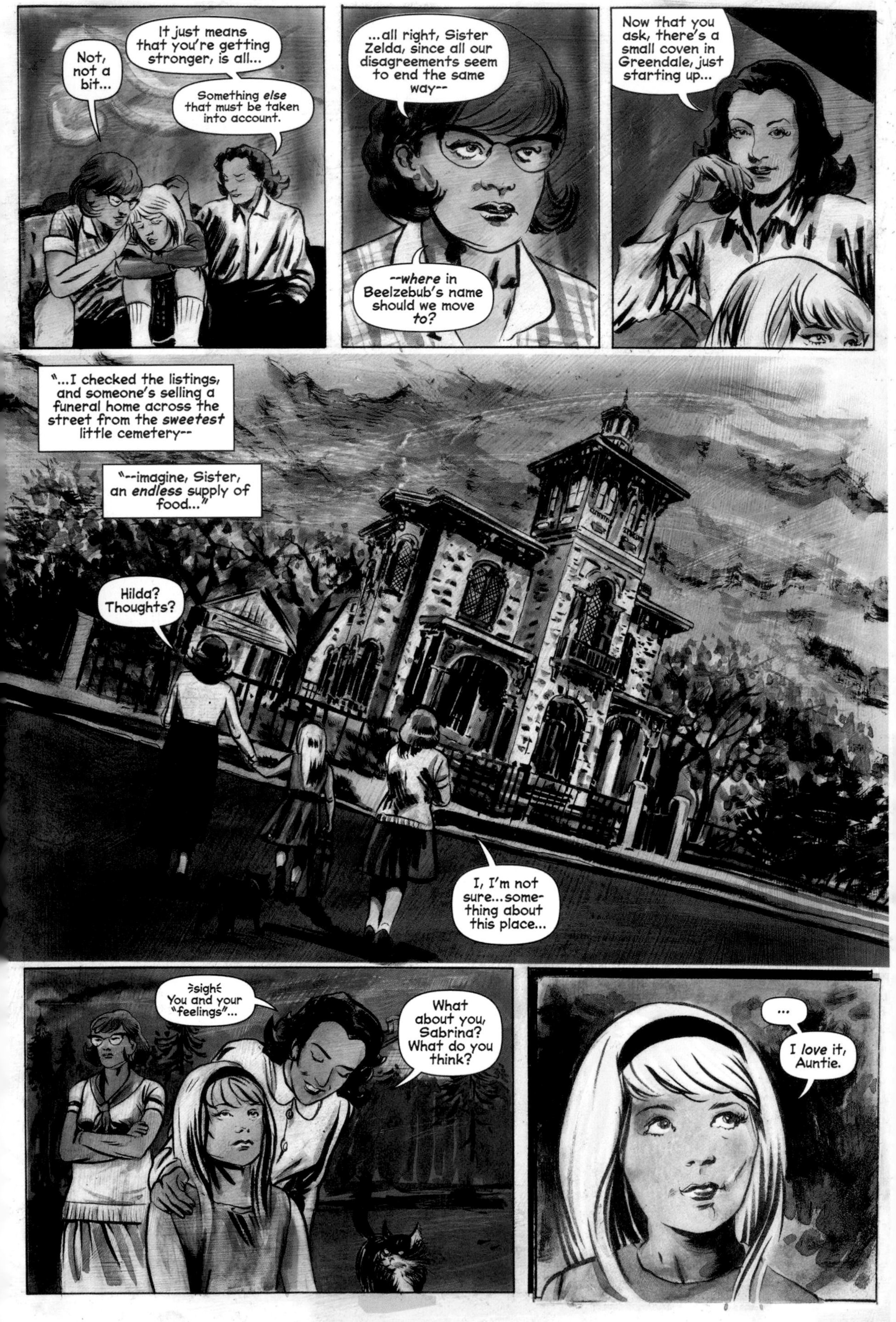

Not, not a bit...
It just means that you're getting stronger, is all...
Something *else* that must be taken into account.
...all right, Sister Zelda, since all our disagreements seem to end the same way--
--*where* in Beelzebub's name should we move *to?*
Now that you ask, there's a small coven in Greendale, just starting up...
"...I checked the listings, and someone's selling a funeral home across the street from the *sweetest* little cemetery--
"--imagine, Sister, an *endless* supply of food..."
Hilda? Thoughts?
I, I'm not sure...some-thing about this place...
sigh You and your "feelings"...
What about you, Sabrina? What do you think?
...
I *love* it, Auntie.

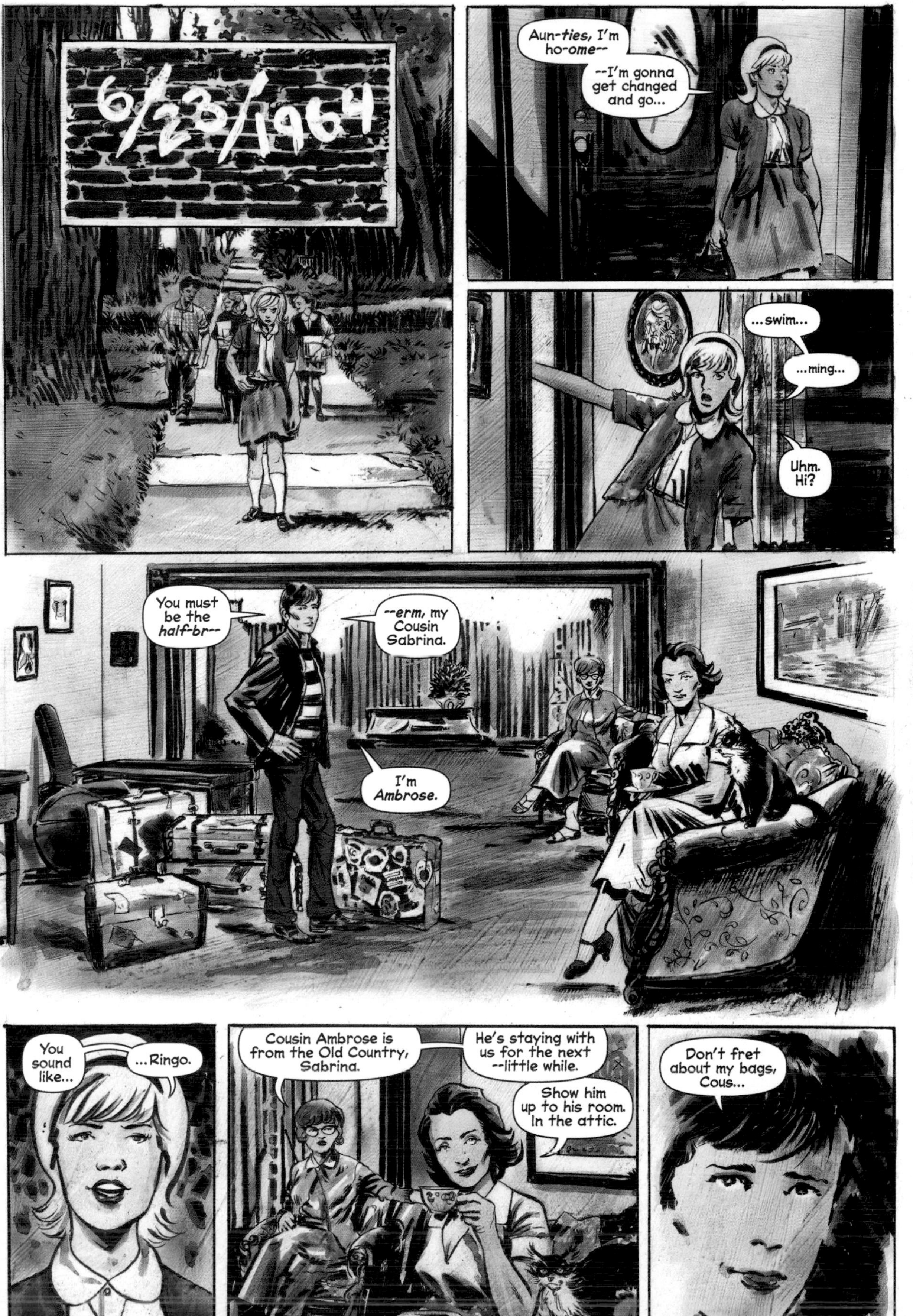
6/23/1964
Aun-ties, I'm ho-ome--
--I'm gonna get changed and go...
...swim...
...ming...
Uhm. Hi?
You must be the half-br--
--erm, my Cousin Sabrina.
I'm Ambrose.
You sound like...
...Ringo.
Cousin Ambrose is from the Old Country, Sabrina.
He's staying with us for the next --little while.
Show him up to his room. In the attic.
Don't fret about my bags, Cous...

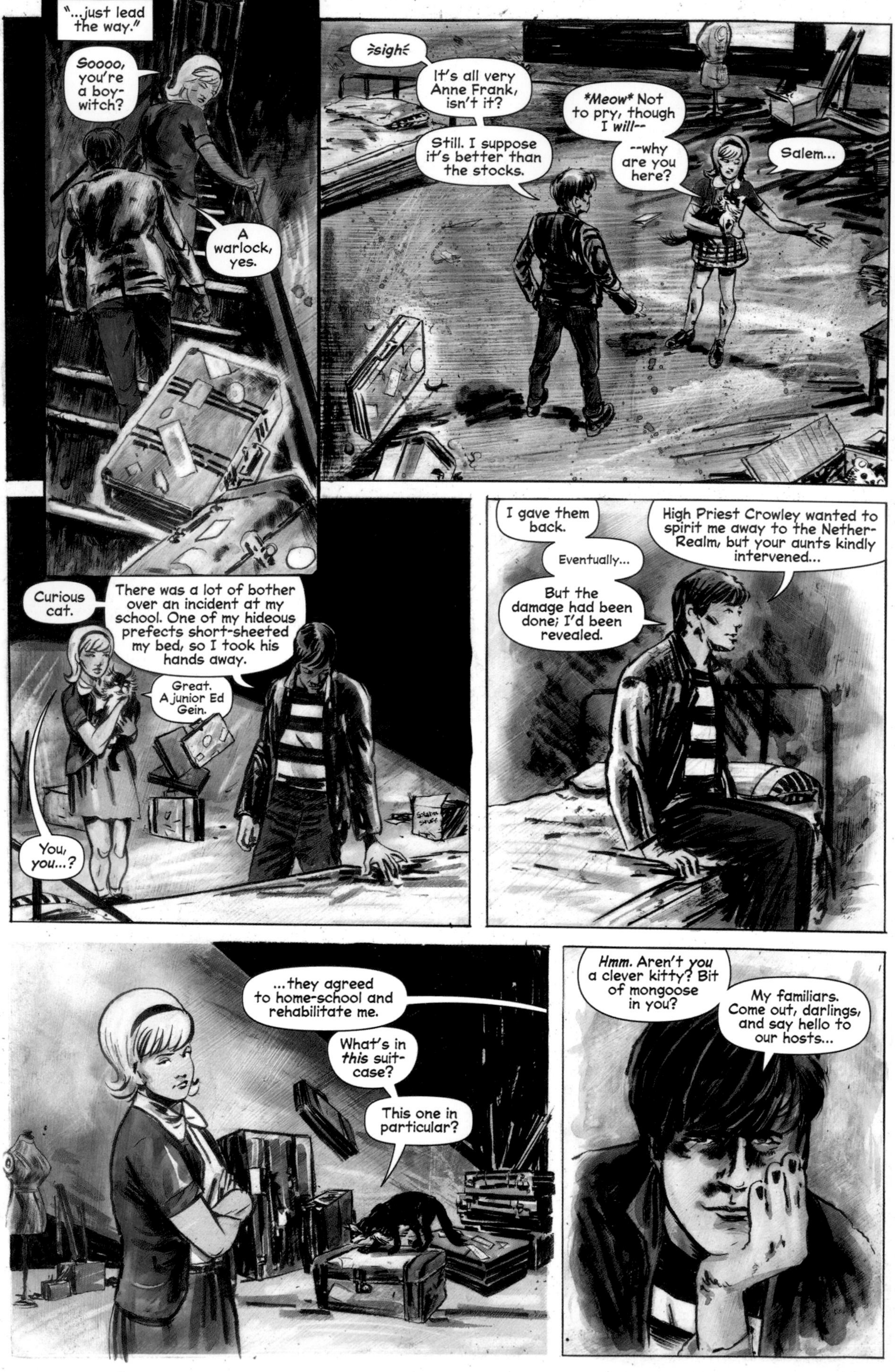

"...just lead the way."
Soooo, you're a boy-witch?
A warlock, yes.
sigh
It's all very Anne Frank, isn't it?
Still. I suppose it's better than the stocks.
Meow Not to pry, though I *will*--
--why are you here?
Salem...
Curious cat.
There was a lot of bother over an incident at my school. One of my hideous prefects short-sheeted my bed, so I took his hands away.
Great. A junior Ed Gein.
You, *you*...?
I gave them back.
Eventually...
But the damage had been done; I'd been revealed.
High Priest Crowley wanted to spirit me away to the Nether-Realm, but your aunts kindly intervened...
...they agreed to home-school and rehabilitate me.
What's in *this* suit-case?
This one in particular?
Hmm. Aren't *you* a clever kitty? Bit of mongoose in you?
My familiars. Come out, darlings, and say hello to our hosts...

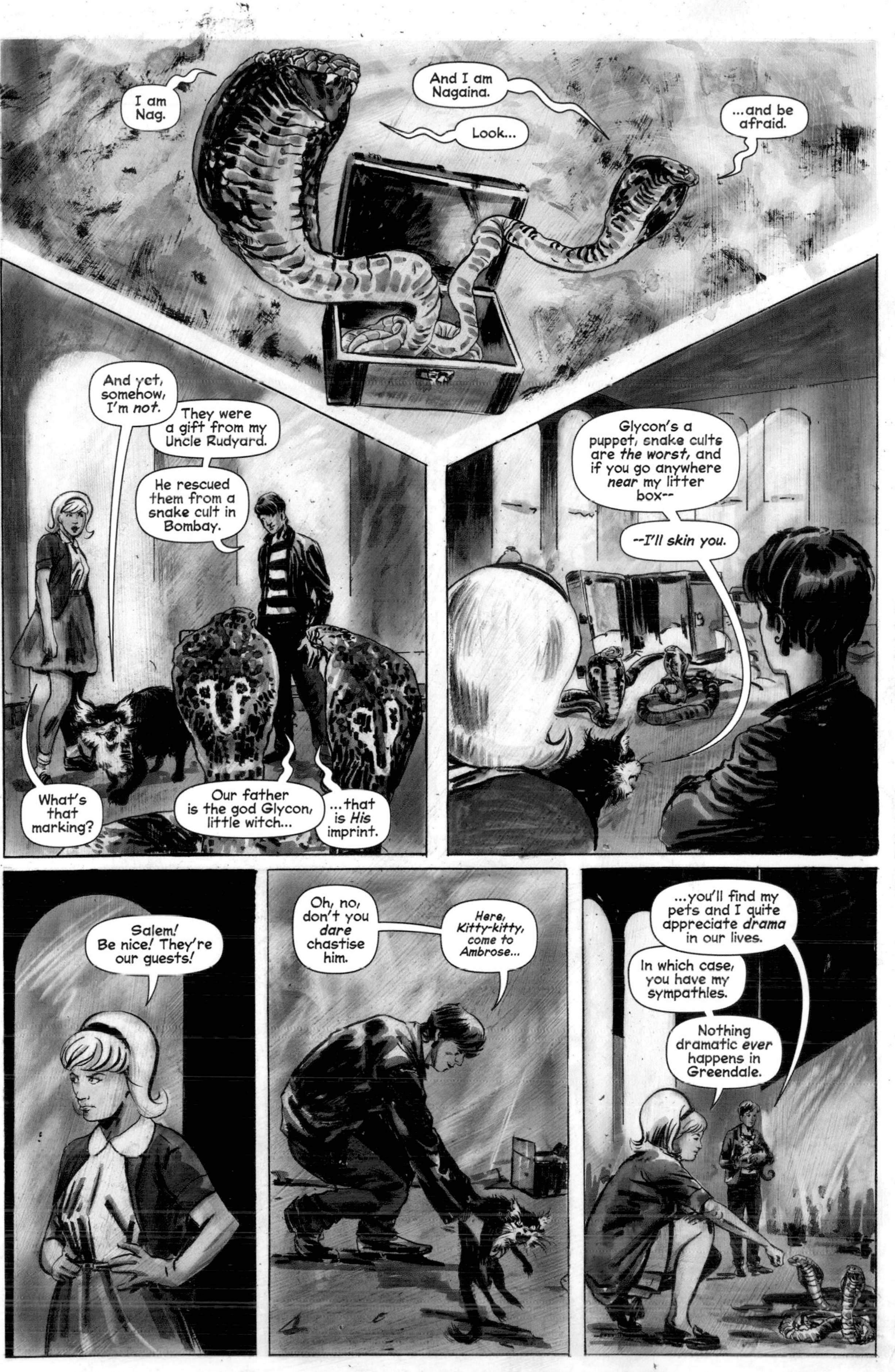
I am Nag.
And I am Nagaina.
Look...
...and be afraid.
And yet, somehow, I'm *not.*
They were a gift from my Uncle Rudyard.
He rescued them from a snake cult in Bombay.
What's that marking?
Our father is the god Glycon, little witch...
...that is *His* imprint.
Glycon's a puppet, snake cults are *the worst,* and if you go anywhere *near* my litter box--
--I'll skin you.
Salem! Be nice! They're our guests!
Oh, no, don't you *dare* chastise him.
Here, Kitty-kitty, come to Ambrose...
...you'll find my pets and I quite appreciate *drama* in our lives.
In which case, you have my sympathies.
Nothing dramatic *ever* happens in Greendale.

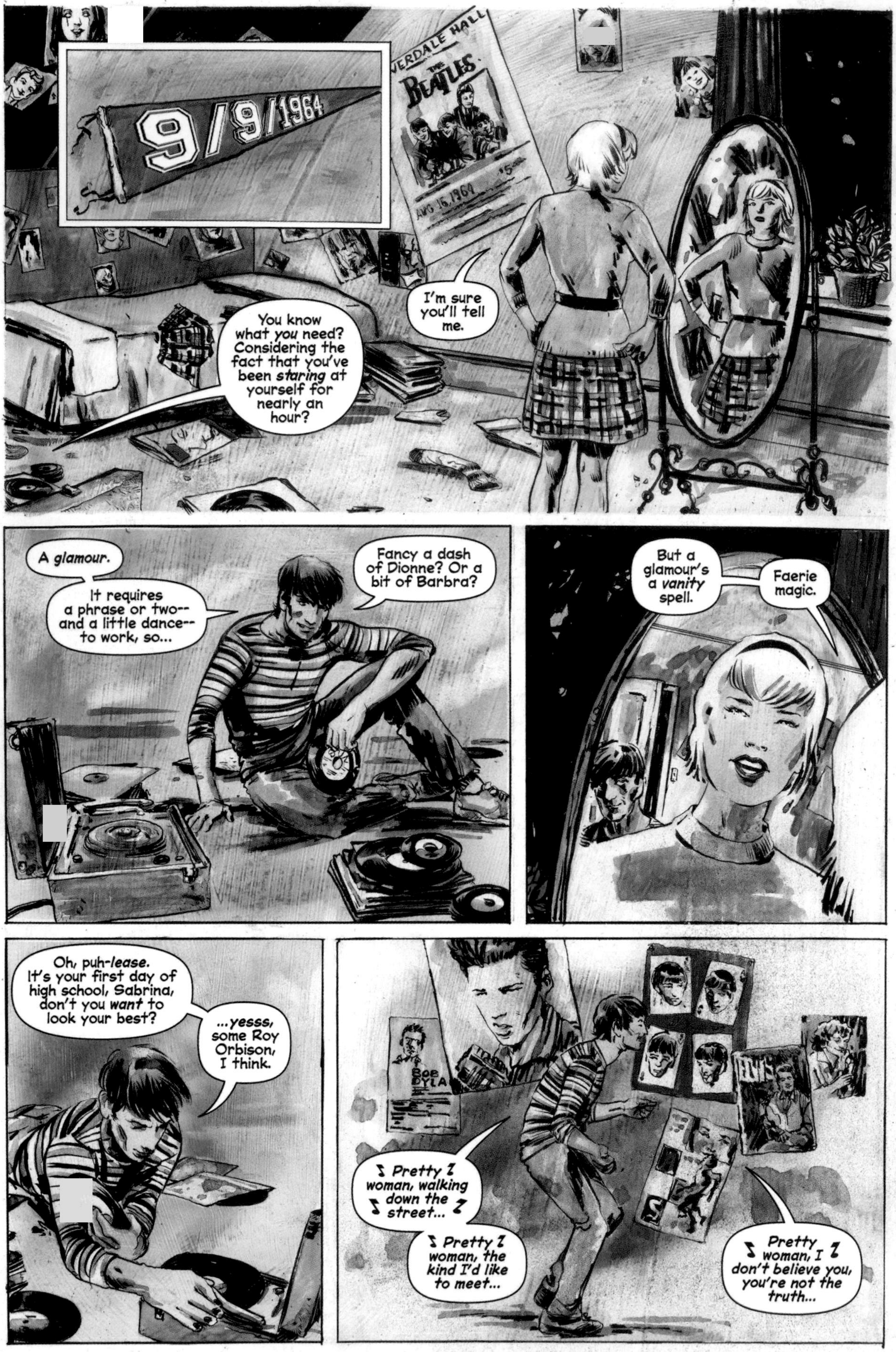

9/9/1964
THE BEATLES
AUG 16, 1964
You know what *you* need? Considering the fact that you've been *staring* at yourself for nearly an hour?
I'm sure you'll tell me.
A *glamour*.
It requires a phrase or two-- and a little dance-- to work, so...
Fancy a dash of Dionne? Or a bit of Barbra?
But a glamour's a *vanity* spell.
Faerie magic.
Oh, puh-*lease*. It's your first day of high school, Sabrina, don't you *want* to look your best?
...*yesss*, some Roy Orbison, I think.
BOB DYLA
♪ *Pretty woman, walking down the street...* ♪
♪ *Pretty woman, the kind I'd like to meet...* ♪
♪ *Pretty woman, I don't believe you, you're not the truth...* ♪

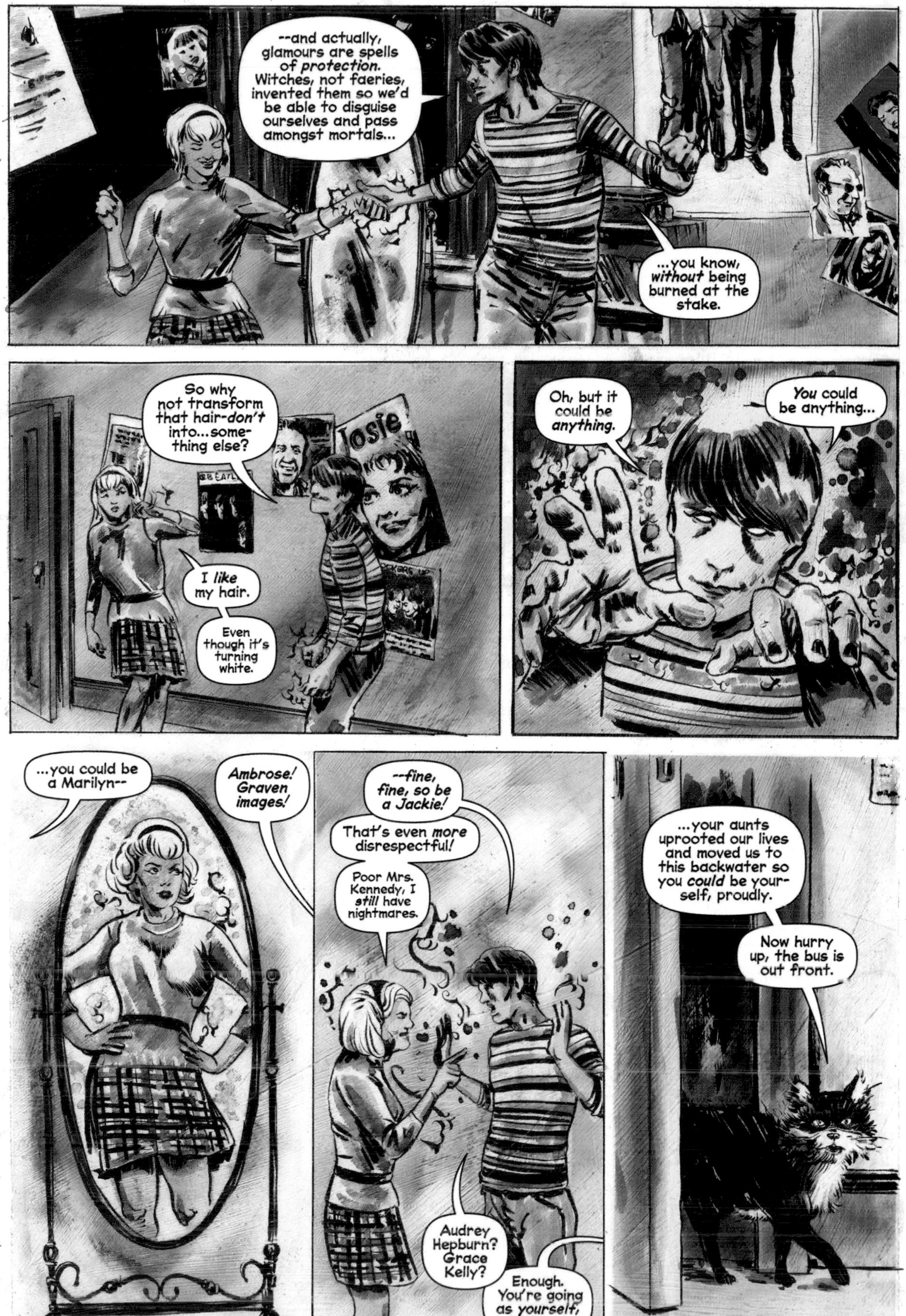
--and actually, glamours are spells of *protection*. Witches, not faeries, invented them so we'd be able to disguise ourselves and pass amongst mortals...
...you know, *without* being burned at the stake.
So why not transform that hair-*don't* into...some-thing else?
I *like* my hair.
Even though it's turning white.
Oh, but it could be *anything*.
You could be anything...
...you could be a Marilyn--
Ambrose! Graven images!
--fine, fine, so be a Jackie!
That's even *more* disrespectful!
Poor Mrs. Kennedy, I *still* have nightmares.
Audrey Hepburn? Grace Kelly?
Enough. You're going as *yourself*, 'Brina...
...your aunts uprooted our lives and moved us to this backwater so you *could* be your-self, proudly.
Now hurry up, the bus is out front.

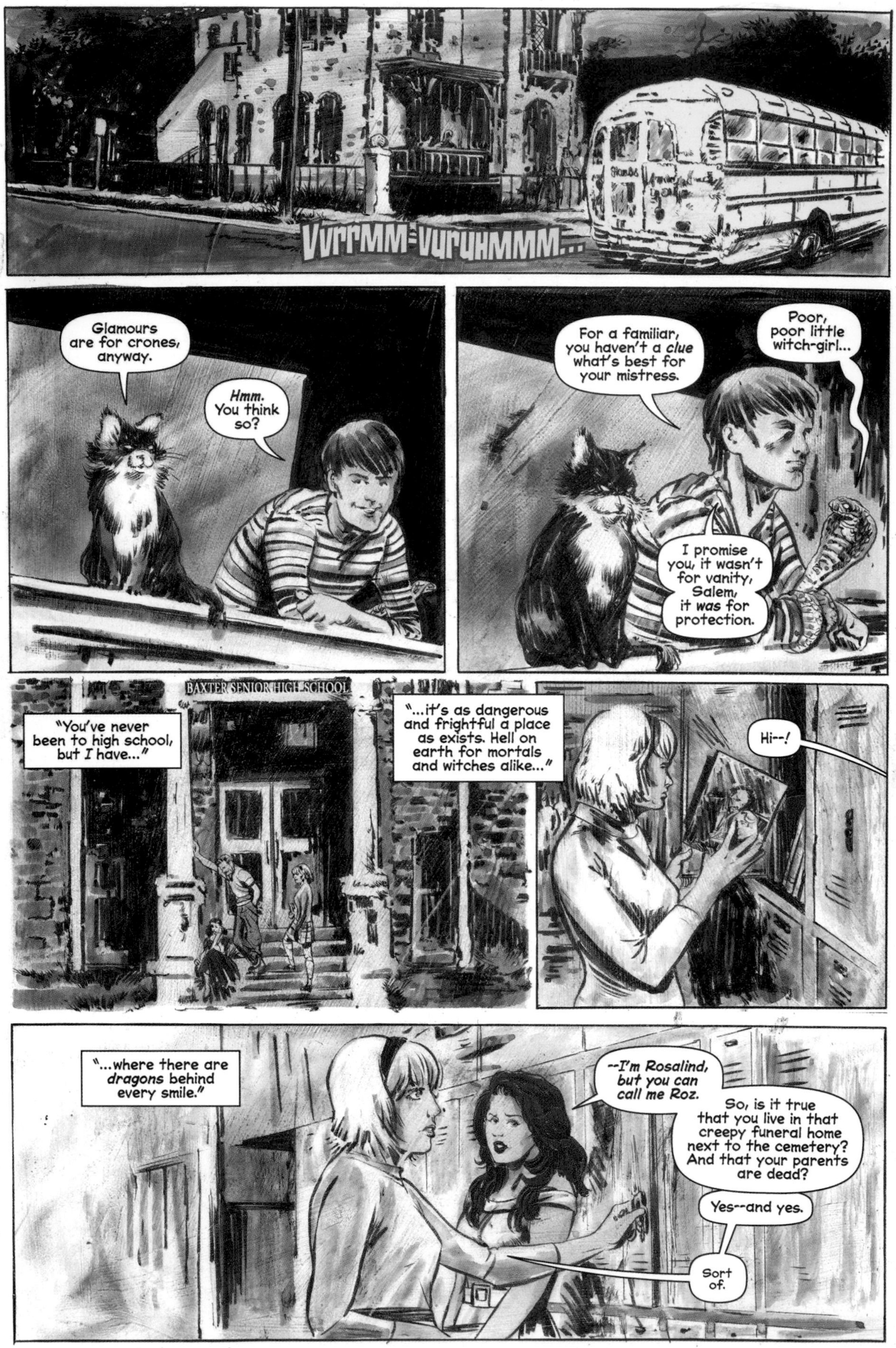
VVRRMM-VVRUHMMM...
Glamours are for crones, anyway.
Hmm. You think so?
For a familiar, you haven't a clue what's best for your mistress.
Poor, poor little witch-girl...
I promise you, it wasn't for vanity, Salem, it was for protection.
BAXTER SENIOR HIGH SCHOOL
"You've never been to high school, but I have..."
"...it's as dangerous and frightful a place as exists. Hell on earth for mortals and witches alike..."
Hi--!
"...where there are dragons behind every smile."
--I'm Rosalind, but you can call me Roz.
So, is it true that you live in that creepy funeral home next to the cemetery? And that your parents are dead?
Yes--and yes.
Sort of.

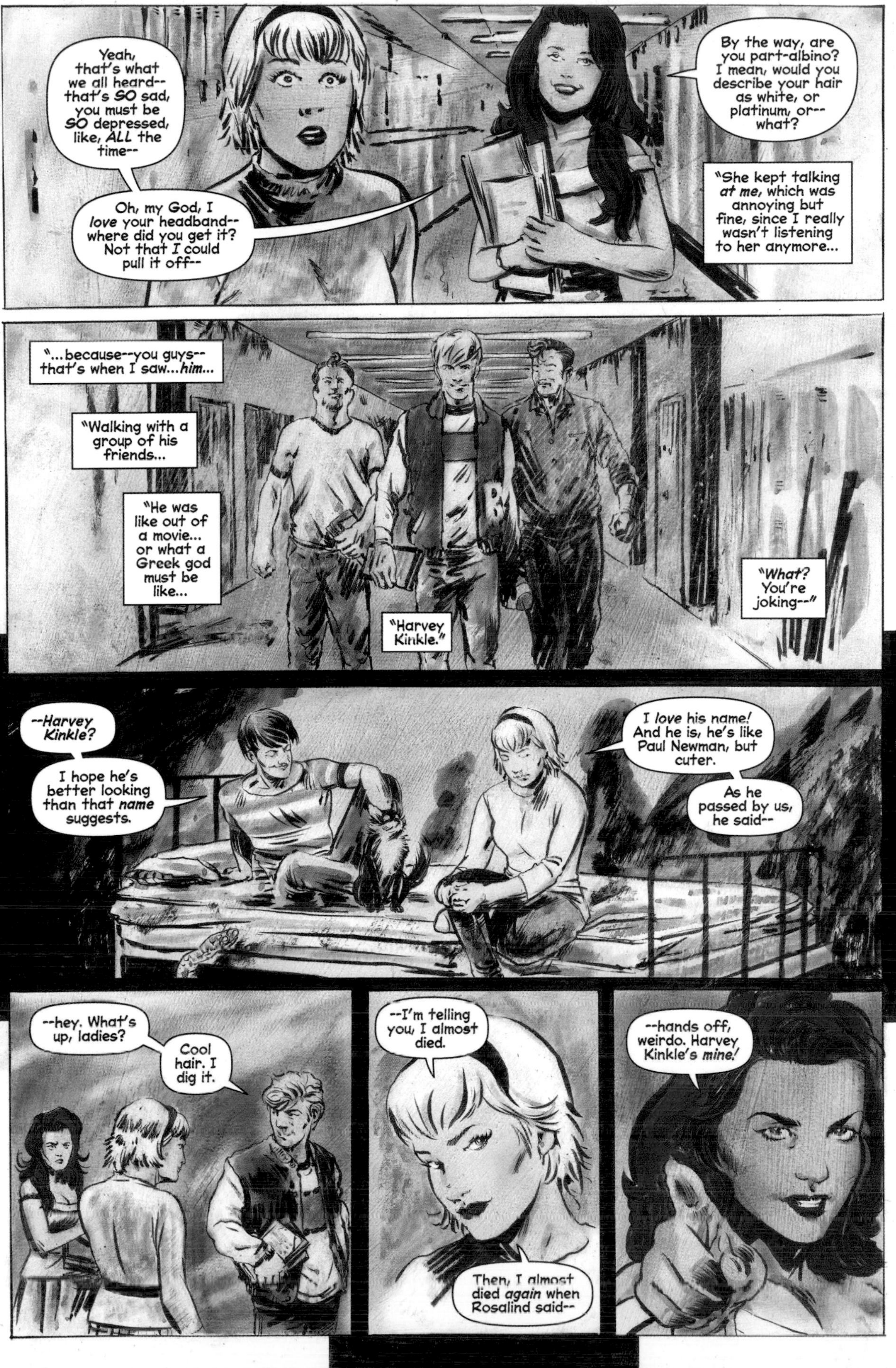

Yeah, that's what we all heard-- that's SO sad, you must be SO depressed, like, ALL the time--
Oh, my God, I love your headband-- where did you get it? Not that I could pull it off--
By the way, are you part-albino? I mean, would you describe your hair as white, or platinum, or-- what?
"She kept talking at me, which was annoying but fine, since I really wasn't listening to her anymore...
"...because--you guys-- that's when I saw...him...
"Walking with a group of his friends...
"He was like out of a movie... or what a Greek god must be like...
"Harvey Kinkle."
"What? You're joking--"
--Harvey Kinkle?
I hope he's better looking than that name suggests.
I love his name! And he is, he's like Paul Newman, but cuter.
As he passed by us, he said--
--hey. What's up, ladies?
Cool hair. I dig it.
--I'm telling you, I almost died.
Then, I almost died again when Rosalind said--
--hands off, weirdo. Harvey Kinkle's mine!

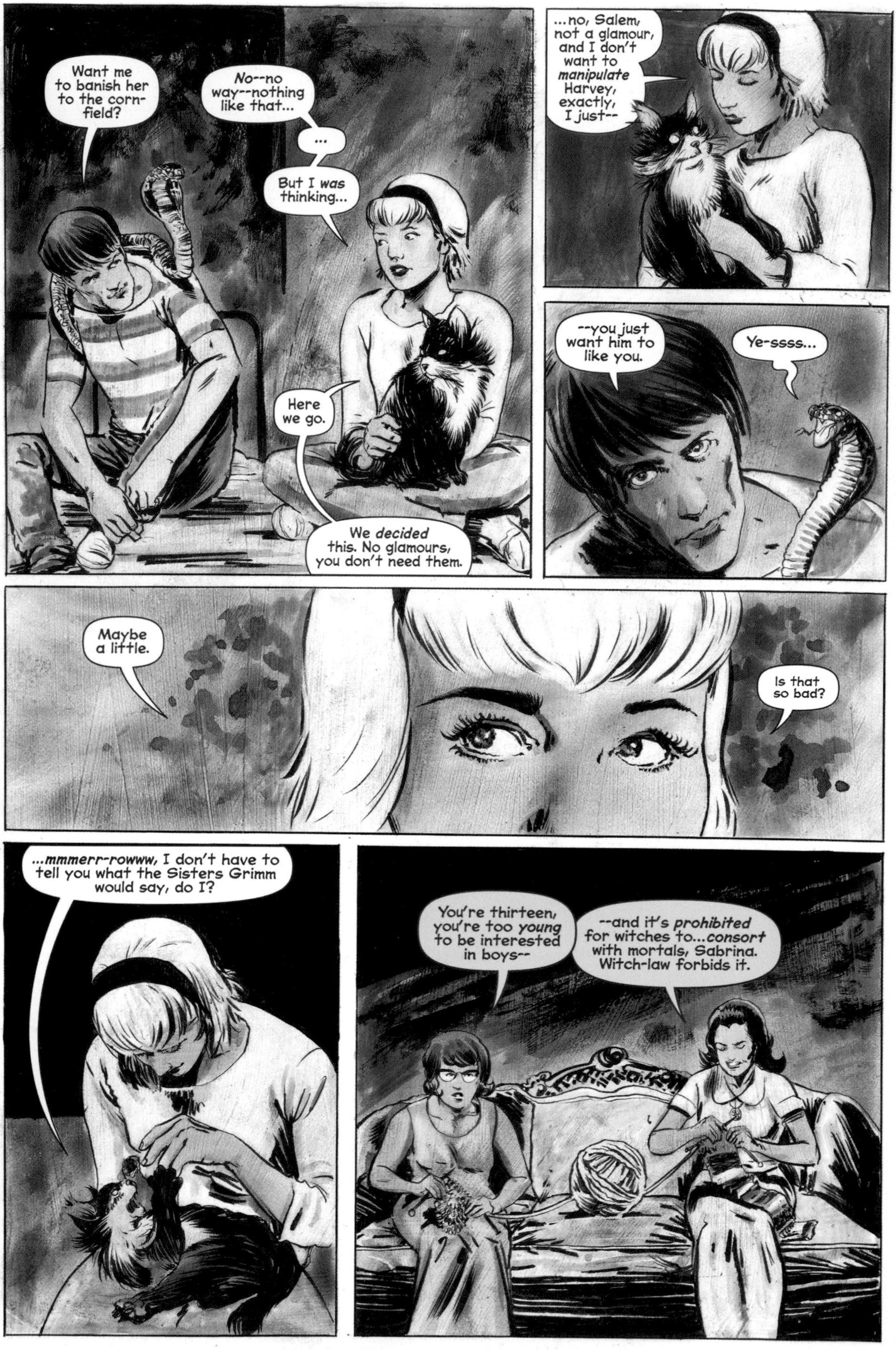

Want me to banish her to the corn-field?
No--no way--nothing like that...
...
But I was thinking...
Here we go.
We decided this. No glamours, you don't need them.
...no, Salem, not a glamour, and I don't want to manipulate Harvey, exactly, I just--
--you just want him to like you.
Ye-ssss...
Maybe a little.
Is that so bad?
...mmmerr-rowww, I don't have to tell you what the Sisters Grimm would say, do I?
You're thirteen, you're too young to be interested in boys--
--and it's prohibited for witches to...consort with mortals, Sabrina. Witch-law forbids it.

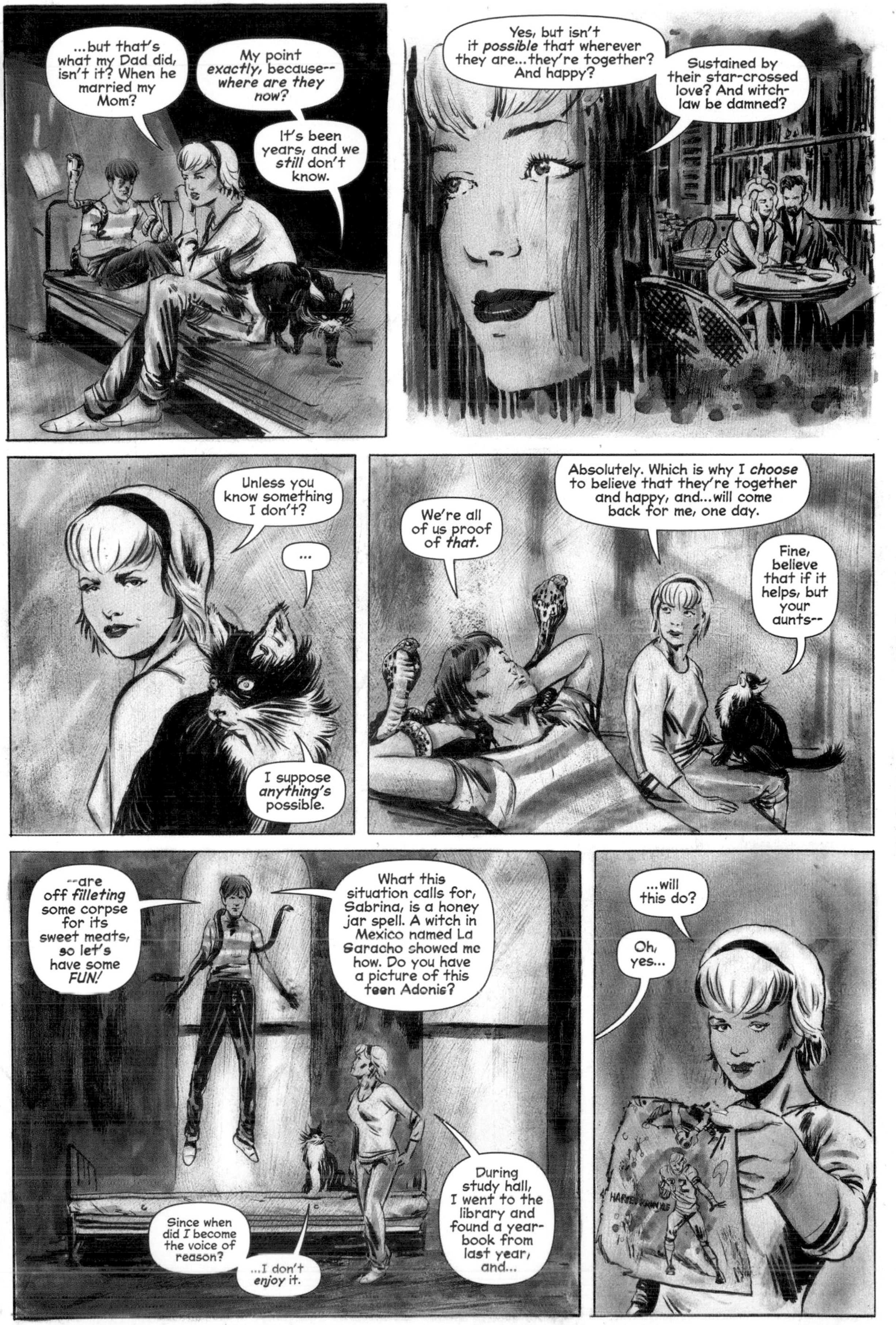
...but that's what my Dad did, isn't it? When he married my Mom?
My point exactly, because--where are they now?
It's been years, and we still don't know.
Yes, but isn't it possible that wherever they are...they're together? And happy?
Sustained by their star-crossed love? And witch-law be damned?
Unless you know something I don't?
...
I suppose anything's possible.
We're all of us proof of that.
Absolutely. Which is why I choose to believe that they're together and happy, and...will come back for me, one day.
Fine, believe that if it helps, but your aunts--
--are off filleting some corpse for its sweet meats, so let's have some FUN!
What this situation calls for, Sabrina, is a honey jar spell. A witch in Mexico named La Saracho showed me how. Do you have a picture of this teen Adonis?
Since when did I become the voice of reason?
...I don't enjoy it.
During study hall, I went to the library and found a year-book from last year, and...
...will this do?
Oh, yes...

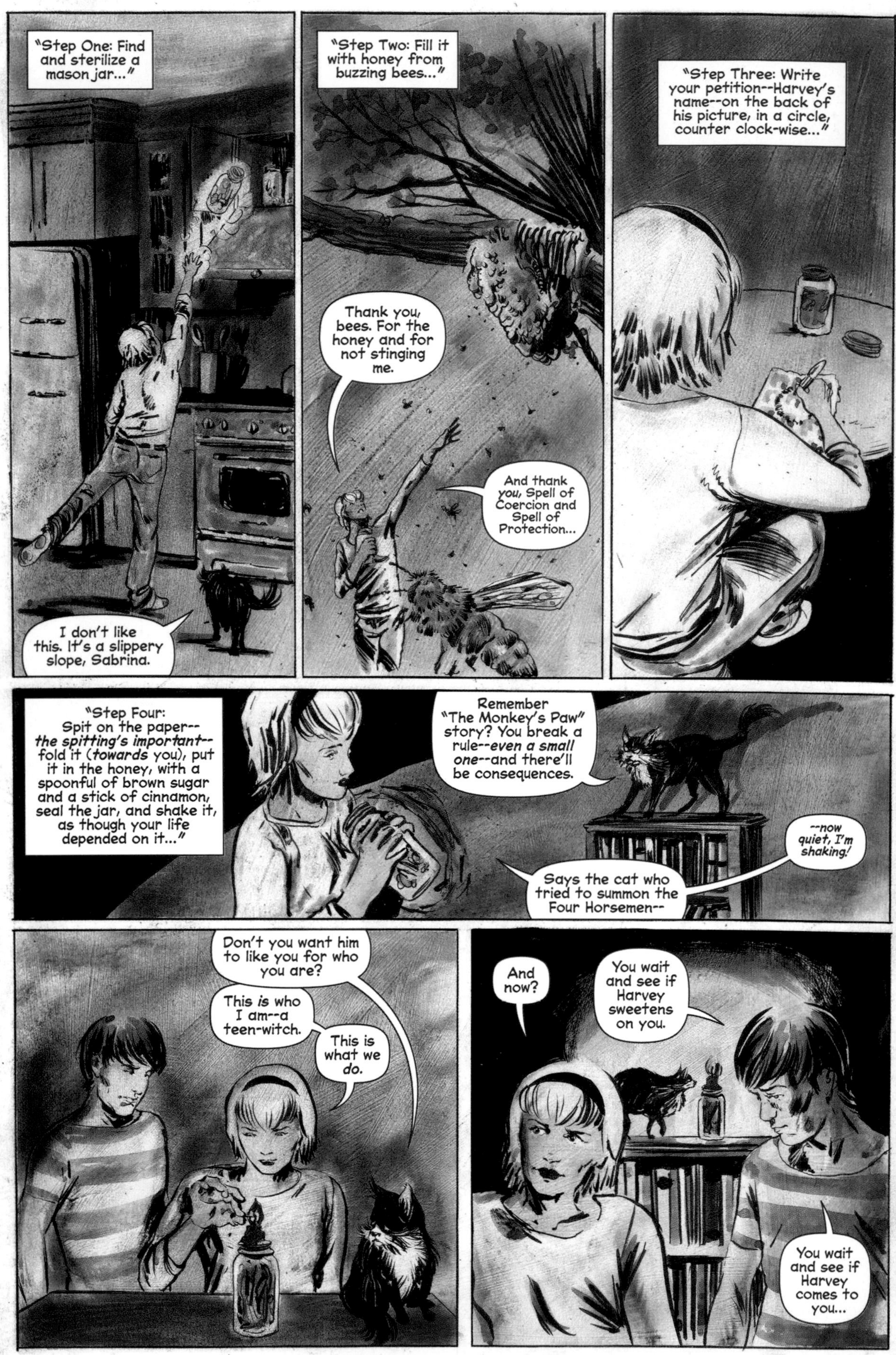

"Step One: Find and sterilize a mason jar..."
I don't like this. It's a slippery slope, Sabrina.
"Step Two: Fill it with honey from buzzing bees..."
Thank you, bees. For the honey and for not stinging me.
And thank *you*, Spell of Coercion and Spell of Protection...
"Step Three: Write your petition--Harvey's name--on the back of his picture, in a circle, counter clock-wise..."
"Step Four: Spit on the paper-- *the spitting's important*-- fold it (*towards* you), put it in the honey, with a spoonful of brown sugar and a stick of cinnamon, seal the jar, and shake it, as though your life depended on it..."
Remember "The Monkey's Paw" story? You break a rule--*even a small one*--and there'll be consequences.
Says the cat who tried to summon the Four Horsemen--
--now quiet, I'm shaking!
Don't you want him to like you for who you are?
This *is* who I am--a teen-witch.
This is what we *do*.
And now?
You wait and see if Harvey sweetens on you.
You wait and see if Harvey comes to you...

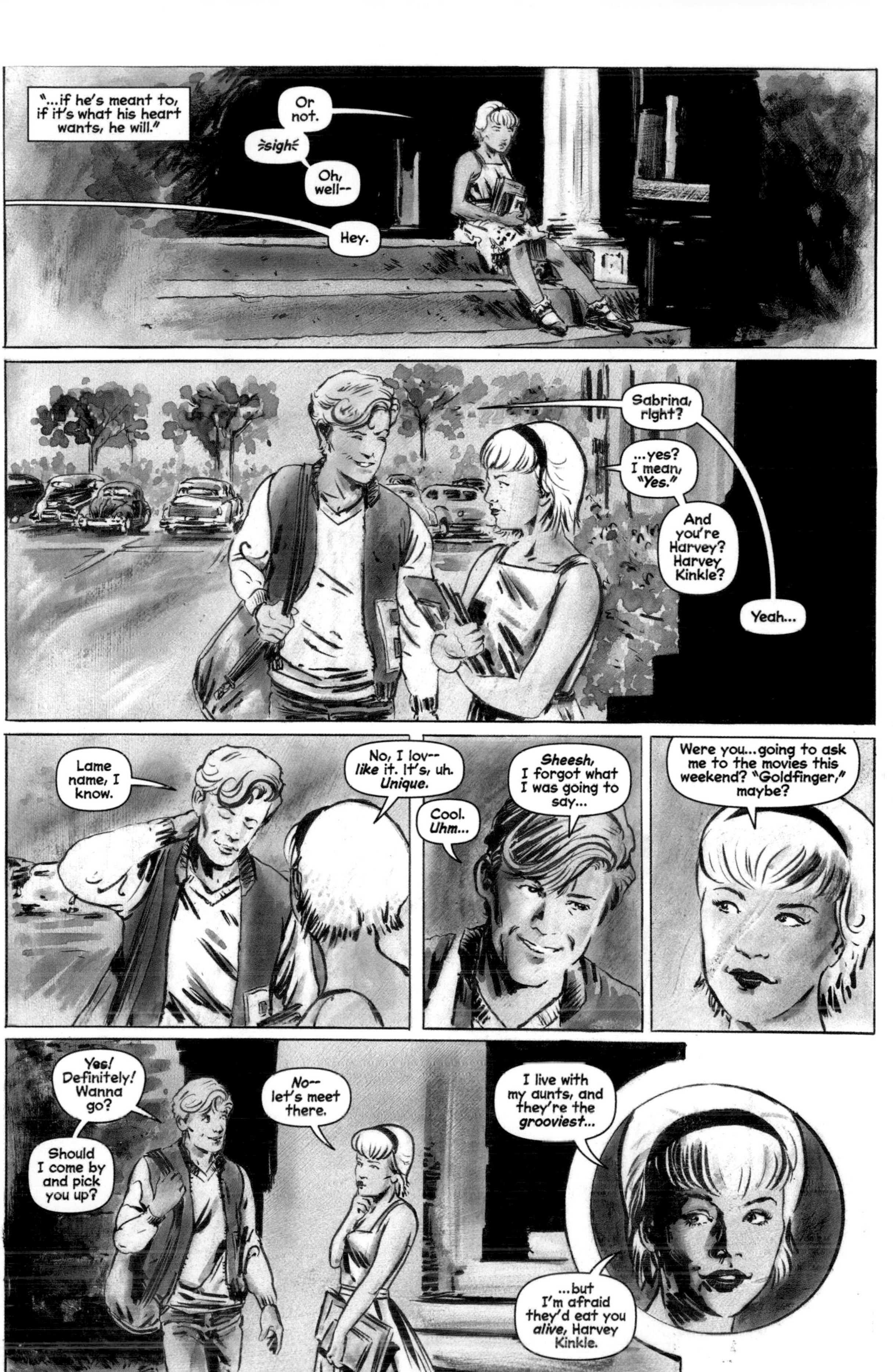
"...if he's meant to, if it's what his heart wants, he will."
Or not.
sigh
Oh, well--
Hey.
Sabrina, right?
...yes? I mean, "Yes."
And you're Harvey? Harvey Kinkle?
Yeah...
Lame name, I know.
No, I lov-- like it. It's, uh. Unique.
Cool. Uhm...
Sheesh, I forgot what I was going to say...
Were you...going to ask me to the movies this weekend? "Goldfinger," maybe?
Yes! Definitely! Wanna go?
Should I come by and pick you up?
No-- let's meet there.
I live with my aunts, and they're the grooviest...
...but I'm afraid they'd eat you alive, Harvey Kinkle.

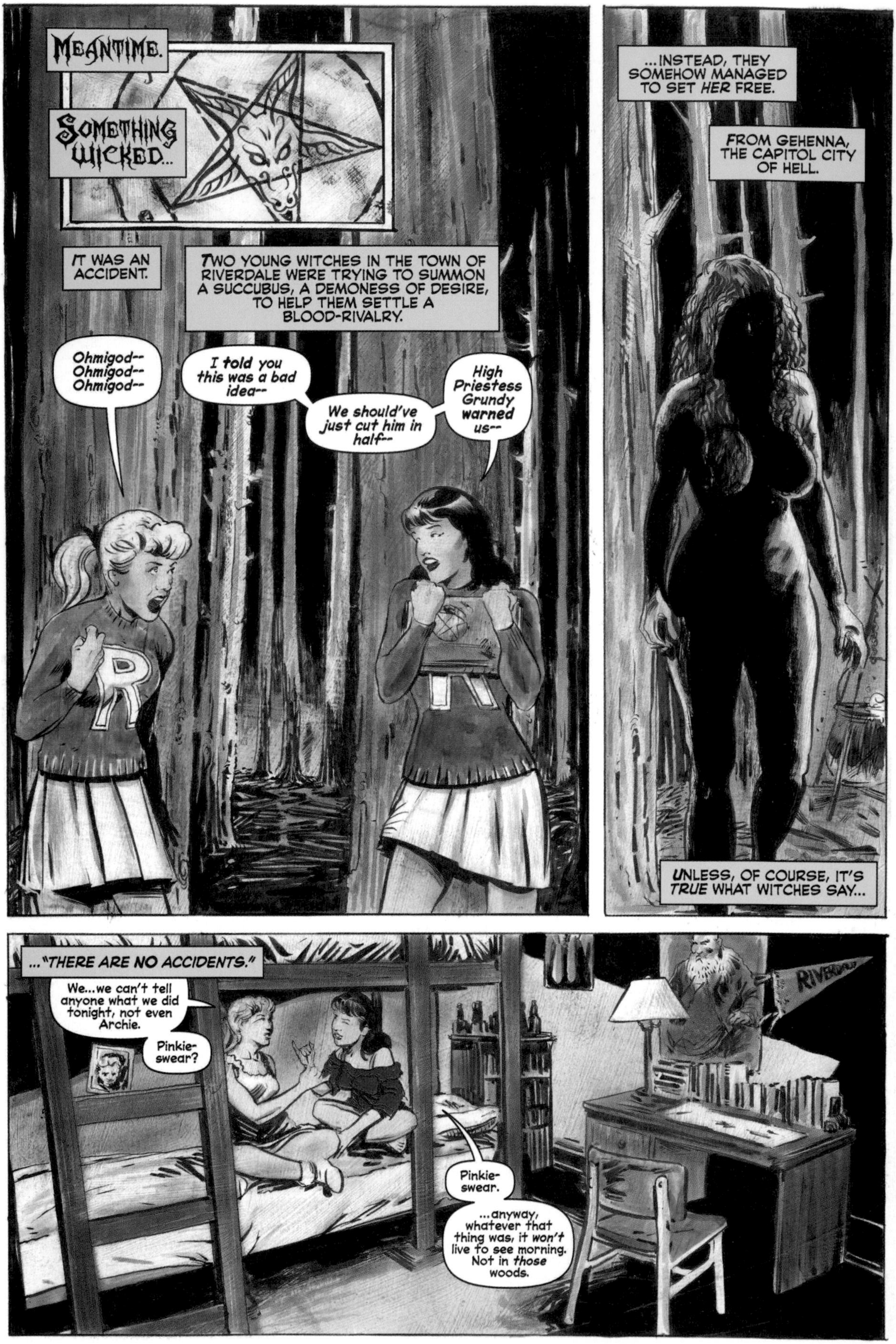
MEANTIME.
SOMETHING WICKED...
IT WAS AN ACCIDENT.
TWO YOUNG WITCHES IN THE TOWN OF RIVERDALE WERE TRYING TO SUMMON A SUCCUBUS, A DEMONESS OF DESIRE, TO HELP THEM SETTLE A BLOOD-RIVALRY.
Ohmigod-- Ohmigod-- Ohmigod--
I told you this was a bad idea--
We should've just cut him in half--
High Priestess Grundy warned us--
...INSTEAD, THEY SOMEHOW MANAGED TO SET HER FREE.
FROM GEHENNA, THE CAPITOL CITY OF HELL.
UNLESS, OF COURSE, IT'S TRUE WHAT WITCHES SAY...
..."THERE ARE NO ACCIDENTS."
We...we can't tell anyone what we did tonight, not even Archie.
Pinkie-swear?
Pinkie-swear.
...anyway, whatever that thing was, it won't live to see morning. Not in those woods.
RIVERDALE

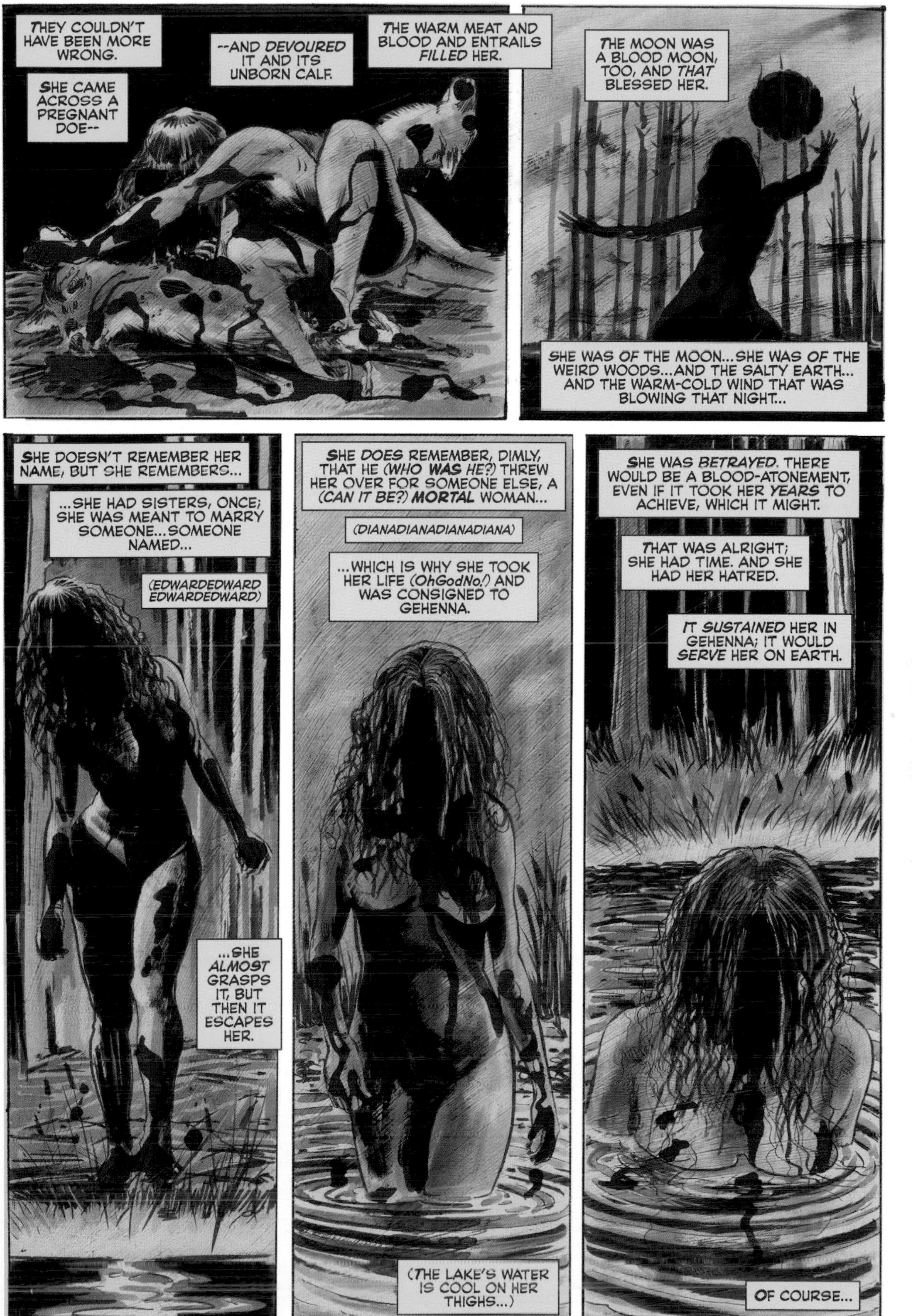
THEY COULDN'T HAVE BEEN MORE WRONG.
SHE CAME ACROSS A PREGNANT DOE--
--AND DEVOURED IT AND ITS UNBORN CALF.
THE WARM MEAT AND BLOOD AND ENTRAILS FILLED HER.
THE MOON WAS A BLOOD MOON, TOO, AND THAT BLESSED HER.
SHE WAS OF THE MOON...SHE WAS OF THE WEIRD WOODS...AND THE SALTY EARTH... AND THE WARM-COLD WIND THAT WAS BLOWING THAT NIGHT...
SHE DOESN'T REMEMBER HER NAME, BUT SHE REMEMBERS...
...SHE HAD SISTERS, ONCE; SHE WAS MEANT TO MARRY SOMEONE...SOMEONE NAMED...
(EDWARDEDWARD EDWARDEDWARD)
...SHE ALMOST GRASPS IT, BUT THEN IT ESCAPES HER.
SHE DOES REMEMBER, DIMLY, THAT HE (WHO WAS HE?) THREW HER OVER FOR SOMEONE ELSE, A (CAN IT BE?) MORTAL WOMAN...
(DIANADIANADIANADIANA)
...WHICH IS WHY SHE TOOK HER LIFE (OhGodNo!) AND WAS CONSIGNED TO GEHENNA.
(THE LAKE'S WATER IS COOL ON HER THIGHS...)
SHE WAS BETRAYED. THERE WOULD BE A BLOOD-ATONEMENT, EVEN IF IT TOOK HER YEARS TO ACHIEVE, WHICH IT MIGHT.
THAT WAS ALRIGHT; SHE HAD TIME. AND SHE HAD HER HATRED.
IT SUSTAINED HER IN GEHENNA; IT WOULD SERVE HER ON EARTH.
OF COURSE...

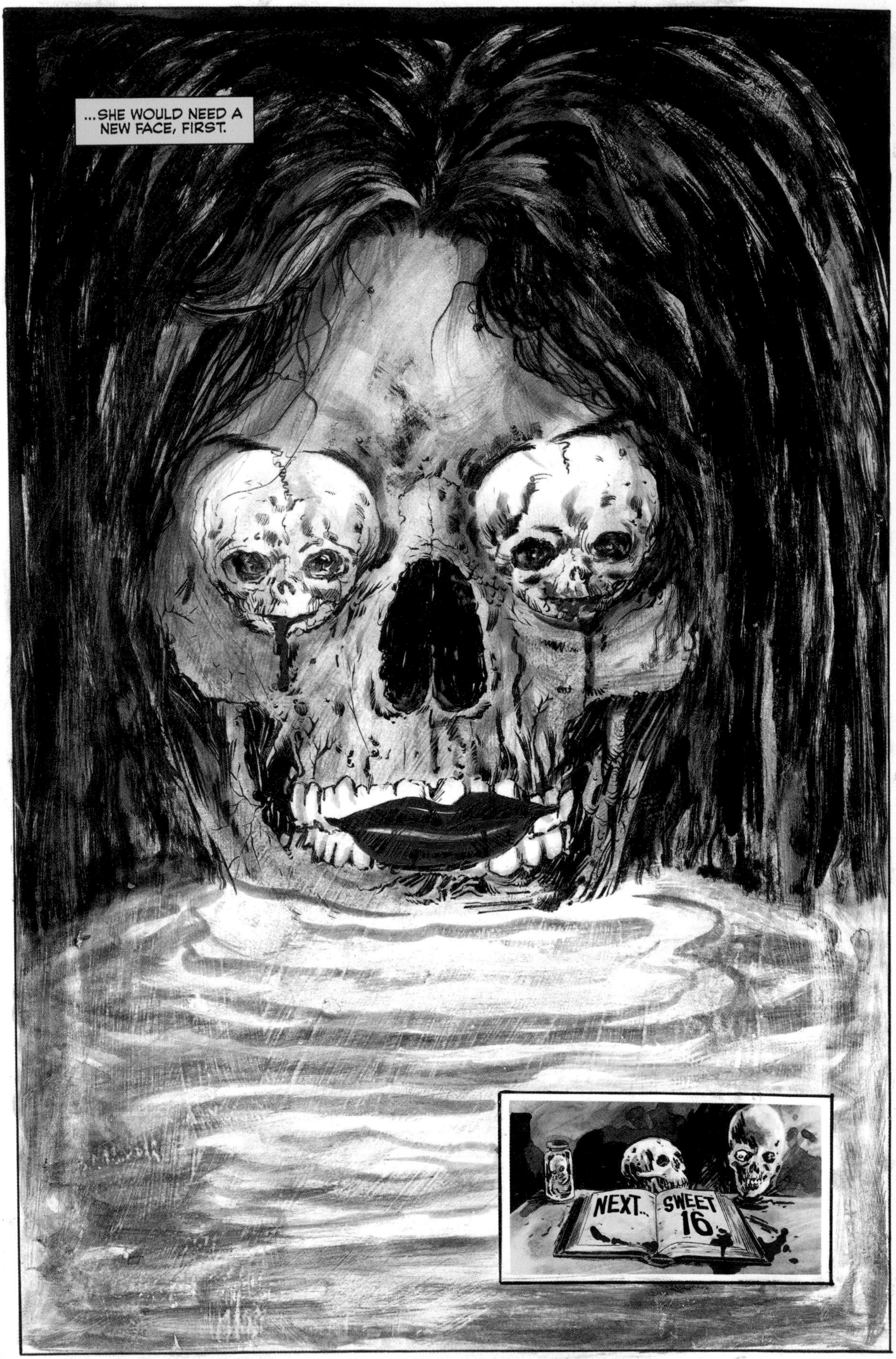
...SHE WOULD NEED A NEW FACE, FIRST.
NEXT...
SWEET 16.

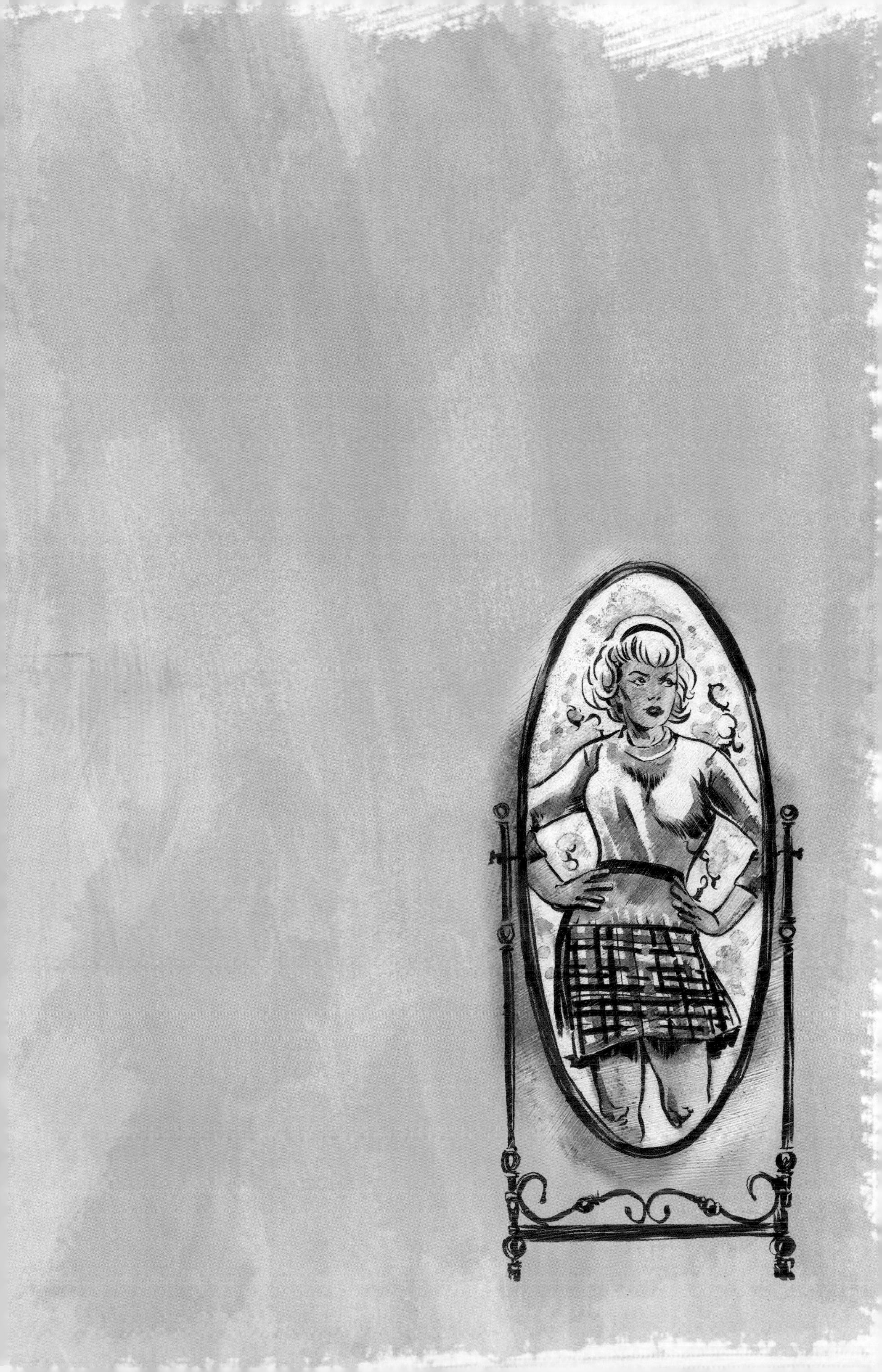

CHAPTER #2

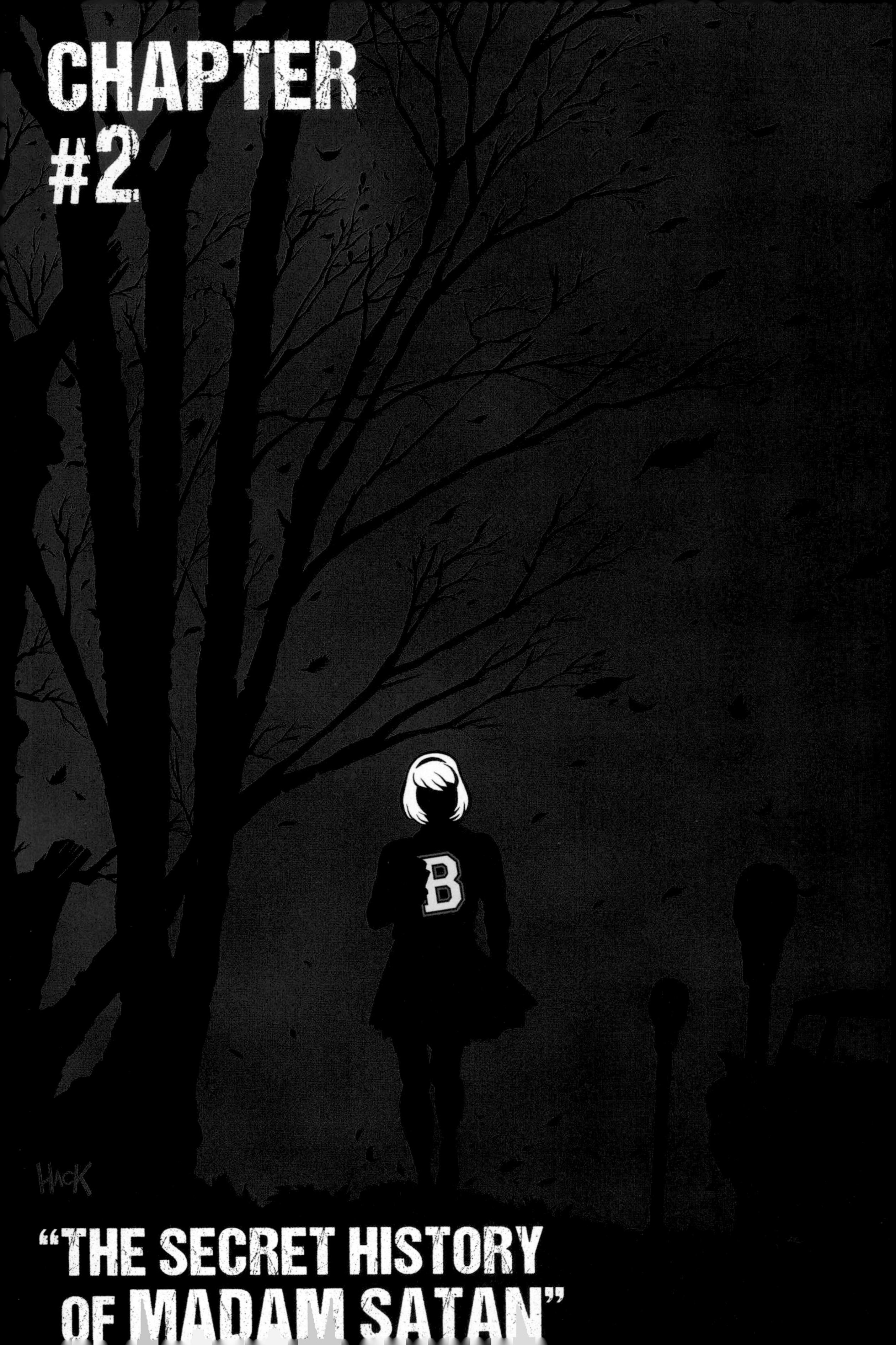

"THE SECRET HISTORY OF MADAM SATAN"

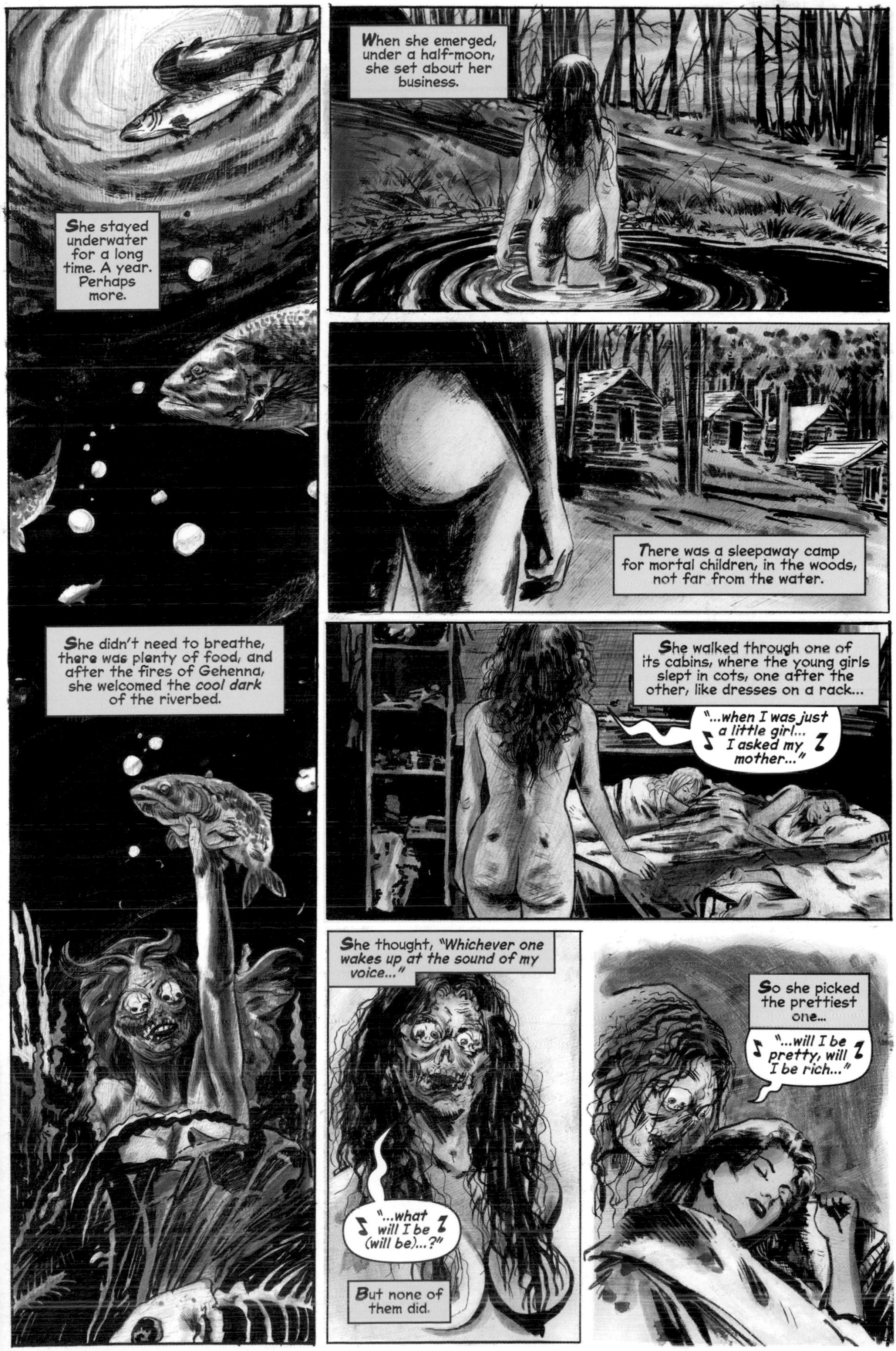
She stayed underwater for a long time. A year. Perhaps more.
She didn't need to breathe, there was plenty of food, and after the fires of Gehenna, she welcomed the *cool dark* of the riverbed.
When she emerged, under a half-moon, she set about her business.
There was a sleepaway camp for mortal children, in the woods, not far from the water.
She walked through one of its cabins, where the young girls slept in cots, one after the other, like dresses on a rack...
"...when I was just a little girl... I asked my mother..."
She thought, "Whichever one wakes up at the sound of my voice..."
"...what will I be (will be)...?"
But none of them did.
So she picked the prettiest one...
"...will I be pretty, will I be rich..."

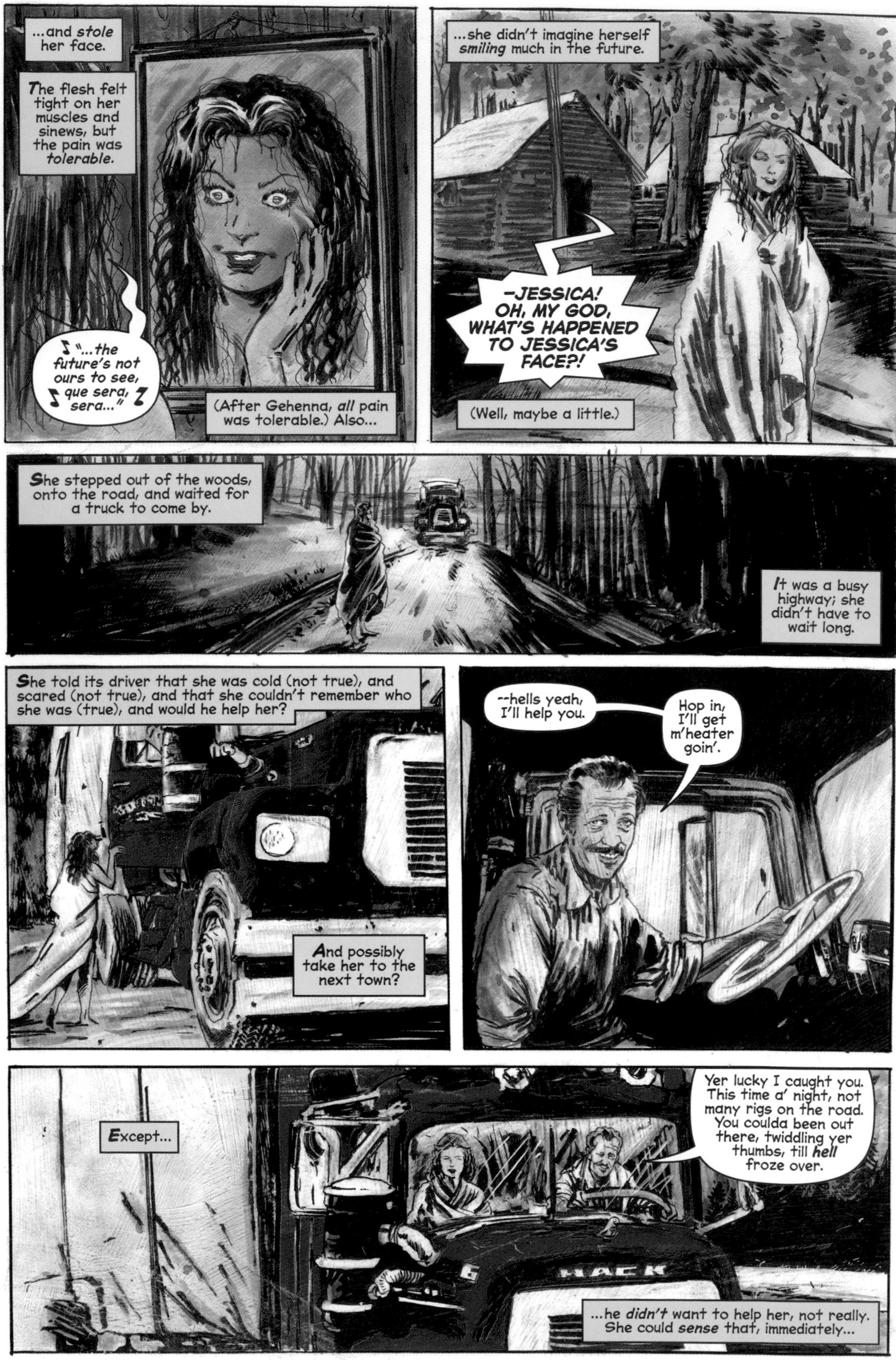
...and *stole* her face.
*T*he flesh felt tight on her muscles and sinews, but the pain was *tolerable.*
♪ "...the future's not ours to see, ♪ que sera, sera..." ♪
(After Gehenna, *all* pain was tolerable.) Also...
...she didn't imagine herself *smiling* much in the future.
–JESSICA! OH, MY GOD, WHAT'S HAPPENED TO JESSICA'S FACE?!
(Well, maybe a little.)
*S*he stepped out of the woods, onto the road, and waited for a truck to come by.
*I*t was a busy highway; she didn't have to wait long.
*S*he told its driver that she was cold (not true), and scared (not true), and that she couldn't remember who she was (true), and would he help her?
*A*nd possibly take her to the next town?
--hells yeah, I'll help you.
Hop in, I'll get m'heater goin'.
*E*xcept...
Yer lucky I caught you. This time a' night, not many rigs on the road. You coulda been out there, twiddling yer thumbs, till *hell* froze over.
...he *didn't* want to help her, not really. She could *sense* that, immediately...

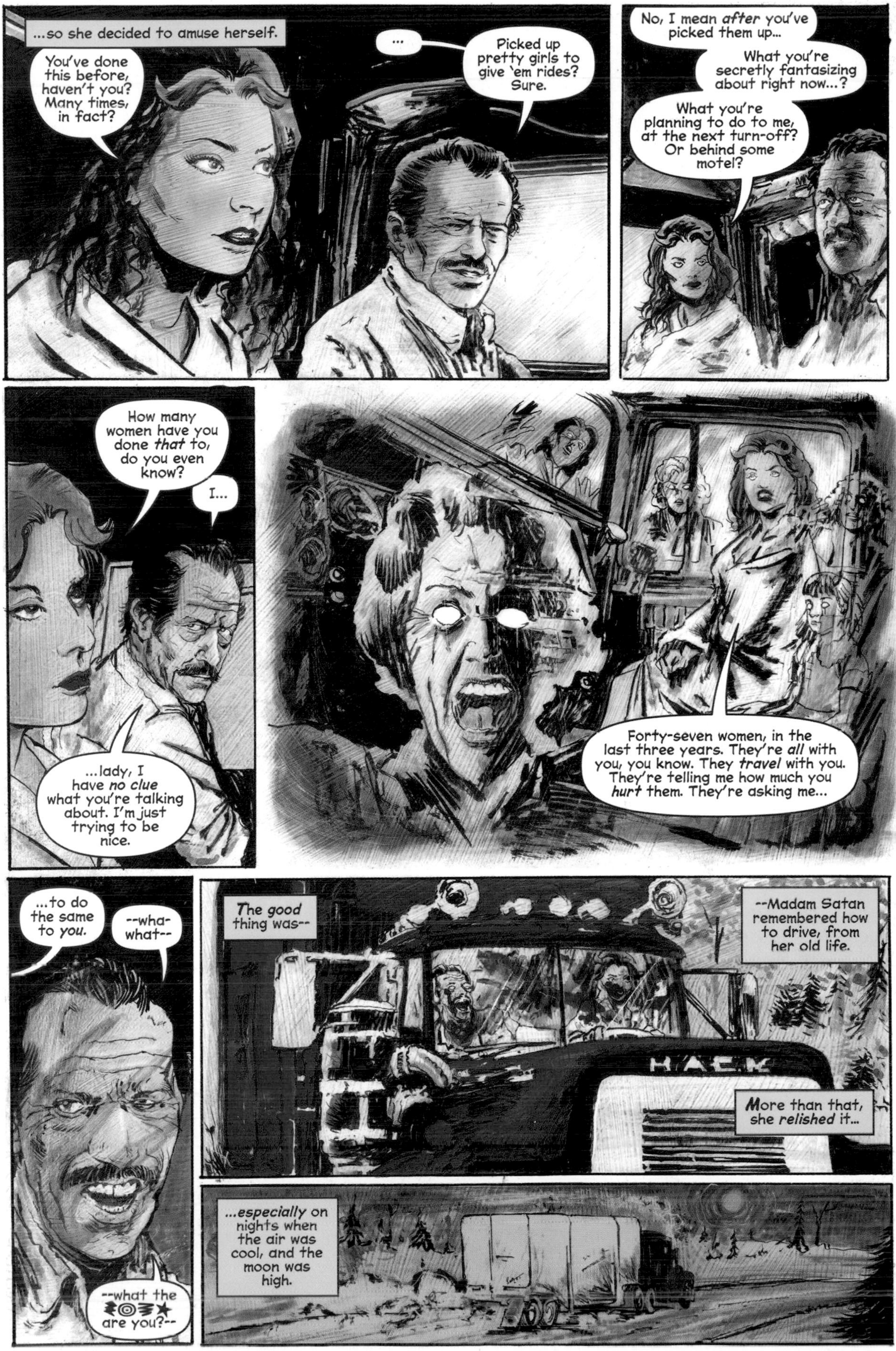
...so she decided to amuse herself.
You've done this before, haven't you? Many times, in fact?
...
Picked up pretty girls to give 'em rides? Sure.
No, I mean *after* you've picked them up...
What you're secretly fantasizing about right now...?
What you're planning to do to me, at the next turn-off? Or behind some motel?
How many women have you done *that* to, do you even know?
I...
...lady, I have *no clue* what you're talking about. I'm just trying to be nice.
Forty-seven women, in the last three years. They're *all* with you, you know. They *travel* with you. They're telling me how much you *hurt* them. They're asking me...
...to do the same to *you.*
--wha-what--
--what the are you?--
The good thing was--
--Madam Satan remembered how to drive, from her old life.
MACK
More than that, she *relished* it...
...*especially* on nights when the air was cool, and the moon was high.

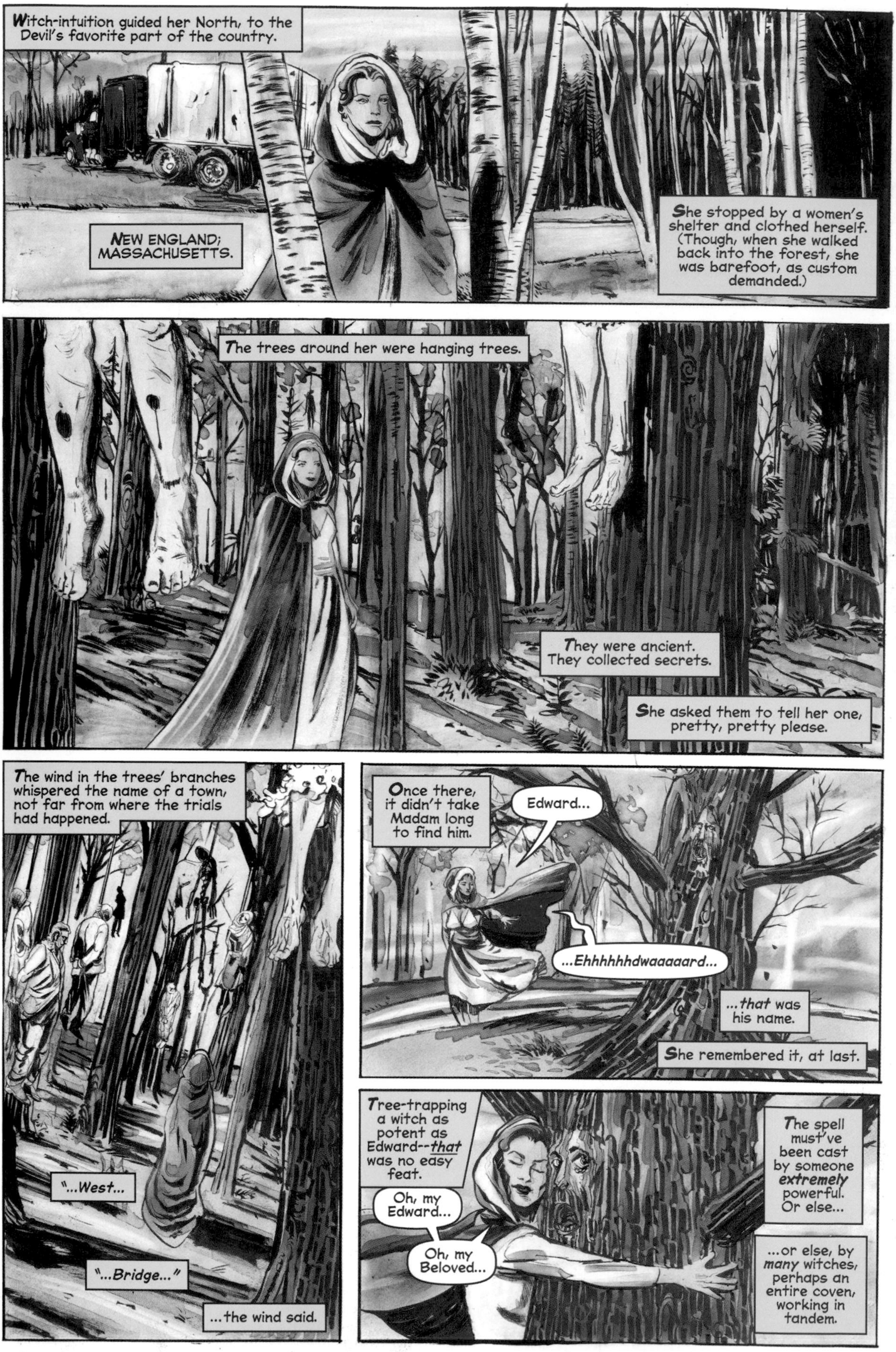

Witch-intuition guided her North, to the Devil's favorite part of the country.
NEW ENGLAND; MASSACHUSETTS.
She stopped by a women's shelter and clothed herself. (Though, when she walked back into the forest, she was barefoot, as custom demanded.)
The trees around her were hanging trees.
They were ancient. They collected secrets.
She asked them to tell her one, pretty, pretty please.
The wind in the trees' branches whispered the name of a town, not far from where the trials had happened.
"...West...
"...Bridge..."
...the wind said.
Once there, it didn't take Madam long to find him.
Edward...
...Ehhhhhhdwaaaaard...
...that was his name.
She remembered it, at last.
Tree-trapping a witch as potent as Edward--that was no easy feat.
Oh, my Edward...
Oh, my Beloved...
The spell must've been cast by someone extremely powerful. Or else...
...or else, by many witches, perhaps an entire coven, working in tandem.

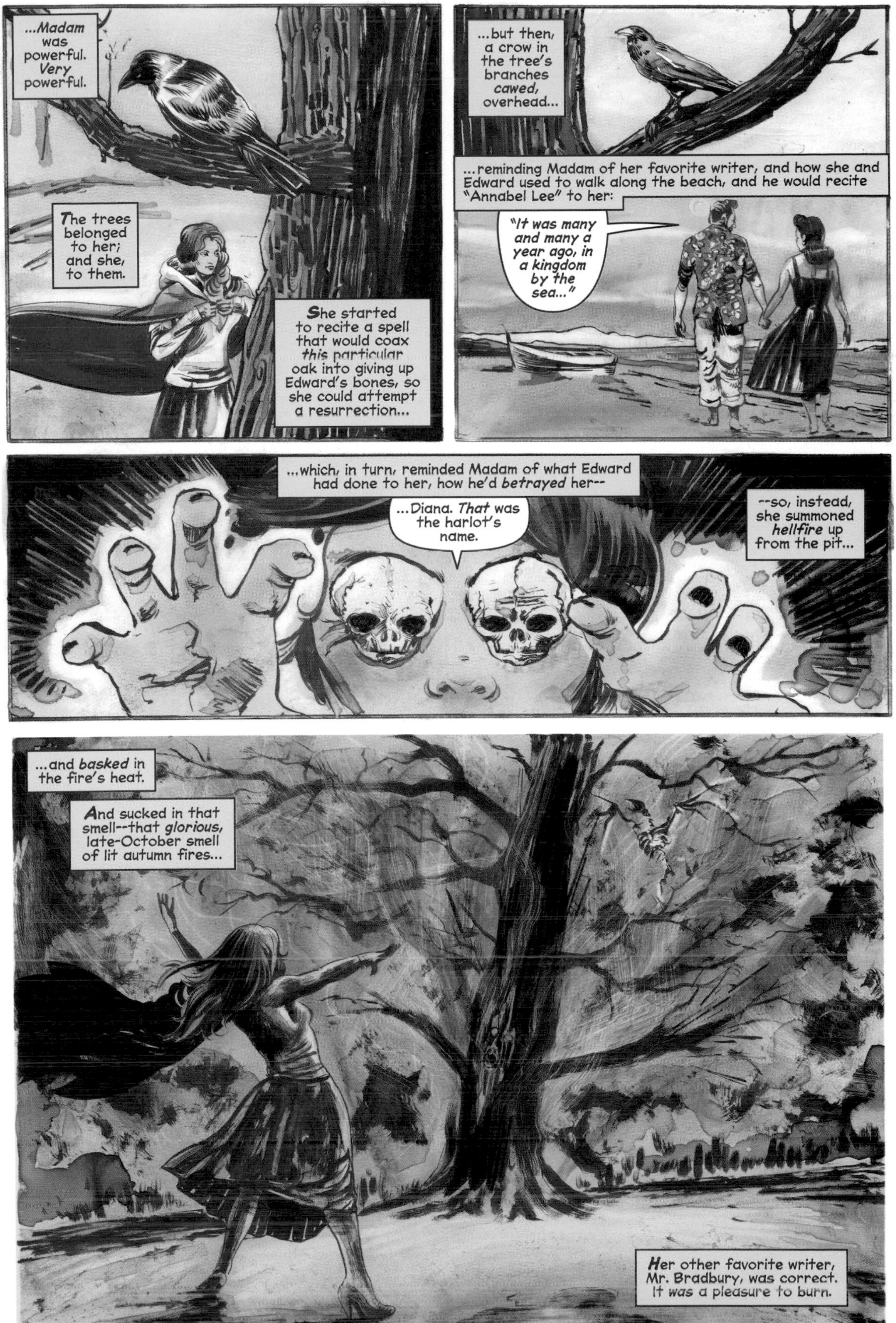

...Madam was powerful. Very powerful.
The trees belonged to her; and she, to them.
She started to recite a spell that would coax this particular oak into giving up Edward's bones, so she could attempt a resurrection...
...but then, a crow in the tree's branches cawed, overhead...
...reminding Madam of her favorite writer, and how she and Edward used to walk along the beach, and he would recite "Annabel Lee" to her:
"It was many and many a year ago, in a kingdom by the sea..."
...which, in turn, reminded Madam of what Edward had done to her, how he'd betrayed her--
...Diana. That was the harlot's name.
--so, instead, she summoned hellfire up from the pit...
...and basked in the fire's heat.
And sucked in that smell--that glorious, late-October smell of lit autumn fires...
Her other favorite writer, Mr. Bradbury, was correct. It was a pleasure to burn.

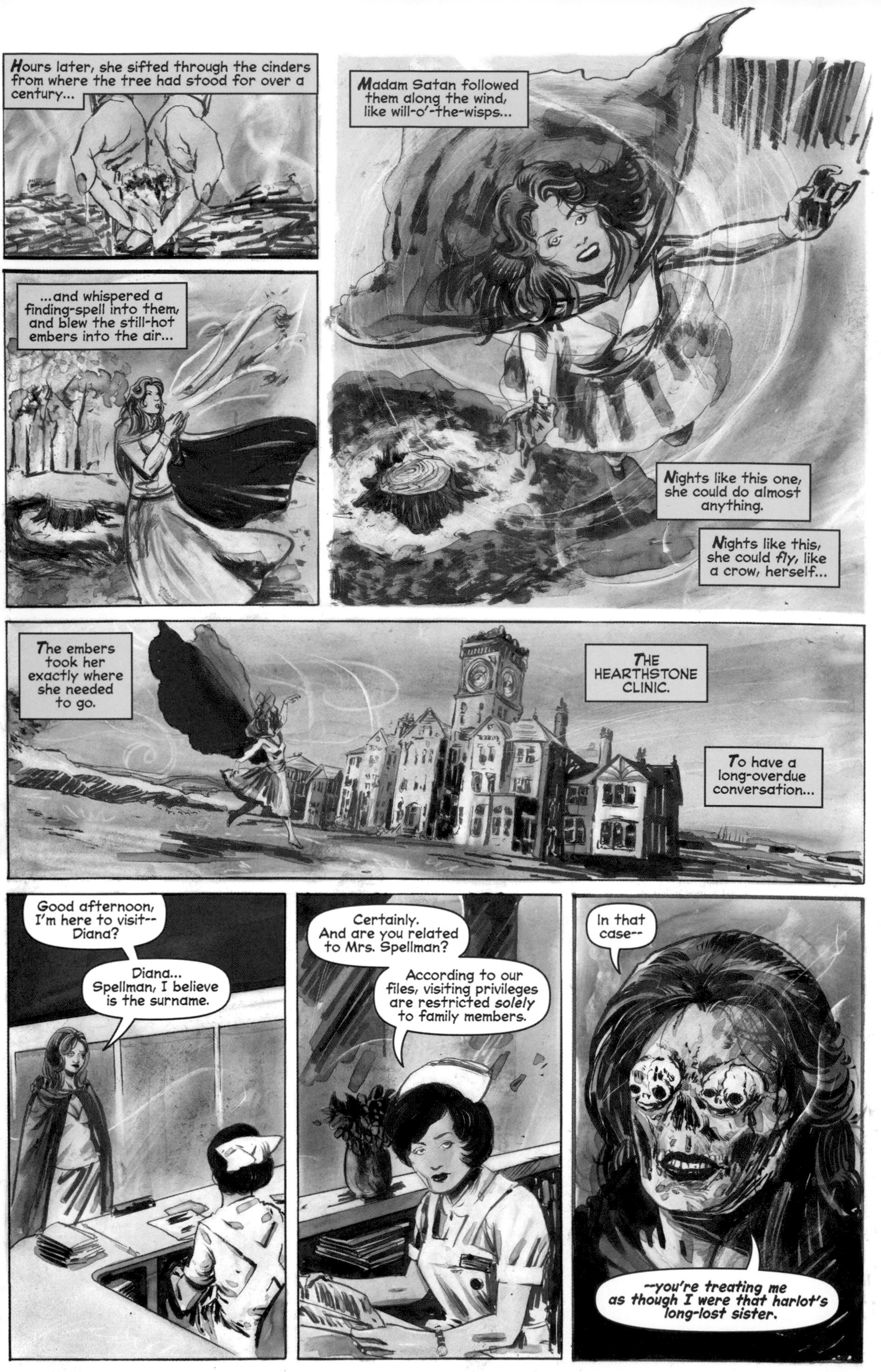
Hours later, she sifted through the cinders from where the tree had stood for over a century...
Madam Satan followed them along the wind, like will-o'-the-wisps...
...and whispered a finding-spell into them, and blew the still-hot embers into the air...
Nights like this one, she could do almost anything.
Nights like this, she could *fly*, like a crow, herself...
The embers took her exactly where she needed to go.
THE HEARTHSTONE CLINIC.
To have a long-overdue conversation...
Good afternoon, I'm here to visit-- Diana?
Diana... Spellman, I believe is the surname.
Certainly. And are you related to Mrs. Spellman?
According to our files, visiting privileges are restricted *solely* to family members.
In that case--
--you're treating me as though I were that harlot's long-lost sister.

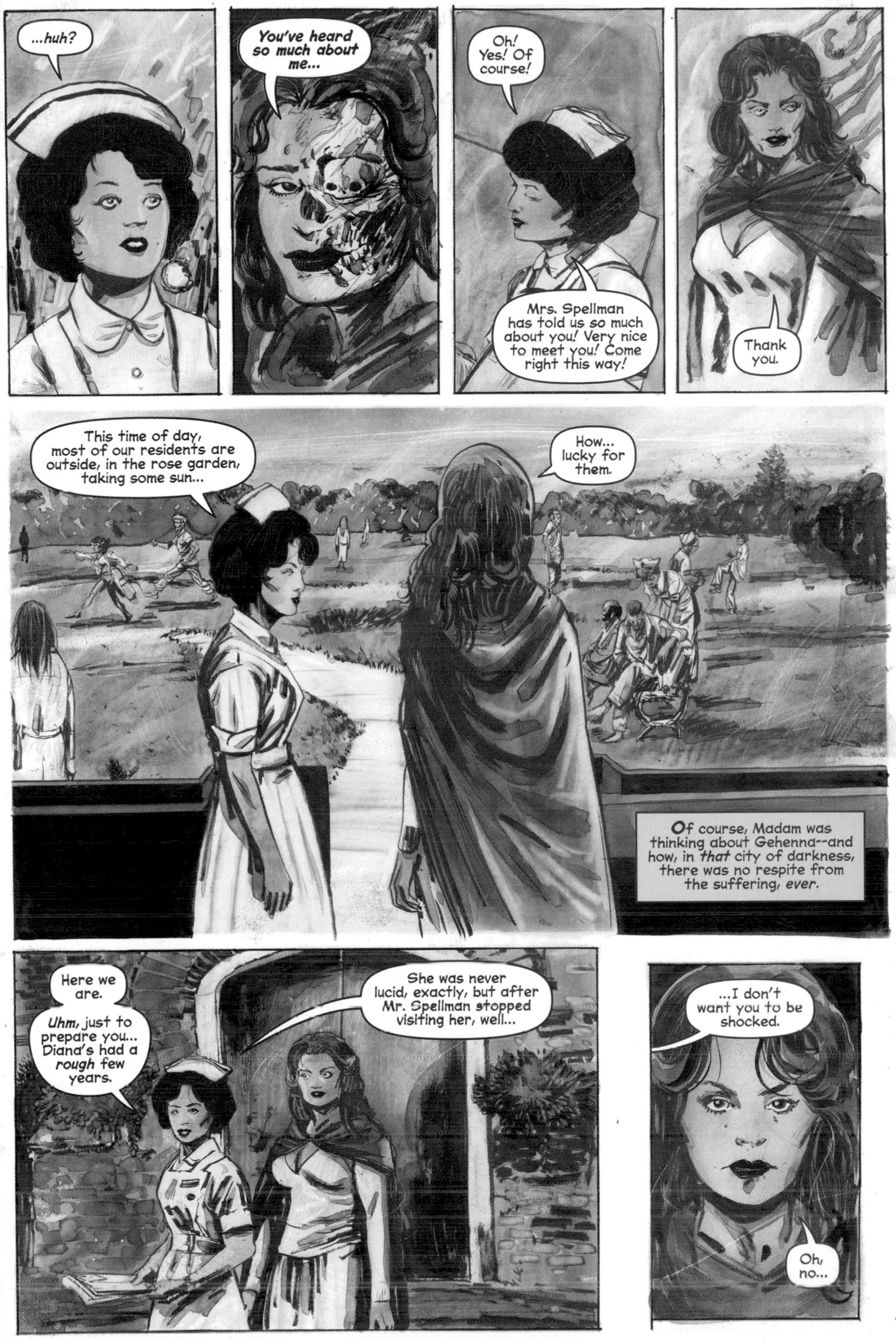
...huh?
You've heard so much about me...
Oh! Yes! Of course!
Mrs. Spellman has told us so much about you! Very nice to meet you! Come right this way!
Thank you.
This time of day, most of our residents are outside, in the rose garden, taking some sun...
How... lucky for them.
Of course, Madam was thinking about Gehenna--and how, in that city of darkness, there was no respite from the suffering, ever.
Here we are.
Uhm, just to prepare you... Diana's had a rough few years.
She was never lucid, exactly, but after Mr. Spellman stopped visiting her, well...
...I don't want you to be shocked.
Oh, no...

...I'm incapable of being shocked, Nurse.

Good afternoon, Diana, you're looking well.

...hhn...

...hhurr...

You'll excuse yourself now.

...I'll let you two be.

Ta-ta.

...hhRRRR...

--hhrr--hrrrr --hhnnghhh...

Not to worry, dear Diana...

...I'll do the talking.

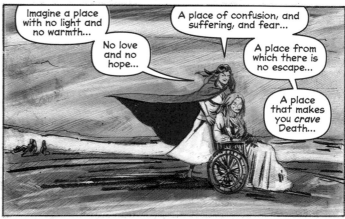

Imagine a place with no light and no warmth...

No love and no hope...

A place of confusion, and suffering, and fear...

A place from which there is no escape...

A place that makes you crave Death...

You're probably thinking, "She's talking about hell," and do you know what?

I am.

Not literal Hell, mind you... Maestro Alighieri's Infierno ...but where I found myself, one day, some years ago...

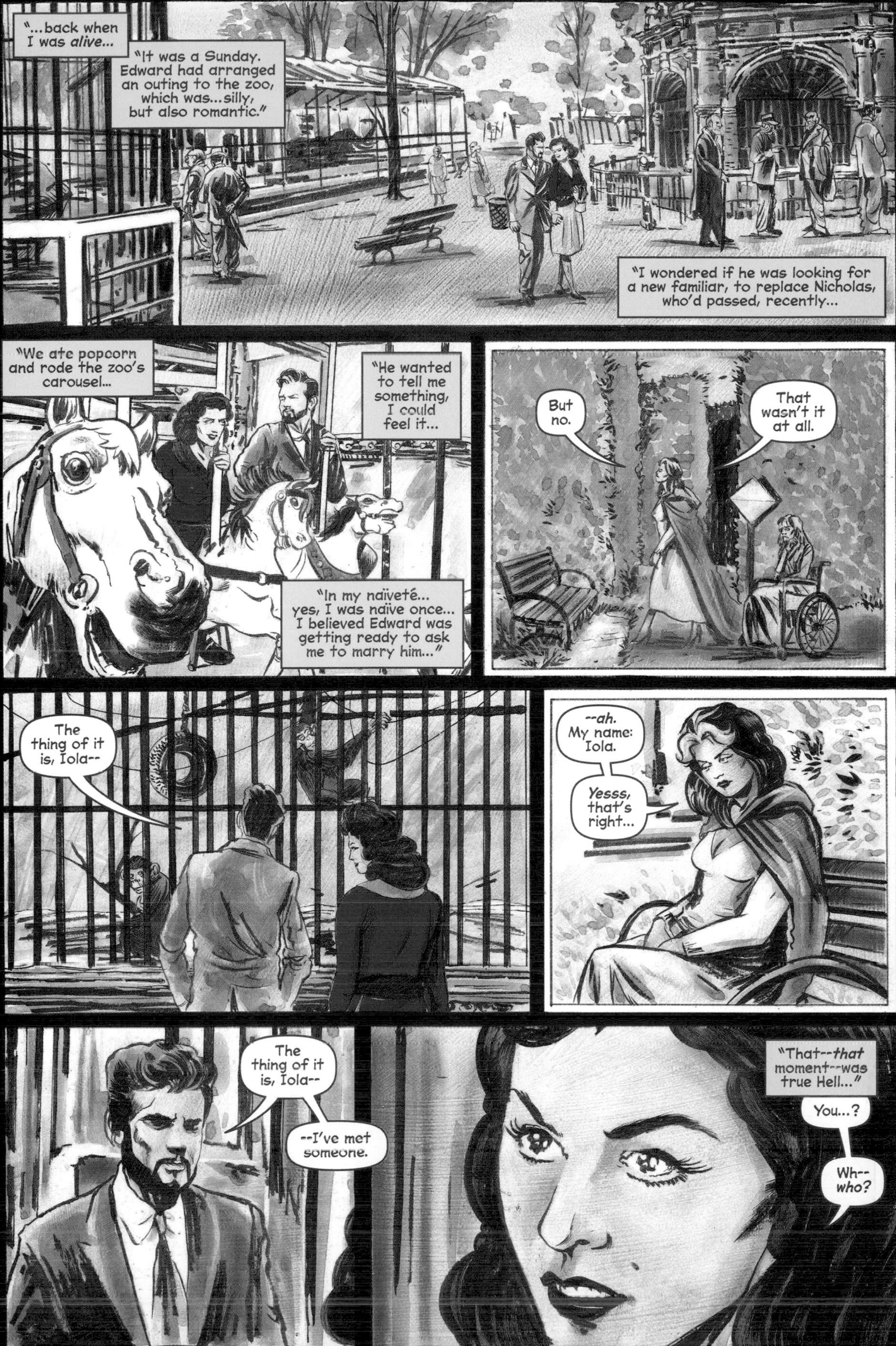
"...back when I was *alive*...
"It was a Sunday. Edward had arranged an outing to the zoo, which was...silly, but also romantic."
"I wondered if he was looking for a new familiar, to replace Nicholas, who'd passed, recently...
"We ate popcorn and rode the zoo's carousel...
"He wanted to tell me something, I could feel it...
"In my naïveté... yes, I was naïve once... I believed Edward was getting ready to ask me to marry him..."
But no.
That wasn't it at all.
The thing of it is, Iola--
--ah. My name: Iola.
Yesss, that's right...
The thing of it is, Iola--
--I've met someone.
"That--*that* moment--was true Hell..."
You...?
Wh-- *who?*

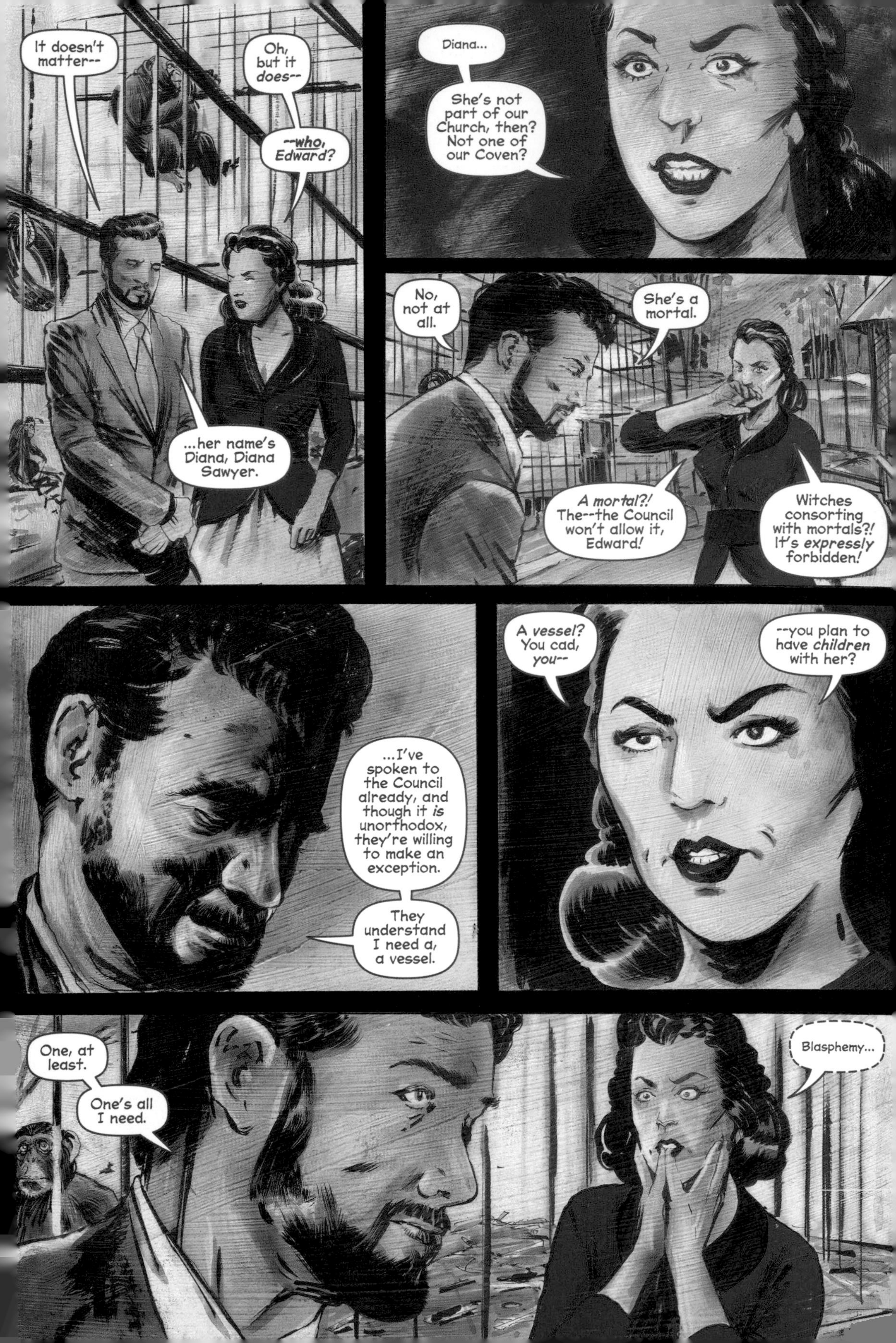
It doesn't matter--
Oh, but it *does*--
--*who*, Edward?
...her name's Diana, Diana Sawyer.
Diana...
She's not part of our Church, then? Not one of our Coven?
No, not at all.
She's a mortal.
A mortal?! The--the Council won't allow it, Edward!
Witches consorting with mortals?! It's *expressly* forbidden!
...I've spoken to the Council already, and though it *is* unorthodox, they're willing to make an exception.
They understand I need a, a vessel.
A *vessel*? You cad, *you*--
--you plan to have *children* with her?
One, at least.
One's all I need.
Blasphemy...

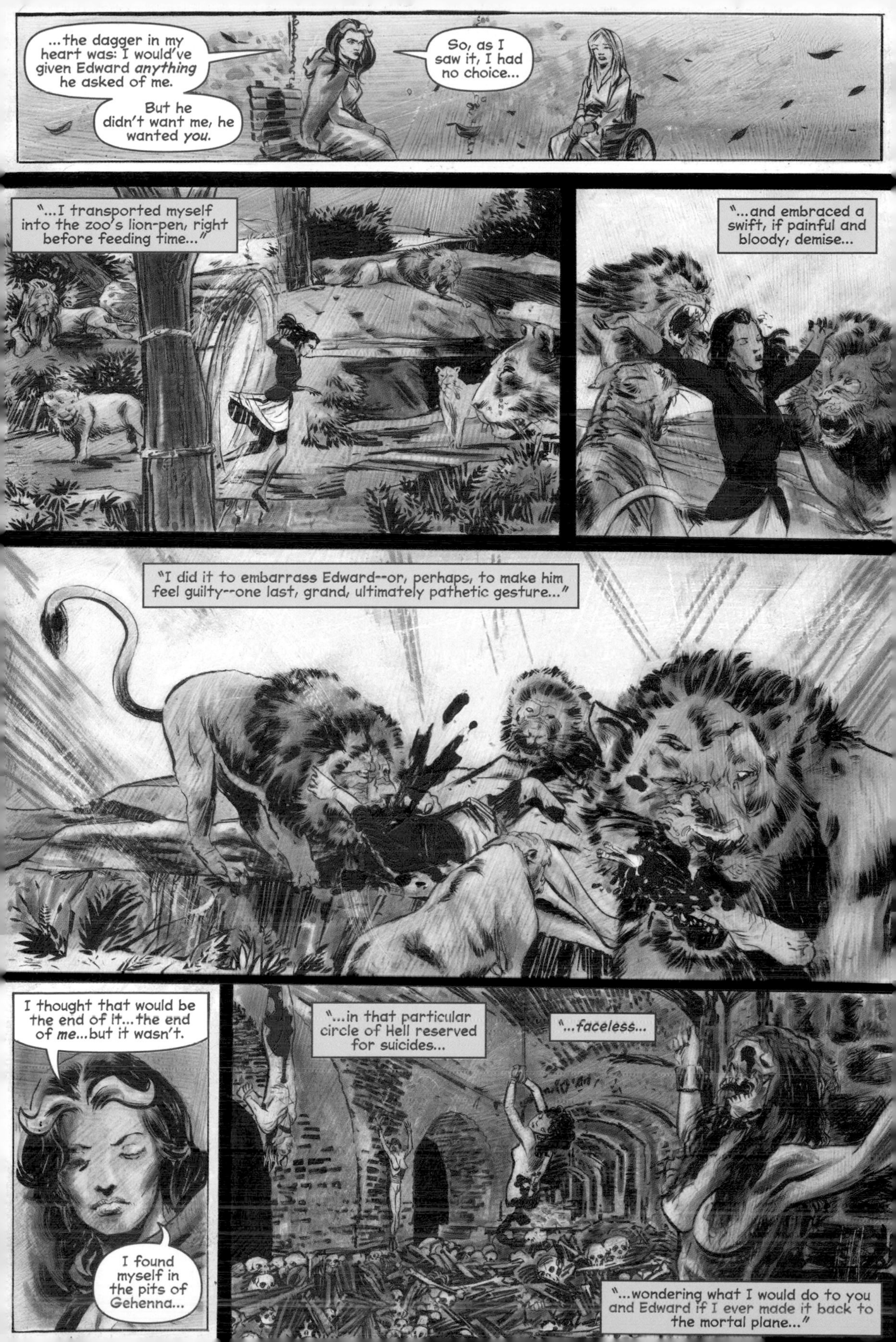
...the dagger in my heart was: I would've given Edward *anything* he asked of me.
But he didn't want me, he wanted *you.*
So, as I saw it, I had no choice...
"...I transported myself into the zoo's lion-pen, right before feeding time..."
"...and embraced a swift, if painful and bloody, demise...
"I did it to embarrass Edward--or, perhaps, to make him feel guilty--one last, grand, ultimately pathetic gesture..."
I thought that would be the end of it...the end of *me*...but it wasn't.
I found myself in the pits of Gehenna...
"...in that particular circle of Hell reserved for suicides...
"...*faceless*...
"...wondering what I would do to you and Edward if I ever made it back to the mortal plane..."

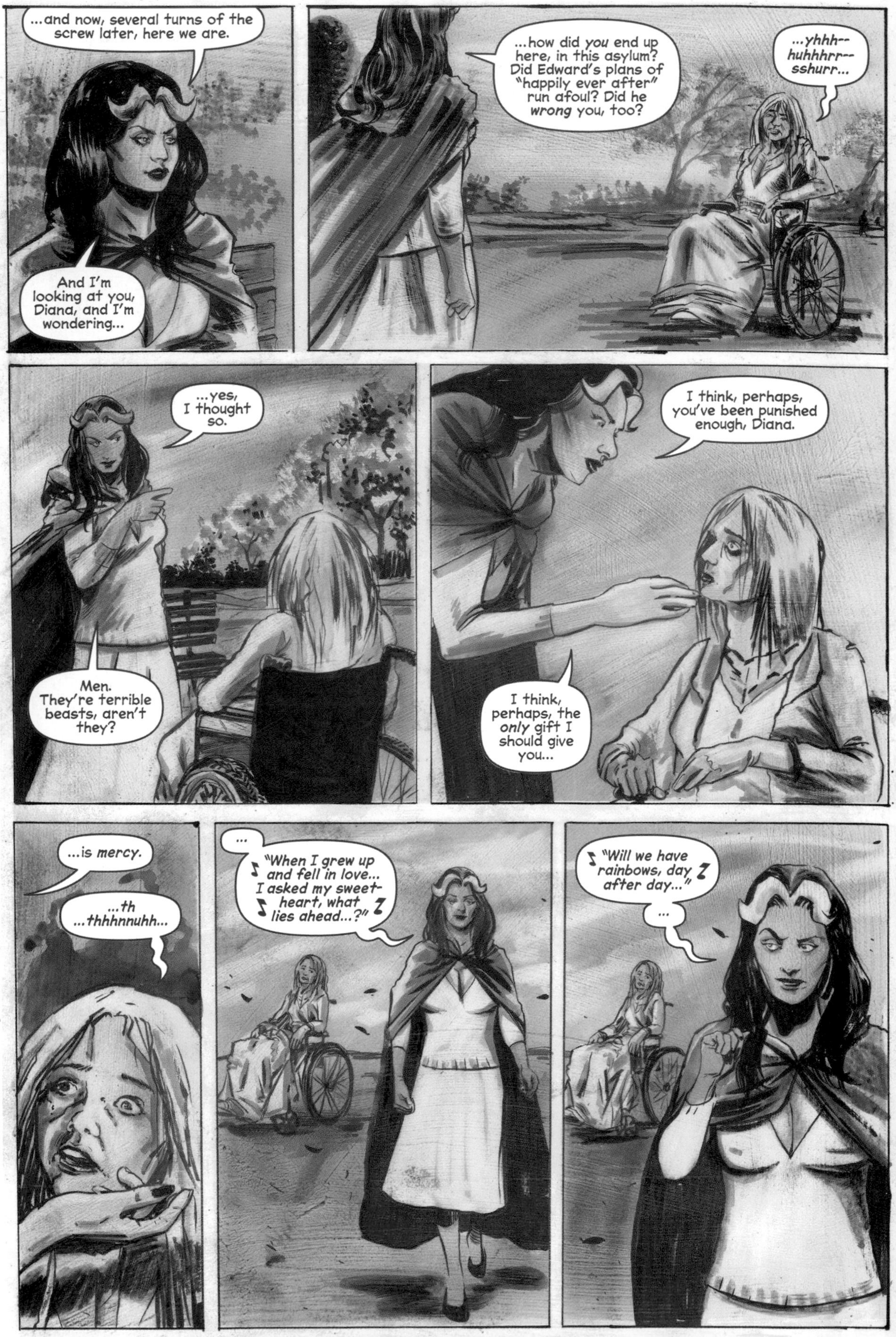
...and now, several turns of the screw later, here we are.
And I'm looking at you, Diana, and I'm wondering...
...how did *you* end up here, in this asylum? Did Edward's plans of "happily ever after" run afoul? Did he *wrong* you, too?
...yhhh--huhhhrr--sshurr...
...yes, I thought so.
Men. They're terrible beasts, aren't they?
I think, perhaps, you've been punished enough, Diana.
I think, perhaps, the *only* gift I should give you...
...is *mercy*.
...th ...thhhnnuhh...
...
"When I grew up and fell in love... I asked my sweet-heart, what lies ahead...?"
"Will we have rainbows, day after day..."
...

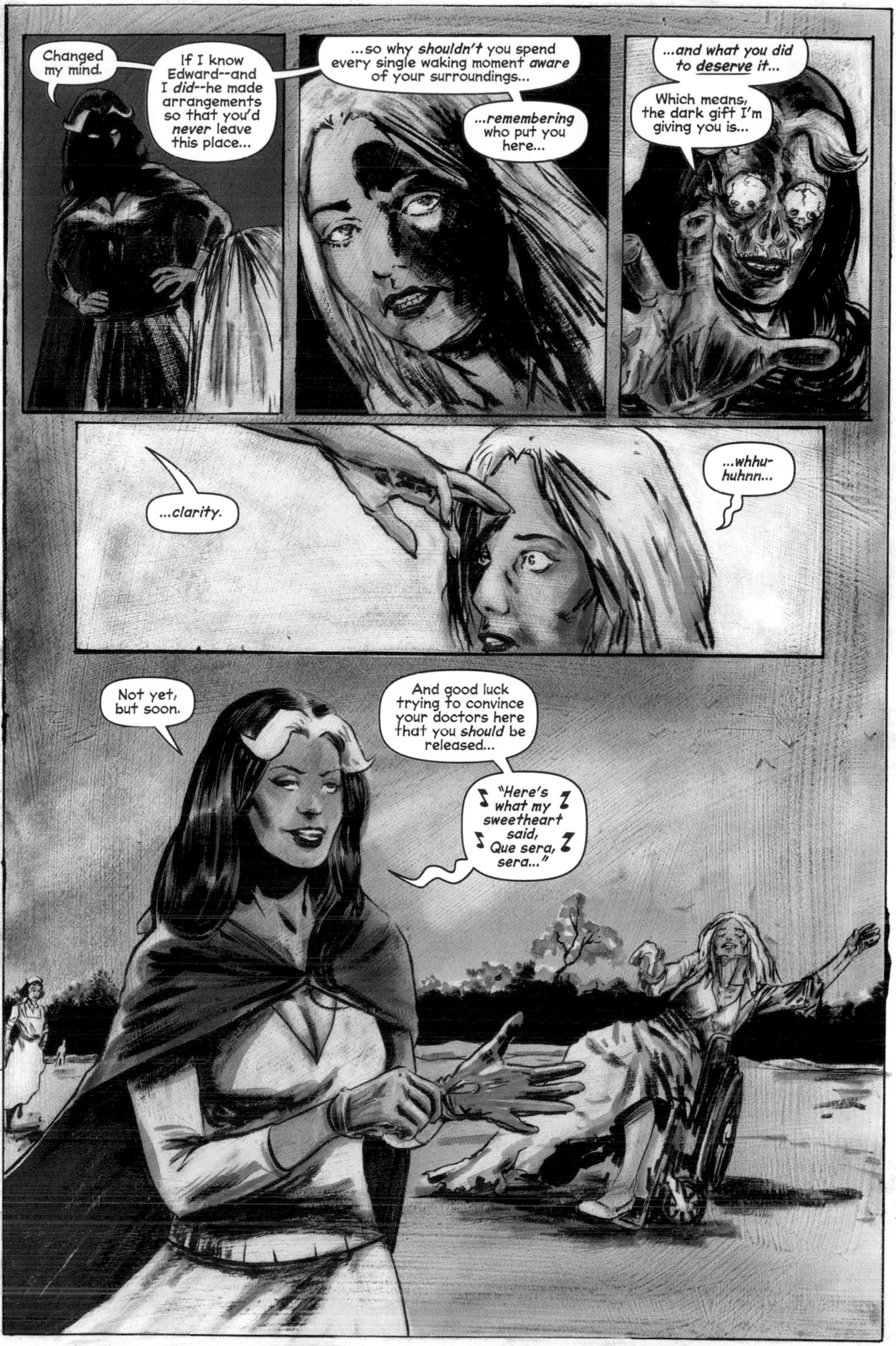
Changed my mind.
If I know Edward--and I *did*--he made arrangements so that you'd *never* leave this place...
...so why *shouldn't* you spend every single waking moment *aware* of your surroundings...
...remembering who put you here...
*...and what you did to **deserve** it...*
Which means, the dark gift I'm giving you is...
...clarity.
...whhu-huhnn...
Not yet, but soon.
And good luck trying to convince your doctors here that you *should* be released...
"Here's what my sweetheart said, Que sera, sera..."

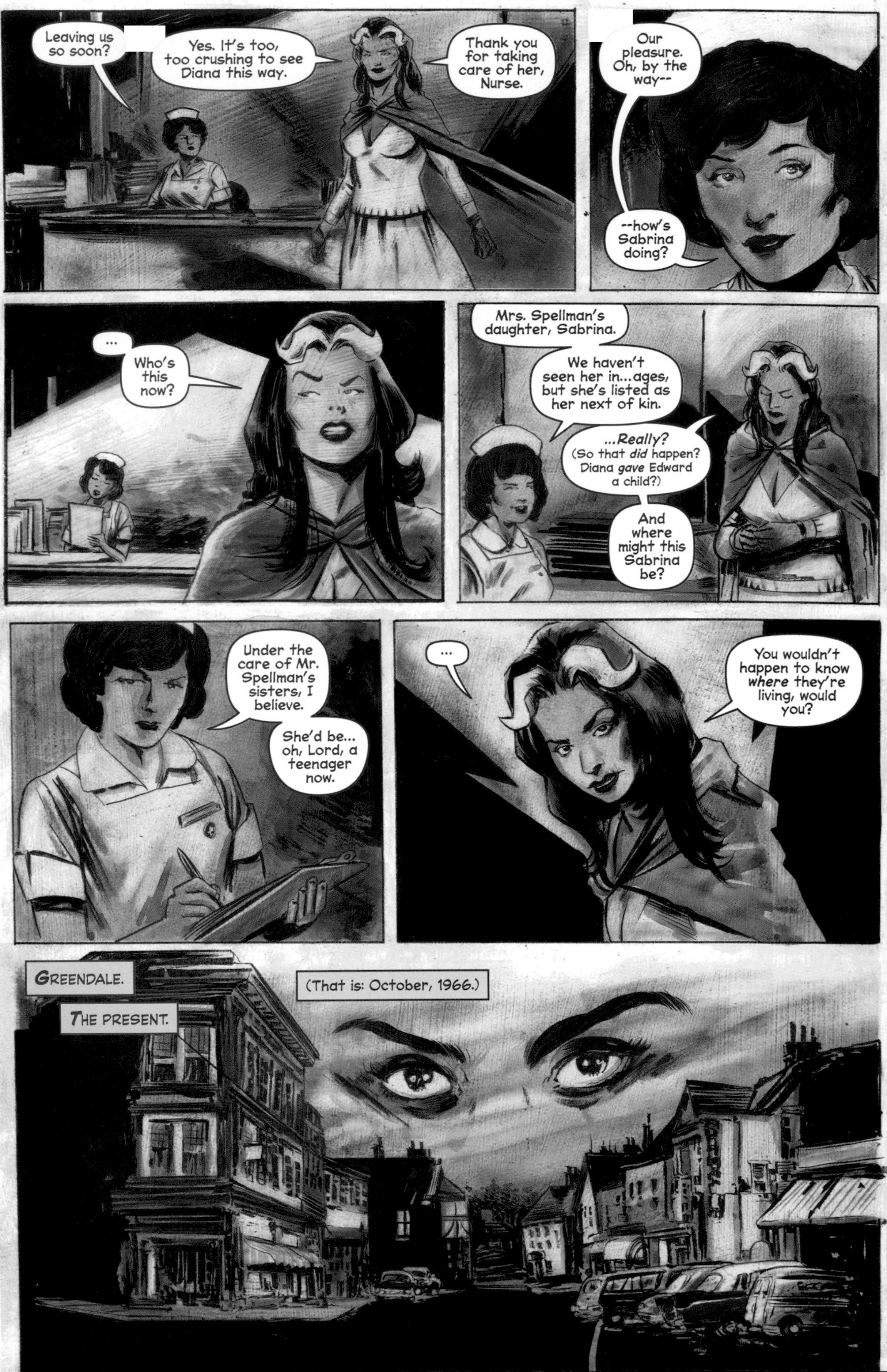
Leaving us so soon?
Yes. It's too, too crushing to see Diana this way.
Thank you for taking care of her, Nurse.
Our pleasure. Oh, by the way--
--how's Sabrina doing?
...
Who's this now?
Mrs. Spellman's daughter, Sabrina.
We haven't seen her in...ages, but she's listed as her next of kin.
...Really?
(So that did happen? Diana gave Edward a child?)
And where might this Sabrina be?
Under the care of Mr. Spellman's sisters, I believe.
She'd be... oh, Lord, a teenager now.
...
You wouldn't happen to know where they're living, would you?
GREENDALE.
THE PRESENT.
(That is: October, 1966.)

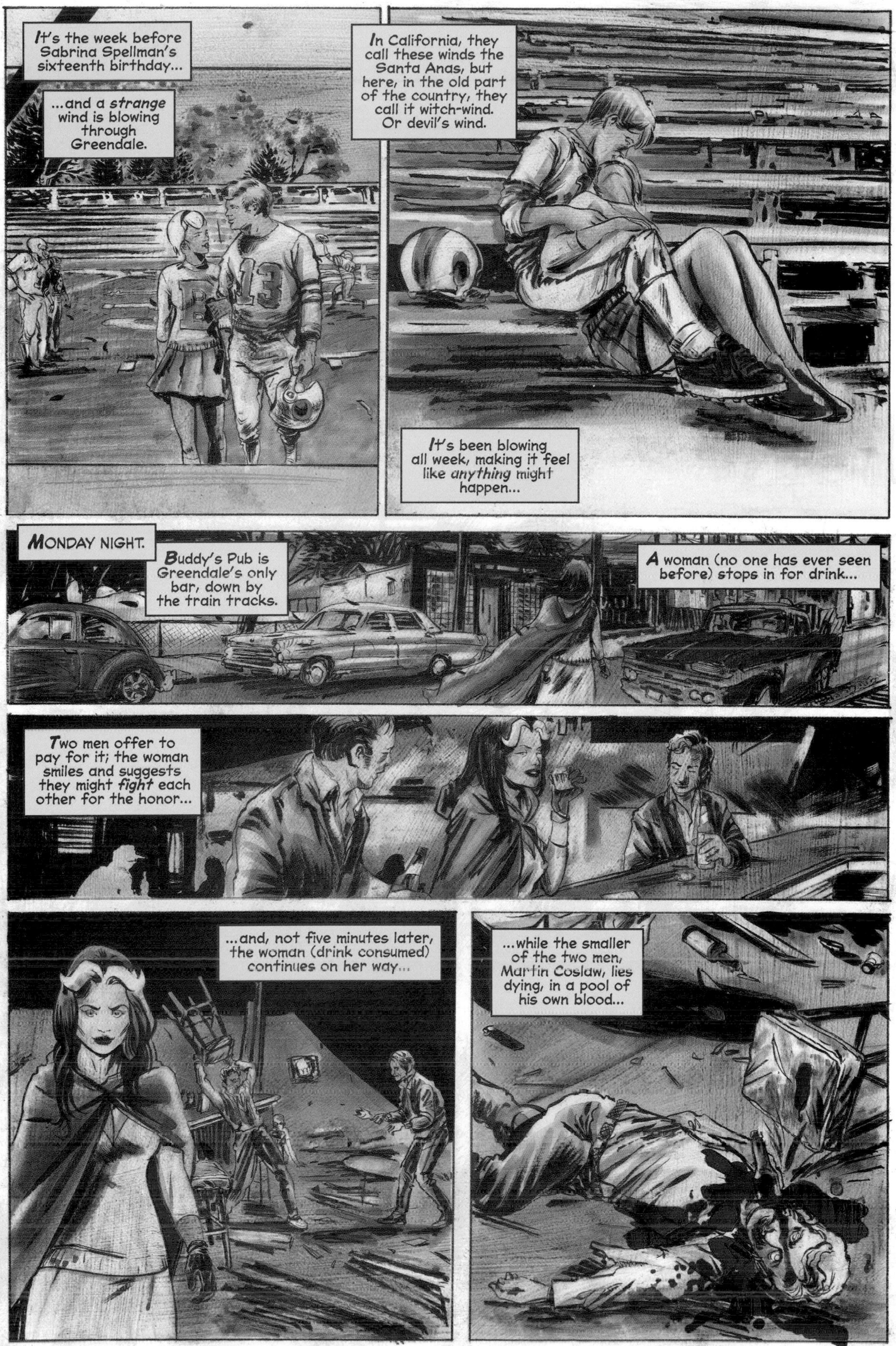
It's the week before Sabrina Spellman's sixteenth birthday...
...and a *strange* wind is blowing through Greendale.
In California, they call these winds the Santa Anas, but here, in the old part of the country, they call it witch-wind. Or devil's wind.
It's been blowing all week, making it feel like *anything* might happen...
MONDAY NIGHT.
Buddy's Pub is Greendale's only bar, down by the train tracks.
A woman (no one has ever seen before) stops in for drink...
Two men offer to pay for it; the woman smiles and suggests they might *fight* each other for the honor...
...and, not five minutes later, the woman (drink consumed) continues on her way...
...while the smaller of the two men, Martin Coslaw, lies dying, in a pool of his own blood...

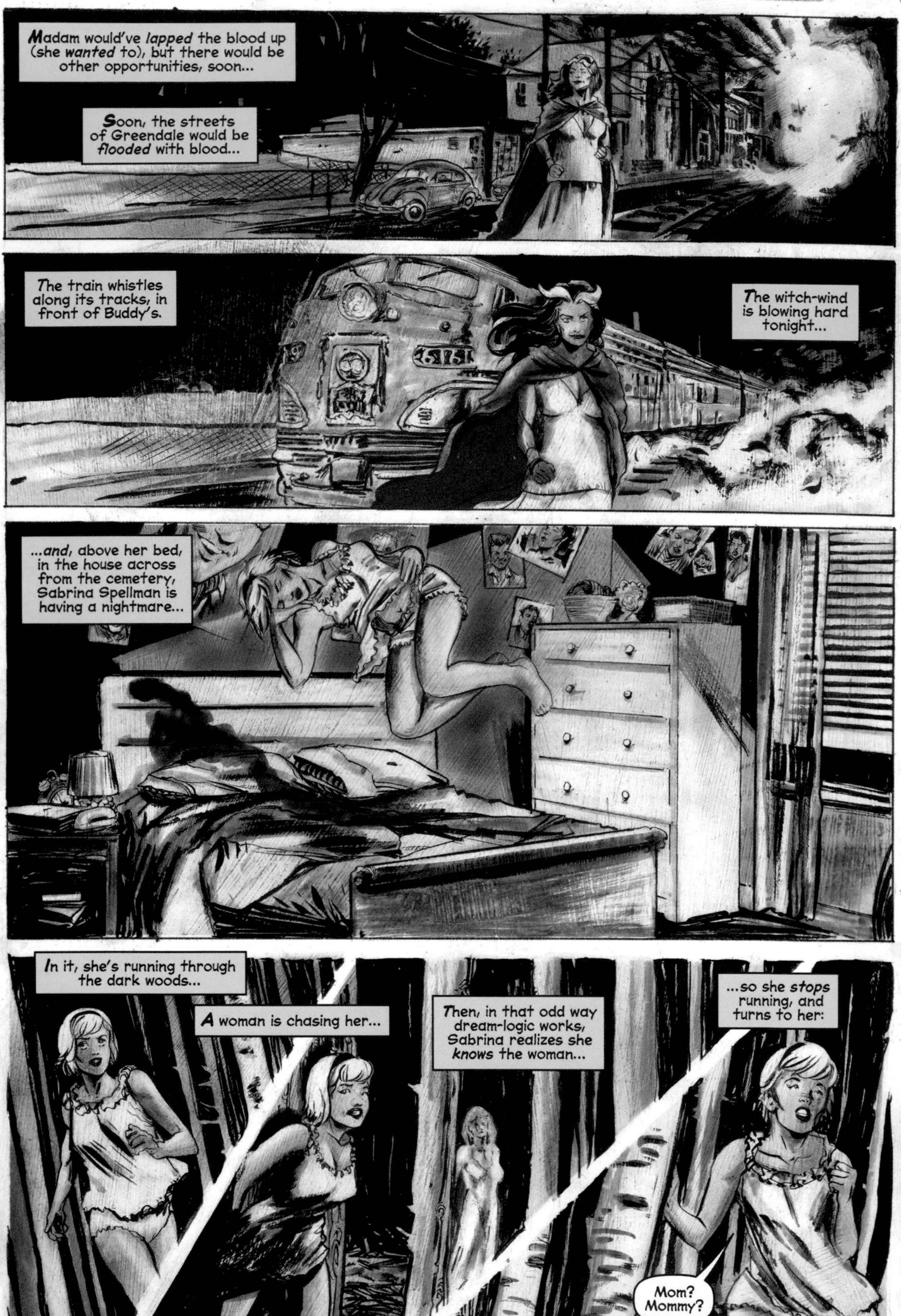
Madam would've lapped the blood up (she wanted to), but there would be other opportunities, soon...
Soon, the streets of Greendale would be flooded with blood...
The train whistles along its tracks, in front of Buddy's.
The witch-wind is blowing hard tonight...
...and, above her bed, in the house across from the cemetery, Sabrina Spellman is having a nightmare...
In it, she's running through the dark woods...
A woman is chasing her...
Then, in that odd way dream-logic works, Sabrina realizes she knows the woman...
...so she stops running, and turns to her:
Mom? Mommy?

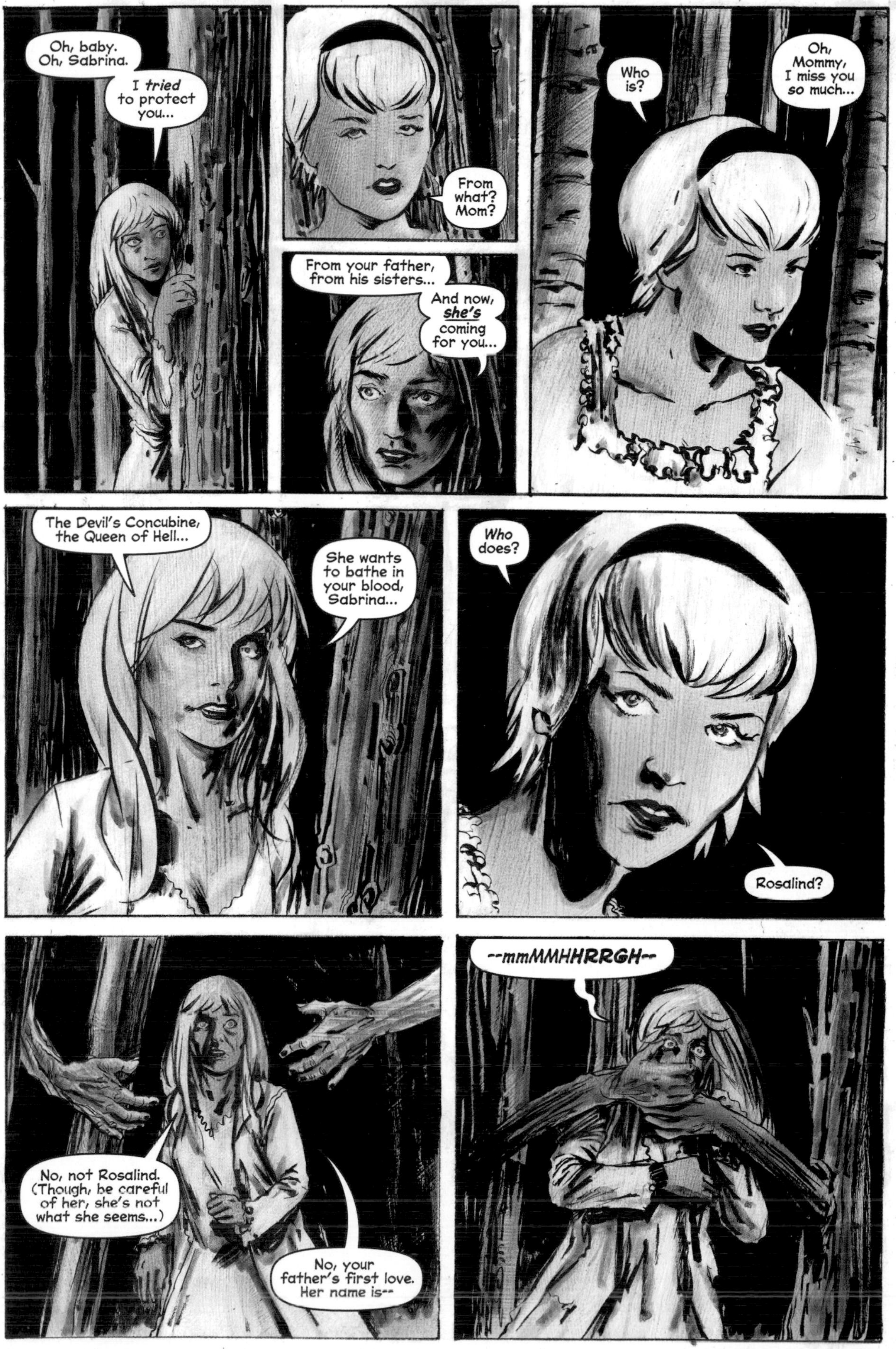

Oh, baby. Oh, Sabrina.
I *tried* to protect you...
From what? Mom?
From your father, from his sisters...
And now, ***she's*** coming for you...
Who is?
Oh, Mommy, I miss you so much...
The Devil's Concubine, the Queen of Hell...
She wants to bathe in your blood, Sabrina...
Who does?
Rosalind?
No, not Rosalind. (Though, be careful of her, she's not what she seems...)
No, your father's first love. Her name is--
--mmMMHHRRGH--

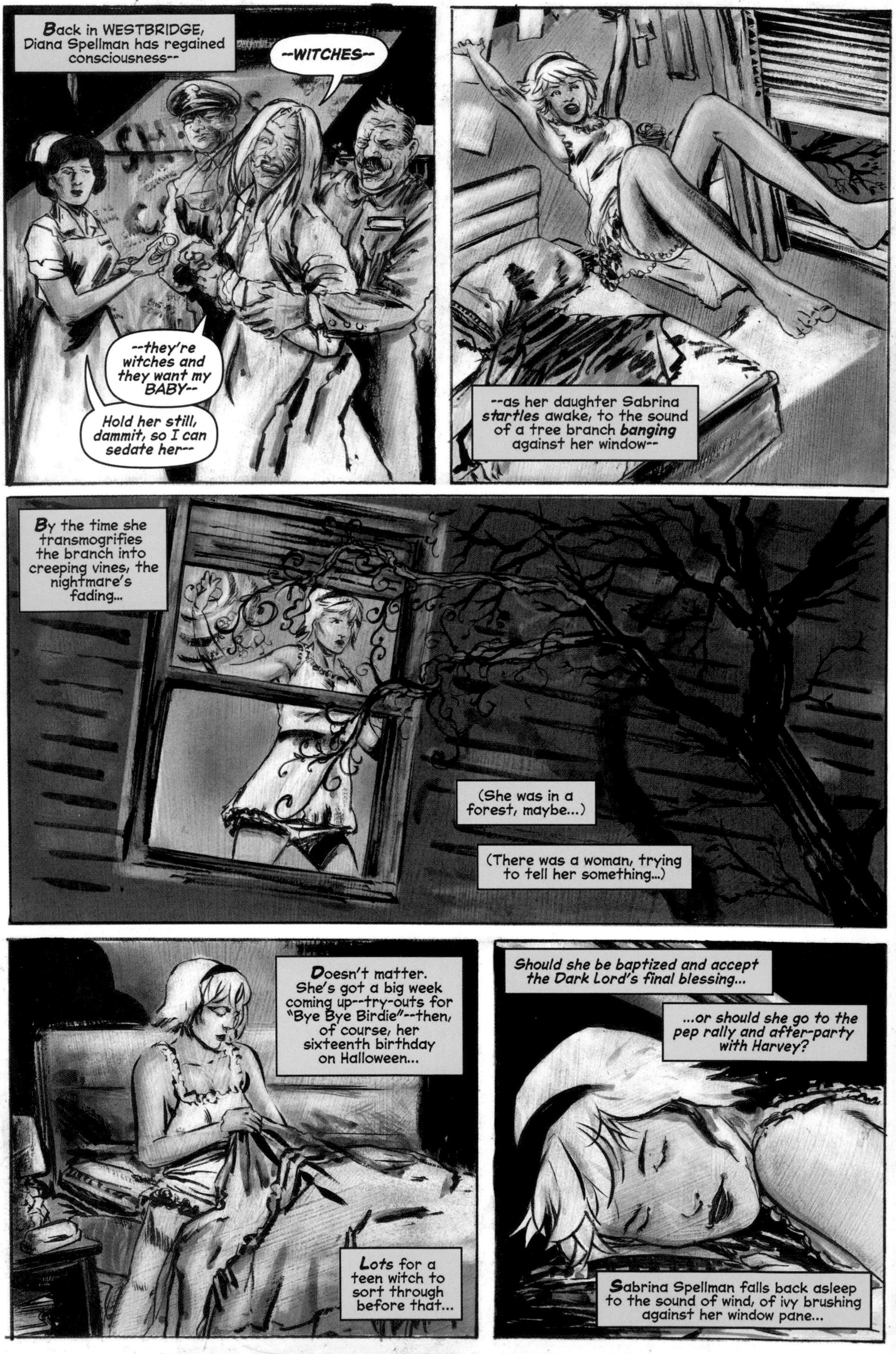
Back in WESTBRIDGE, Diana Spellman has regained consciousness--
--WITCHES--
--they're witches and they want my BABY--
Hold her still, dammit, so I can sedate her--
--as her daughter Sabrina startles awake, to the sound of a tree branch banging against her window--
By the time she transmogrifies the branch into creeping vines, the nightmare's fading...
(She was in a forest, maybe...)
(There was a woman, trying to tell her something...)
Doesn't matter. She's got a big week coming up--try-outs for "Bye Bye Birdie"--then, of course, her sixteenth birthday on Halloween...
Lots for a teen witch to sort through before that...
Should she be baptized and accept the Dark Lord's final blessing...
...or should she go to the pep rally and after-party with Harvey?
Sabrina Spellman falls back asleep to the sound of wind, of ivy brushing against her window pane...

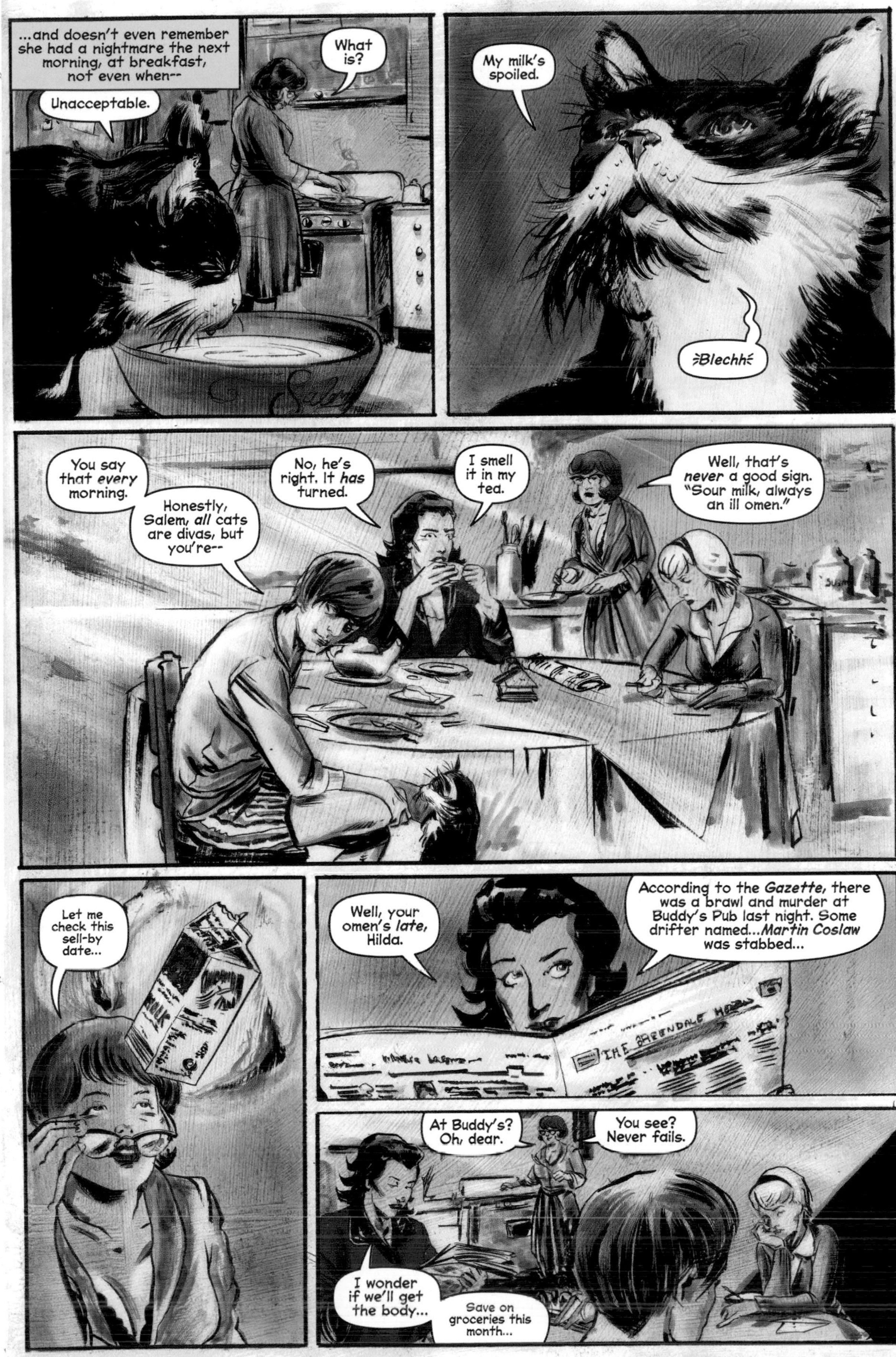
...and doesn't even remember she had a nightmare the next morning, at breakfast, not even when--
What is?
Unacceptable.
My milk's spoiled.
Blechh
You say that *every* morning.
Honestly, Salem, *all* cats are divas, but you're--
No, he's right. It *has* turned.
I smell it in my tea.
Well, that's *never* a good sign. "Sour milk, always an ill omen."
Let me check this sell-by date...
Well, your omen's *late,* Hilda.
According to the *Gazette,* there was a brawl and murder at Buddy's Pub last night. Some drifter named...*Martin Coslaw* was stabbed...
At Buddy's? Oh, dear.
You see? Never fails.
I wonder if we'll get the body...
Save on groceries this month...

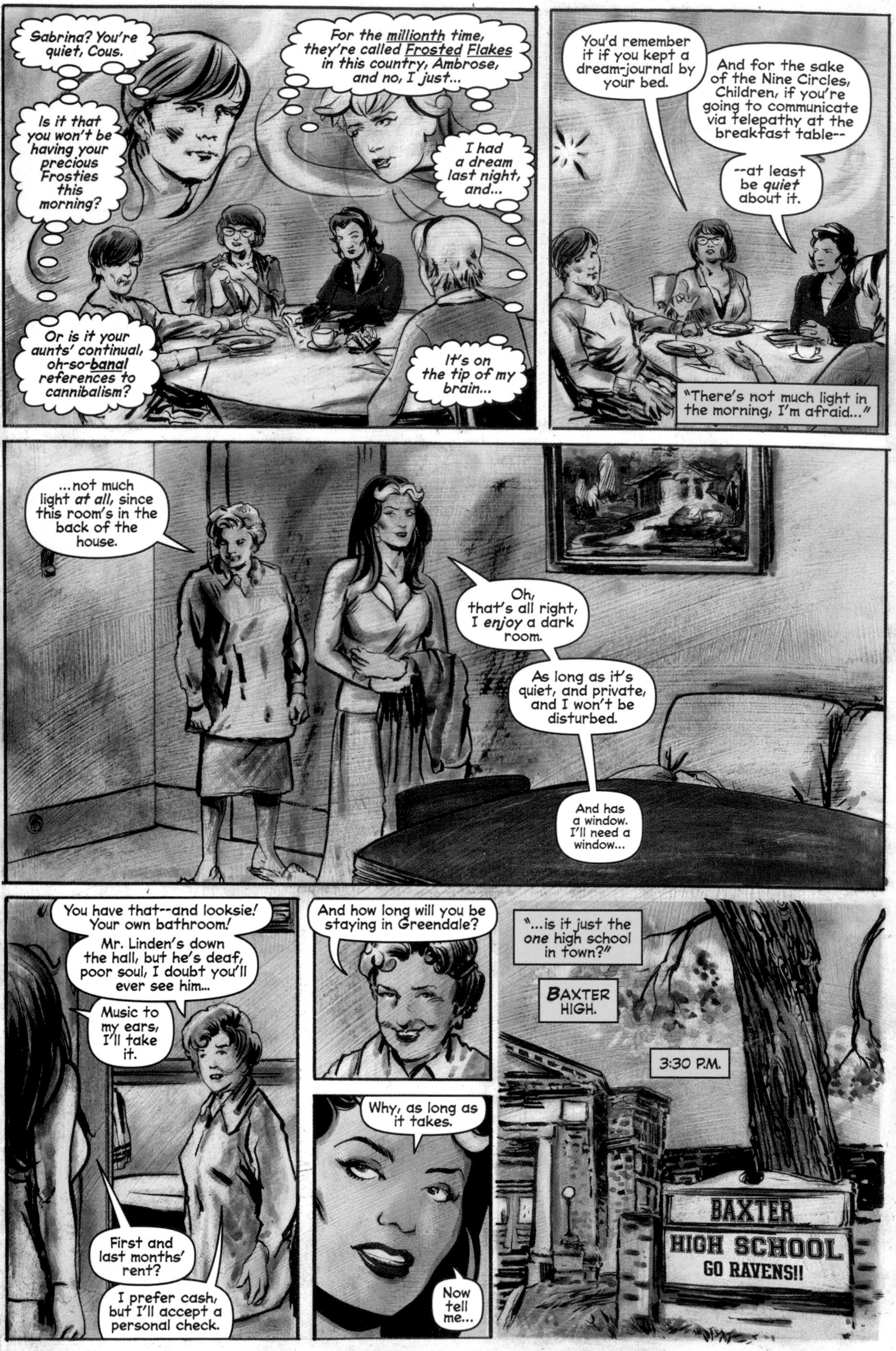
Sabrina? You're quiet, Cous.
Is it that you won't be having your precious Frosties this morning?
Or is it your aunts' continual, oh-so-banal references to cannibalism?
For the millionth time, they're called Frosted Flakes in this country, Ambrose, and no, I just...
I had a dream last night, and...
It's on the tip of my brain...
You'd remember it if you kept a dream-journal by your bed.
And for the sake of the Nine Circles, Children, if you're going to communicate via telepathy at the breakfast table--
--at least be quiet about it.
"There's not much light in the morning, I'm afraid..."
...not much light at all, since this room's in the back of the house.
Oh, that's all right, I enjoy a dark room.
As long as it's quiet, and private, and I won't be disturbed.
And has a window. I'll need a window...
You have that--and looksie! Your own bathroom!
Mr. Linden's down the hall, but he's deaf, poor soul, I doubt you'll ever see him...
Music to my ears, I'll take it.
First and last months' rent?
I prefer cash, but I'll accept a personal check.
And how long will you be staying in Greendale?
Why, as long as it takes.
Now tell me...
"...is it just the one high school in town?"
BAXTER HIGH.
3:30 P.M.
BAXTER
HIGH SCHOOL
GO RAVENS!!

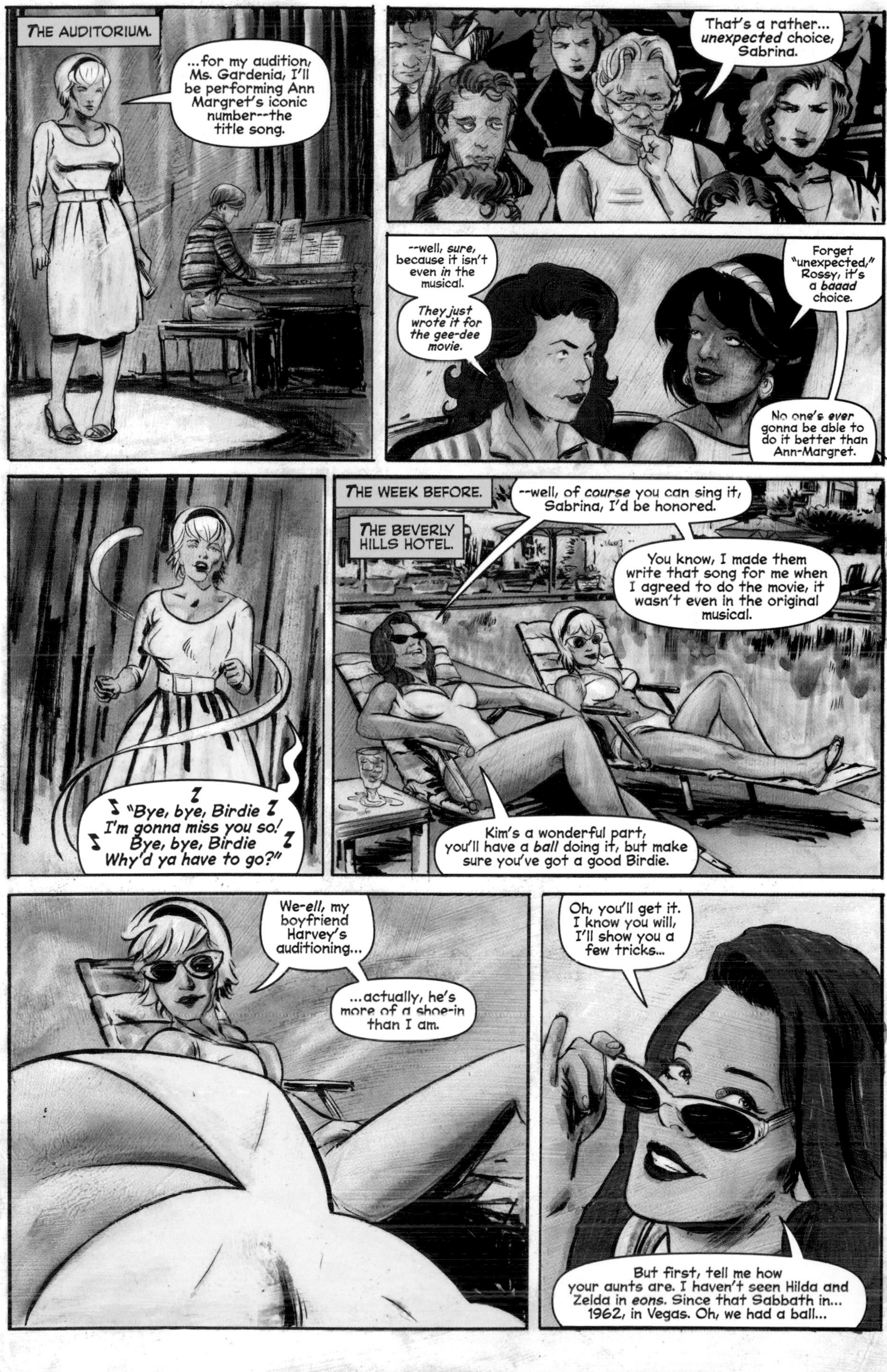
THE AUDITORIUM.
...for my audition, Ms. Gardenia, I'll be performing Ann Margret's iconic number--the title song.
That's a rather... unexpected choice, Sabrina.
--well, sure, because it isn't even in the musical.
They just wrote it for the gee-dee movie.
Forget "unexpected," Rossy, it's a baaad choice.
No one's ever gonna be able to do it better than Ann-Margret.
"Bye, bye, Birdie I'm gonna miss you so! Bye, bye, Birdie Why'd ya have to go?"
THE WEEK BEFORE.
THE BEVERLY HILLS HOTEL.
--well, of course you can sing it, Sabrina, I'd be honored.
You know, I made them write that song for me when I agreed to do the movie, it wasn't even in the original musical.
Kim's a wonderful part, you'll have a ball doing it, but make sure you've got a good Birdie.
We-ell, my boyfriend Harvey's auditioning...
...actually, he's more of a shoe-in than I am.
Oh, you'll get it. I know you will, I'll show you a few tricks...
But first, tell me how your aunts are. I haven't seen Hilda and Zelda in eons. Since that Sabbath in... 1962, in Vegas. Oh, we had a ball...

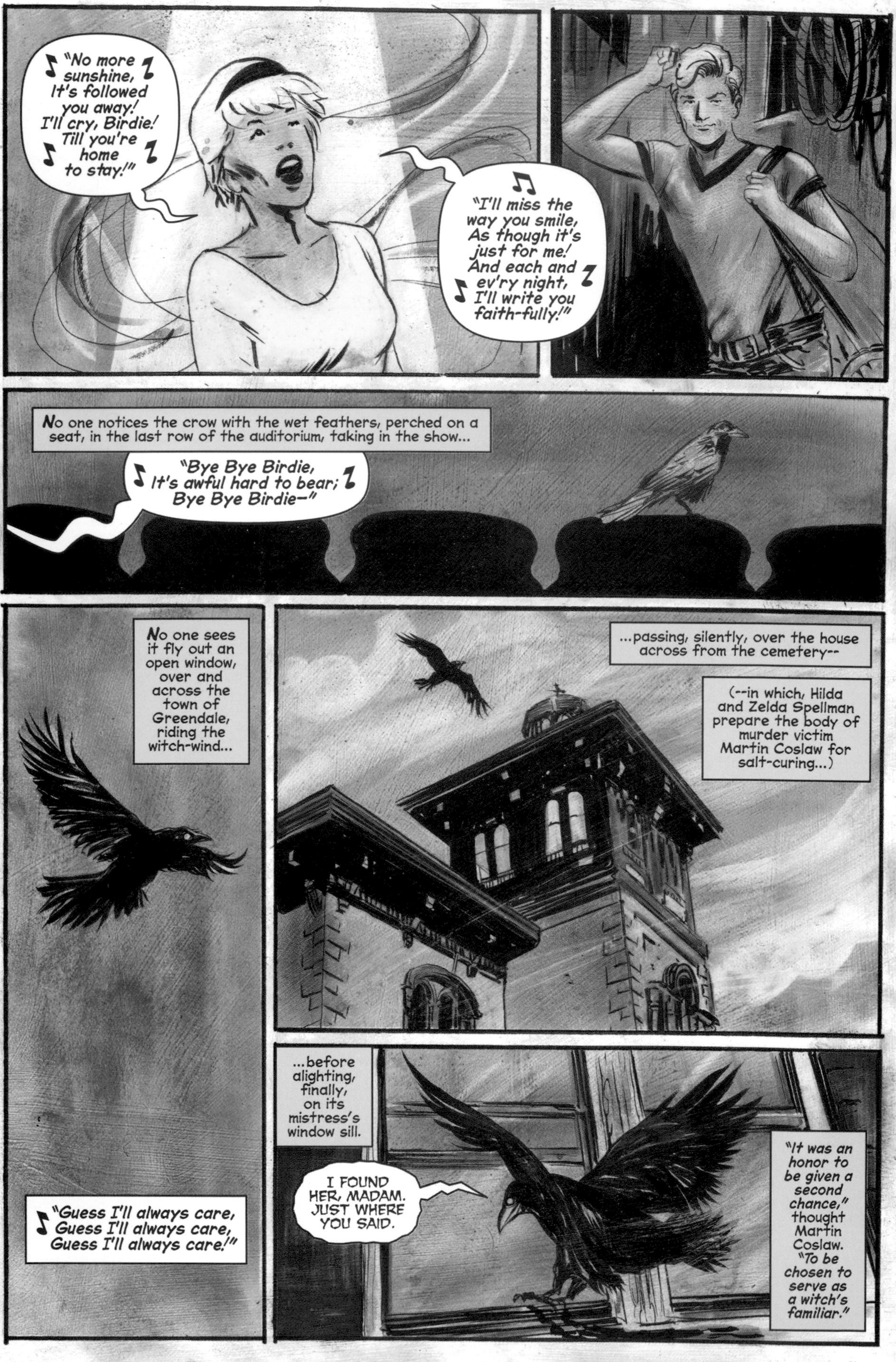
"No more sunshine, It's followed you away! I'll cry, Birdie! Till you're home to stay!"
"I'll miss the way you smile, As though it's just for me! And each and ev'ry night, I'll write you faith-fully!"
No one notices the crow with the wet feathers, perched on a seat, in the last row of the auditorium, taking in the show...
"Bye Bye Birdie, It's awful hard to bear; Bye Bye Birdie--"
No one sees it fly out an open window, over and across the town of Greendale, riding the witch-wind...
...passing, silently, over the house across from the cemetery--
(--in which, Hilda and Zelda Spellman prepare the body of murder victim Martin Coslaw for salt-curing...)
"Guess I'll always care, Guess I'll always care, Guess I'll always care!"
...before alighting, finally, on its mistress's window sill.
I FOUND HER, MADAM. JUST WHERE YOU SAID.
"It was an honor to be given a second chance," thought Martin Coslaw. "To be chosen to serve as a witch's familiar."

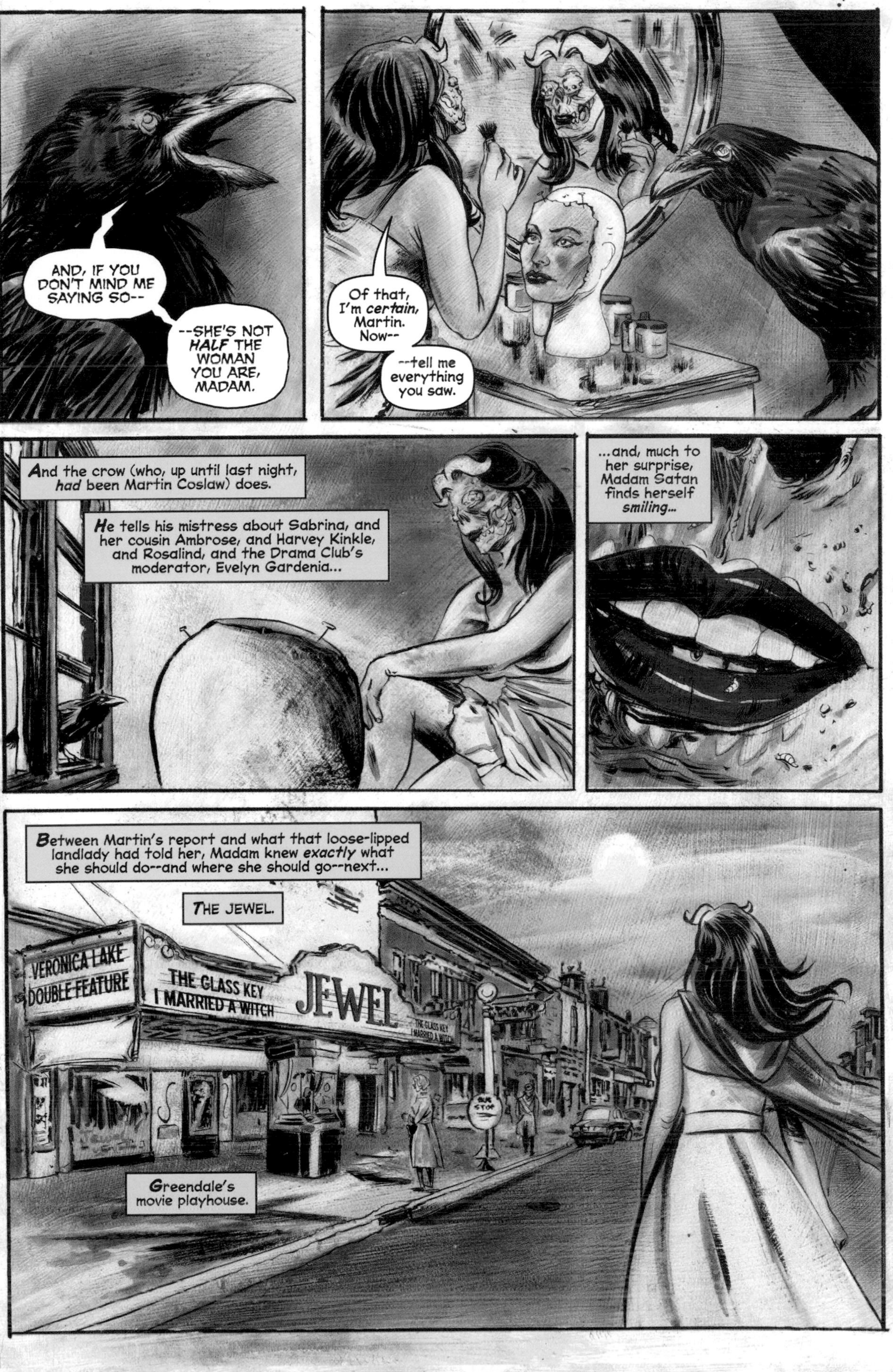
AND, IF YOU DON'T MIND ME SAYING SO--
--SHE'S NOT HALF THE WOMAN YOU ARE, MADAM.
Of that, I'm certain, Martin. Now--
--tell me everything you saw.
And the crow (who, up until last night, had been Martin Coslaw) does.
He tells his mistress about Sabrina, and her cousin Ambrose, and Harvey Kinkle, and Rosalind, and the Drama Club's moderator, Evelyn Gardenia...
...and, much to her surprise, Madam Satan finds herself smiling...
Between Martin's report and what that loose-lipped landlady had told her, Madam knew exactly what she should do--and where she should go--next...
THE JEWEL.
VERONICA LAKE DOUBLE FEATURE
THE GLASS KEY
I MARRIED A WITCH
JEWEL
THE GLASS KEY
I MARRIED A WITCH
BUS STOP
Greendale's movie playhouse.

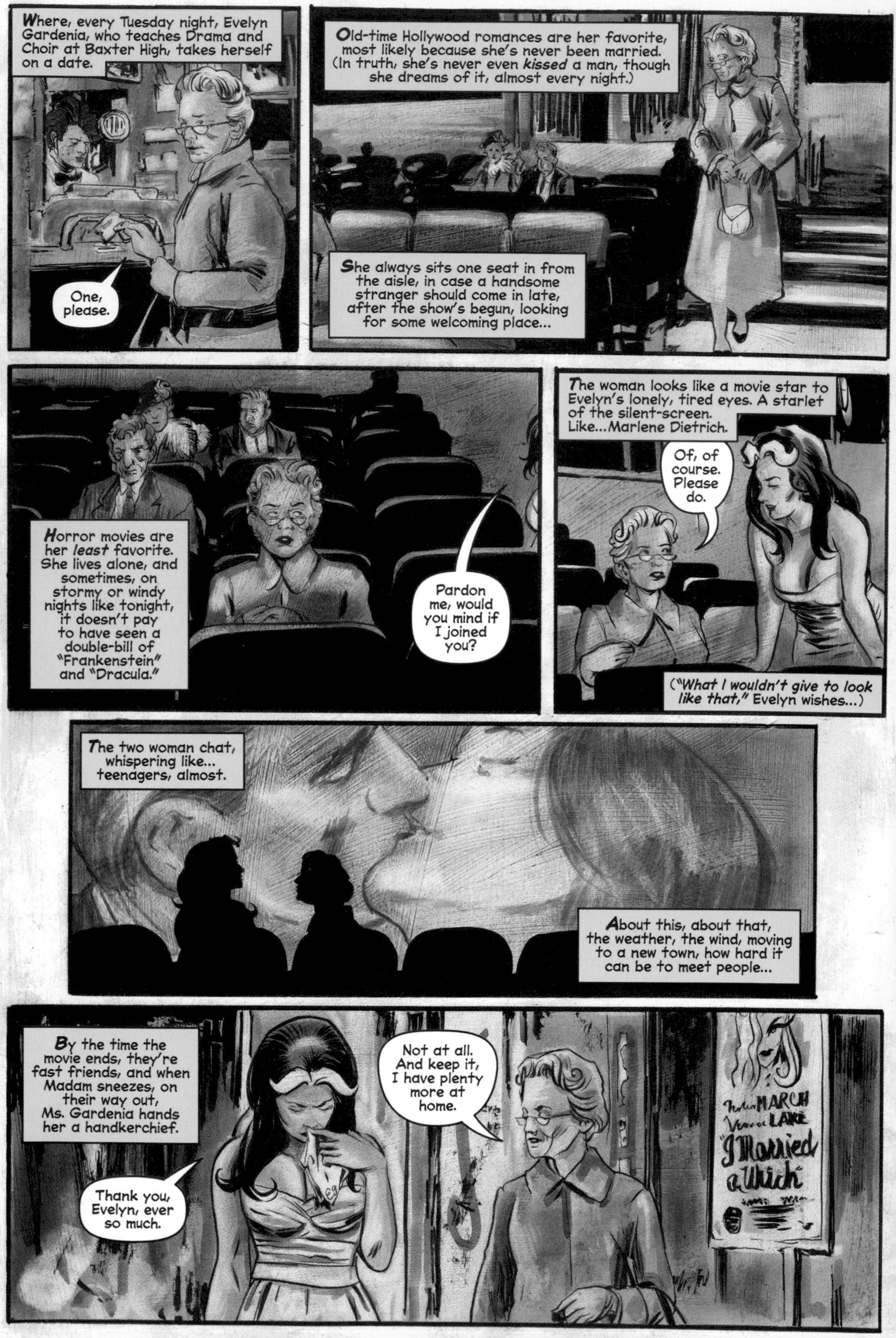
Where, every Tuesday night, Evelyn Gardenia, who teaches Drama and Choir at Baxter High, takes herself on a date.
One, please.
Old-time Hollywood romances are her favorite, most likely because she's never been married. (In truth, she's never even *kissed* a man, though she dreams of it, almost every night.)
She always sits one seat in from the aisle, in case a handsome stranger should come in late, after the show's begun, looking for some welcoming place...
Horror movies are her *least* favorite. She lives alone, and sometimes, on stormy or windy nights like tonight, it doesn't pay to have seen a double-bill of "Frankenstein" and "Dracula."
Pardon me, would you mind if I joined you?
The woman looks like a movie star to Evelyn's lonely, tired eyes. A starlet of the silent-screen. Like...Marlene Dietrich.
Of, of course. Please do.
(*"What I wouldn't give to look like that,"* Evelyn wishes...)
The two woman chat, whispering like... teenagers, almost.
About this, about that, the weather, the wind, moving to a new town, how hard it can be to meet people...
By the time the movie ends, they're fast friends, and when Madam sneezes, on their way out, Ms. Gardenia hands her a handkerchief.
Thank you, Evelyn, ever so much.
Not at all. And keep it, I have plenty more at home.
MARCH
LAKE
"I Married a Witch"

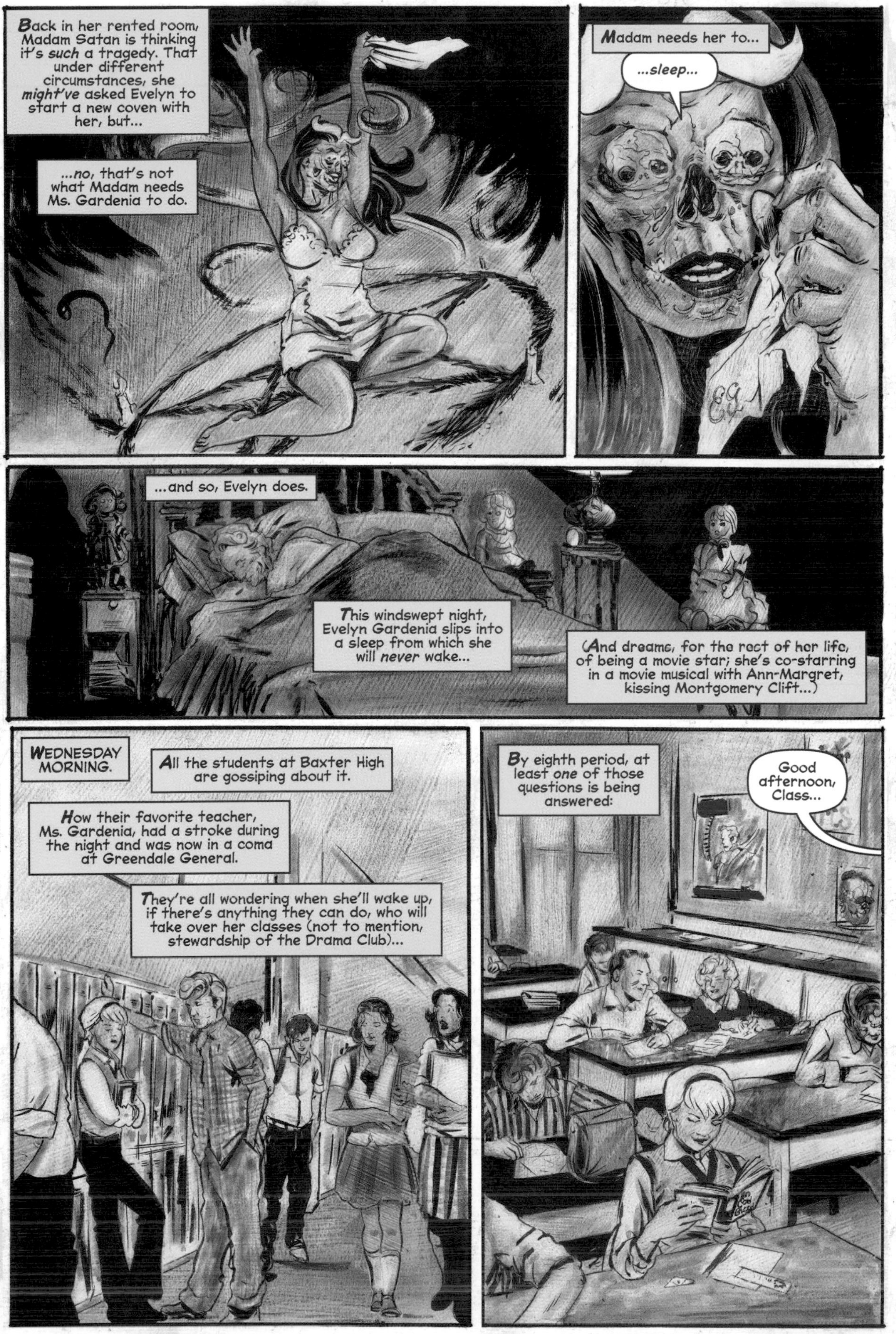
Back in her rented room, Madam Satan is thinking it's *such* a tragedy. That under different circumstances, she *might've* asked Evelyn to start a new coven with her, but...
...*no*, that's not what Madam needs Ms. Gardenia to do.
Madam needs her to...
...*sleep*...
...and so, Evelyn does.
This windswept night, Evelyn Gardenia slips into a sleep from which she will *never* wake...
(And dreams, for the rest of her life, of being a movie star; she's co-starring in a movie musical with Ann-Margret, kissing Montgomery Clift...)
WEDNESDAY MORNING.
All the students at Baxter High are gossiping about it.
How their favorite teacher, Ms. Gardenia, had a stroke during the night and was now in a coma at Greendale General.
They're all wondering when she'll wake up, if there's anything they can do, who will take over her classes (not to mention, stewardship of the Drama Club)...
By eighth period, at least *one* of those questions is being answered:
Good afternoon, Class...

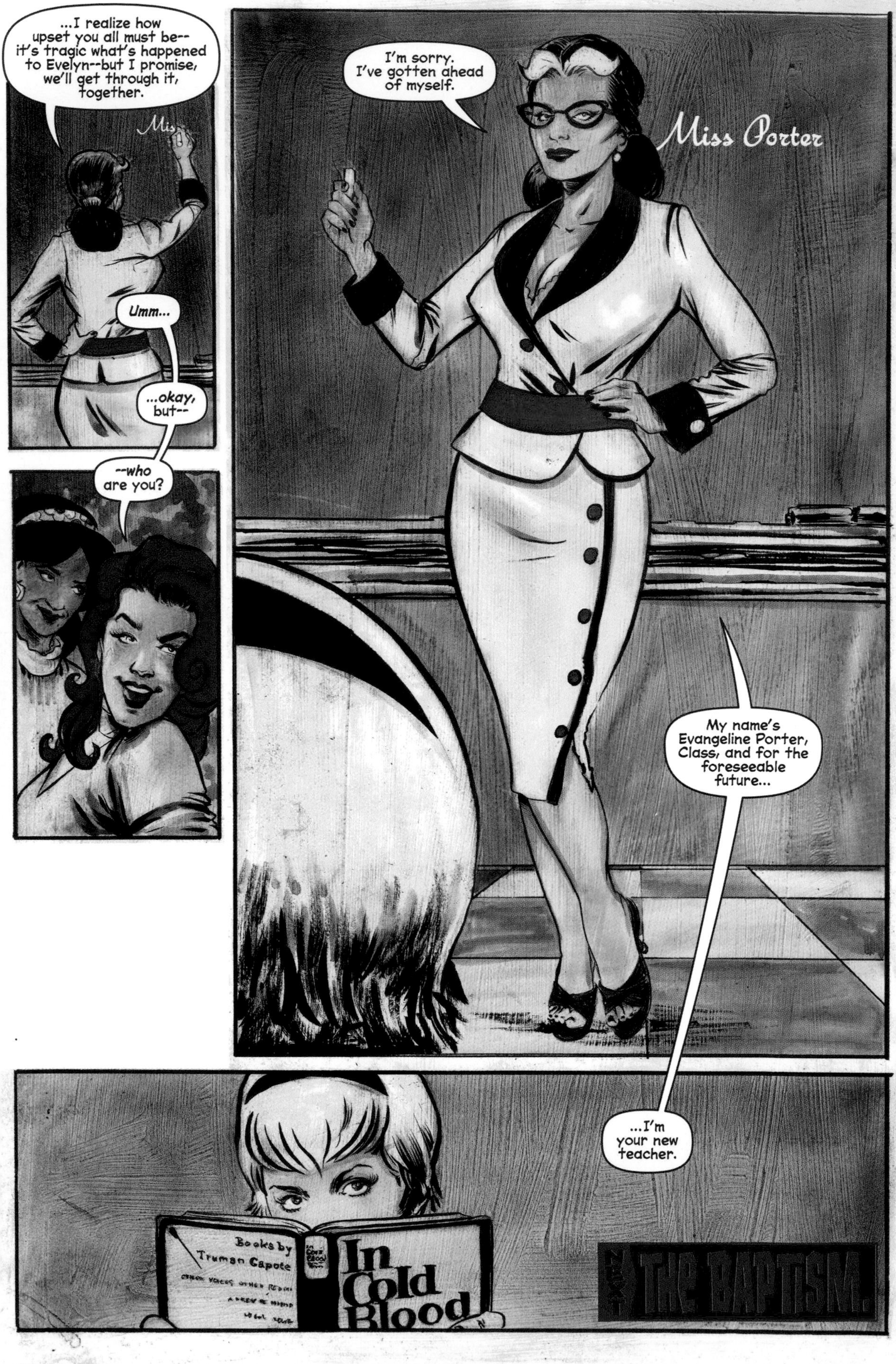
...I realize how upset you all must be--it's tragic what's happened to Evelyn--but I promise, we'll get through it, together.
Mis
Umm...
...okay, but--
--who are you?
I'm sorry. I've gotten ahead of myself.
Miss Porter
My name's Evangeline Porter, Class, and for the foreseeable future...
...I'm your new teacher.
Books by Truman Capote
In Cold Blood
NEXT: THE BAPTISM.

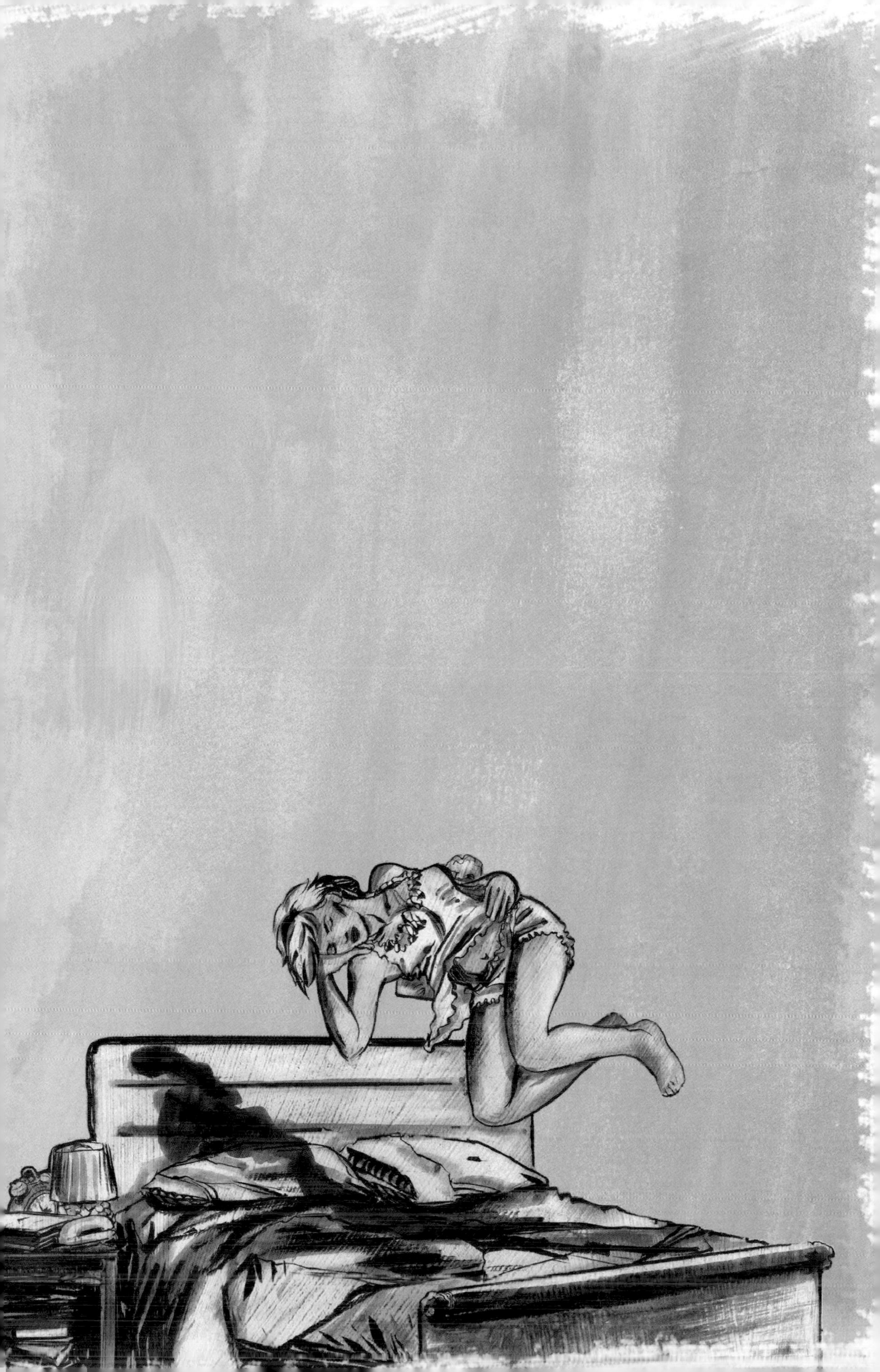

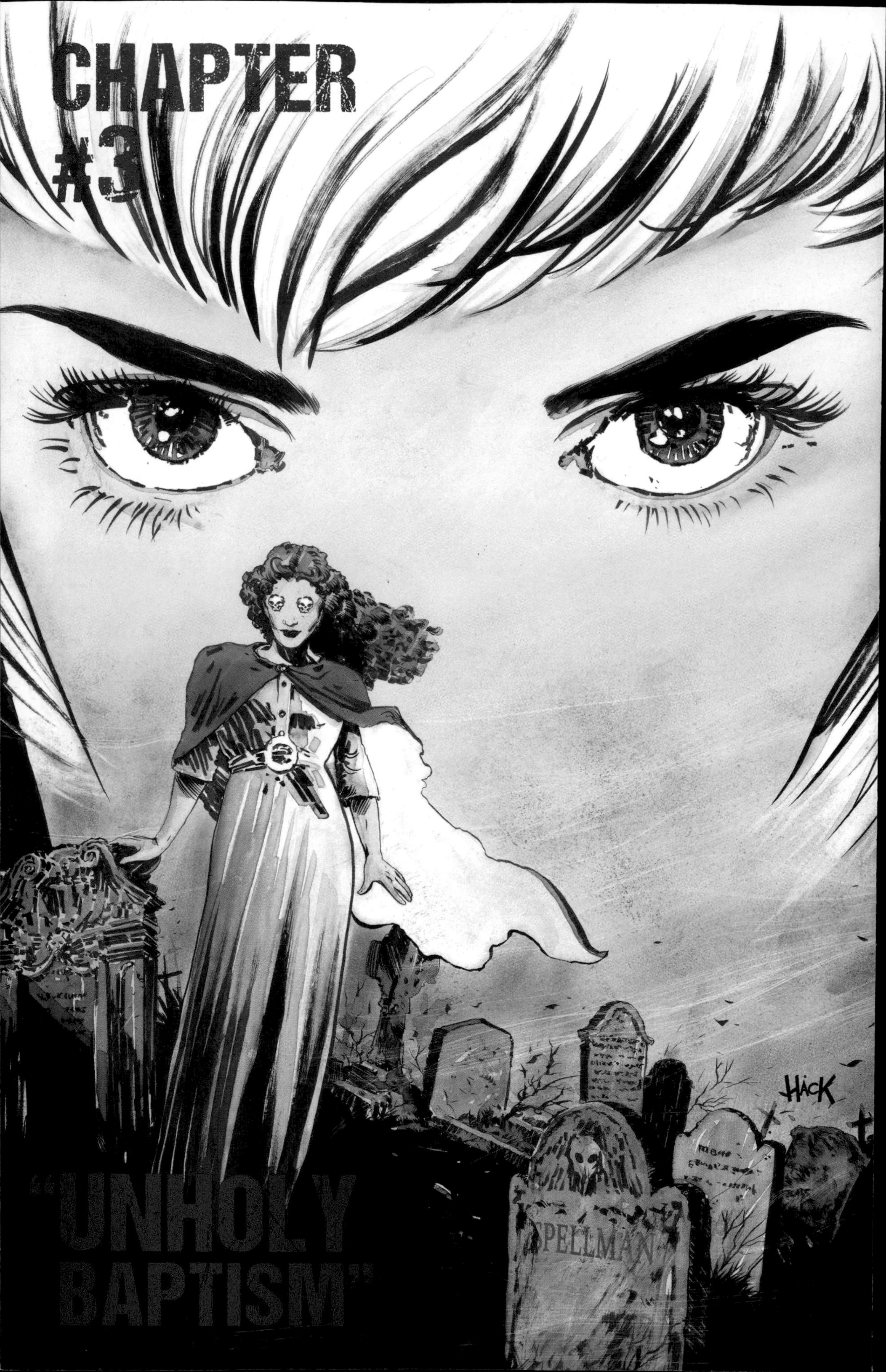
CHAPTER #3
HACK
"UNHOLY BAPTISM"
SPELLMAN

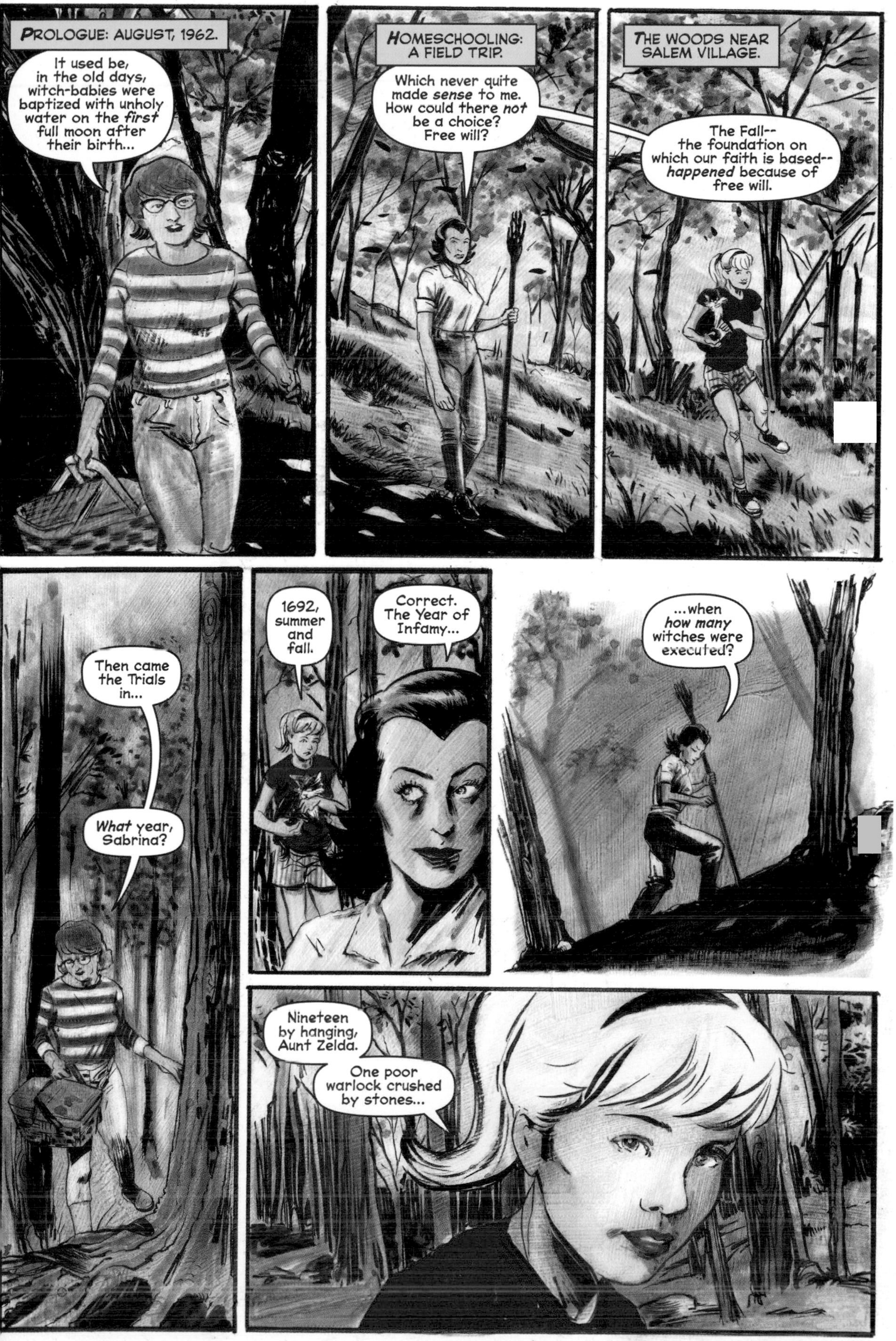
PROLOGUE: AUGUST, 1962.
It used be, in the old days, witch-babies were baptized with unholy water on the *first* full moon after their birth...
HOMESCHOOLING: A FIELD TRIP.
Which never quite made *sense* to me. How could there *not* be a choice? Free will?
THE WOODS NEAR SALEM VILLAGE.
The Fall-- the foundation on which our faith is based-- *happened* because of free will.
Then came the Trials in...
What year, Sabrina?
1692, summer and fall.
Correct. The Year of Infamy...
...when *how many* witches were executed?
Nineteen by hanging, Aunt Zelda.
One poor warlock crushed by stones...

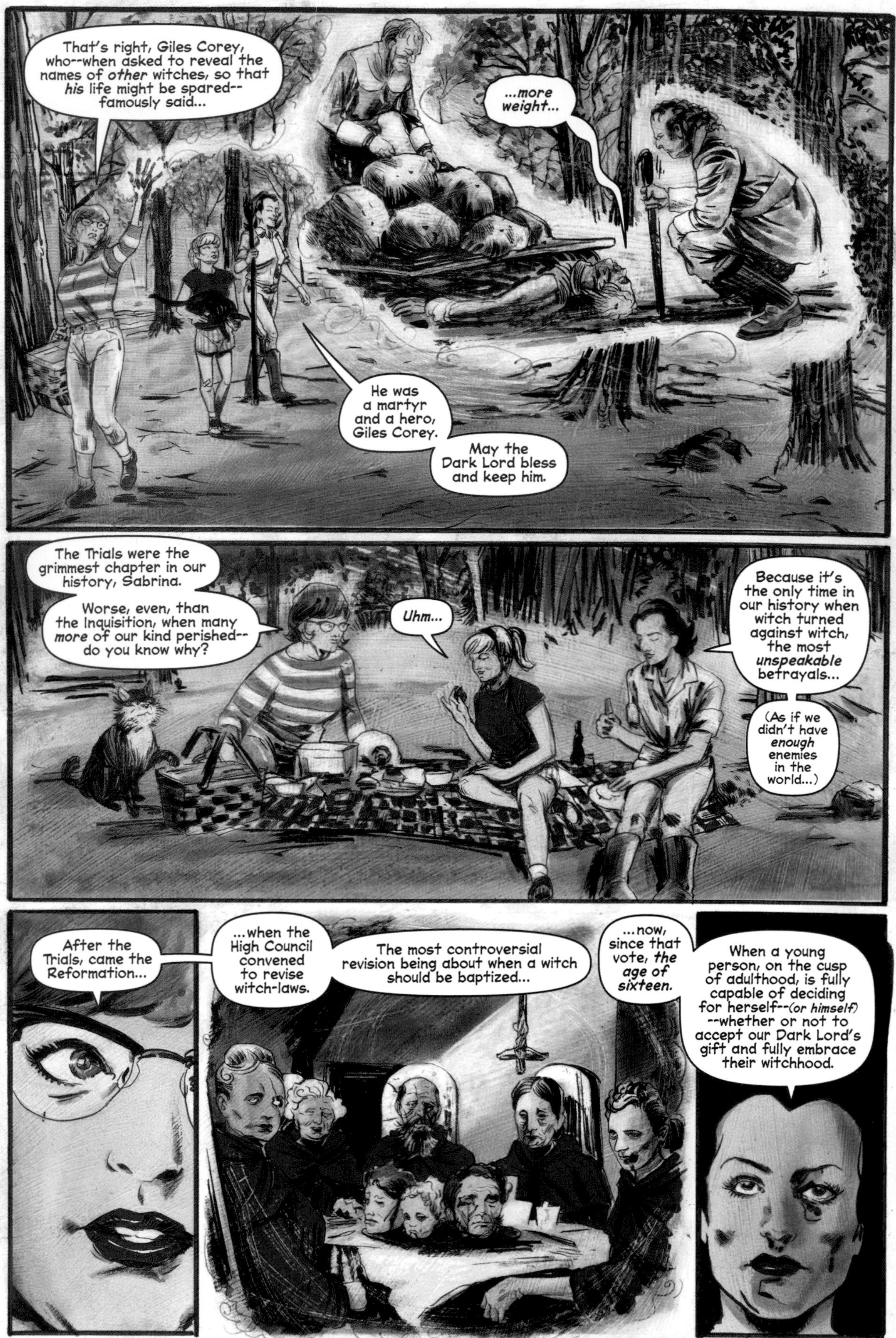
That's right, Giles Corey, who--when asked to reveal the names of *other* witches, so that *his* life might be spared--famously said...
...*more weight*...
He was a martyr and a hero, Giles Corey.
May the Dark Lord bless and keep him.
The Trials were the grimmest chapter in our history, Sabrina.
Worse, even, than the Inquisition, when many *more* of our kind perished--do you know why?
Uhm...
Because it's the only time in our history when witch turned against witch, the most *unspeakable* betrayals...
(As if we didn't have *enough* enemies in the world...)
After the Trials, came the Reformation...
...when the High Council convened to revise witch-laws.
The most controversial revision being about when a witch should be baptized...
...now, since that vote, *the age of sixteen.*
When a young person, on the cusp of adulthood, is fully capable of deciding for herself--*(or himself)* --whether or not to accept our Dark Lord's gift and fully embrace their witchhood.

It will be the *single* most important decision of your life, Sabrina.

For many, it's a *straw law*, but you...you actually *can* choose, Sabrina, to live as a mortal.

Your father... ensured that.

And, *whichever* path you decide to follow, the path of light or the path of *night*, your Aunt Zelda and I want you to know--

--we'll love and support you, no matter what.

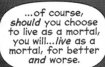

...of course, *should* you choose to live as a mortal, you will...*live* as a mortal, for better *and* worse.

You'll grow older, at the same rate they do. Your powers will fade, over the years, the way paintings do in the sun... Your whole life will be less...I don't want to say *remarkable*...

You'll know love, true love.

The possibility of it, at least...

But aunties... I'm *eleven*.

Sixteen's *forever* away.

≶sniff≷

Be here before we know it...

Merciful Mephistopheles, Hilda, witches are *incapable* of producing tears, so don't even *try*.

END FIELD TRIP.

END PROLOGUE.

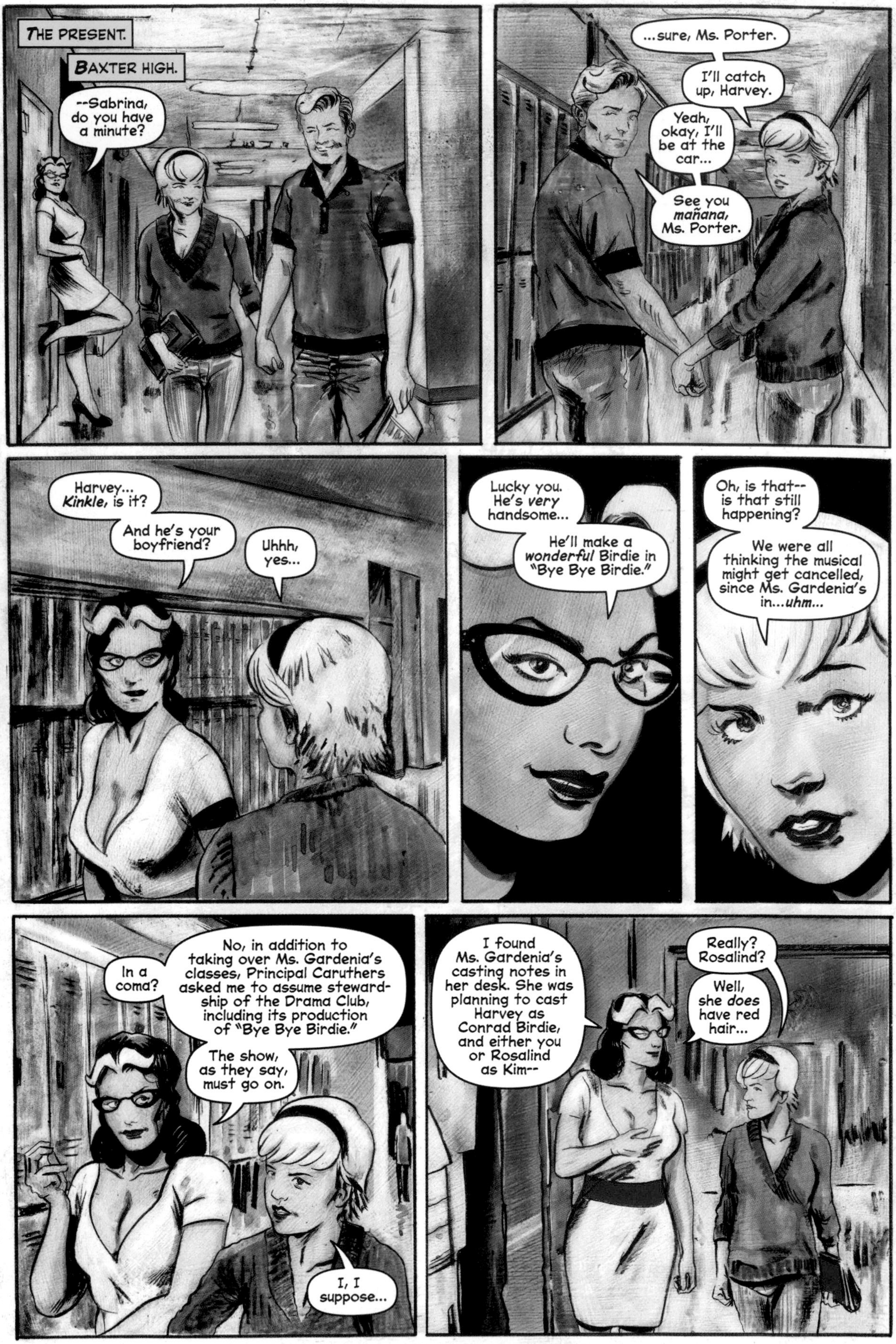
THE PRESENT.
BAXTER HIGH.
--Sabrina, do you have a minute?
...sure, Ms. Porter.
I'll catch up, Harvey.
Yeah, okay, I'll be at the car...
See you *mañana*, Ms. Porter.
Harvey... *Kinkle*, is it?
And he's your boyfriend?
Uhhh, yes...
Lucky you. He's *very* handsome...
He'll make a *wonderful* Birdie in "Bye Bye Birdie."
Oh, is that-- is that still happening?
We were all thinking the musical might get cancelled, since Ms. Gardenia's in...*uhm*...
In a coma?
No, in addition to taking over Ms. Gardenia's classes, Principal Caruthers asked me to assume steward-ship of the Drama Club, including its production of "Bye Bye Birdie."
The show, as they say, must go on.
I, I suppose...
I found Ms. Gardenia's casting notes in her desk. She was planning to cast Harvey as Conrad Birdie, and either you or Rosalind as Kim--
Really? Rosalind?
Well, she *does* have red hair...

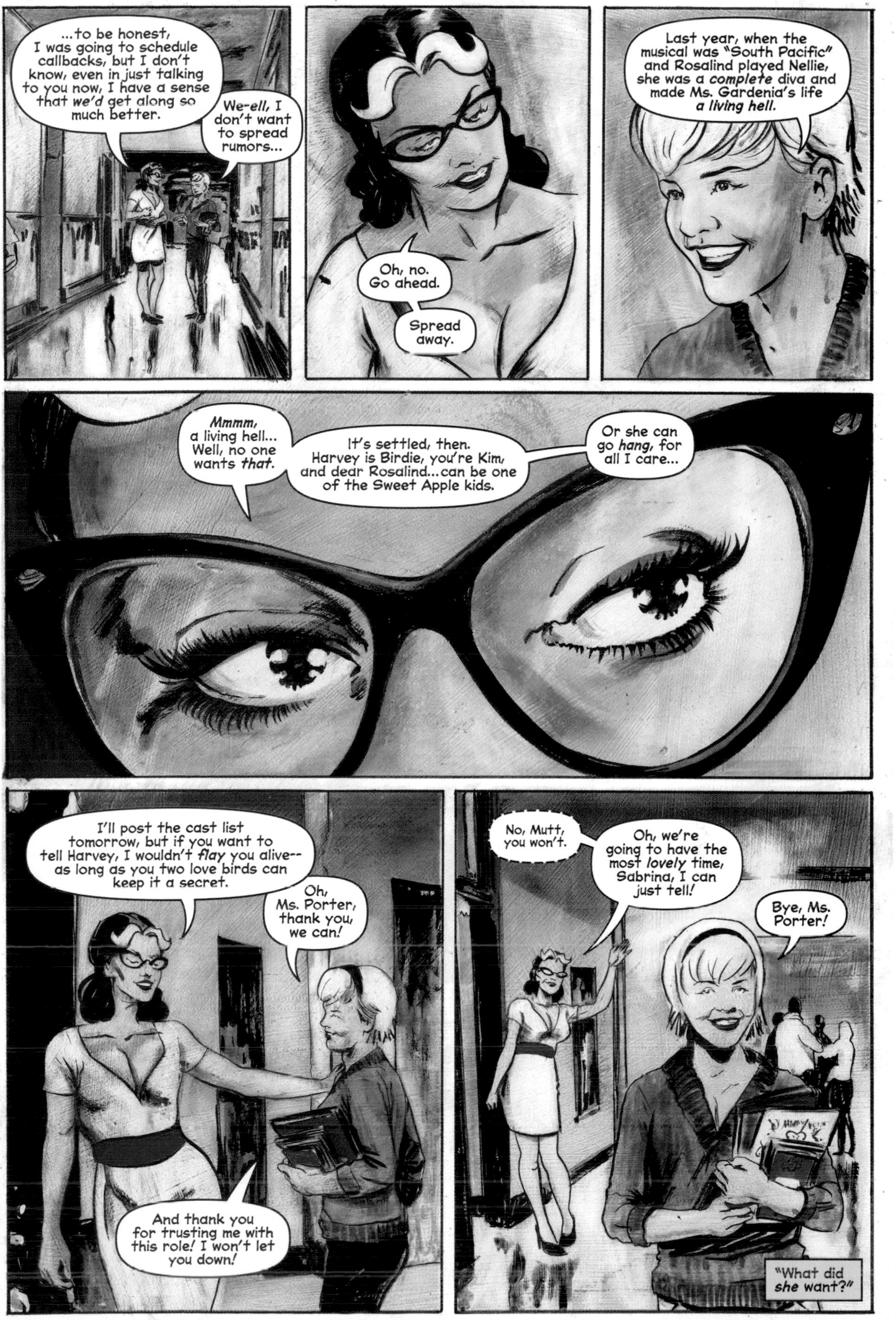
...to be honest, I was going to schedule callbacks, but I don't know, even in just talking to you now, I have a sense that *we'd* get along so much better.
We-*ell*, I don't want to spread rumors...
Oh, no. Go ahead.
Spread away.
Last year, when the musical was "South Pacific" and Rosalind played Nellie, she was a *complete* diva and made Ms. Gardenia's life *a living hell.*
Mmmm, a living hell... Well, no one wants *that.*
It's settled, then. Harvey is Birdie, you're Kim, and dear Rosalind...can be one of the Sweet Apple kids.
Or she can go *hang,* for all I care...
I'll post the cast list tomorrow, but if you want to tell Harvey, I wouldn't *flay* you alive-- as long as you two love birds can keep it a secret.
Oh, Ms. Porter, thank you, we can!
And thank you for trusting me with this role! I won't let you down!
No, Mutt, you won't.
Oh, we're going to have the most *lovely* time, Sabrina, I can just tell!
Bye, Ms. Porter!
"What did *she* want?"

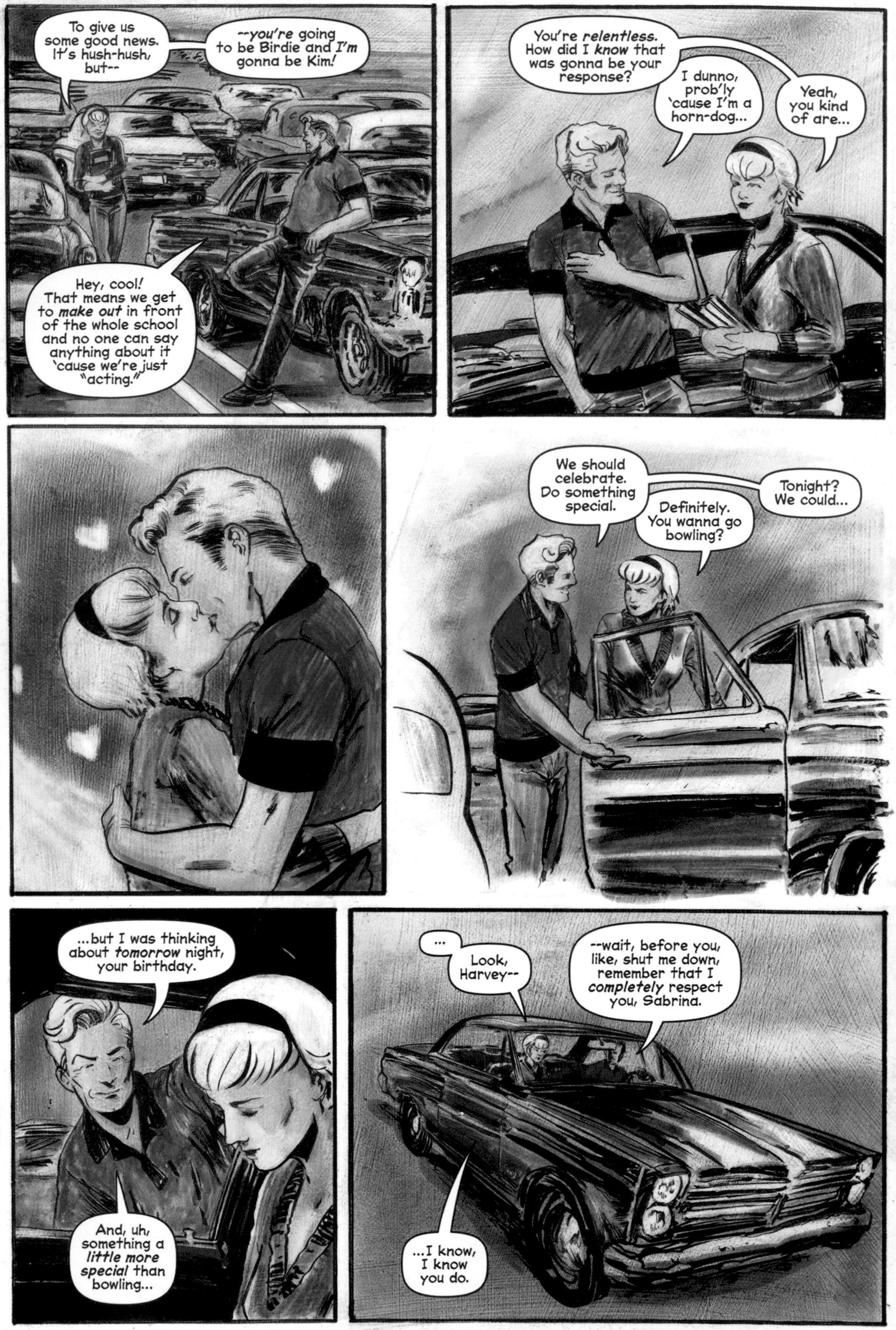
To give us some good news. It's hush-hush, but--
--*you're* going to be Birdie and *I'm* gonna be Kim!
Hey, cool! That means we get to *make out* in front of the whole school and no one can say anything about it 'cause we're just "acting."
You're *relentless.* How did I *know* that was gonna be your response?
I dunno, prob'ly 'cause I'm a horn-dog...
Yeah, you kind of are...
We should celebrate. Do something special.
Tonight? We could...
Definitely. You wanna go bowling?
...but I was thinking about *tomorrow* night, your birthday.
And, uh, something a *little more special* than bowling...
...
Look, Harvey--
--wait, before you, like, shut me down, remember that I *completely* respect you, Sabrina.
...I know, I know you do.

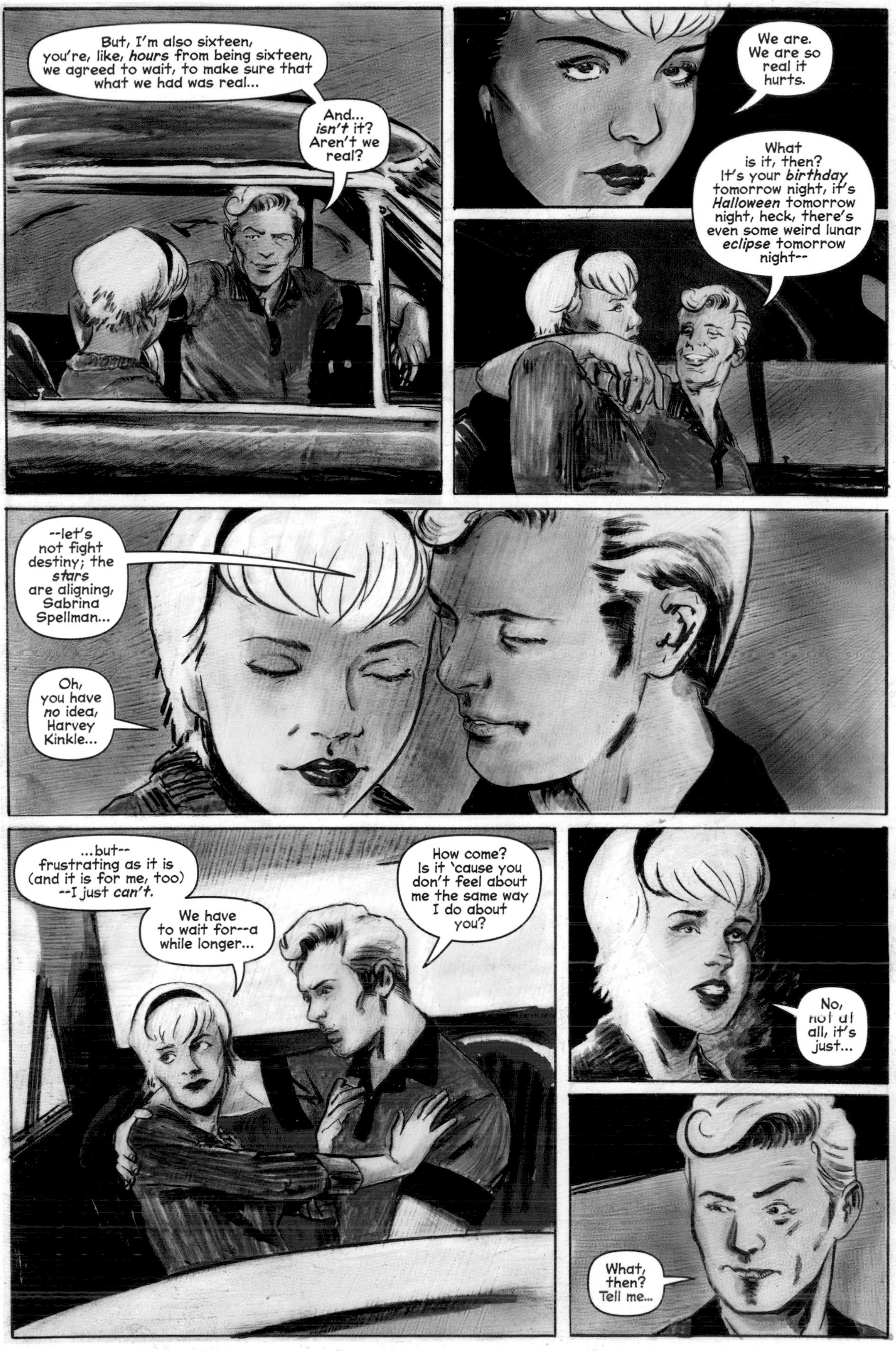

But, I'm also sixteen, you're, like, *hours* from being sixteen, we agreed to wait, to make sure that what we had was real...
And... *isn't* it? Aren't we real?
We are. We are so real it hurts.
What is it, then? It's your *birthday* tomorrow night, it's *Halloween* tomorrow night, heck, there's even some weird lunar *eclipse* tomorrow night--
--let's not fight destiny; the *stars* are aligning, Sabrina Spellman...
Oh, you have *no* idea, Harvey Kinkle...
...but-- frustrating as it is (and it is for me, too) --I just *can't*.
We have to wait for--a while longer...
How come? Is it 'cause you don't feel about me the same way I do about you?
No, not at all, it's just...
What, then? Tell me...

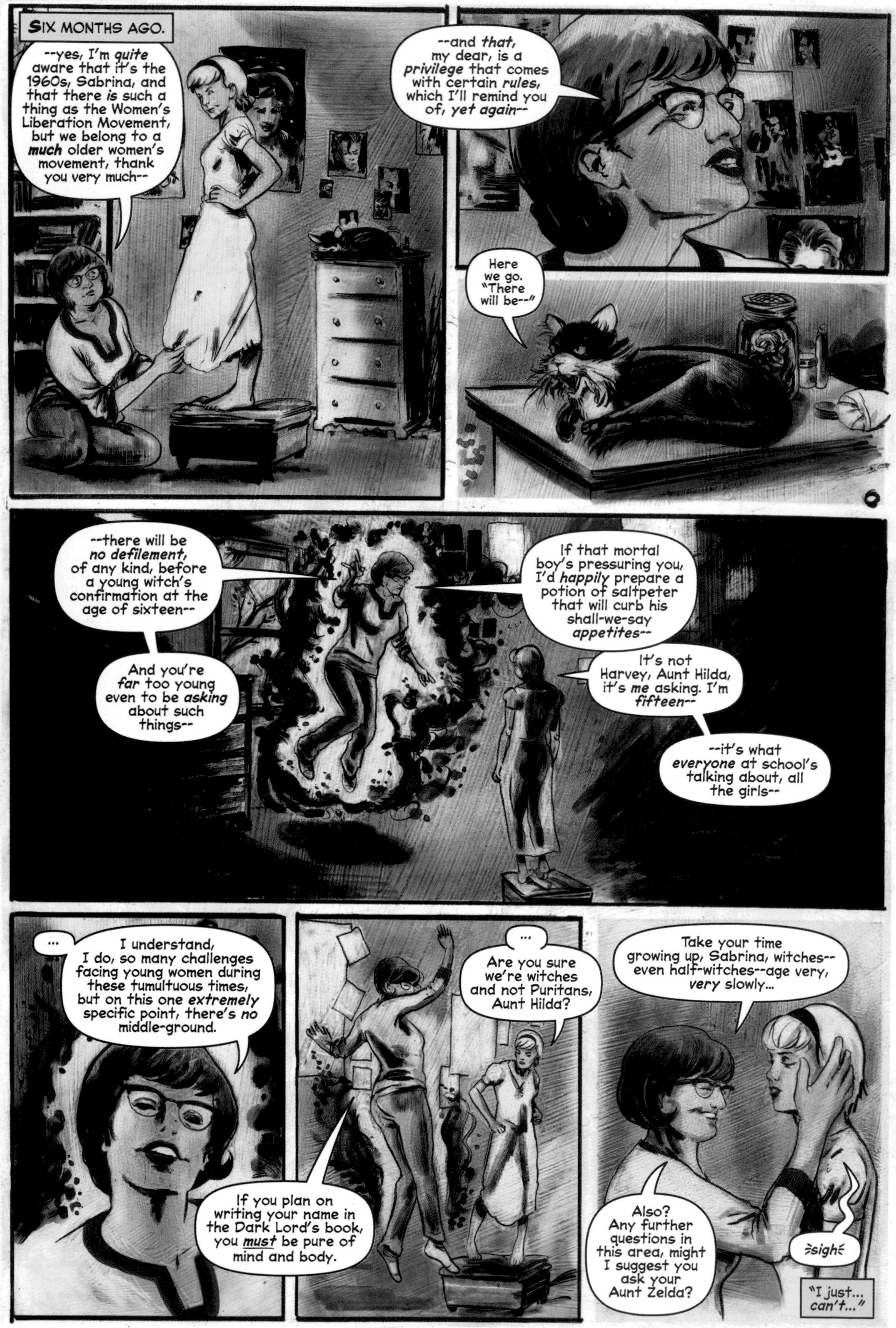
SIX MONTHS AGO.
--yes, I'm quite aware that it's the 1960s, Sabrina, and that there is such a thing as the Women's Liberation Movement, but we belong to a much older women's movement, thank you very much--
--and that, my dear, is a privilege that comes with certain rules, which I'll remind you of, yet again--
Here we go. "There will be--"
--there will be no defilement, of any kind, before a young witch's confirmation at the age of sixteen--
And you're far too young even to be asking about such things--
If that mortal boy's pressuring you, I'd happily prepare a potion of saltpeter that will curb his shall-we-say appetites--
It's not Harvey, Aunt Hilda, it's me asking. I'm fifteen--
--it's what everyone at school's talking about, all the girls--
...
I understand, I do, so many challenges facing young women during these tumultuous times, but on this one extremely specific point, there's no middle-ground.
If you plan on writing your name in the Dark Lord's book, you must be pure of mind and body.
...
Are you sure we're witches and not Puritans, Aunt Hilda?
Take your time growing up, Sabrina, witches--even half-witches--age very, very slowly...
Also? Any further questions in this area, might I suggest you ask your Aunt Zelda?
sigh
"I just... can't..."

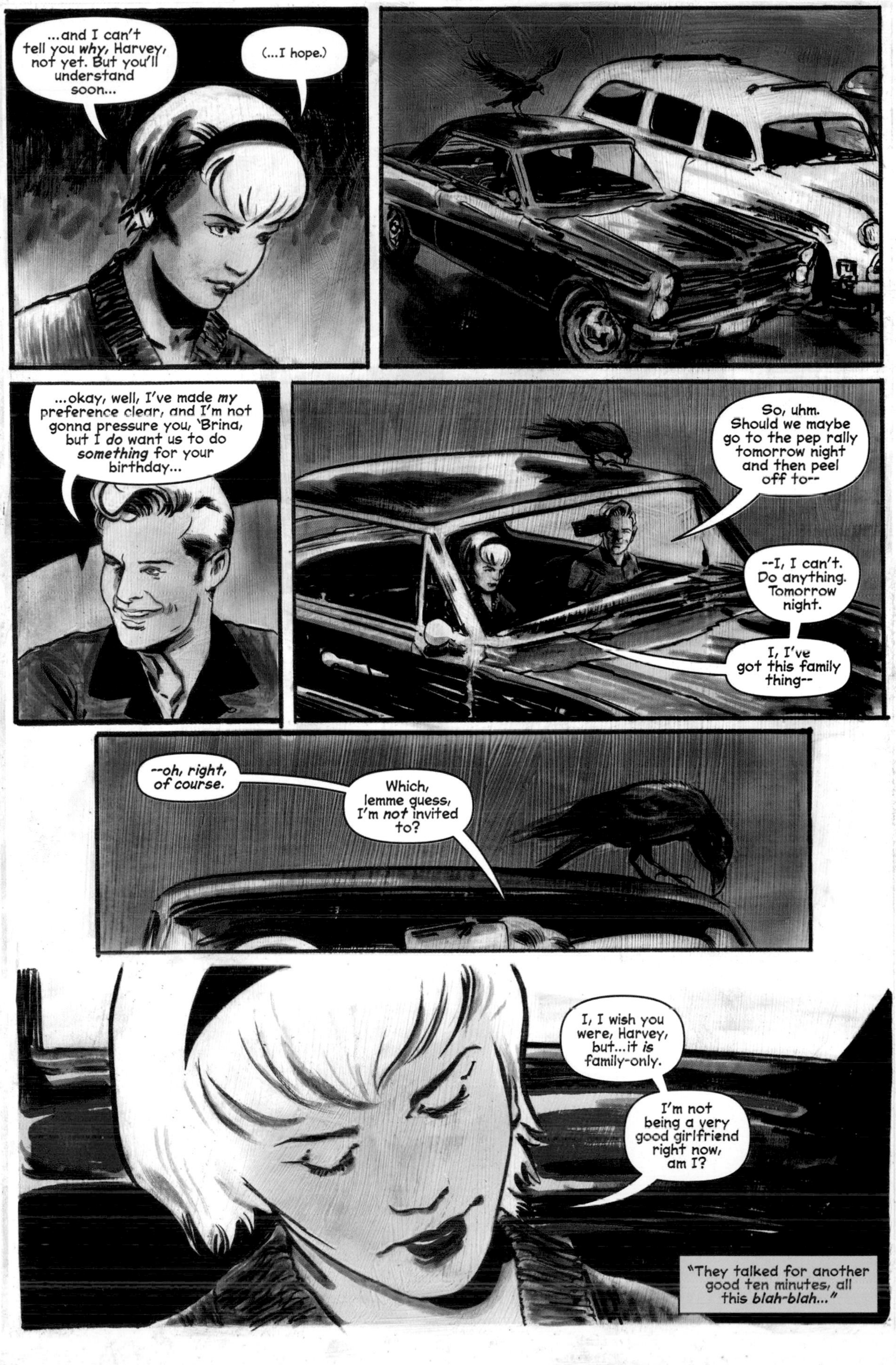
...and I can't tell you *why*, Harvey, not yet. But you'll understand soon...
(...I hope.)
...okay, well, I've made *my* preference clear, and I'm not gonna pressure you, 'Brina, but I *do* want us to do *something* for your birthday...
So, uhm. Should we maybe go to the pep rally tomorrow night and then peel off to--
--I, I can't. Do anything. Tomorrow night.
I, I've got this family thing--
--oh, right, of course.
Which, lemme guess, I'm *not* invited to?
I, I wish you were, Harvey, but...it *is* family-only.
I'm not being a very good girlfriend right now, am I?
"They talked for another good ten minutes, all this *blah-blah*..."

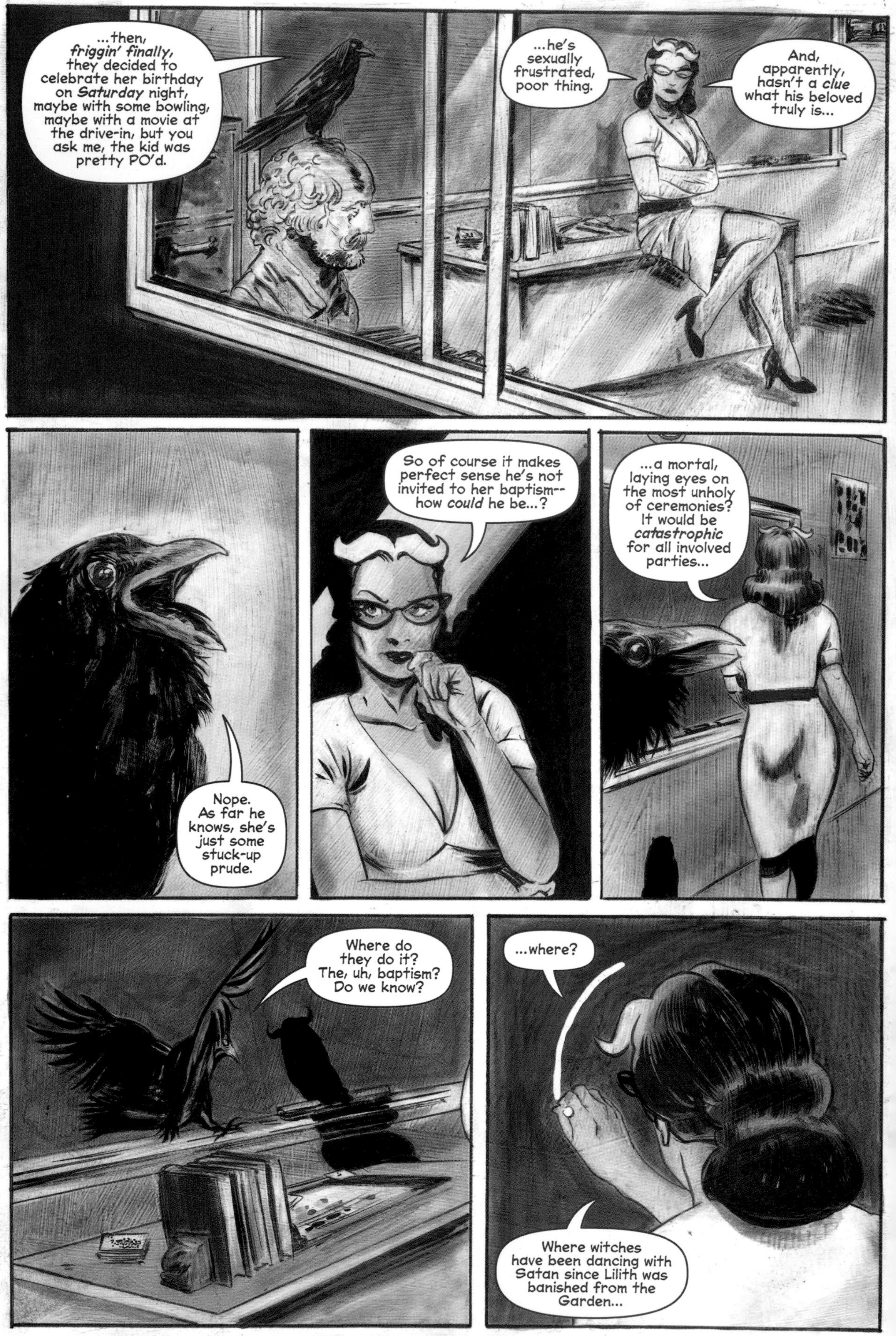
...then, friggin' finally, they decided to celebrate her birthday on Saturday night, maybe with some bowling, maybe with a movie at the drive-in, but you ask me, the kid was pretty PO'd.
...he's sexually frustrated, poor thing.
And, apparently, hasn't a clue what his beloved truly is...
Nope. As far he knows, she's just some stuck-up prude.
So of course it makes perfect sense he's not invited to her baptism--how could he be...?
...a mortal, laying eyes on the most unholy of ceremonies? It would be catastrophic for all involved parties...
Where do they do it? The, uh, baptism? Do we know?
...where?
Where witches have been dancing with Satan since Lilith was banished from the Garden...

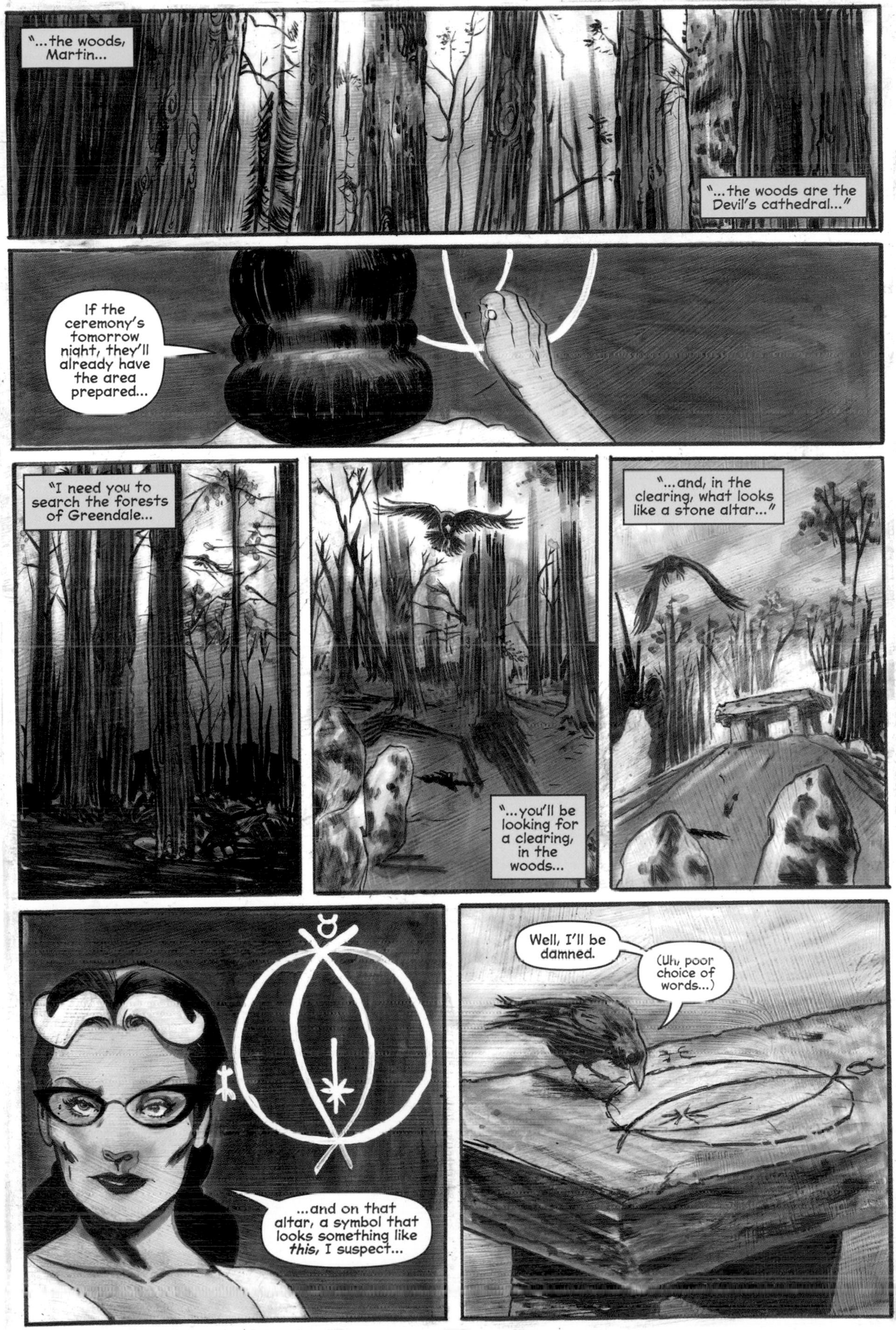
"...the woods, Martin...
"...the woods are the Devil's cathedral..."
If the ceremony's tomorrow night, they'll already have the area prepared...
"I need you to search the forests of Greendale...
"...you'll be looking for a clearing, in the woods...
"...and, in the clearing, what looks like a stone altar..."
...and on that altar, a symbol that looks something like *this,* I suspect...
Well, I'll be damned.
(Uh, poor choice of words...)

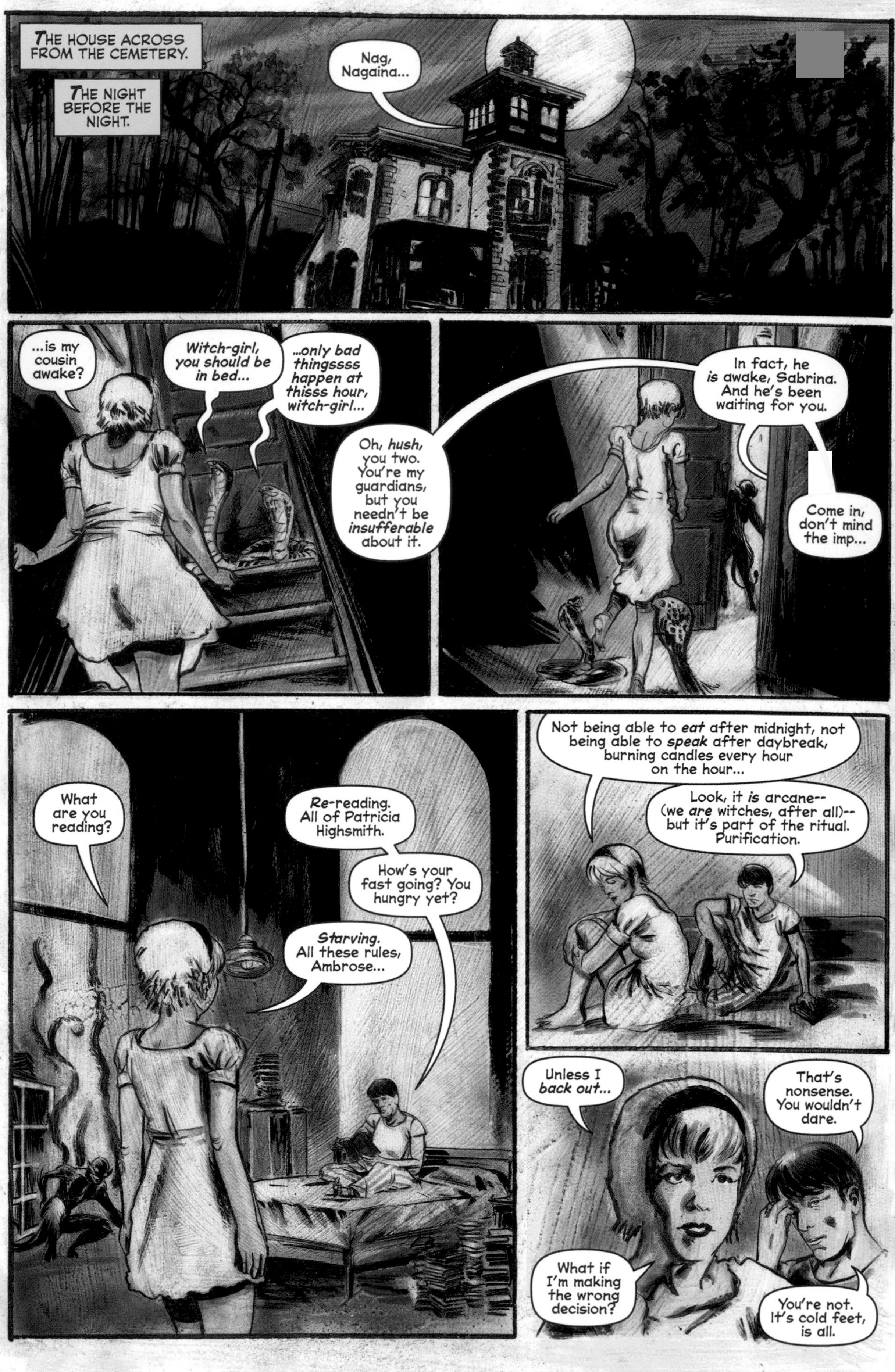
The house across from the cemetery.
The night before the night.
Nag, Nagaina...
...is my cousin awake?
Witch-girl, you should be in bed...
...only bad thingssss happen at thisss hour, witch-girl...
Oh, *hush,* you two. You're my guardians, but you needn't be *insufferable* about it.
In fact, he *is* awake, Sabrina. And he's been waiting for you.
Come in, don't mind the imp...
What are you reading?
Re-reading. All of Patricia Highsmith.
How's your fast going? You hungry yet?
Starving. All these rules, Ambrose...
Not being able to *eat* after midnight, not being able to *speak* after daybreak, burning candles every hour on the hour...
Look, it *is* arcane-- (we *are* witches, after all)-- but it's part of the ritual. Purification.
Unless I *back out...*
That's nonsense. You wouldn't dare.
What if I'm making the wrong decision?
You're not. It's cold feet, is all.

Listen, it's natural to be unnerved.

...I was before *my* baptism.

But...it's *different* for boys, isn't it?

I mean, it *matters* less, doesn't it?

...*hmm*, is that true?

Yes, I suppose so...

And then there's the Harvey of it all.

He can *feel* something's wrong-- he can *sense* this wall going up between us-- but, of course, I can't *tell* him anything...

And then, after tomorrow night...

Oh, Cous.

J'adore Harvey, he's sweet and nice (especially for a football player), but let me ask you: Was he going to be forever?

That's the thing! I *DON'T* know!

(I thought... maybe... possibly...)

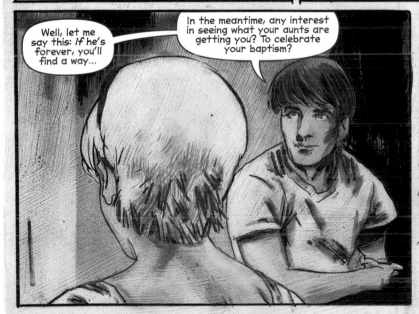

Well, let me say this: *If he's* forever, you'll find a way...

In the meantime, any interest in seeing what your aunts are getting you? To celebrate your baptism?

You mean--

--like a gift?

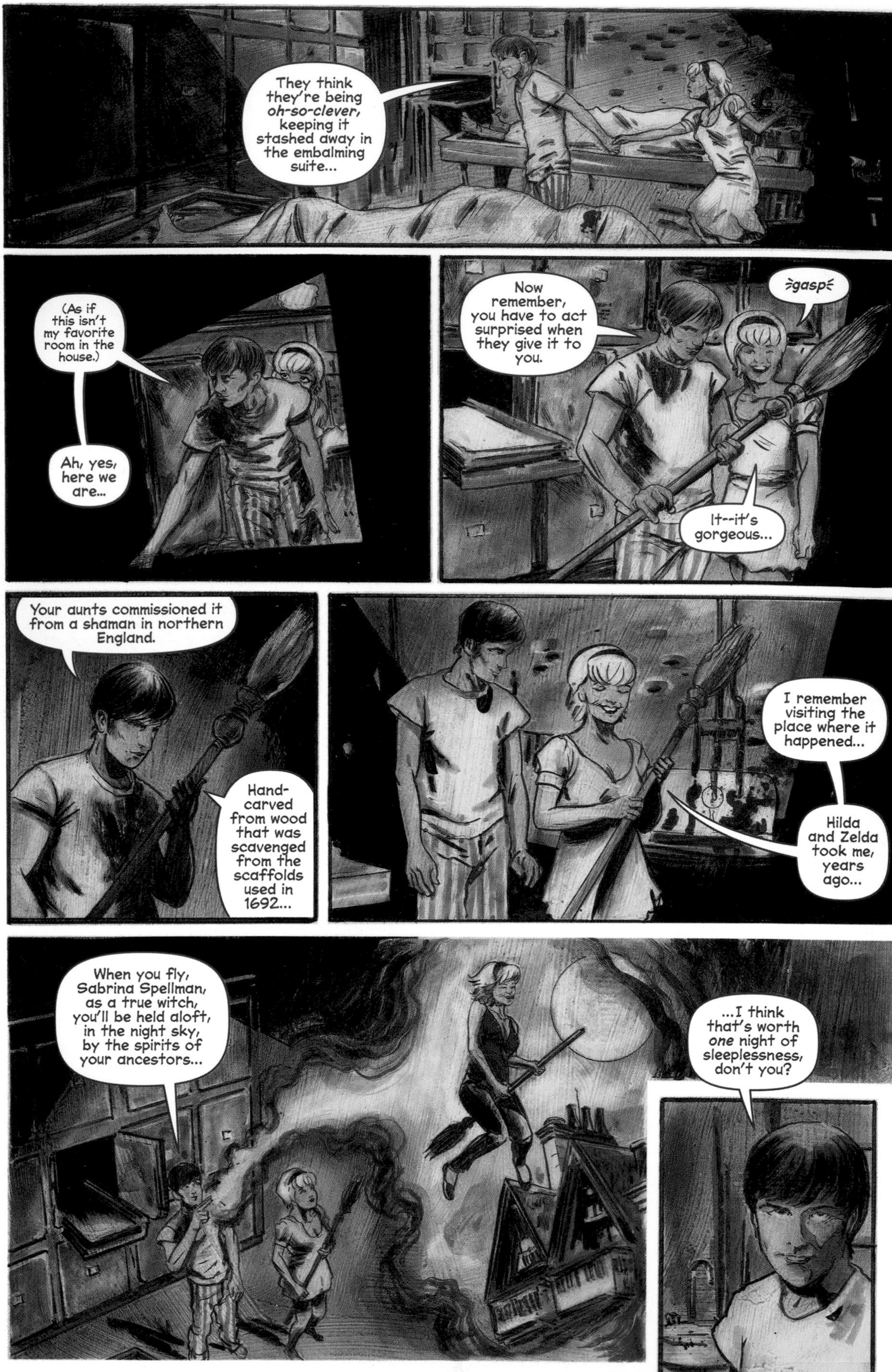
They think they're being *oh-so-clever,* keeping it stashed away in the embalming suite...
(As if this isn't my favorite room in the house.)
Ah, yes, here we are...
Now remember, you have to act surprised when they give it to you.
gasp
It--it's gorgeous...
Your aunts commissioned it from a shaman in northern England.
Hand-carved from wood that was scavenged from the scaffolds used in 1692...
I remember visiting the place where it happened...
Hilda and Zelda took me, years ago...
When you fly, Sabrina Spellman, as a true witch, you'll be held aloft, in the night sky, by the spirits of your ancestors...
...I think that's worth *one* night of sleeplessness, don't you?

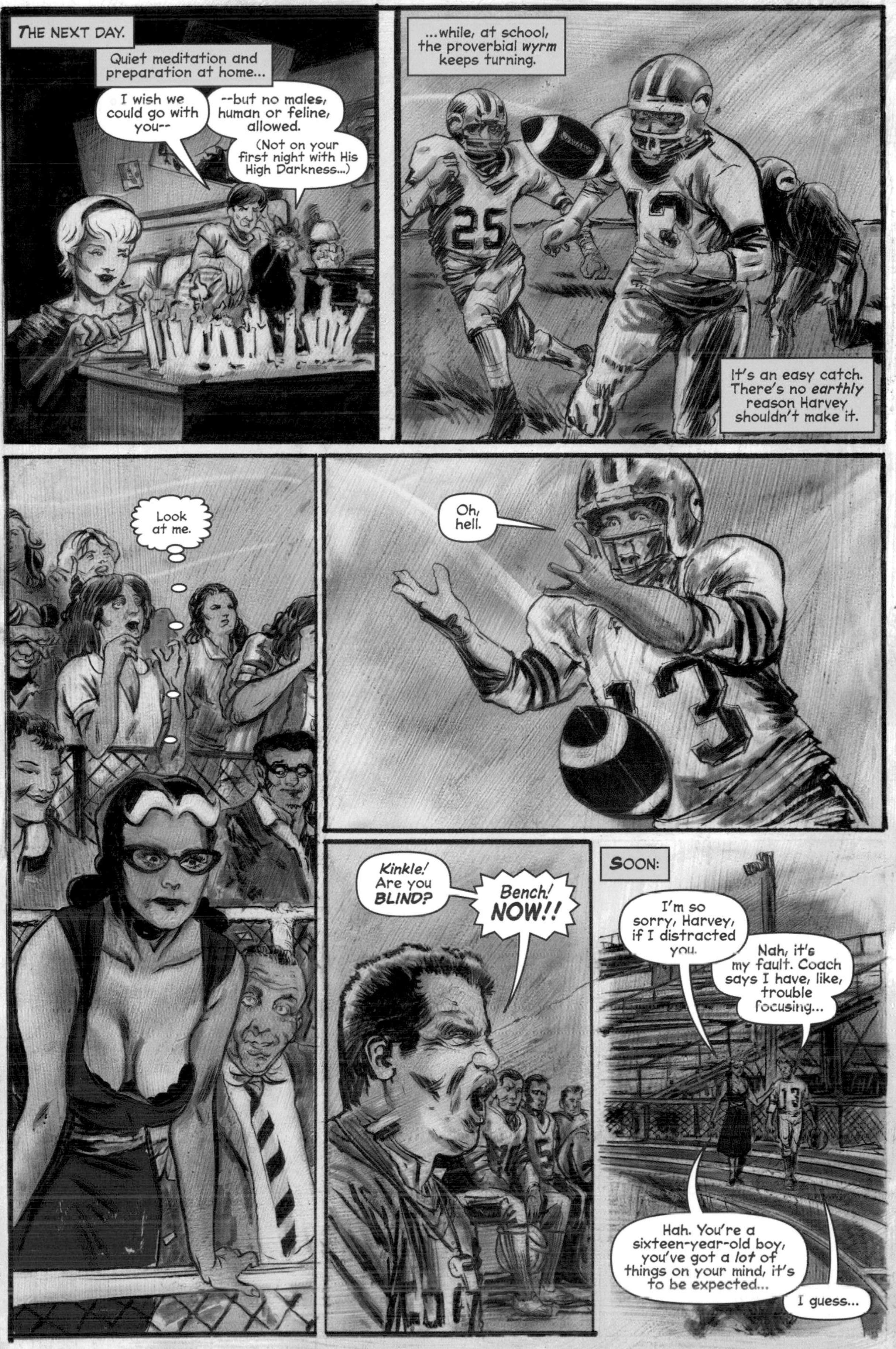
THE NEXT DAY.
Quiet meditation and preparation at home...
I wish we could go with you--
--but no males, human or feline, allowed.
(Not on your first night with His High Darkness...)
...while, at school, the proverbial *wyrm* keeps turning.
25
13
It's an easy catch. There's no *earthly* reason Harvey shouldn't make it.
Look at me.
Oh, hell.
13
Kinkle! Are you *BLIND?*
Bench! NOW!!
SOON:
I'm so sorry, Harvey, if I distracted you.
Nah, it's my fault. Coach says I have, like, trouble focusing...
13
Hah. You're a sixteen-year-old boy, you've got a *lot* of things on your mind, it's to be expected...
I guess...

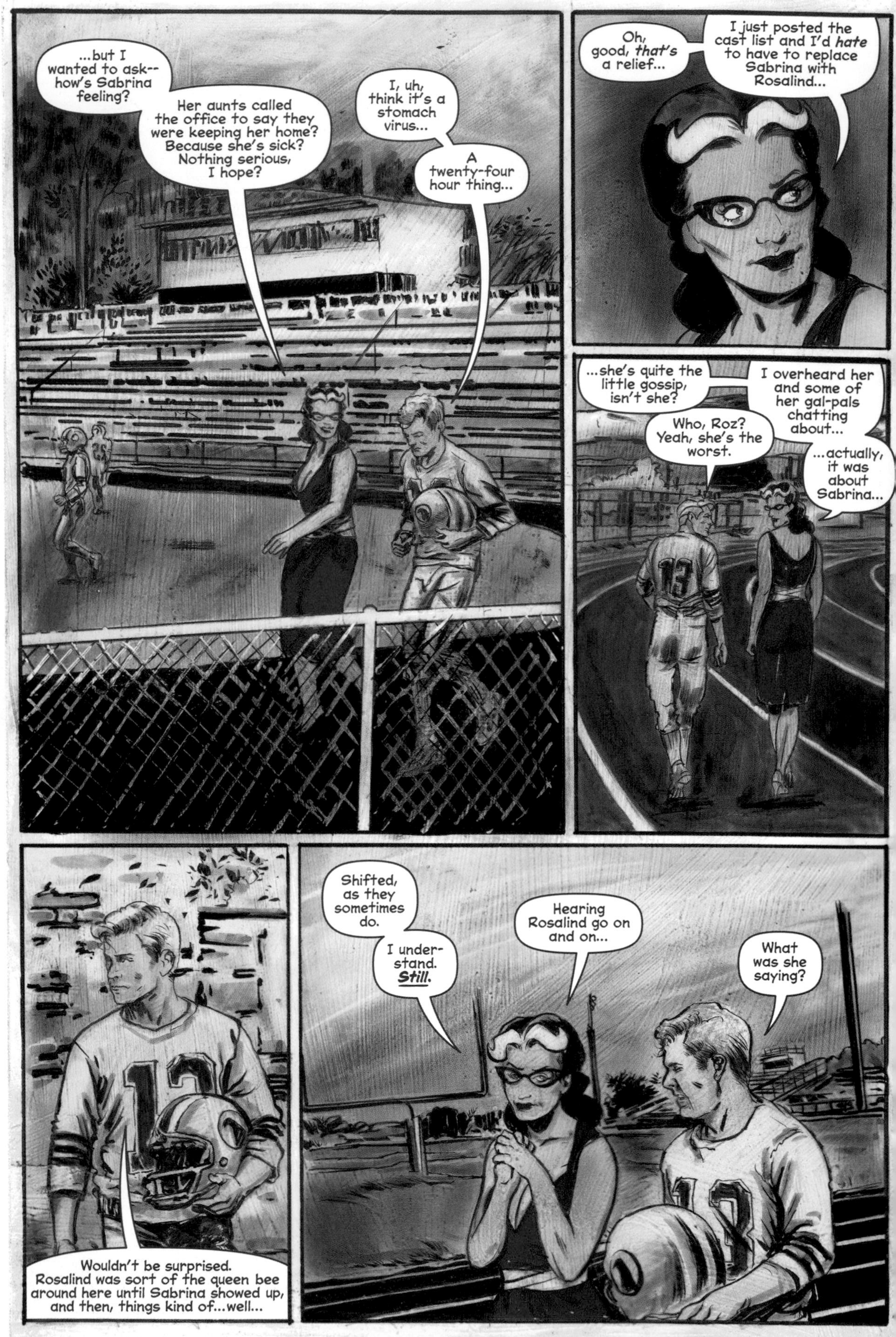
...but I wanted to ask--how's Sabrina feeling?
Her aunts called the office to say they were keeping her home? Because she's sick? Nothing serious, I hope?
I, uh, think it's a stomach virus...
A twenty-four hour thing...
Oh, good, *that's* a relief...
I just posted the cast list and I'd *hate* to have to replace Sabrina with Rosalind...
...she's quite the little gossip, isn't she?
Who, Roz? Yeah, she's the worst.
I overheard her and some of her gal-pals chatting about...
...actually, it was about Sabrina...
Wouldn't be surprised. Rosalind was sort of the queen bee around here until Sabrina showed up, and then, things kind of...well...
Shifted, as they sometimes do.
I understand. ***Still.***
Hearing Rosalind go on and on...
What was she saying?

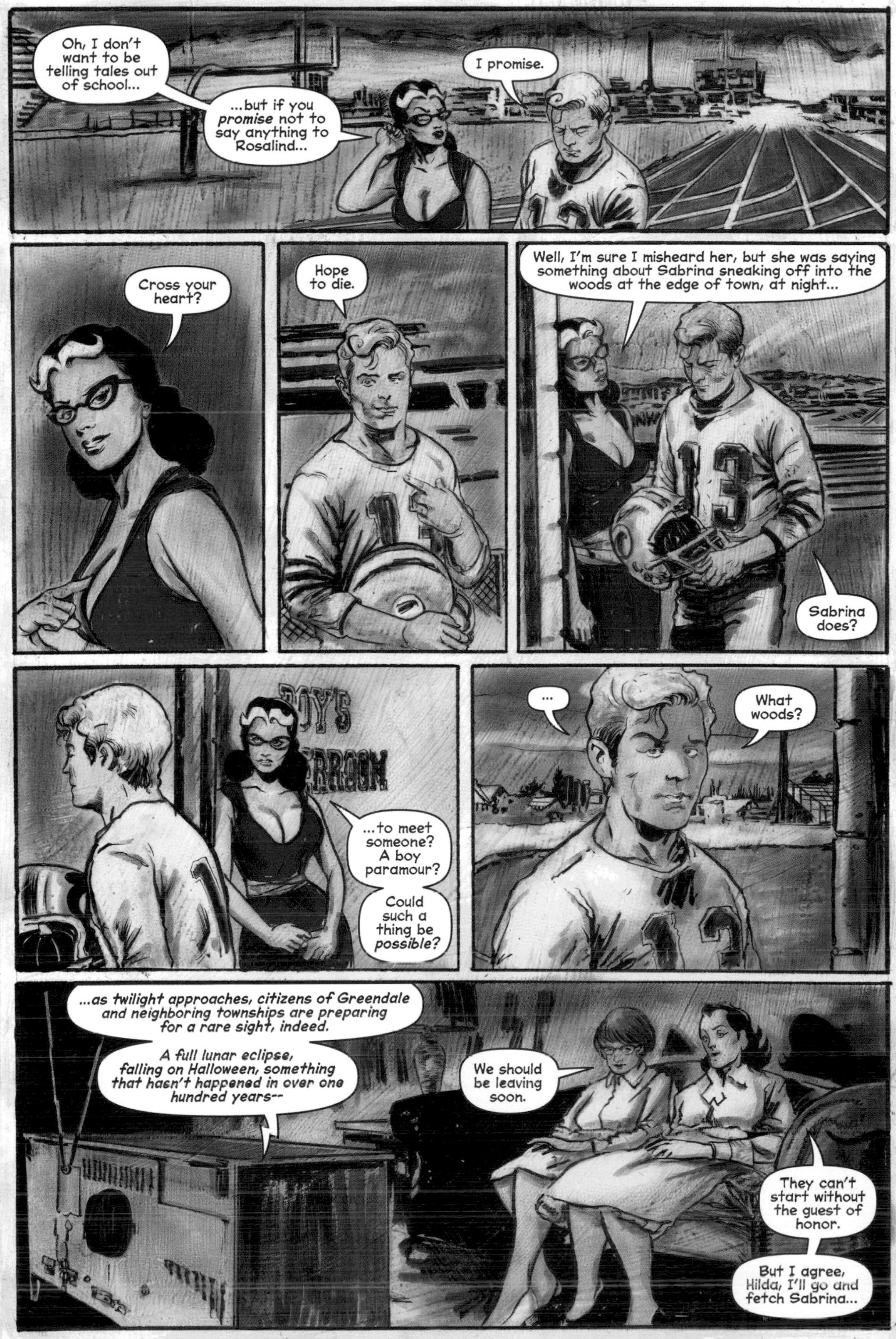

Oh, I don't want to be telling tales out of school...
...but if you *promise* not to say anything to Rosalind...
I promise.
Cross your heart?
Hope to die.
Well, I'm sure I misheard her, but she was saying something about Sabrina sneaking off into the woods at the edge of town, at night...
Sabrina does?
...to meet someone? A boy paramour?
Could such a thing be *possible*?
...
What woods?
...as twilight approaches, citizens of Greendale and neighboring townships are preparing for a rare sight, indeed.
A full lunar eclipse, falling on Halloween, something that hasn't happened in over one hundred years--
We should be leaving soon.
They can't start without the guest of honor.
But I agree, Hilda, I'll go and fetch Sabrina...

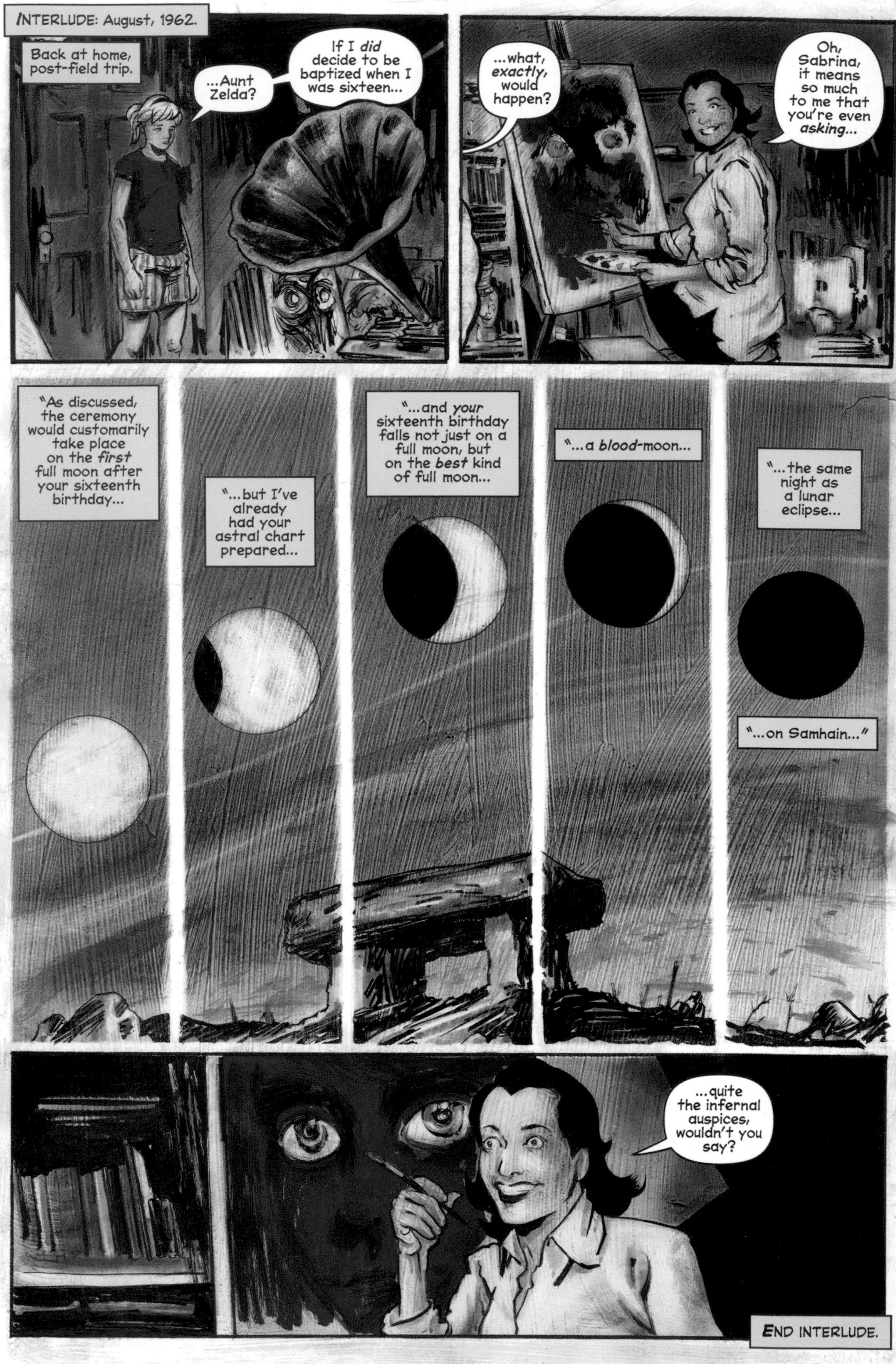
INTERLUDE: August, 1962.
Back at home, post-field trip.
...Aunt Zelda?
If I did decide to be baptized when I was sixteen...
...what, exactly, would happen?
Oh, Sabrina, it means so much to me that you're even asking...
"As discussed, the ceremony would customarily take place on the first full moon after your sixteenth birthday...
"...but I've already had your astral chart prepared...
"...and your sixteenth birthday falls not just on a full moon, but on the best kind of full moon...
"...a blood-moon...
"...the same night as a lunar eclipse...
"...on Samhain..."
...quite the infernal auspices, wouldn't you say?
END INTERLUDE.

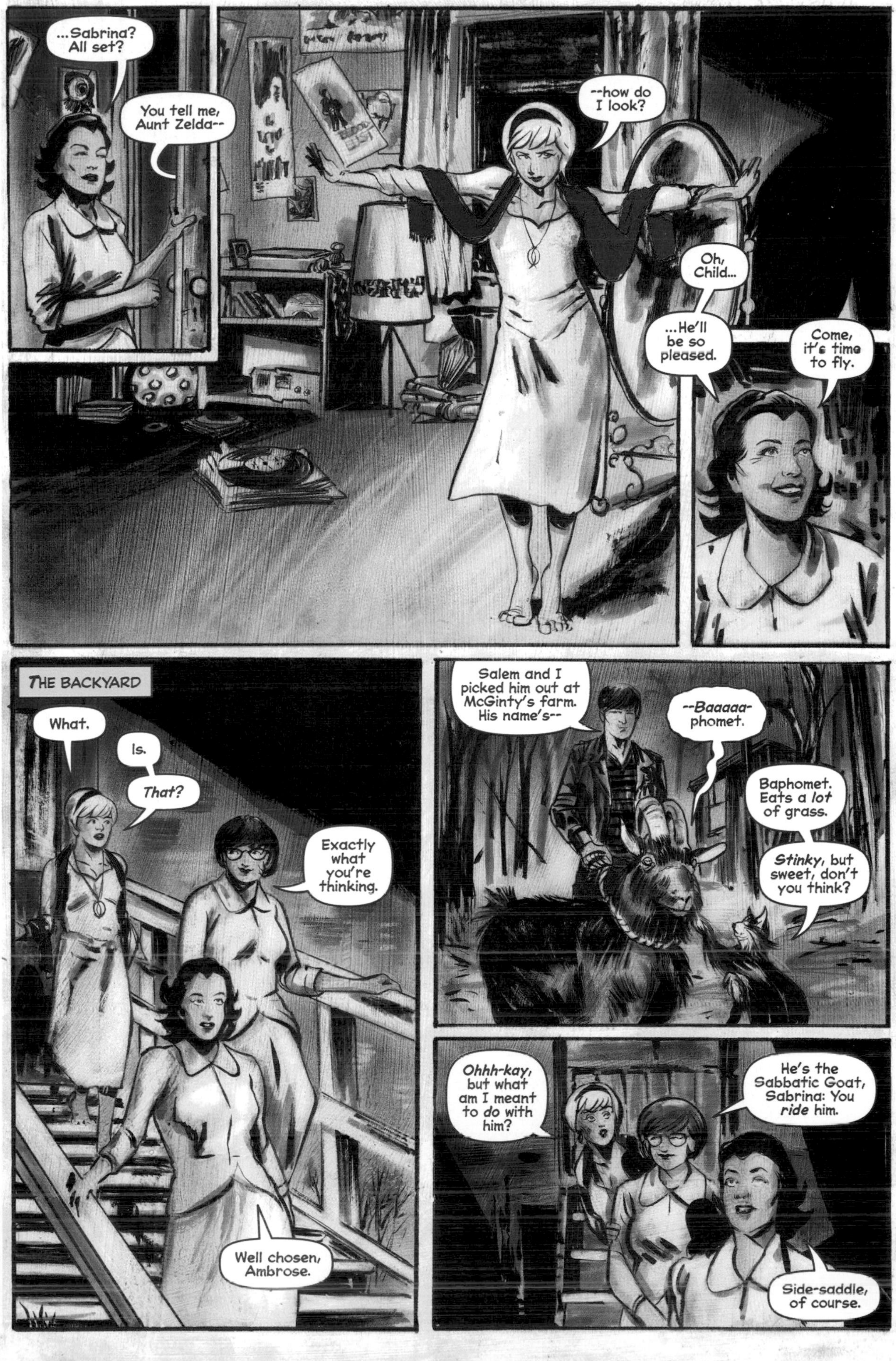
...Sabrina? All set?
You tell me, Aunt Zelda--
--how do I look?
Oh, Child...
...He'll be so pleased.
Come, it's time to fly.
THE BACKYARD
What.
Is.
That?
Exactly what you're thinking.
Well chosen, Ambrose.
Salem and I picked him out at McGinty's farm. His name's--
--Baaaaa-phomet.
Baphomet. Eats a lot of grass.
Stinky, but sweet, don't you think?
Ohhh-kay, but what am I meant to do with him?
He's the Sabbatic Goat, Sabrina: You ride him.
Side-saddle, of course.

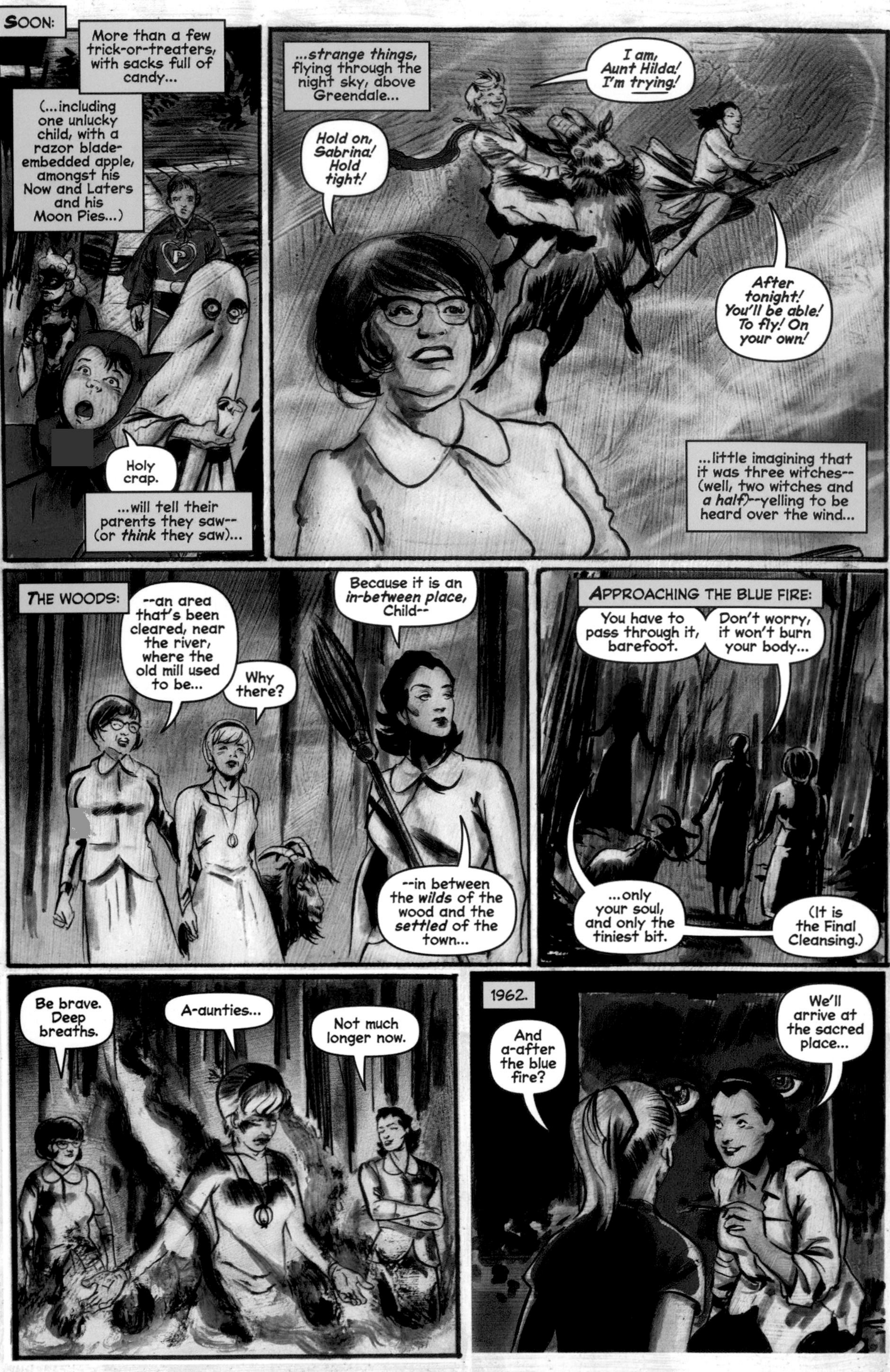
SOON:
More than a few trick-or-treaters, with sacks full of candy...
(...including one unlucky child, with a razor blade-embedded apple, amongst his Now and Laters and his Moon Pies...)
Holy crap.
...will tell their parents they saw-- (or *think* they saw)...
...*strange things,* flying through the night sky, above Greendale...
I am, Aunt Hilda! I'm *trying!*
Hold on, Sabrina! Hold tight!
After tonight! You'll be able! To fly! On your own!
...little imagining that it was three witches-- (well, two witches and *a half*)--yelling to be heard over the wind...
THE WOODS:
--an area that's been cleared, near the river, where the old mill used to be...
Why there?
Because it is an *in-between place,* Child--
--in between the *wilds* of the wood and the *settled* of the town...
APPROACHING THE BLUE FIRE:
You have to pass through it, barefoot.
Don't worry, it won't burn your body...
...only your soul, and only the tiniest bit.
(It is the Final Cleansing.)
Be brave. Deep breaths.
A-aunties...
Not much longer now.
1962.
And a-after the blue fire?
We'll arrive at the sacred place...

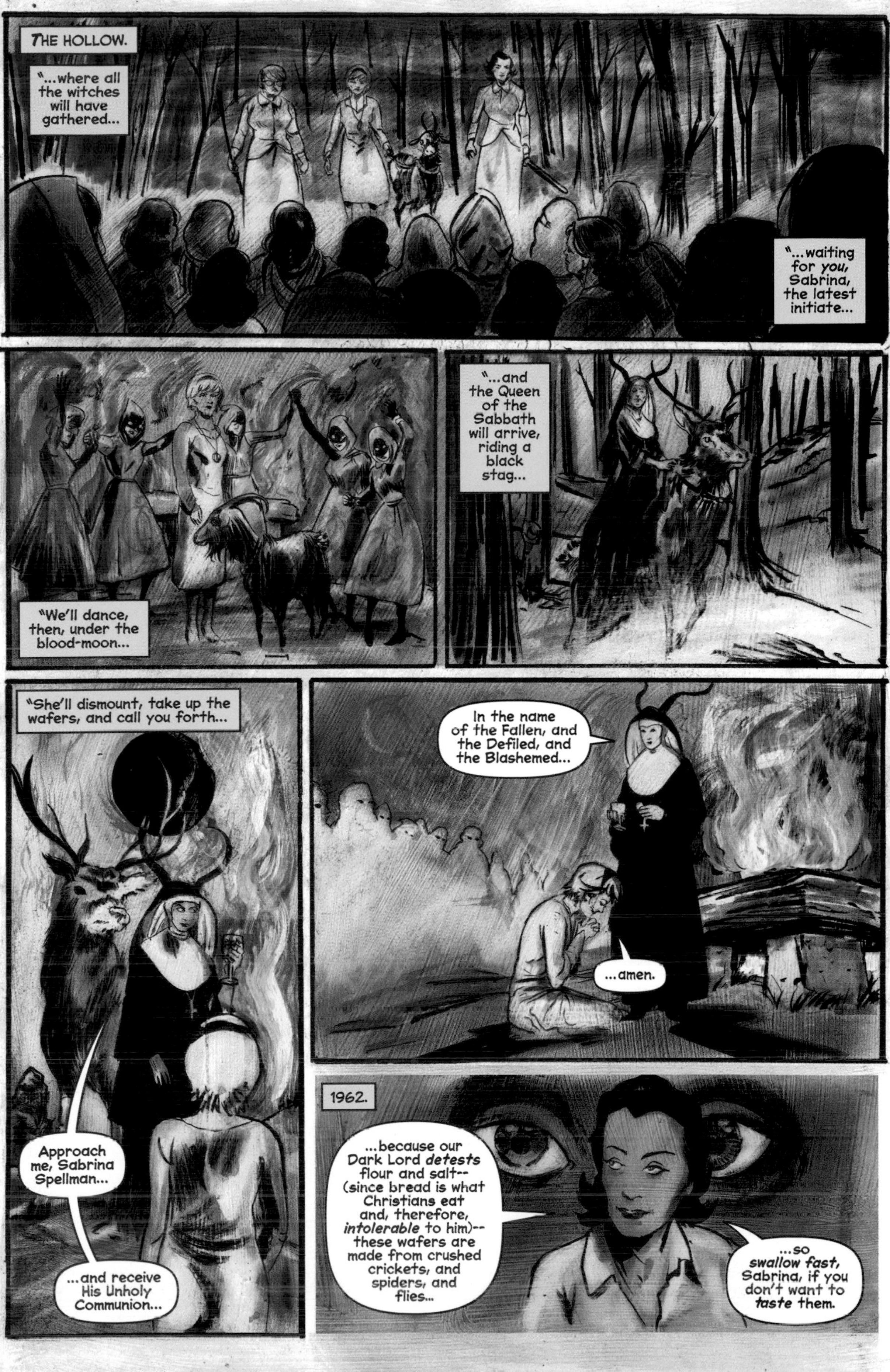
THE HOLLOW.
"...where all the witches will have gathered...
"...waiting for you, Sabrina, the latest initiate...
"We'll dance, then, under the blood-moon...
"...and the Queen of the Sabbath will arrive, riding a black stag...
"She'll dismount, take up the wafers, and call you forth...
Approach me, Sabrina Spellman...
...and receive His Unholy Communion...
In the name of the Fallen, and the Defiled, and the Blashemed...
...amen.
1962.
...because our Dark Lord detests flour and salt-- (since bread is what Christians eat and, therefore, intolerable to him)-- these wafers are made from crushed crickets, and spiders, and flies...
...so swallow fast, Sabrina, if you don't want to taste them.

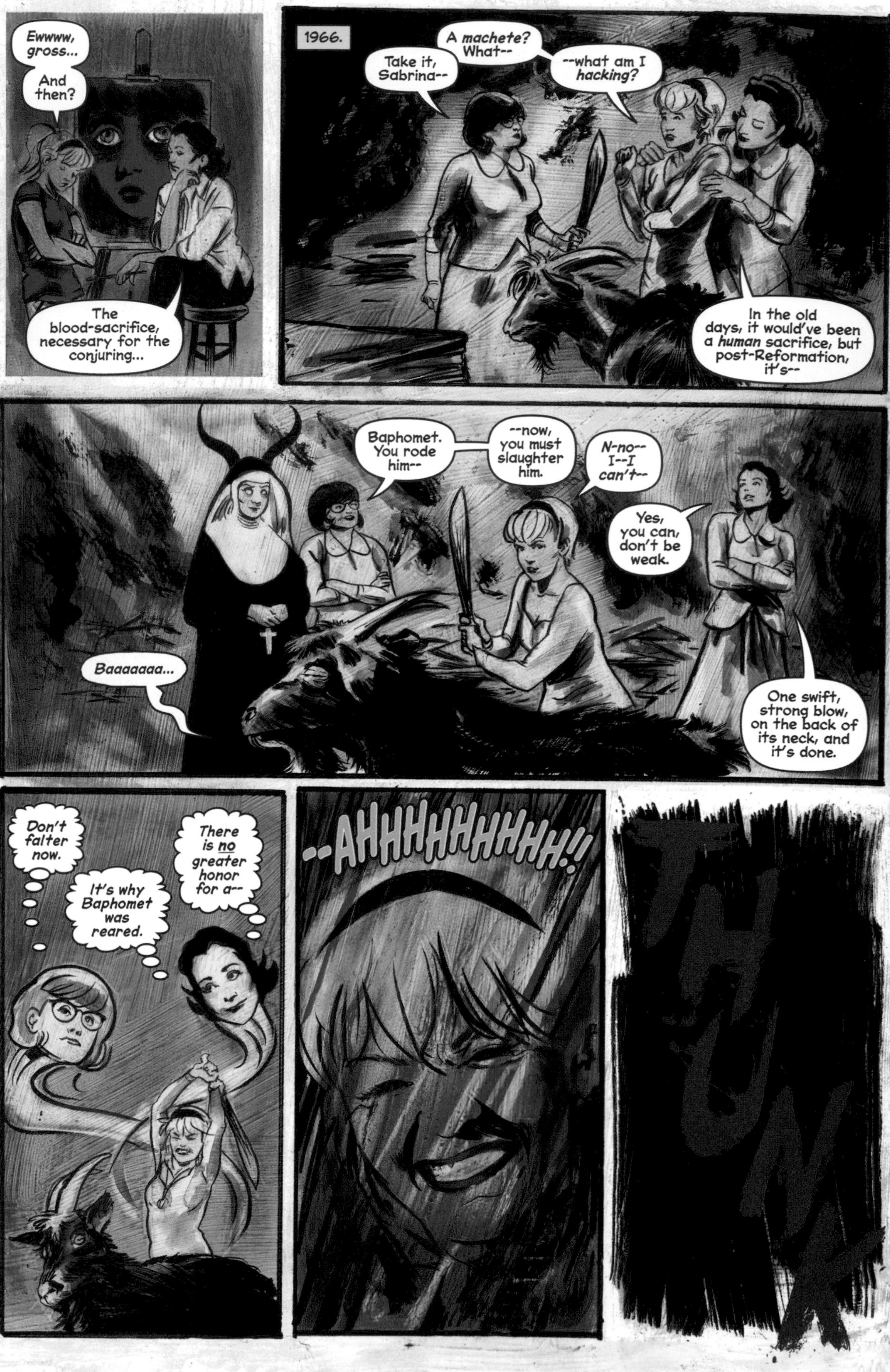
Ewwww, gross...
And then?
The blood-sacrifice, necessary for the conjuring...
1966.
Take it, Sabrina--
A *machete?* What--
--what am I *hacking?*
In the old days, it would've been a *human* sacrifice, but post-Reformation, it's--
Baphomet. You rode him--
--now, you must slaughter him.
N-no-- I--I can't--
Yes, you can, don't be weak.
Baaaaaaa...
One swift, strong blow, on the back of its neck, and it's done.
Don't falter now.
It's why Baphomet was reared.
There is no greater honor for a--
--AHHHHHHHHHH!!

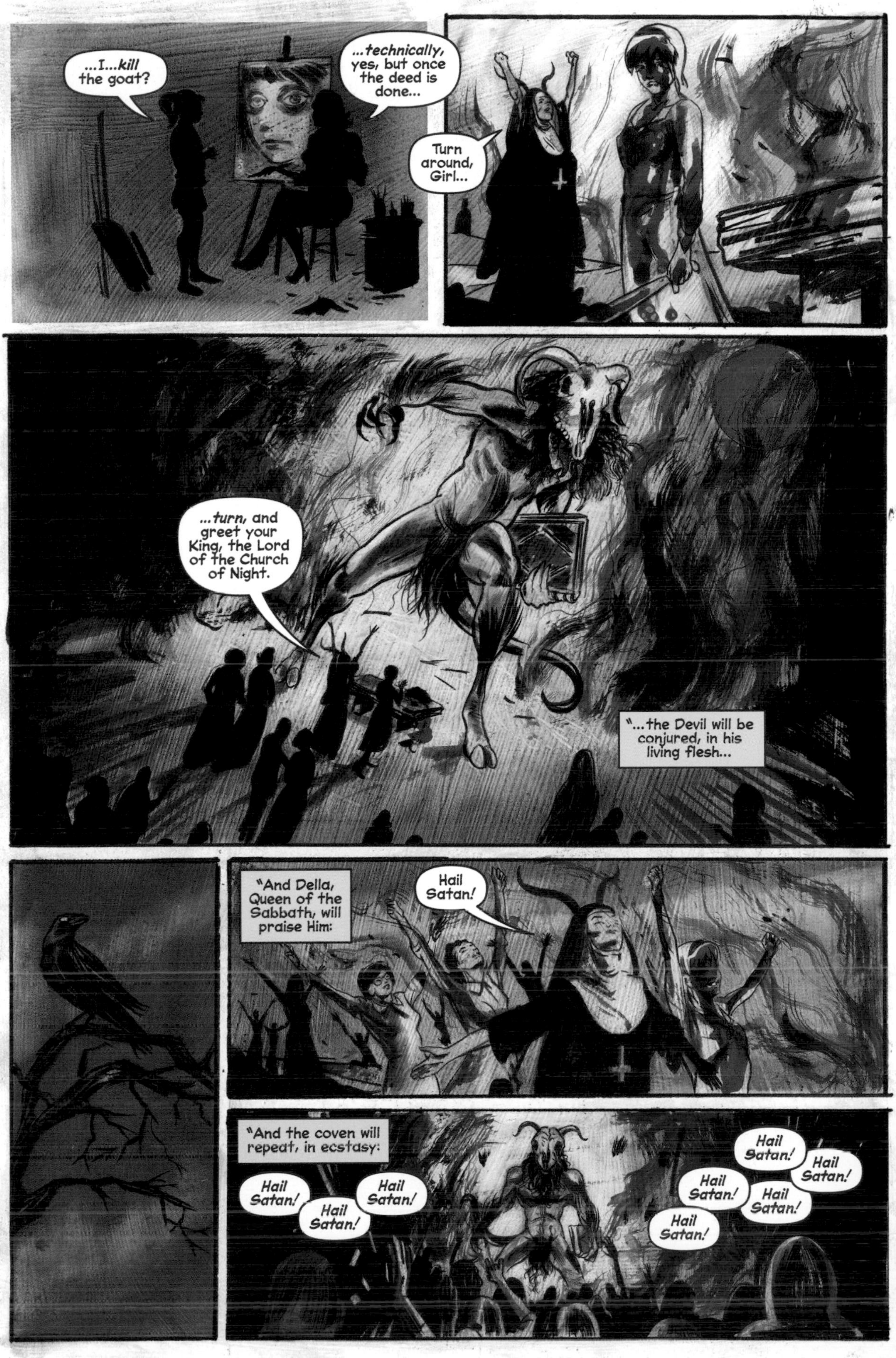

...I...kill the goat?
...technically, yes, but once the deed is done...
Turn around, Girl...
...turn, and greet your King, the Lord of the Church of Night.
"...the Devil will be conjured, in his living flesh...
"And Della, Queen of the Sabbath, will praise Him:
Hail Satan!
"And the coven will repeat, in ecstasy:
Hail Satan!
Hail Satan!
Hail Satan!
Hail Satan!
Hail Satan!
Hail Satan!
Hail Satan!
Hail Satan!

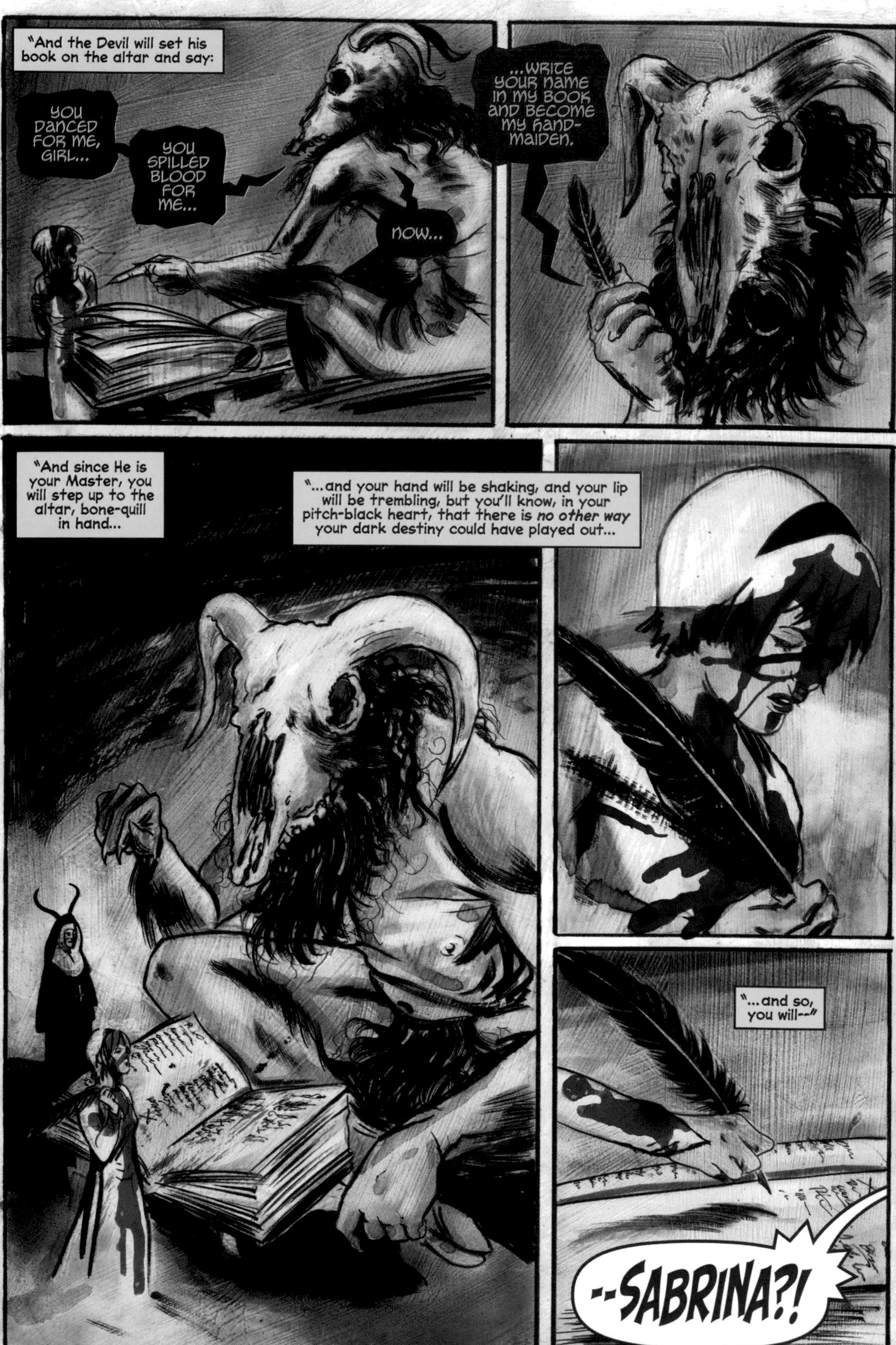
"And the Devil will set his book on the altar and say:
YOU DANCED FOR ME, GIRL...
YOU SPILLED BLOOD FOR ME...
NOW...
...WRITE YOUR NAME IN MY BOOK AND BECOME MY HAND-MAIDEN.
"And since He is your Master, you will step up to the altar, bone-quill in hand...
"...and your hand will be shaking, and your lip will be trembling, but you'll know, in your pitch-black heart, that there is *no other way* your dark destiny could have played out...
"...and so, you will--"
--SABRINA?!

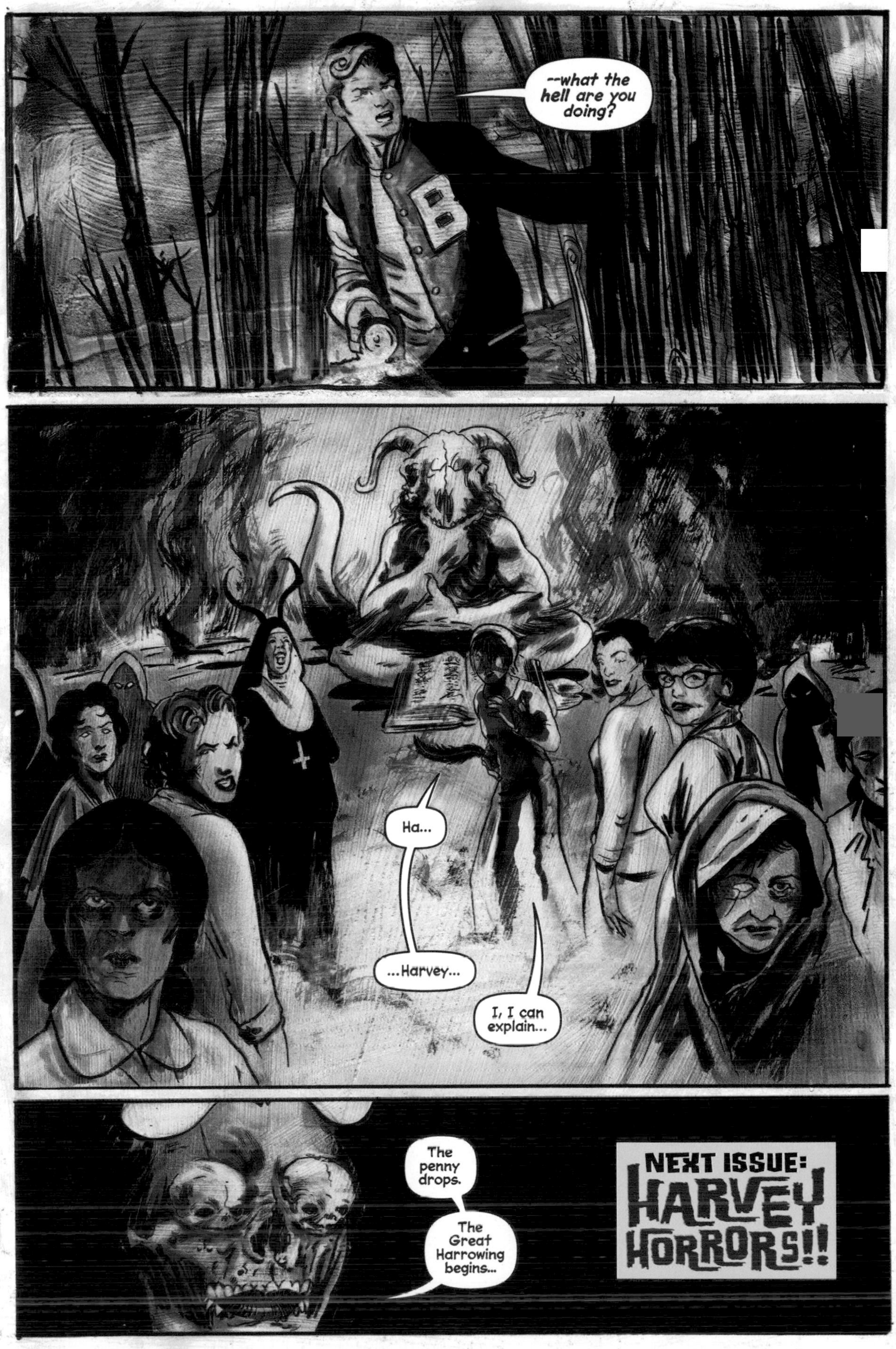
--what the hell are you doing?
Ha...
...Harvey...
I, I can explain...
The penny drops.
The Great Harrowing begins...
NEXT ISSUE:
HARVEY HORRORS!!

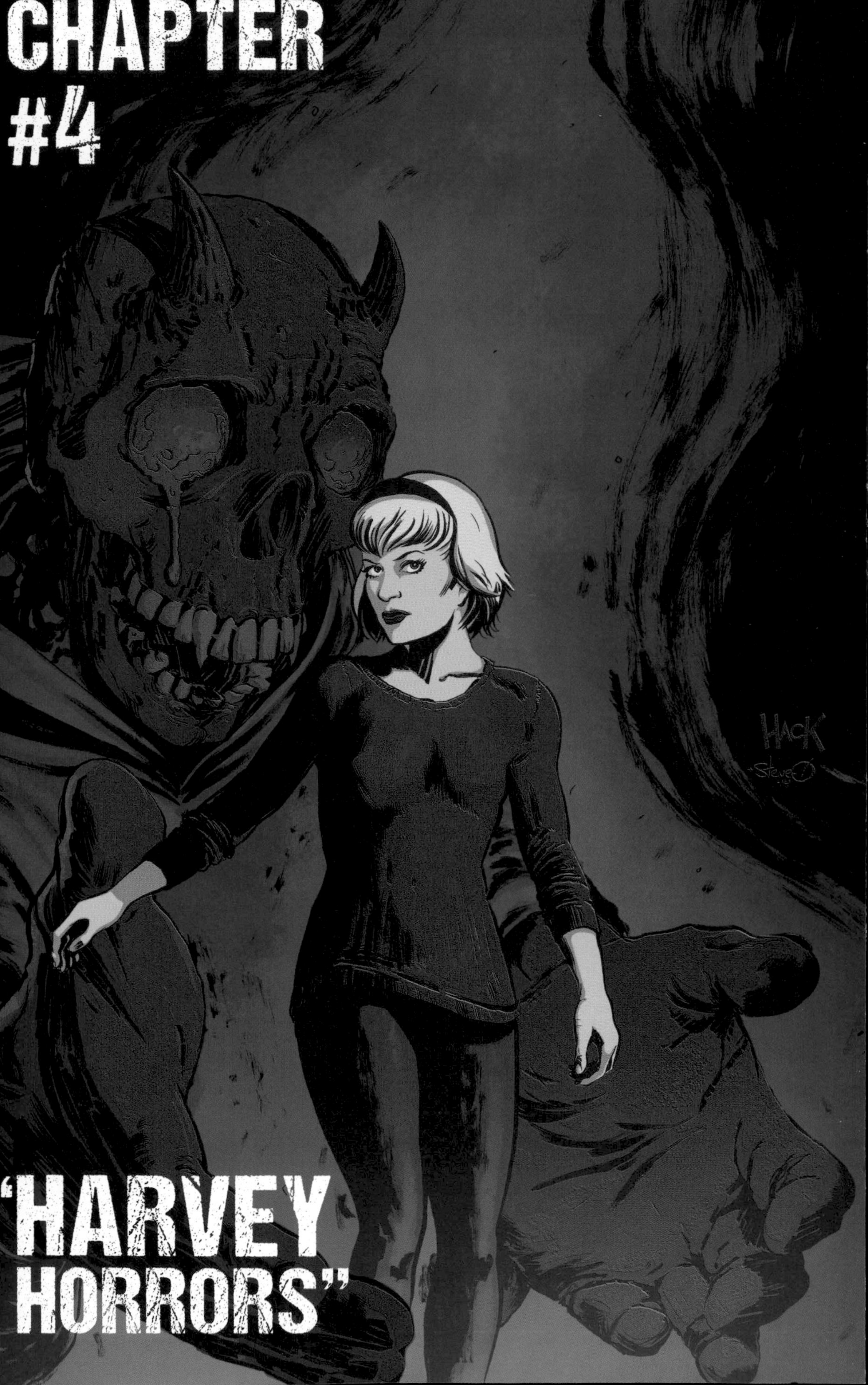
CHAPTER
#4
'HARVEY
HORRORS"
HACK

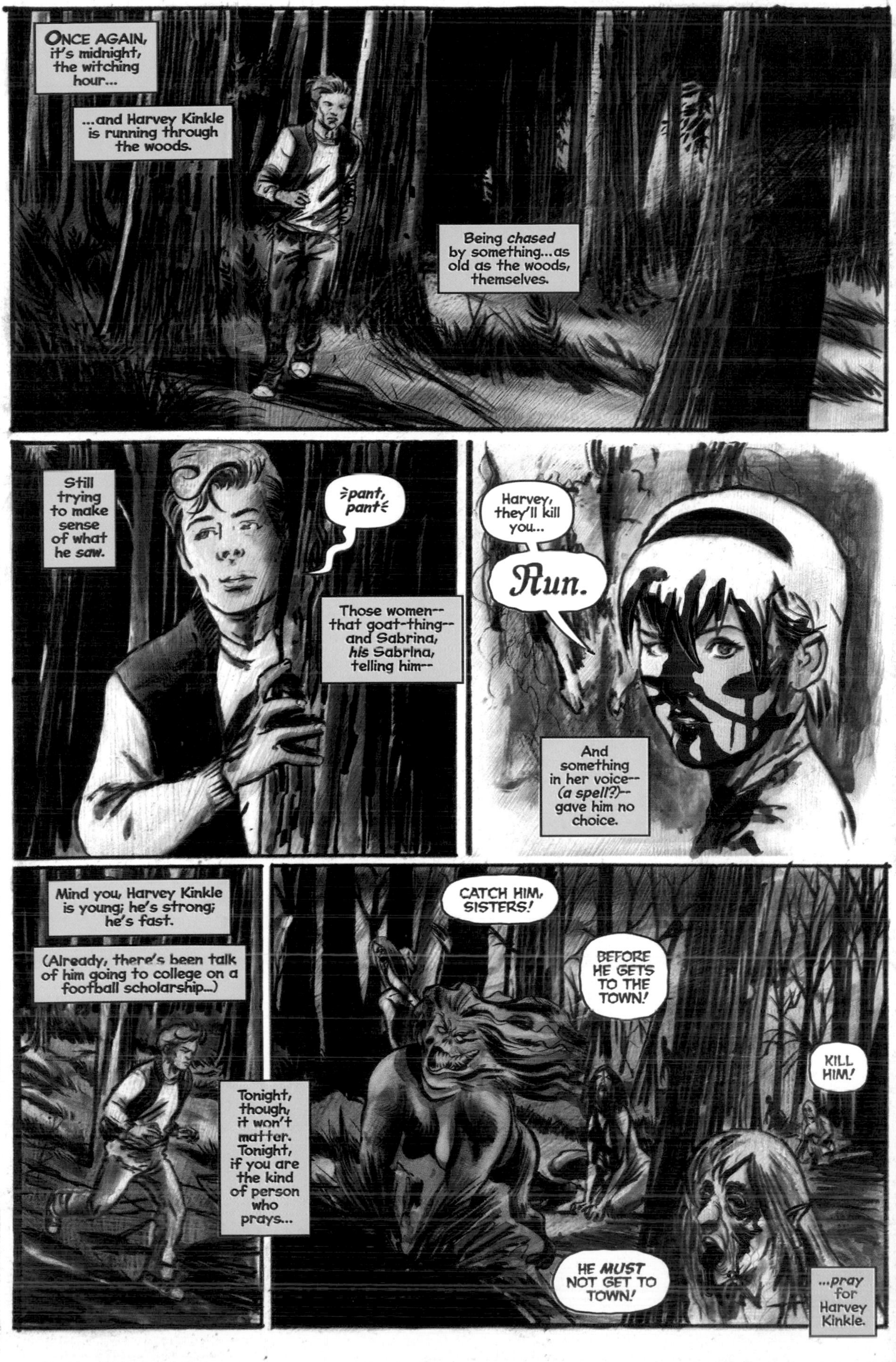
ONCE AGAIN, it's midnight, the witching hour...
...and Harvey Kinkle is running through the woods.
Being *chased* by something...as old as the woods, themselves.
Still trying to make sense of what he *saw*.
pant, pant
Those women--that goat-thing--and Sabrina, *his* Sabrina, telling him--
Harvey, they'll kill you...
Run.
And something in her voice--(*a spell?*)--gave him no choice.
Mind you, Harvey Kinkle is young; he's strong; he's fast.
(Already, there's been talk of him going to college on a football scholarship...)
Tonight, though, it won't matter. Tonight, if you are the kind of person who prays...
CATCH HIM, SISTERS!
BEFORE HE GETS TO THE TOWN!
KILL HIM!
HE *MUST* NOT GET TO TOWN!
...*pray* for Harvey Kinkle.

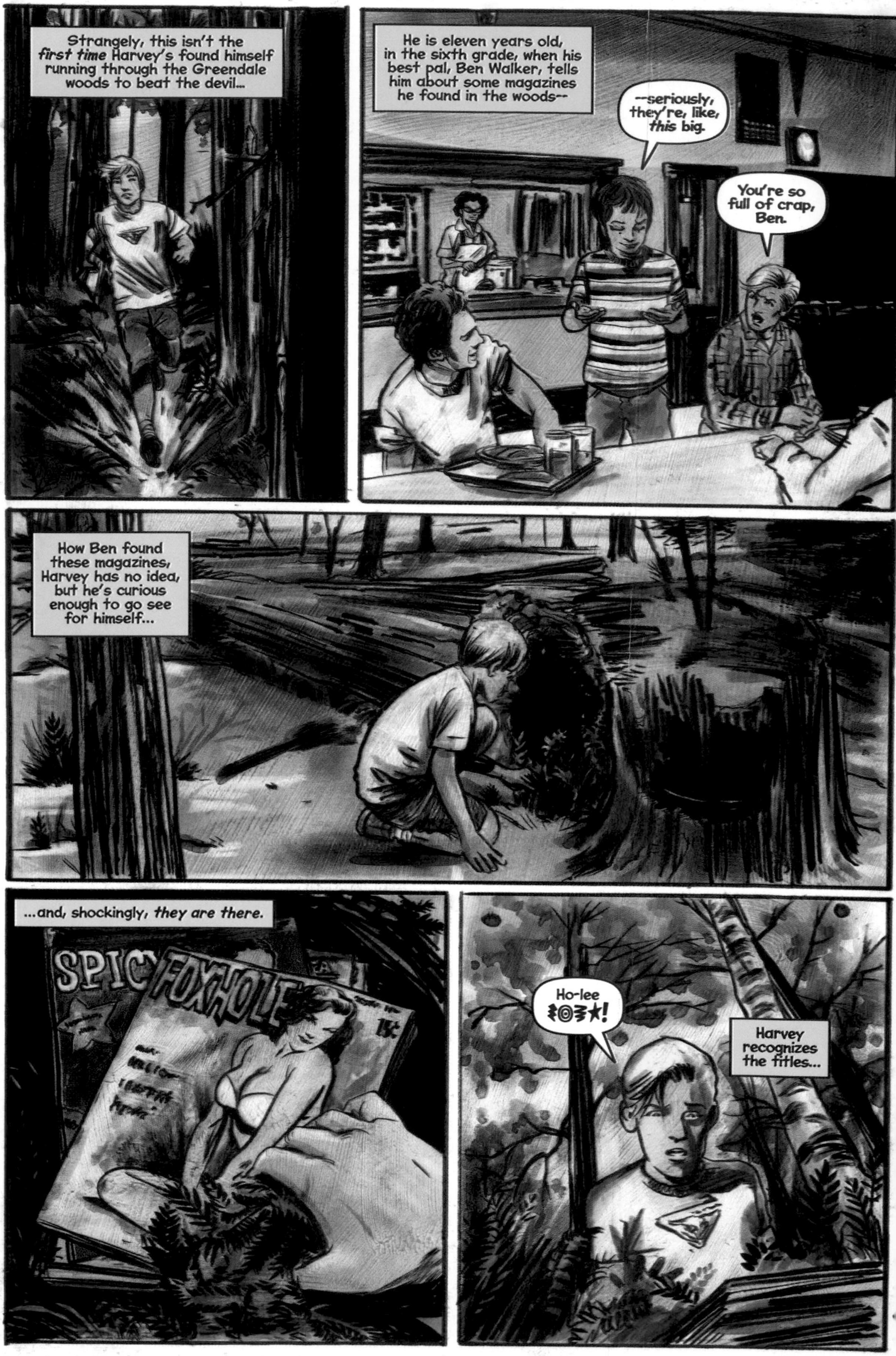
Strangely, this isn't the *first time* Harvey's found himself running through the Greendale woods to beat the devil...
He is eleven years old, in the sixth grade, when his best pal, Ben Walker, tells him about some magazines he found in the woods--
--seriously, they're, like, *this* big.
You're so full of crap, Ben.
How Ben found these magazines, Harvey has no idea, but he's curious enough to go see for himself...
...and, shockingly, *they are there.*
SPIC
FOXHOLE
15¢
Ho-lee
Harvey recognizes the titles...

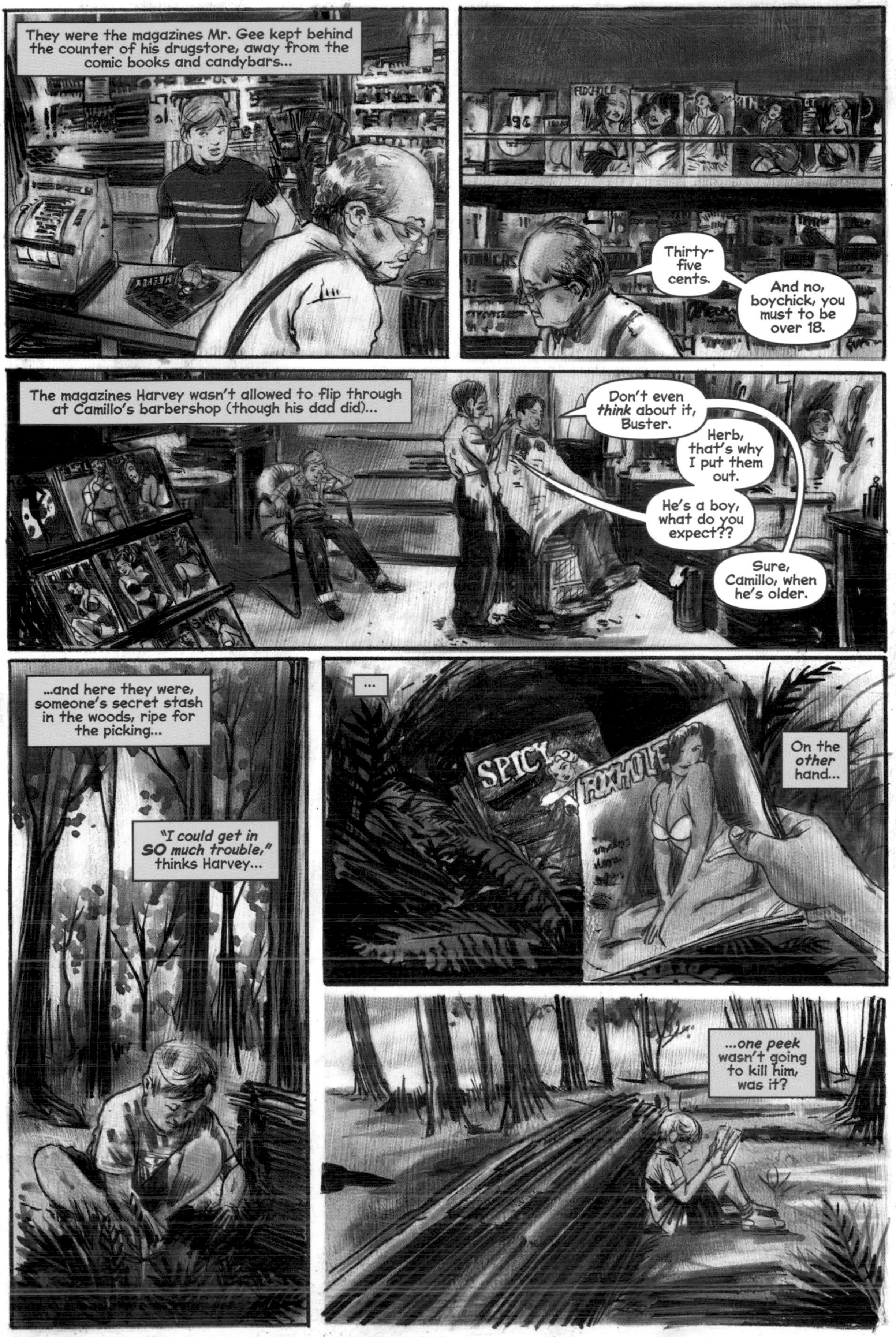
They were the magazines Mr. Gee kept behind the counter of his drugstore, away from the comic books and candybars...
Thirty-five cents.
And no, boychick, you must to be over 18.
The magazines Harvey wasn't allowed to flip through at Camillo's barbershop (though his dad did)...
Don't even *think* about it, Buster.
Herb, that's why I put them out.
He's a boy, what do you expect??
Sure, Camillo, when he's older.
...and here they were, someone's secret stash in the woods, ripe for the picking...
"I could get in SO much trouble," thinks Harvey...
...
SPICY
FOXHOLE
On the *other* hand...
...*one peek* wasn't going to kill him, was it?

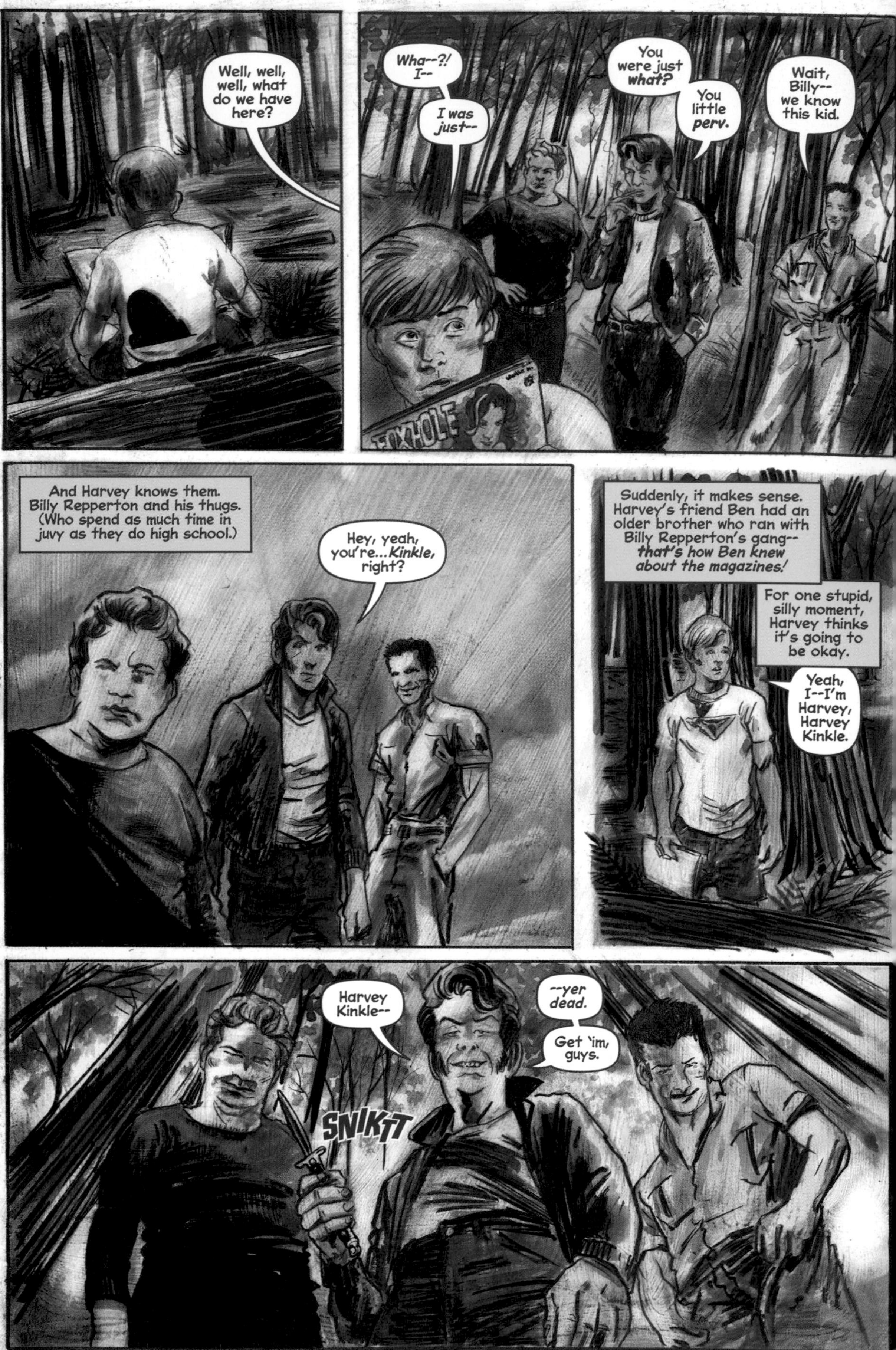
Well, well, well, what do we have here?
Wha--?! I--
I was just--
You were just *what?*
You little *perv.*
Wait, Billy-- we know this kid.
FOXHOLE
And Harvey knows them. Billy Repperton and his thugs. (Who spend as much time in juvy as they do high school.)
Hey, yeah, you're...*Kinkle,* right?
Suddenly, it makes sense. Harvey's friend Ben had an older brother who ran with Billy Repperton's gang-- *that's how Ben knew about the magazines!*
For one stupid, silly moment, Harvey thinks it's going to be okay.
Yeah, I--I'm Harvey, Harvey Kinkle.
Harvey Kinkle--
--yer dead.
Get 'im, guys.
SNIKTT

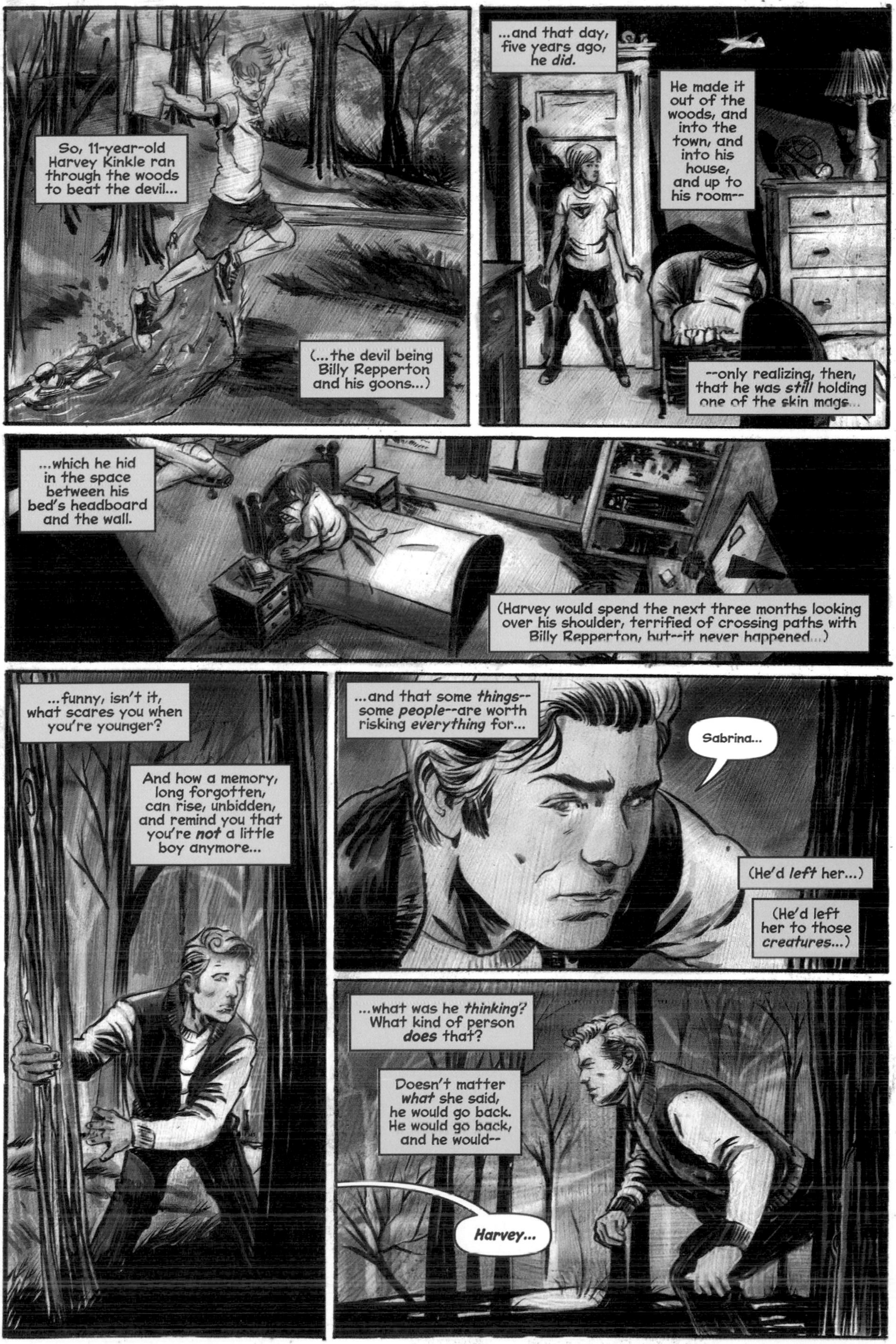

So, 11-year-old Harvey Kinkle ran through the woods to beat the devil...
(...the devil being Billy Repperton and his goons...)
...and that day, five years ago, he *did.*
He made it out of the woods, and into the town, and into his house, and up to his room--
--only realizing, then, that he was *still* holding one of the skin mags...
...which he hid in the space between his bed's headboard and the wall.
(Harvey would spend the next three months looking over his shoulder, terrified of crossing paths with Billy Repperton, but--it never happened...)
...funny, isn't it, what scares you when you're younger?
And how a memory, long forgotten, can rise, unbidden, and remind you that you're *not* a little boy anymore...
...and that some *things*--some *people*--are worth risking *everything* for...
Sabrina...
(He'd *left* her...)
(He'd left her to those *creatures*...)
...what was he *thinking?* What kind of person *does* that?
Doesn't matter *what* she said, he would go back. He would go back, and he would--
Harvey...

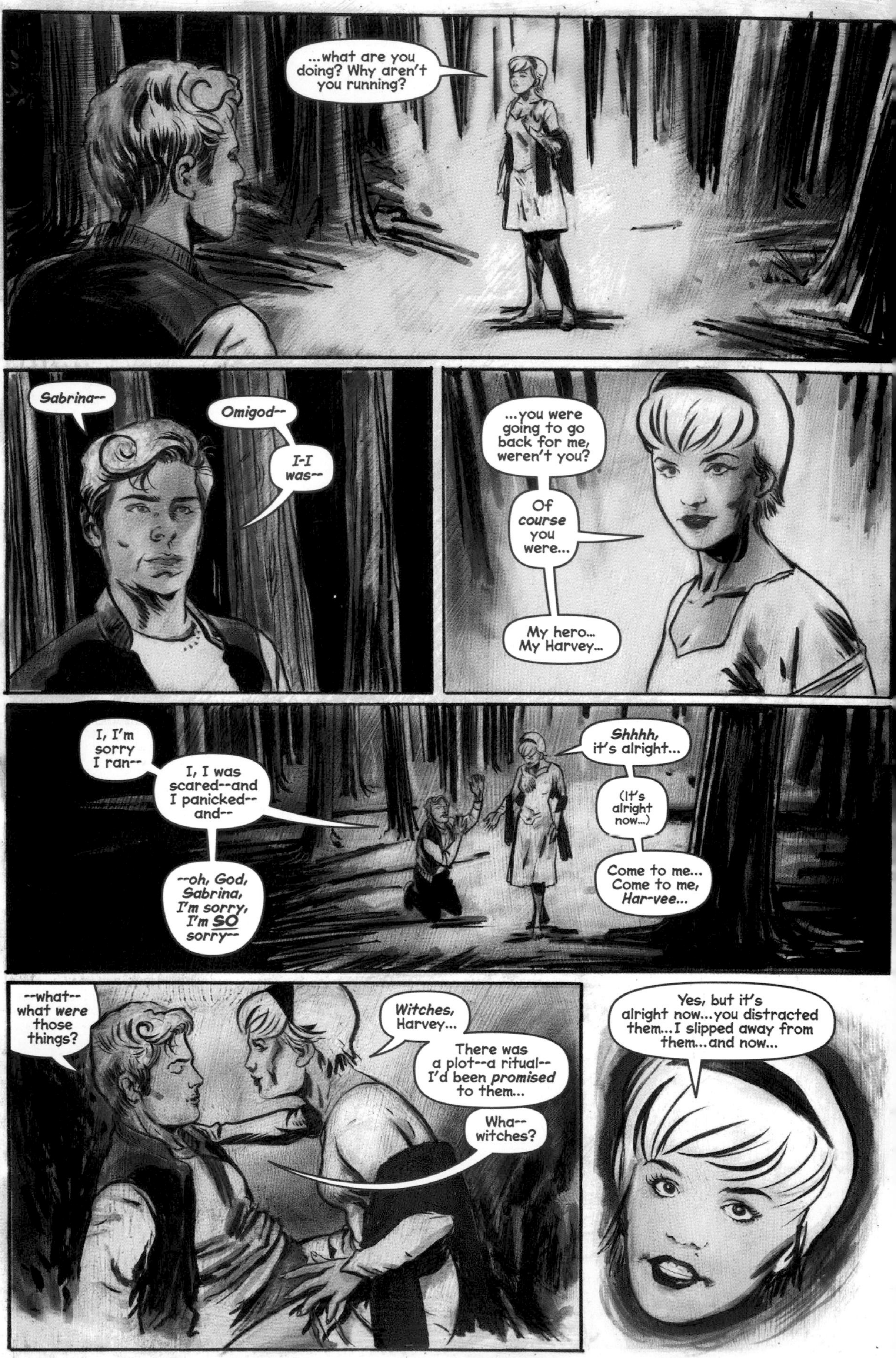
...what are you doing? Why aren't you running?
Sabrina--
Omigod--
I-I was--
...you were going to go back for me, weren't you?
Of course you were...
My hero... My Harvey...
I, I'm sorry I ran--
I, I was scared--and I panicked--and--
--oh, God, Sabrina, I'm sorry, I'm SO sorry--
Shhhh, it's alright...
(It's alright now...)
Come to me... Come to me, Har-vee...
--what--what were those things?
Witches, Harvey...
There was a plot--a ritual--I'd been promised to them...
Wha--witches?
Yes, but it's alright now...you distracted them...I slipped away from them...and now...

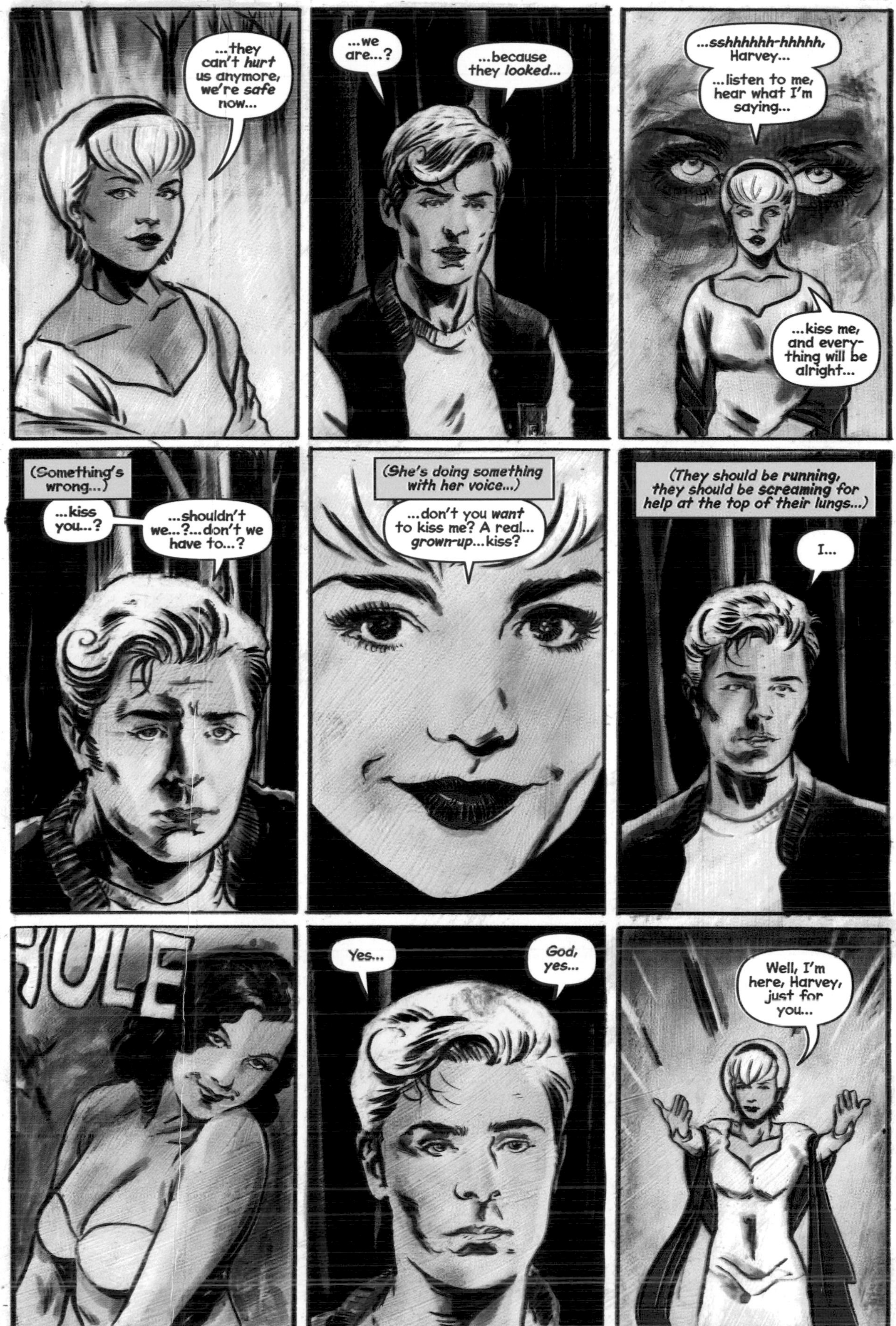

...they can't hurt us anymore, we're safe now...
...we are...?
...because they looked...
...sshhhhhh-hhhhh, Harvey...
...listen to me, hear what I'm saying...
...kiss me, and every-thing will be alright...
(Something's wrong...)
...kiss you...?
...shouldn't we...?...don't we have to...?
(She's doing something with her voice...)
...don't you want to kiss me? A real... grown-up...kiss?
(They should be running, they should be screaming for help at the top of their lungs...)
I...
HULE
Yes...
God, yes...
Well, I'm here, Harvey, just for you...

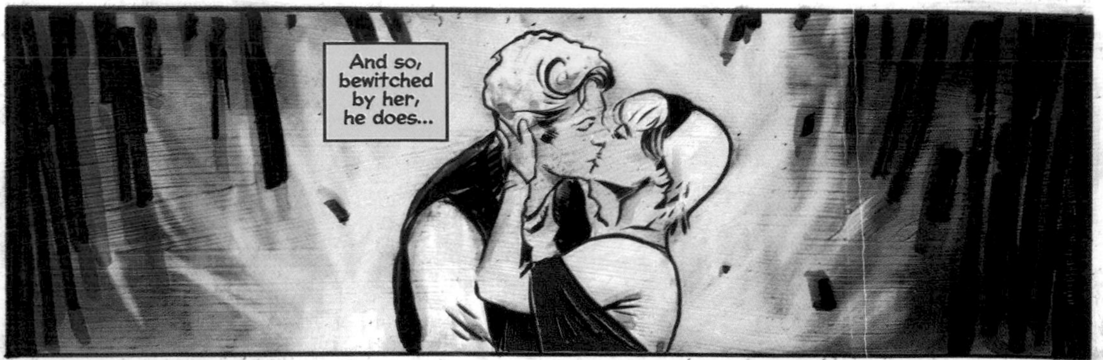
And so, bewitched by her, he does...

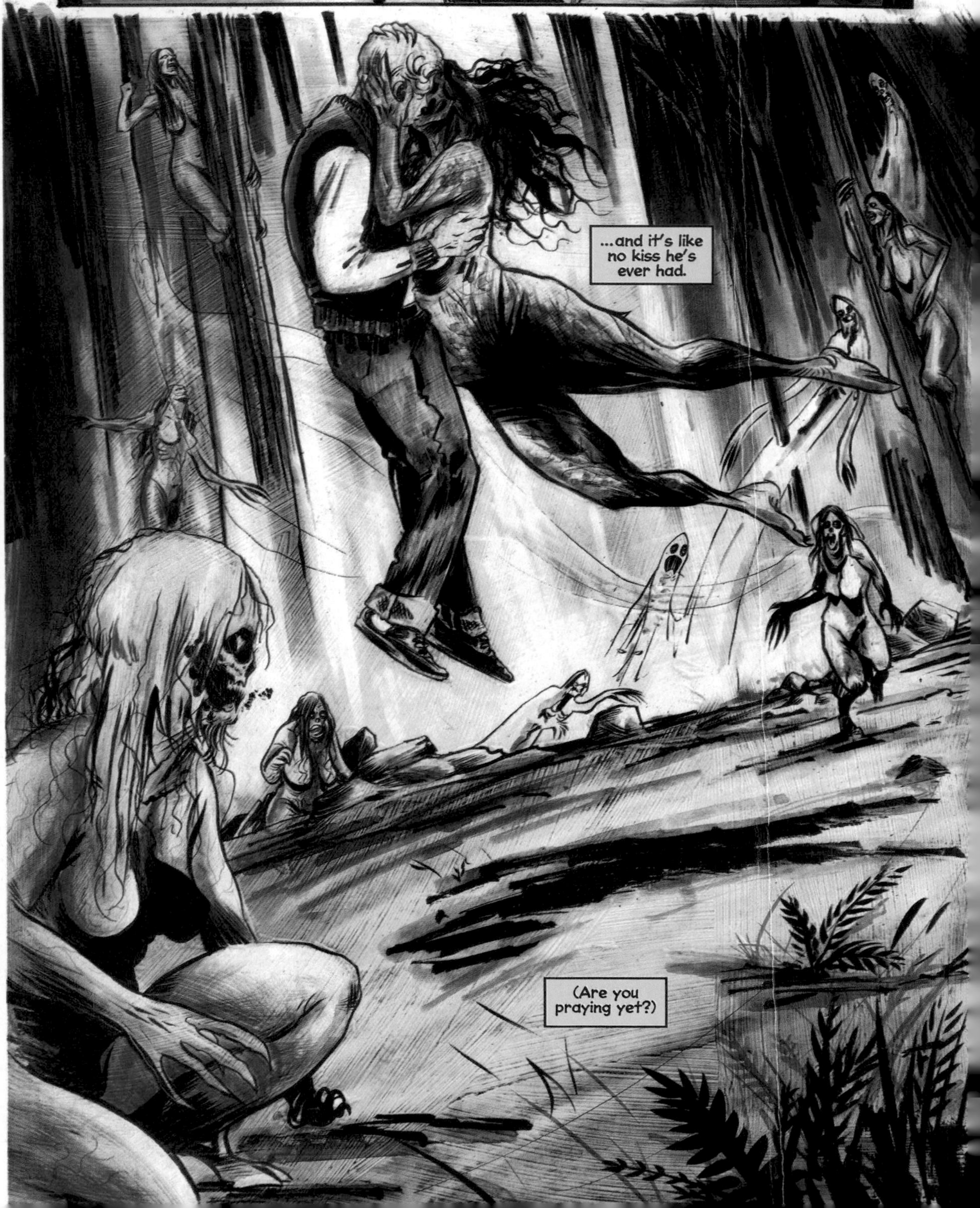
...and it's like no kiss he's ever had.
(Are you praying yet?)

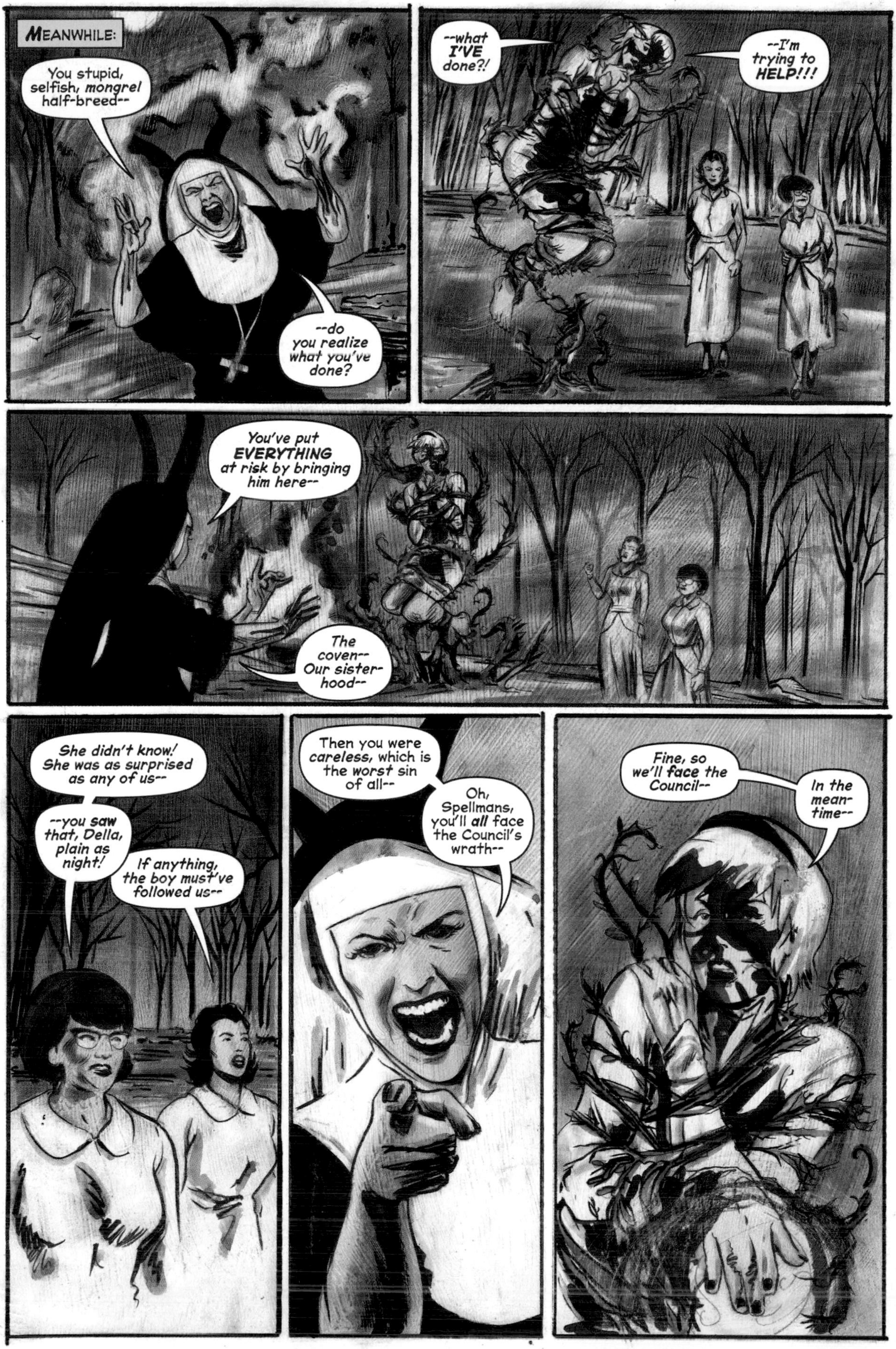
MEANWHILE:
You stupid, selfish, mongrel half-breed--
--do you realize what you've done?
--what I'VE done?!
--I'm trying to HELP!!!
You've put EVERYTHING at risk by bringing him here--
The coven-- Our sisterhood--
She didn't know! She was as surprised as any of us--
--you saw that, Della, plain as night!
If anything, the boy must've followed us--
Then you were careless, which is the worst sin of all--
Oh, Spellmans, you'll all face the Council's wrath--
Fine, so we'll face the Council--
In the mean-time--

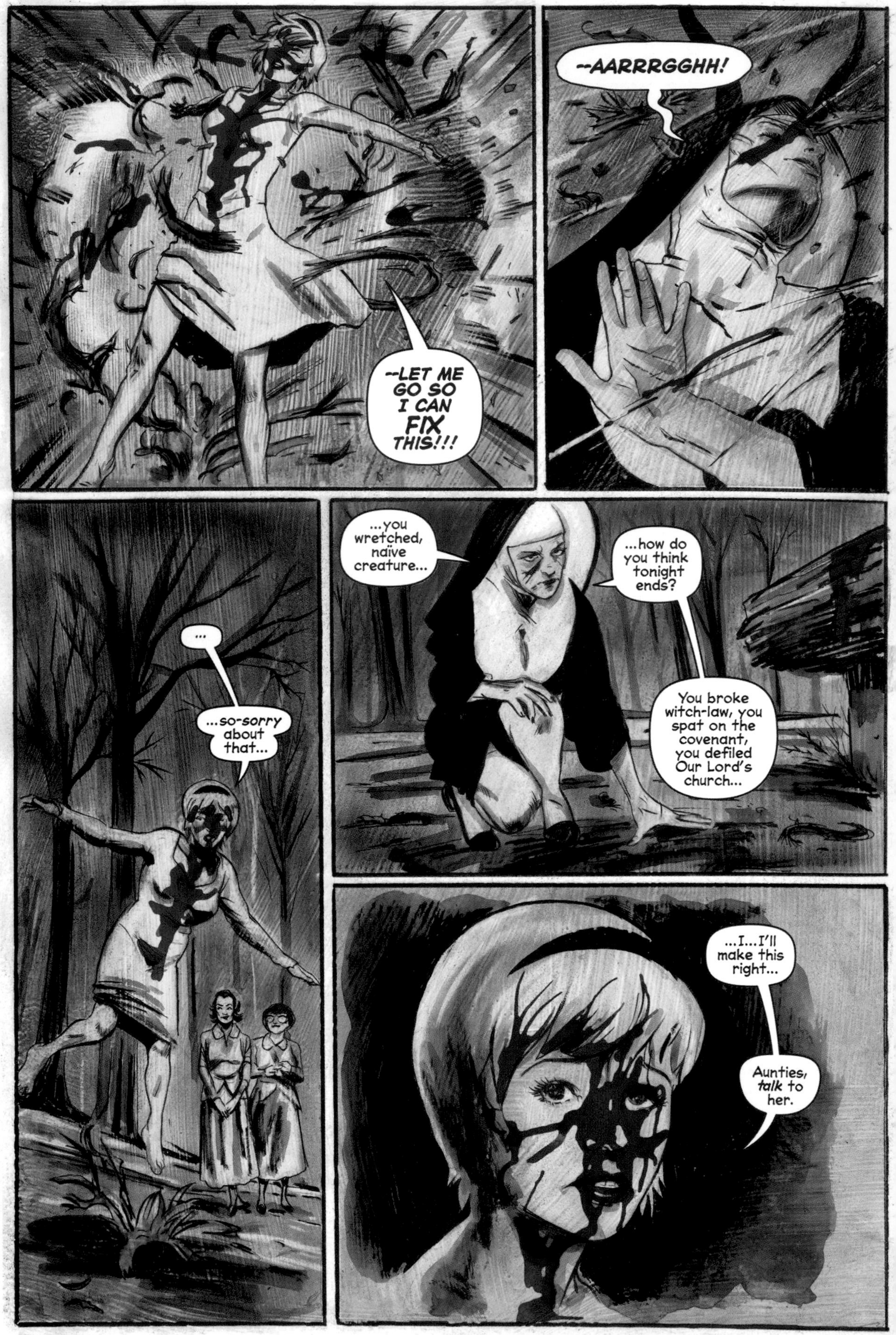
--LET ME GO SO I CAN FIX THIS!!!
--AARRRGGHH!
...
...so-sorry about that...
...you wretched, naïve creature...
...how do you think tonight ends?
You broke witch-law, you spat on the covenant, you defiled Our Lord's church...
...I...I'll make this right...
Aunties, talk to her.

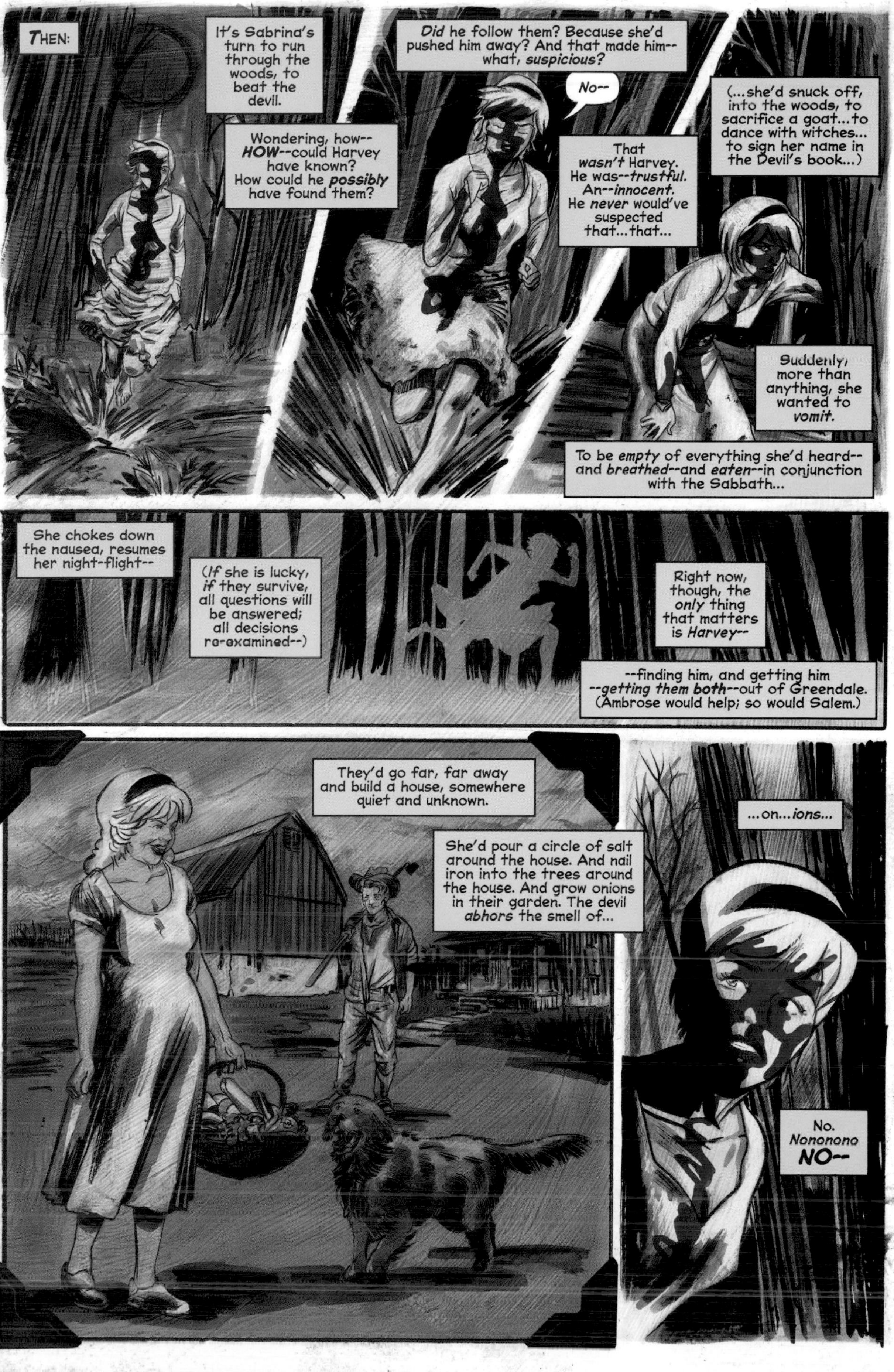
THEN:
It's Sabrina's turn to run through the woods, to beat the devil.
Wondering, how--HOW--could Harvey have known? How could he possibly have found them?
Did he follow them? Because she'd pushed him away? And that made him--what, suspicious?
No--
That wasn't Harvey. He was--trustful. An--innocent. He never would've suspected that...that...
(...she'd snuck off, into the woods, to sacrifice a goat...to dance with witches... to sign her name in the Devil's book...)
Suddenly, more than anything, she wanted to vomit.
To be empty of everything she'd heard--and breathed--and eaten--in conjunction with the Sabbath...
She chokes down the nausea, resumes her night-flight--
(If she is lucky, if they survive, all questions will be answered; all decisions re-examined--)
Right now, though, the only thing that matters is Harvey--
--finding him, and getting him --getting them both--out of Greendale. (Ambrose would help; so would Salem.)
They'd go far, far away and build a house, somewhere quiet and unknown.
She'd pour a circle of salt around the house. And nail iron into the trees around the house. And grow onions in their garden. The devil abhors the smell of...
...on...ions...
No. Nonononono NO--

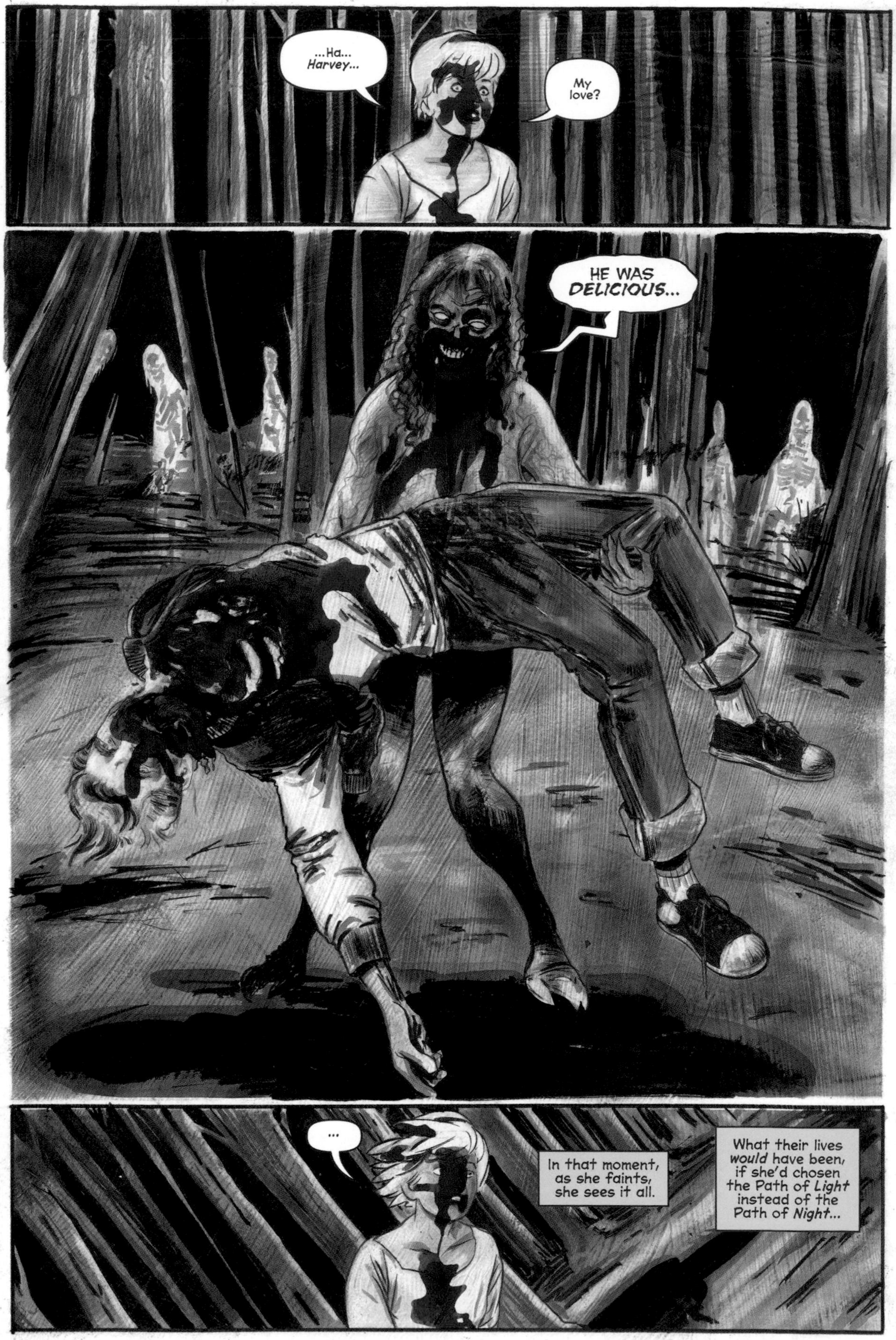

...Ha... *Harvey*...
My love?
HE WAS *DELICIOUS*...
...
In that moment, as she faints, she sees it all.
What their lives *would* have been, if she'd chosen the Path of *Light* instead of the Path of *Night*...

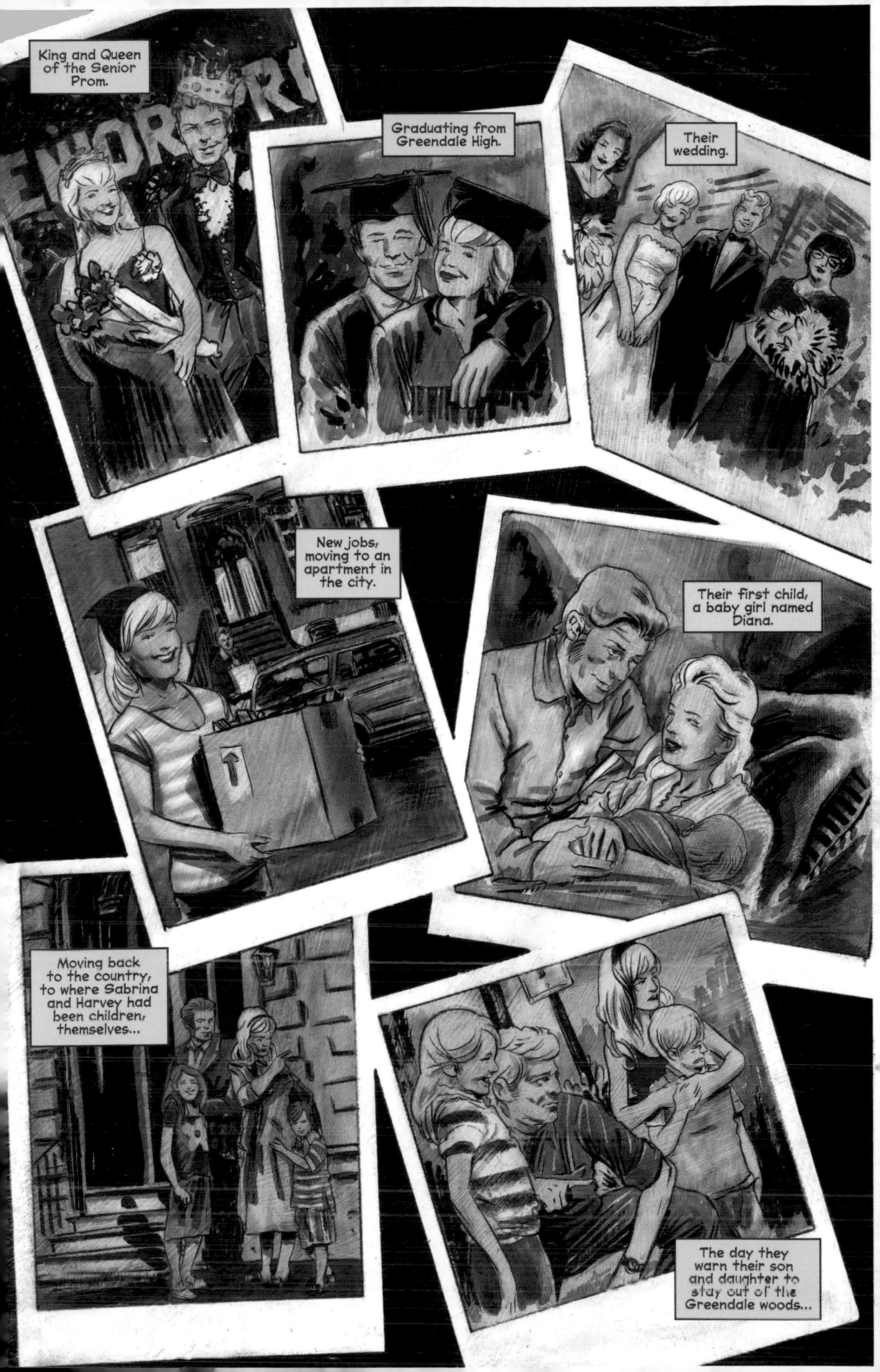

King and Queen of the Senior Prom.
Graduating from Greendale High.
Their wedding.
New jobs, moving to an apartment in the city.
Their first child, a baby girl named Diana.
Moving back to the country, to where Sabrina and Harvey had been children, themselves...
The day they warn their son and daughter to stay out of the Greendale woods...

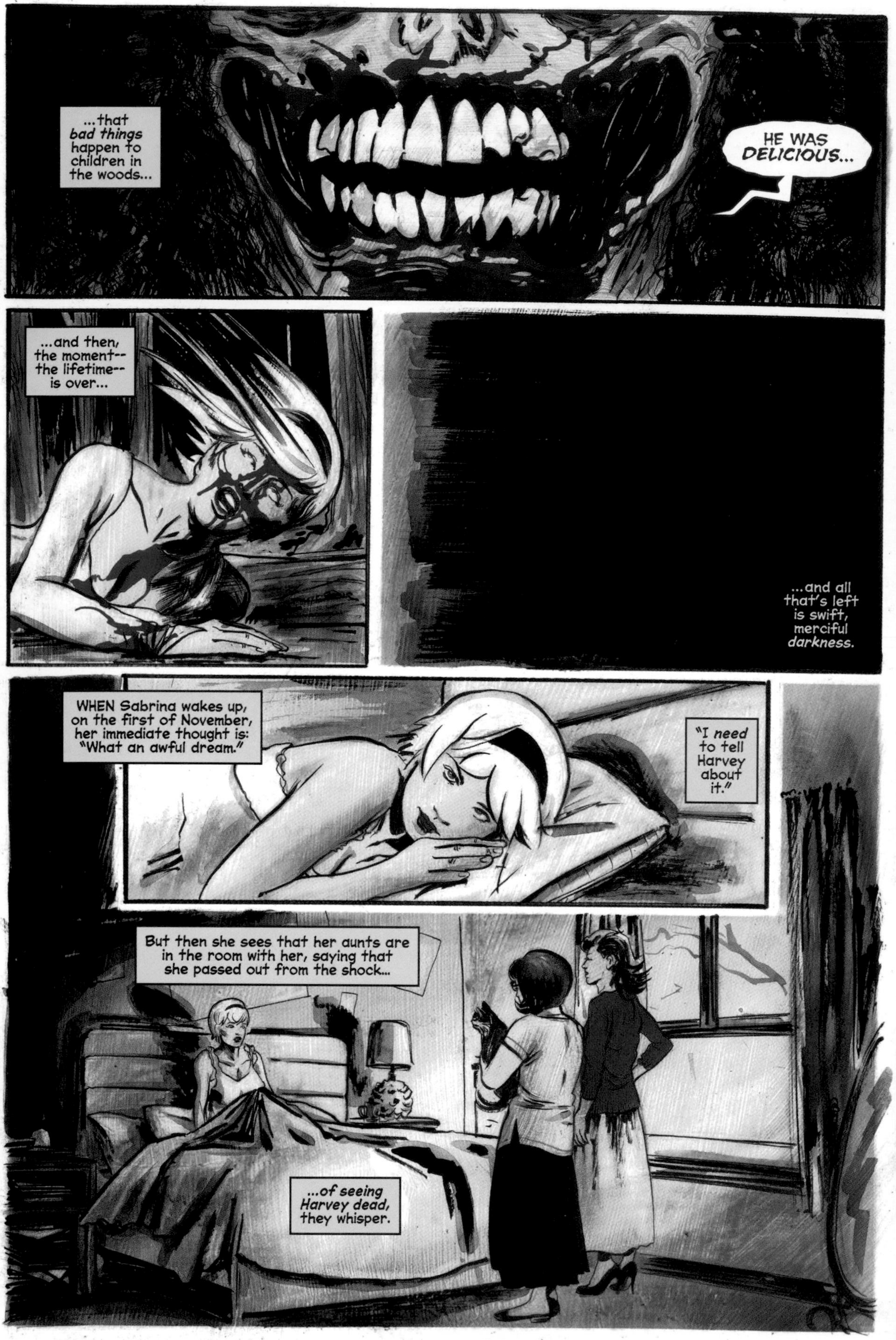
...that *bad things* happen to children in the woods...
HE WAS **DELICIOUS...**
...and then, the moment-- the lifetime-- is over...
...and all that's left is swift, merciful *darkness.*
WHEN Sabrina wakes up, on the first of November, her immediate thought is: "What an awful dream."
"I *need* to tell Harvey about it."
But then she sees that her aunts are in the room with her, saying that she passed out from the shock...
...*of seeing Harvey dead,* they whisper.

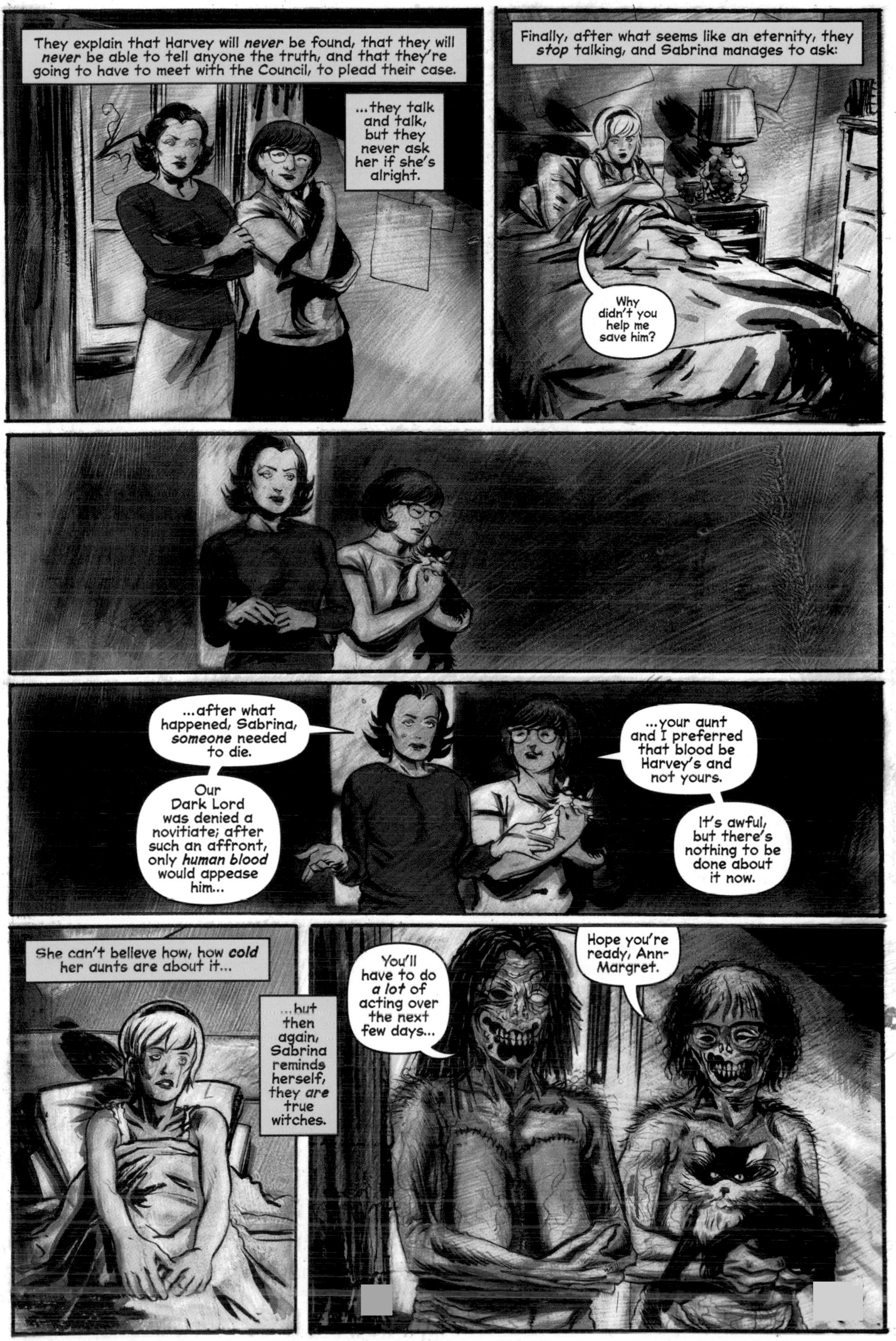
They explain that Harvey will *never* be found, that they will *never* be able to tell anyone the truth, and that they're going to have to meet with the Council, to plead their case.
...they talk and talk, but they never ask her if she's alright.
Finally, after what seems like an eternity, they *stop* talking, and Sabrina manages to ask:
Why didn't you help me save him?
...after what happened, Sabrina, *someone* needed to die.
Our Dark Lord was denied a novitiate; after such an affront, only *human blood* would appease him...
...your aunt and I preferred that blood be Harvey's and not yours.
It's awful, but there's nothing to be done about it now.
She can't believe how, how *cold* her aunts are about it...
...but then again, Sabrina reminds herself, they *are* true witches.
You'll have to do *a lot* of acting over the next few days...
Hope you're ready, Ann-Margret.

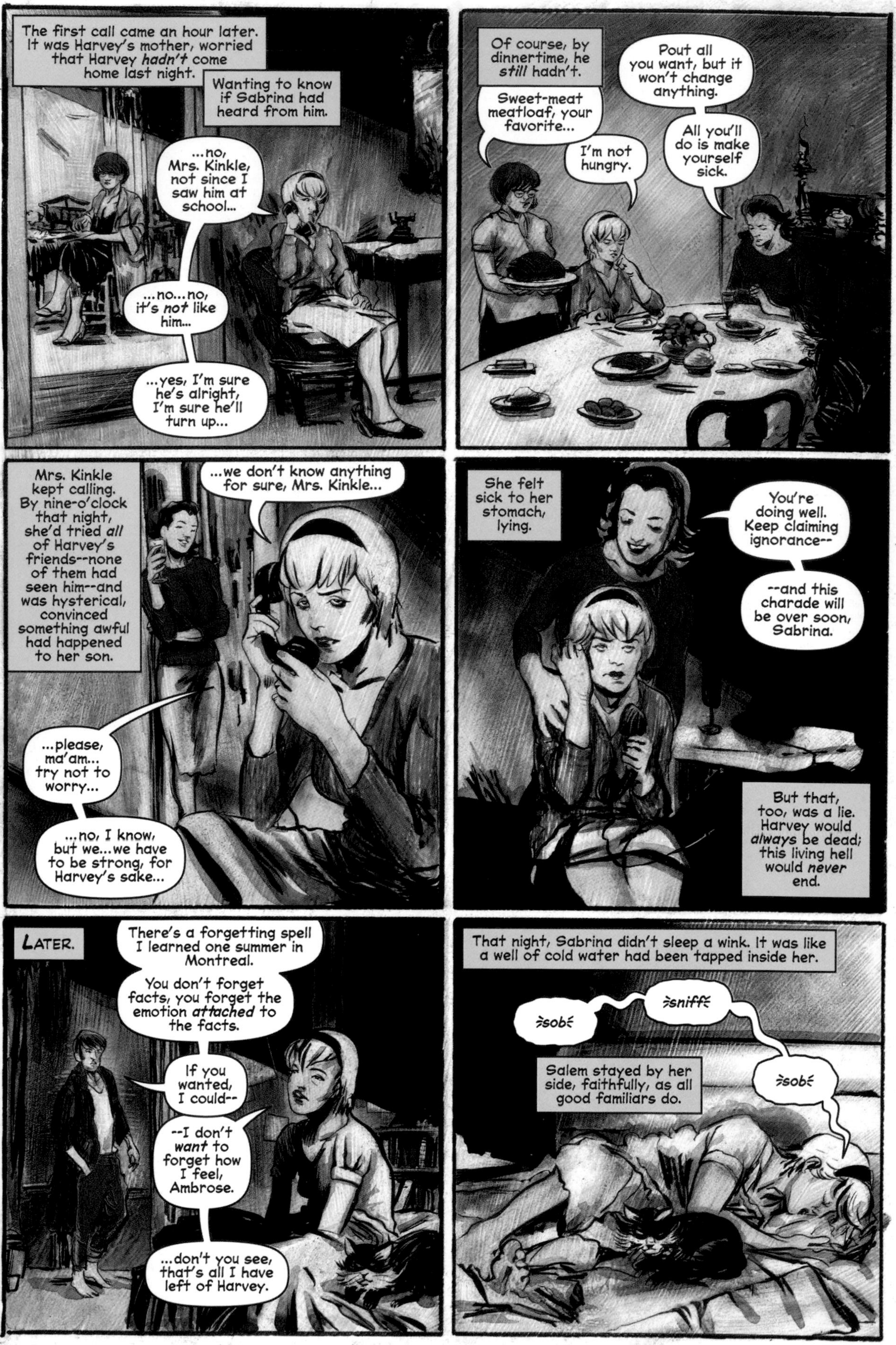
The first call came an hour later. It was Harvey's mother, worried that Harvey *hadn't* come home last night.
Wanting to know if Sabrina had heard from him.
...no, Mrs. Kinkle, not since I saw him at school...
...no...no, it's *not* like him...
...yes, I'm sure he's alright, I'm sure he'll turn up...
Of course, by dinnertime, he *still* hadn't.
Sweet-meat meatloaf, your favorite...
I'm not hungry.
Pout all you want, but it won't change anything.
All you'll do is make yourself sick.
Mrs. Kinkle kept calling. By nine-o'clock that night, she'd tried *all* of Harvey's friends--none of them had seen him--and was hysterical, convinced something awful had happened to her son.
...we don't know anything for sure, Mrs. Kinkle...
...please, ma'am... try not to worry...
...no, I know, but we...we have to be strong, for Harvey's sake...
She felt sick to her stomach, lying.
You're doing well. Keep claiming ignorance--
--and this charade will be over soon, Sabrina.
But that, too, was a lie. Harvey would *always* be dead; this living hell would *never* end.
LATER.
There's a forgetting spell I learned one summer in Montreal.
You don't forget facts, you forget the emotion *attached* to the facts.
If you wanted, I could--
--I don't *want* to forget how I feel, Ambrose.
...don't you see, that's all I have left of Harvey.
That night, Sabrina didn't sleep a wink. It was like a well of cold water had been tapped inside her.
sob
sniff
sob
Salem stayed by her side, faithfully, as all good familiars do.

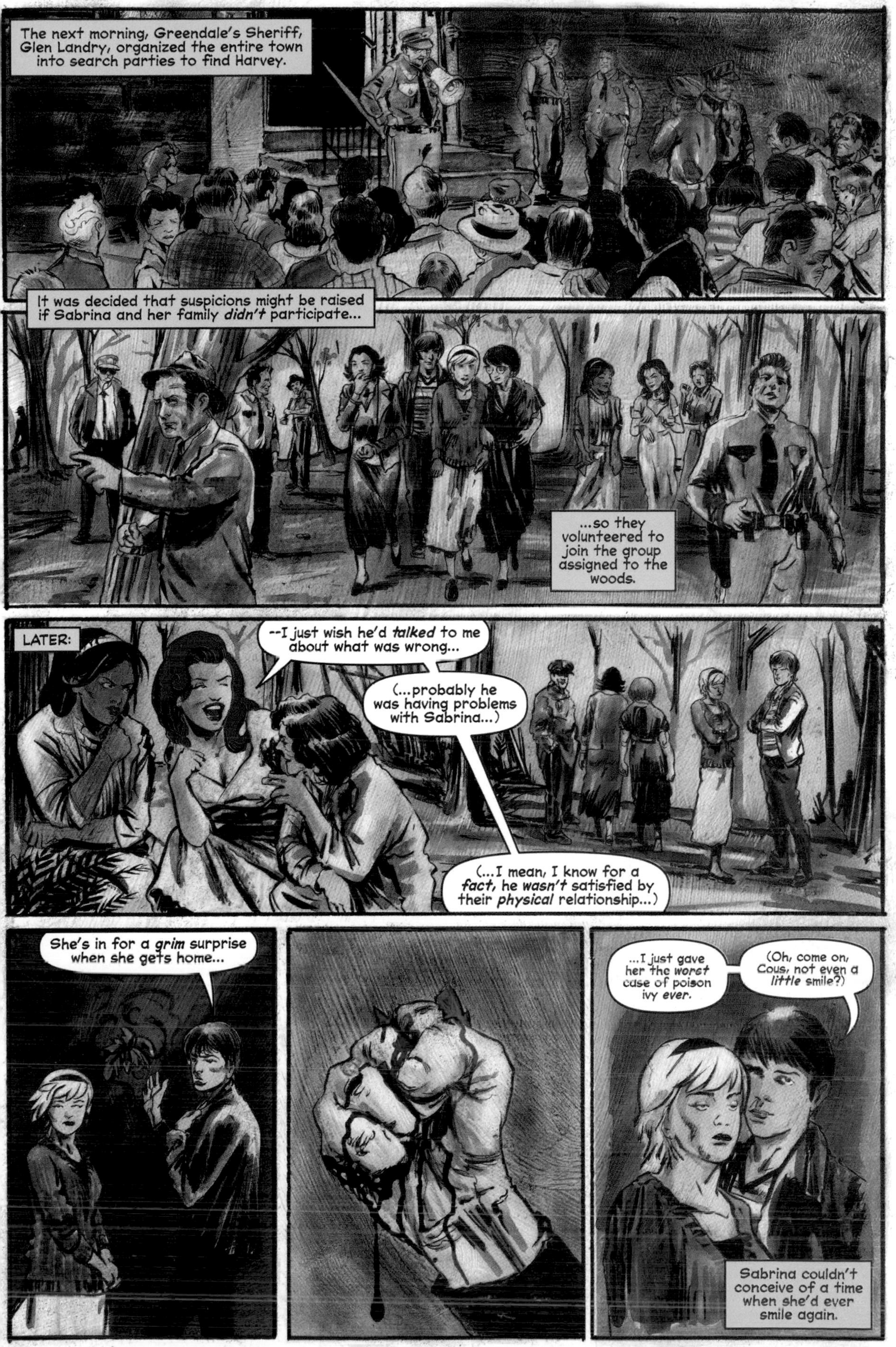

The next morning, Greendale's Sheriff, Glen Landry, organized the entire town into search parties to find Harvey.
It was decided that suspicions might be raised if Sabrina and her family *didn't* participate...
...so they volunteered to join the group assigned to the woods.
LATER:
--I just wish he'd *talked* to me about what was wrong...
(...probably he was having problems with Sabrina...)
(...I mean, I know for a *fact,* he *wasn't* satisfied by their *physical* relationship...)
She's in for a *grim* surprise when she gets home...
...I just gave her the *worst* case of poison ivy *ever.*
(Oh, come on, Cous, not even a *little* smile?)
Sabrina couldn't conceive of a time when she'd ever smile again.

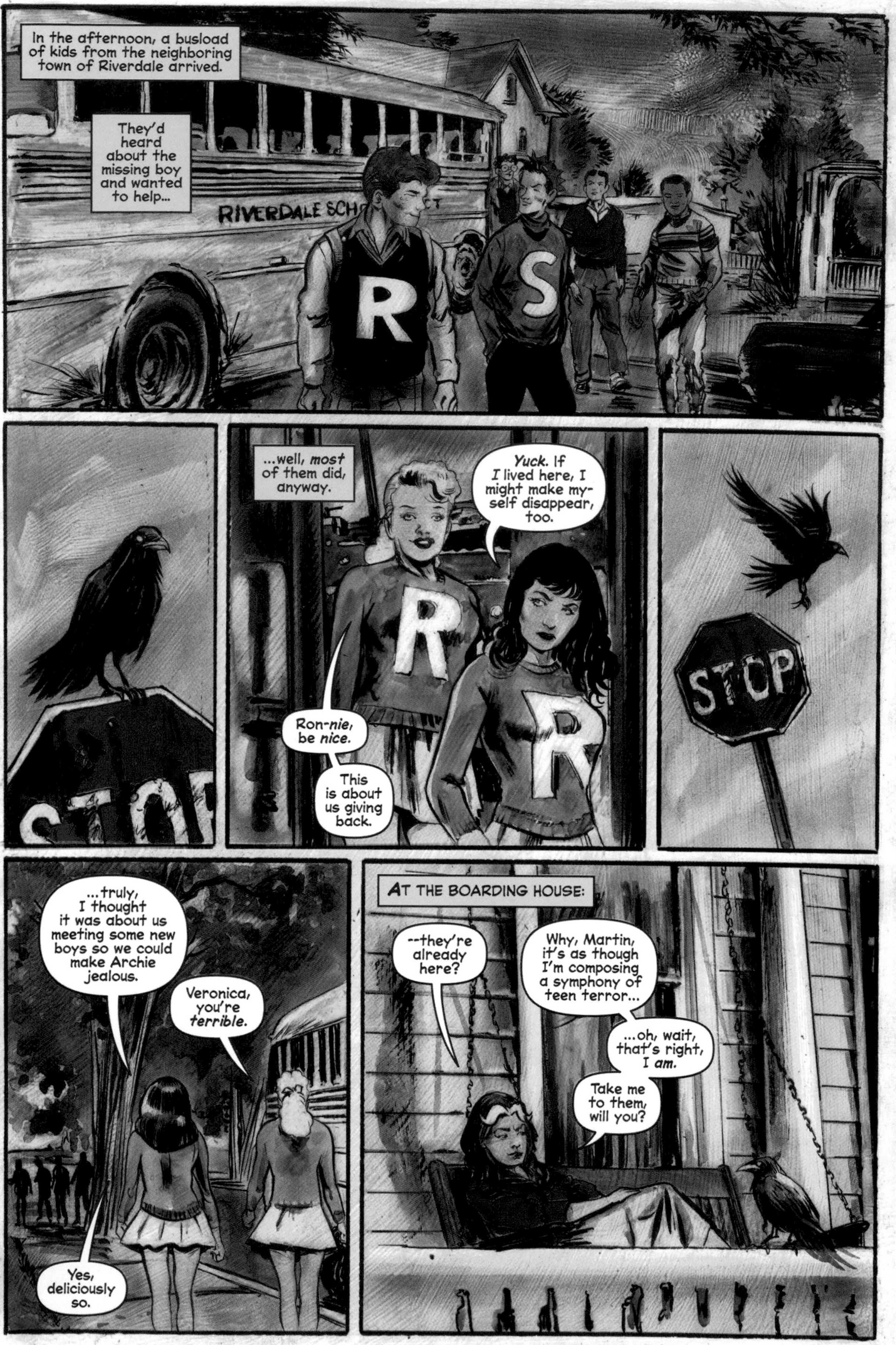
In the afternoon, a busload of kids from the neighboring town of Riverdale arrived.
They'd heard about the missing boy and wanted to help...
RIVERDALE SCHO
R
S
...well, *most* of them did, anyway.
Yuck. If *I* lived here, I might make myself disappear, too.
Ron-*nie*, be *nice*.
This is about us giving back.
STOP
...truly, I thought it was about us meeting some new boys so we could make Archie jealous.
Veronica, you're *terrible*.
Yes, deliciously so.
AT THE BOARDING HOUSE:
--they're already here?
Why, Martin, it's as though I'm composing a symphony of teen terror...
...oh, wait, that's right, I *am*.
Take me to them, will you?

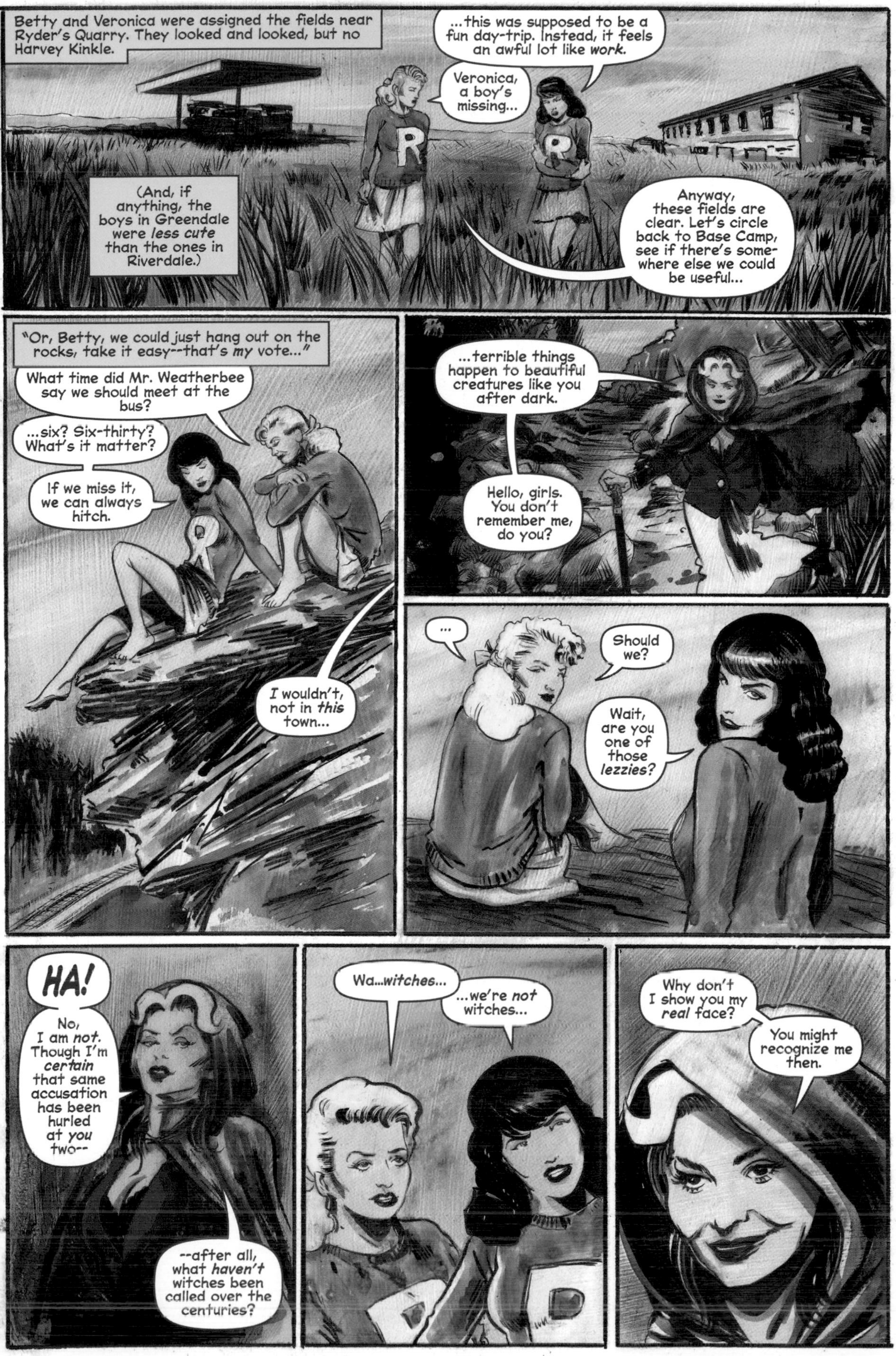

Betty and Veronica were assigned the fields near Ryder's Quarry. They looked and looked, but no Harvey Kinkle.
...this was supposed to be a fun day-trip. Instead, it feels an awful lot like *work.*
Veronica, a boy's missing...
(And, if anything, the boys in Greendale were *less cute* than the ones in Riverdale.)
Anyway, these fields are clear. Let's circle back to Base Camp, see if there's some-where else we could be useful...
"Or, Betty, we could just hang out on the rocks, take it easy--that's *my* vote..."
What time did Mr. Weatherbee say we should meet at the bus?
...six? Six-thirty? What's it matter?
If we miss it, we can always hitch.
I wouldn't, not in *this* town...
...terrible things happen to beautiful creatures like you after dark.
Hello, girls. You don't remember me, do you?
...
Should we?
Wait, are you one of those *lezzies?*
HA!
No, I am *not.* Though I'm *certain* that same accusation has been hurled at *you* two--
--after all, what *haven't* witches been called over the centuries?
Wa...*witches*...
...we're *not* witches...
Why don't I show you my *real* face?
You might recognize me then.

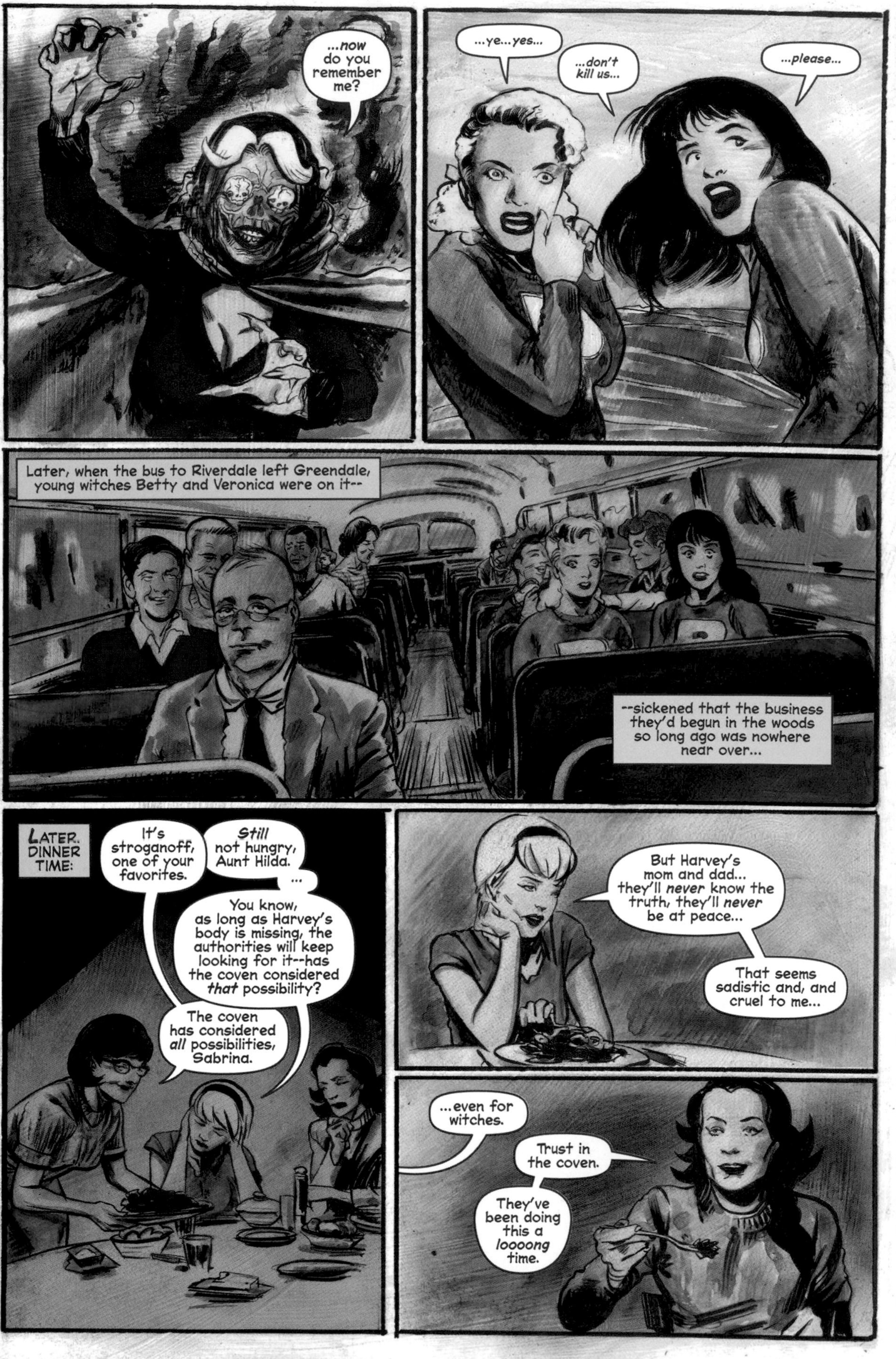

...now do you remember me?
...ye...yes...
...don't kill us...
...please...
Later, when the bus to Riverdale left Greendale, young witches Betty and Veronica were on it--
--sickened that the business they'd begun in the woods so long ago was nowhere near over...
LATER. DINNER TIME:
It's stroganoff, one of your favorites.
Still not hungry, Aunt Hilda.
...
You know, as long as Harvey's body is missing, the authorities will keep looking for it--has the coven considered that possibility?
The coven has considered all possibilities, Sabrina.
But Harvey's mom and dad... they'll never know the truth, they'll never be at peace...
That seems sadistic and, and cruel to me...
...even for witches.
Trust in the coven.
They've been doing this a loooong time.

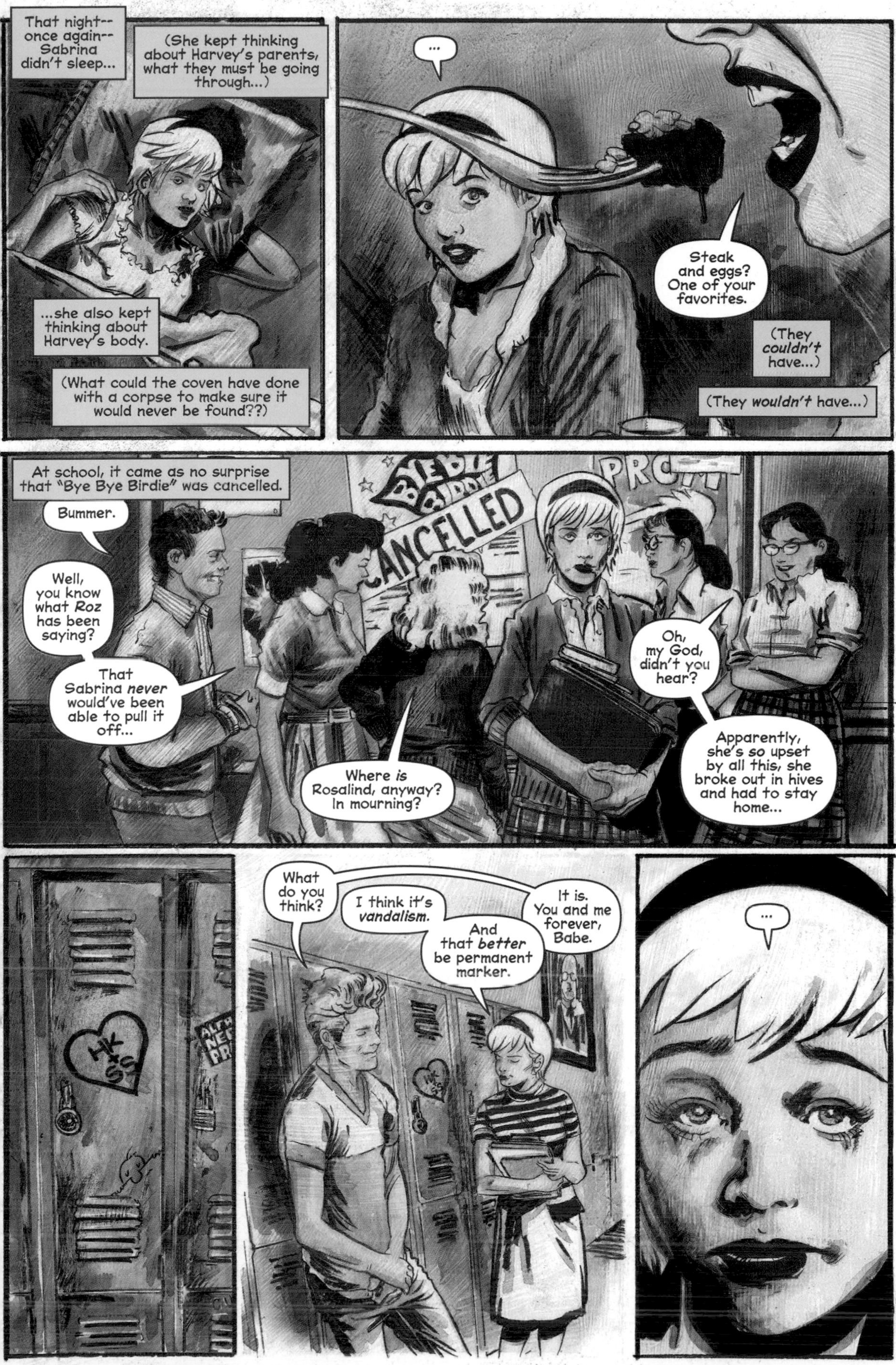

That night-- once again-- Sabrina didn't sleep...
(She kept thinking about Harvey's parents, what they must be going through...)
...she also kept thinking about Harvey's body.
(What could the coven have done with a corpse to make sure it would never be found??)
...
Steak and eggs? One of your favorites.
(They couldn't have...)
(They wouldn't have...)
At school, it came as no surprise that "Bye Bye Birdie" was cancelled.
CANCELLED
Bummer.
Well, you know what Roz has been saying?
That Sabrina never would've been able to pull it off...
Where is Rosalind, anyway? In mourning?
Oh, my God, didn't you hear?
Apparently, she's so upset by all this, she broke out in hives and had to stay home...
What do you think?
I think it's vandalism.
And that better be permanent marker.
It is. You and me forever, Babe.
...

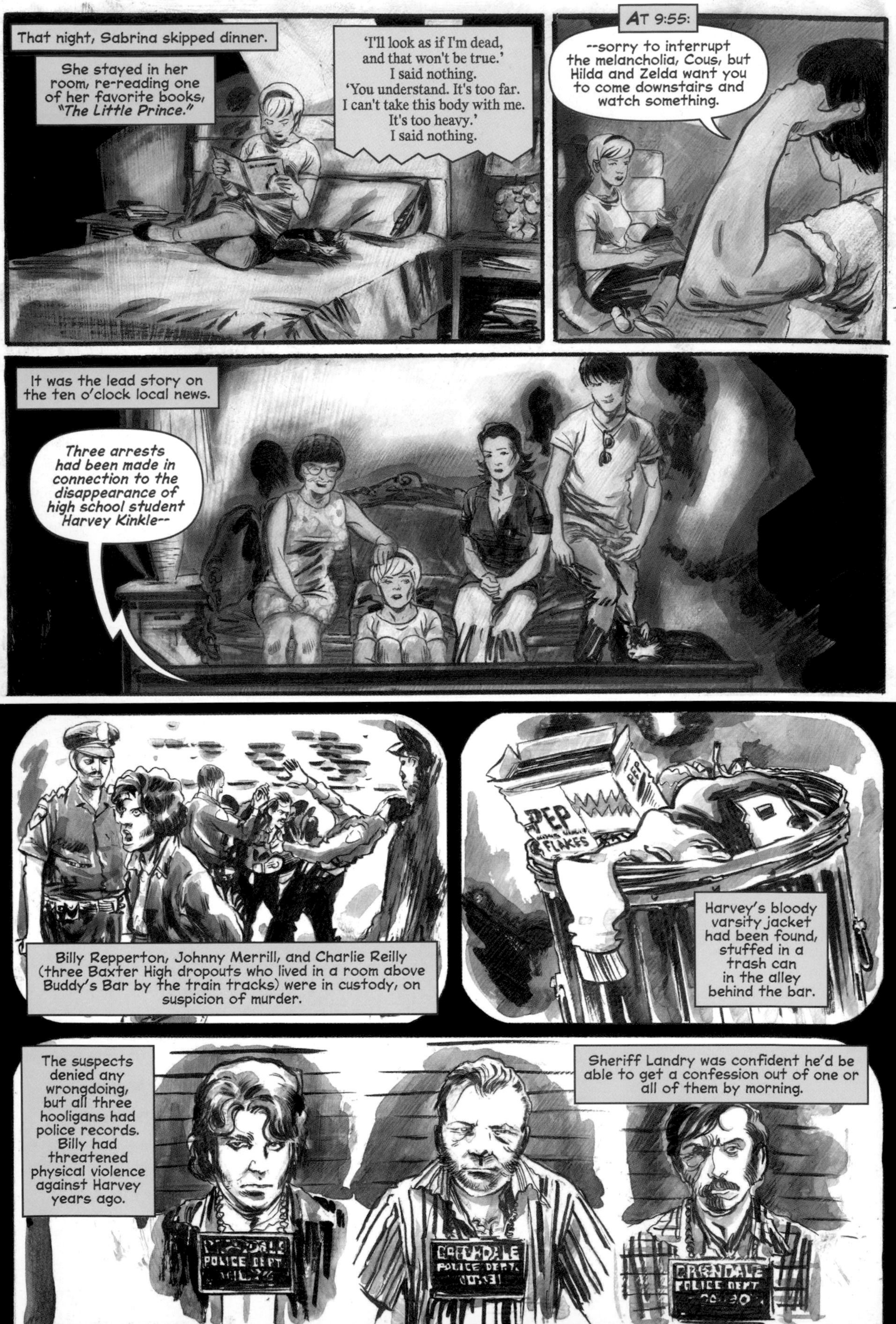

That night, Sabrina skipped dinner.
She stayed in her room, re-reading one of her favorite books, "The Little Prince."
'I'll look as if I'm dead, and that won't be true.' I said nothing. 'You understand. It's too far. I can't take this body with me. It's too heavy.' I said nothing.
AT 9:55:
--sorry to interrupt the melancholia, Cous, but Hilda and Zelda want you to come downstairs and watch something.
It was the lead story on the ten o'clock local news.
Three arrests had been made in connection to the disappearance of high school student Harvey Kinkle--
Billy Repperton, Johnny Merrill, and Charlie Reilly (three Baxter High dropouts who lived in a room above Buddy's Bar by the train tracks) were in custody, on suspicion of murder.
PEP
FLAKES
Harvey's bloody varsity jacket had been found, stuffed in a trash can in the alley behind the bar.
The suspects denied any wrongdoing, but all three hooligans had police records. Billy had threatened physical violence against Harvey years ago.
Sheriff Landry was confident he'd be able to get a confession out of one or all of them by morning.
GREENDALE
POLICE DEPT.

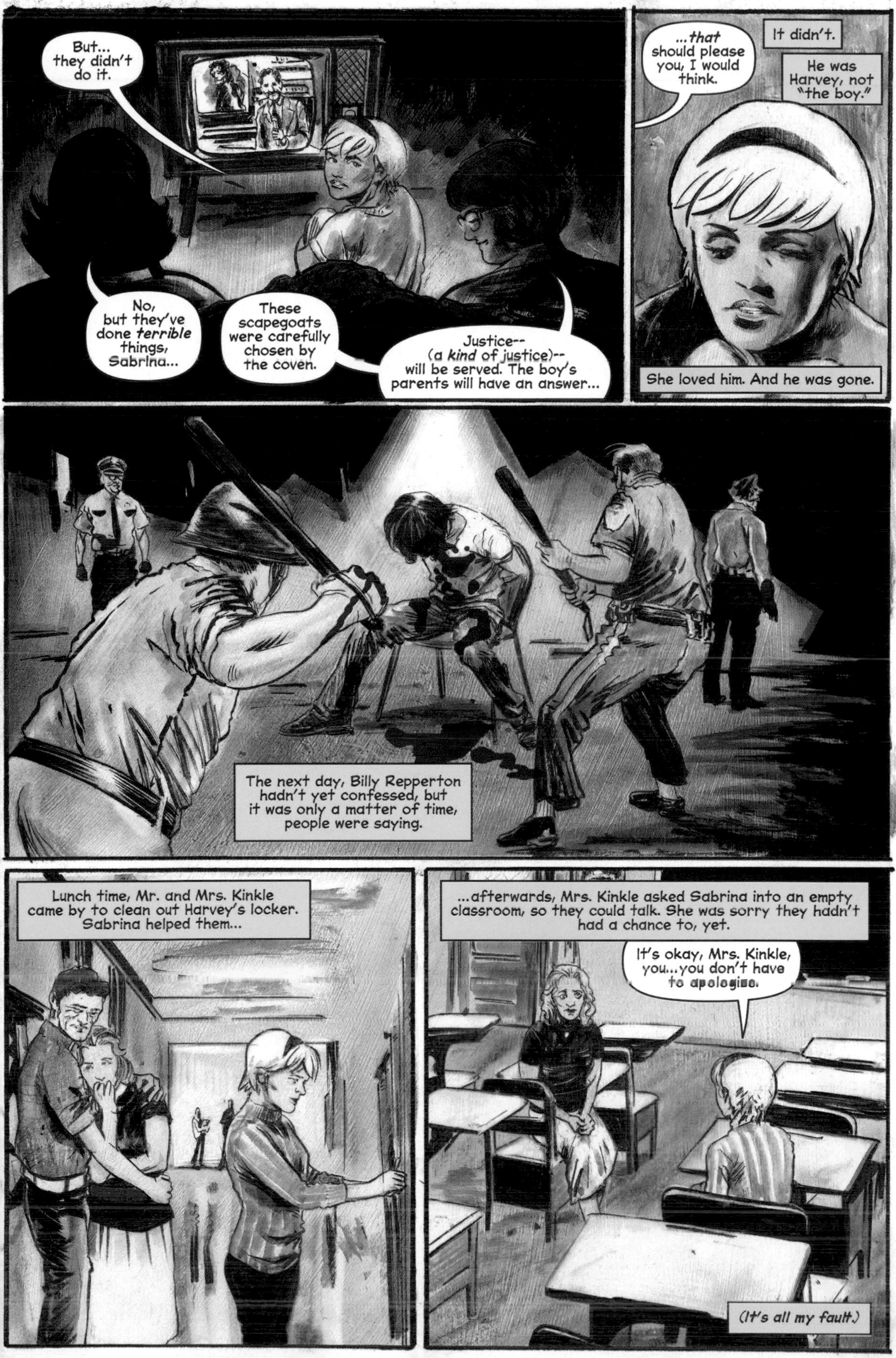
But... they didn't do it.
No, but they've done *terrible* things, Sabrina...
These scapegoats were carefully chosen by the coven.
Justice-- (a *kind* of justice)-- will be served. The boy's parents will have an answer...
...*that* should please you, I would think.
It didn't.
He was Harvey, not "the boy."
She loved him. And he was gone.
The next day, Billy Repperton hadn't yet confessed, but it was only a matter of time, people were saying.
Lunch time, Mr. and Mrs. Kinkle came by to clean out Harvey's locker. Sabrina helped them...
...afterwards, Mrs. Kinkle asked Sabrina into an empty classroom, so they could talk. She was sorry they hadn't had a chance to, yet.
It's okay, Mrs. Kinkle, you...you don't have to apologize.
(It's all my fault.)

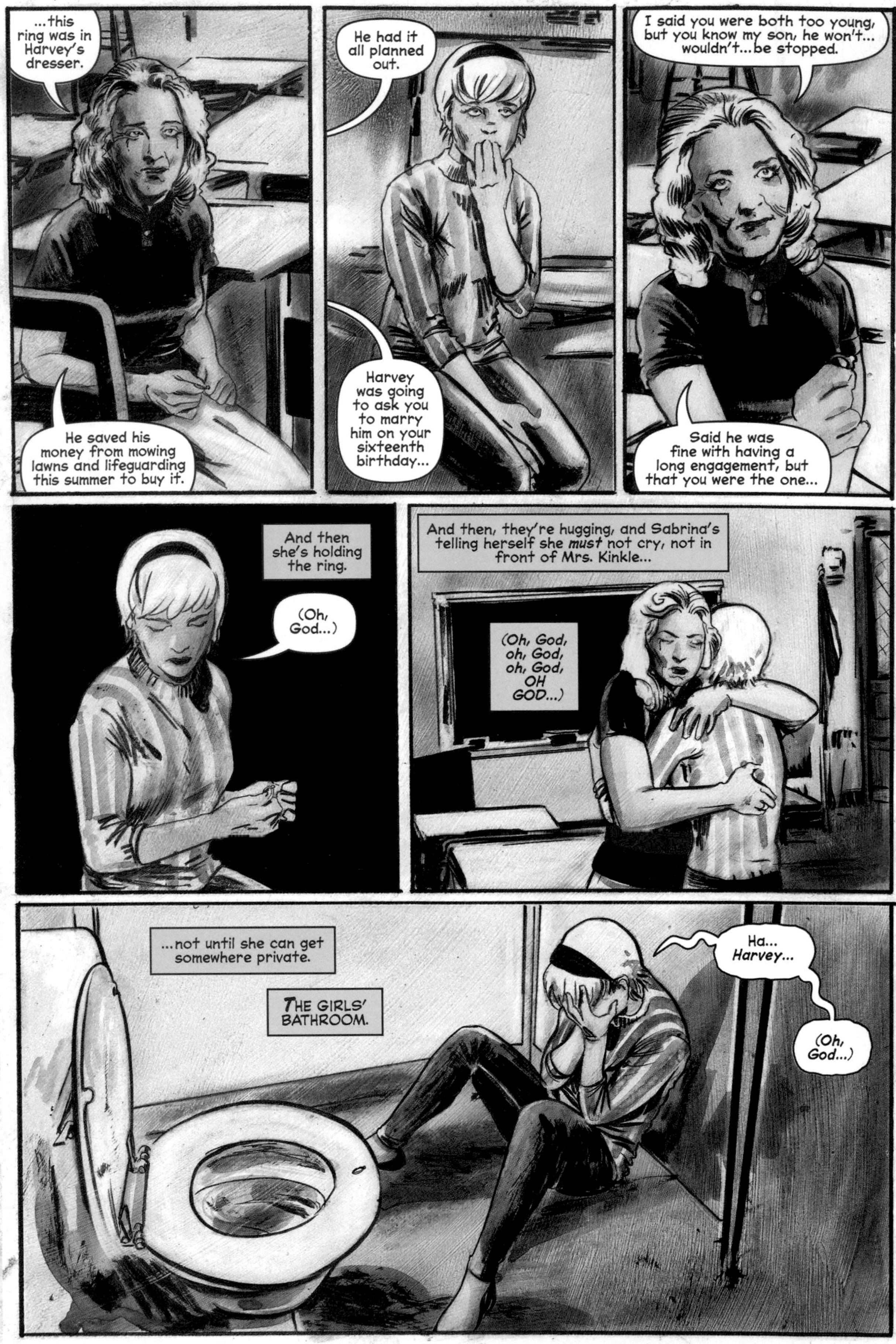
...this ring was in Harvey's dresser.
He saved his money from mowing lawns and lifeguarding this summer to buy it.
He had it all planned out.
Harvey was going to ask you to marry him on your sixteenth birthday...
I said you were both too young, but you know my son, he won't... wouldn't...be stopped.
Said he was fine with having a long engagement, but that you were the one...
And then she's holding the ring.
(Oh, God...)
And then, they're hugging, and Sabrina's telling herself she *must* not cry, not in front of Mrs. Kinkle...
(Oh, God, oh, God, oh, God, OH GOD...)
...not until she can get somewhere private.
THE GIRLS' BATHROOM.
Ha... *Harvey...*
(Oh, God...)

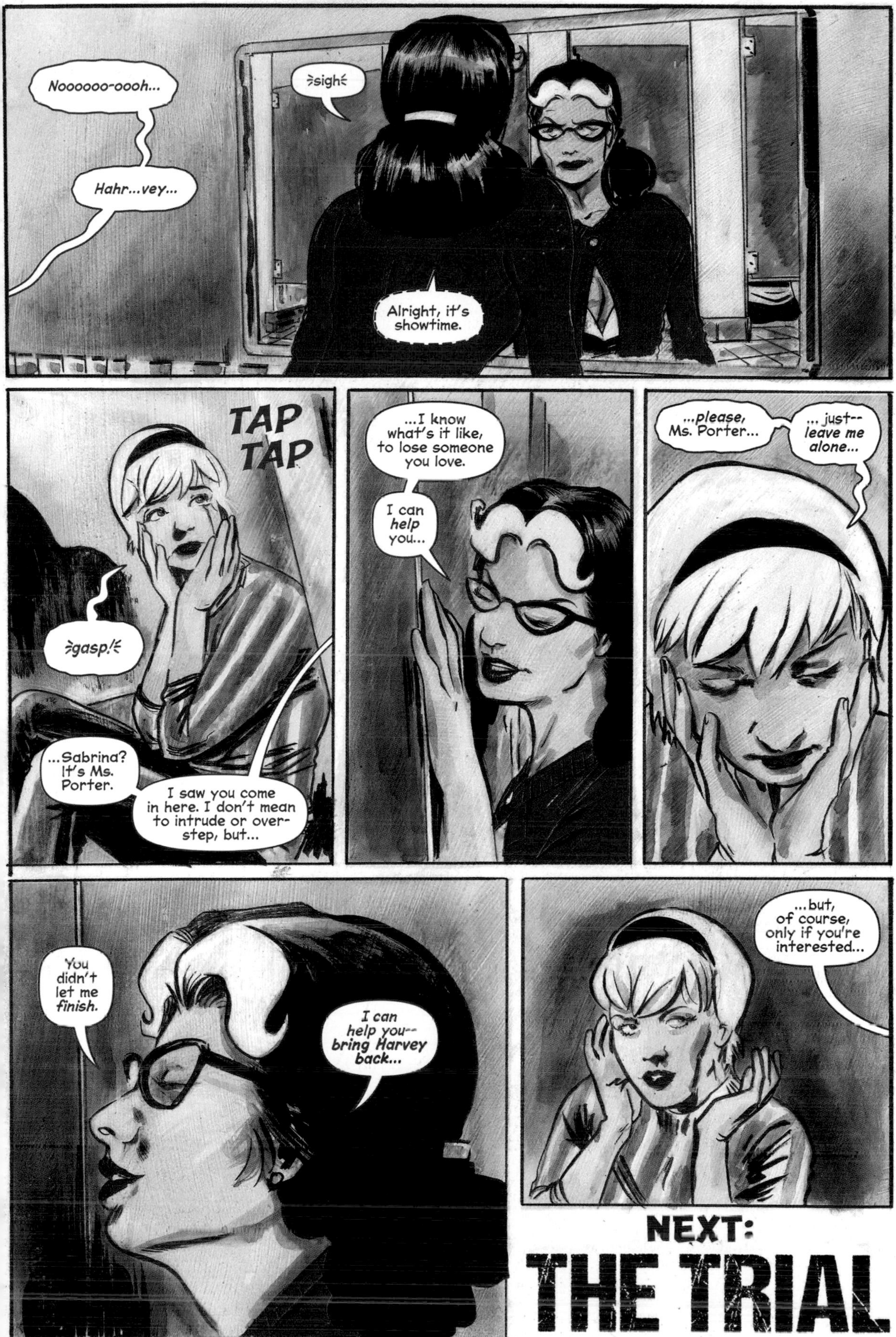
Noooooo-oooh...
Hahr...vey...
sigh
Alright, it's showtime.
TAP TAP
gasp!
...Sabrina? It's Ms. Porter.
I saw you come in here. I don't mean to intrude or over-step, but...
...I know what's it like, to lose someone you love.
I can help you...
...please, Ms. Porter...
... just-- leave me alone...
You didn't let me finish.
I can help you-- bring Harvey back...
...but, of course, only if you're interested...
NEXT:
THE TRIAL

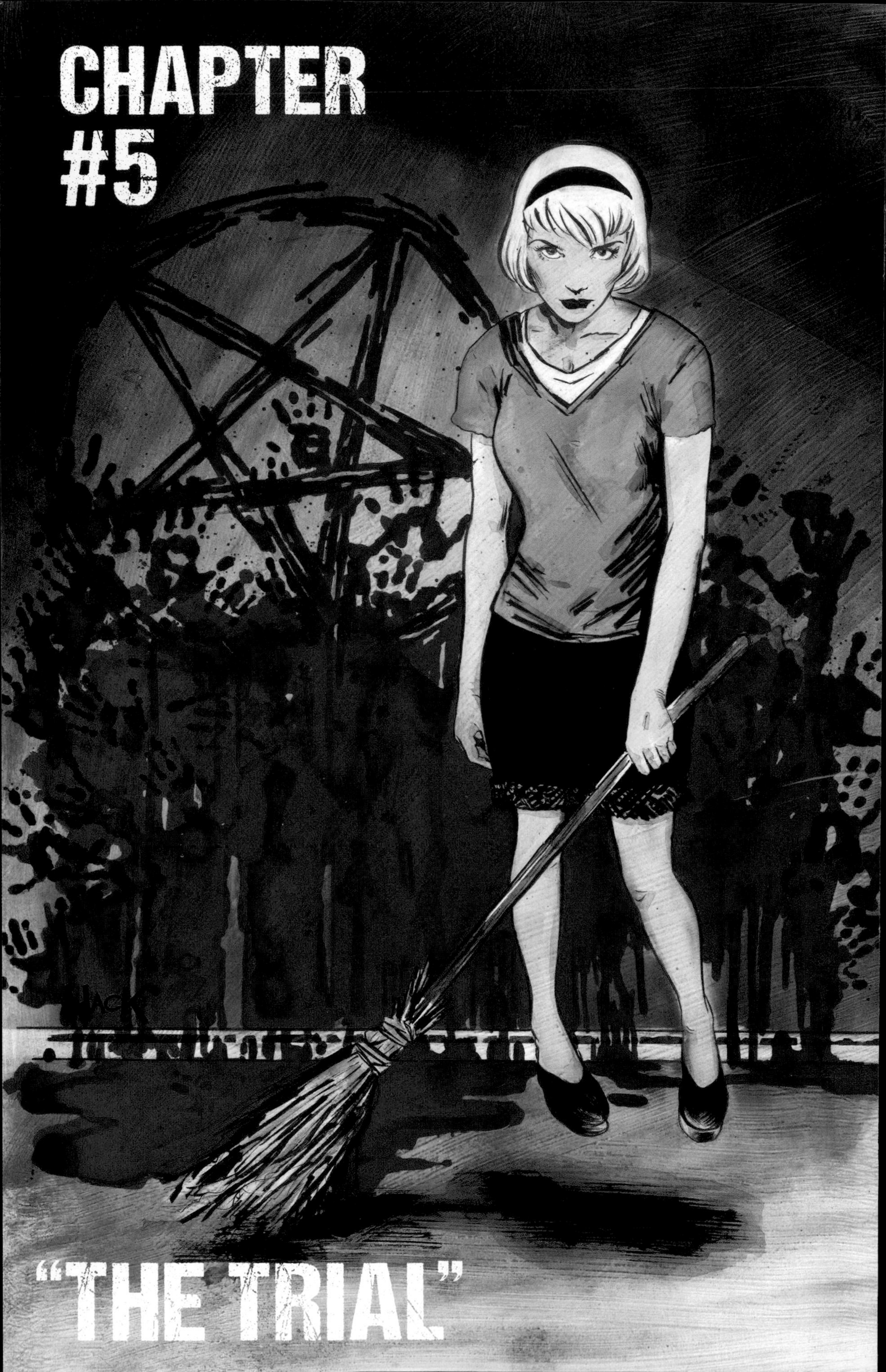
CHAPTER
#5
"THE TRIAL"

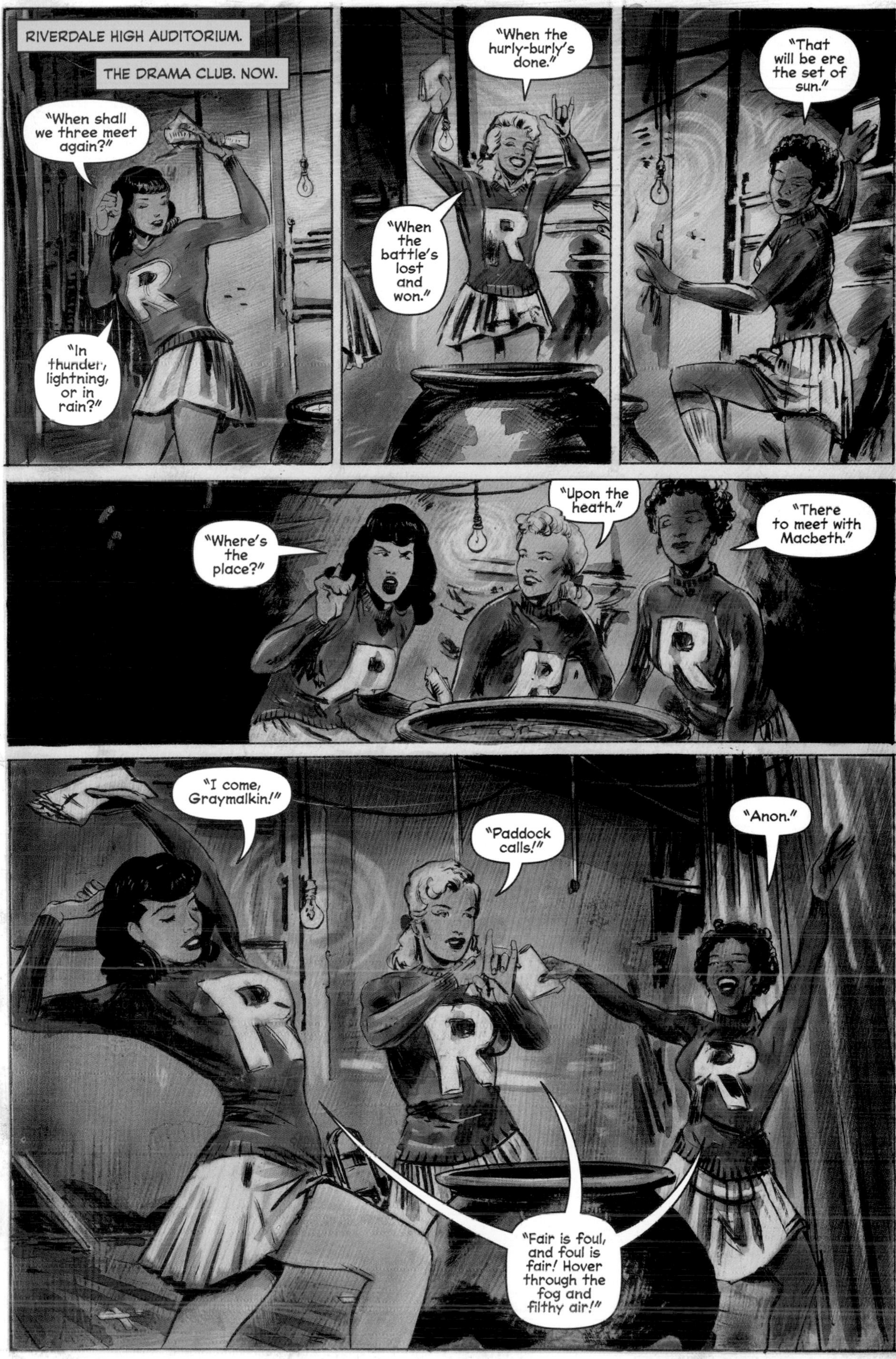
RIVERDALE HIGH AUDITORIUM.
THE DRAMA CLUB. NOW.
"When shall we three meet again?"
"In thunder, lightning, or in rain?"
"When the hurly-burly's done."
"When the battle's lost and won."
"That will be ere the set of sun."
"Where's the place?"
"Upon the heath."
"There to meet with Macbeth."
"I come, Graymalkin!"
"Paddock calls!"
"Anon."
"Fair is foul, and foul is fair! Hover through the fog and filthy air!"

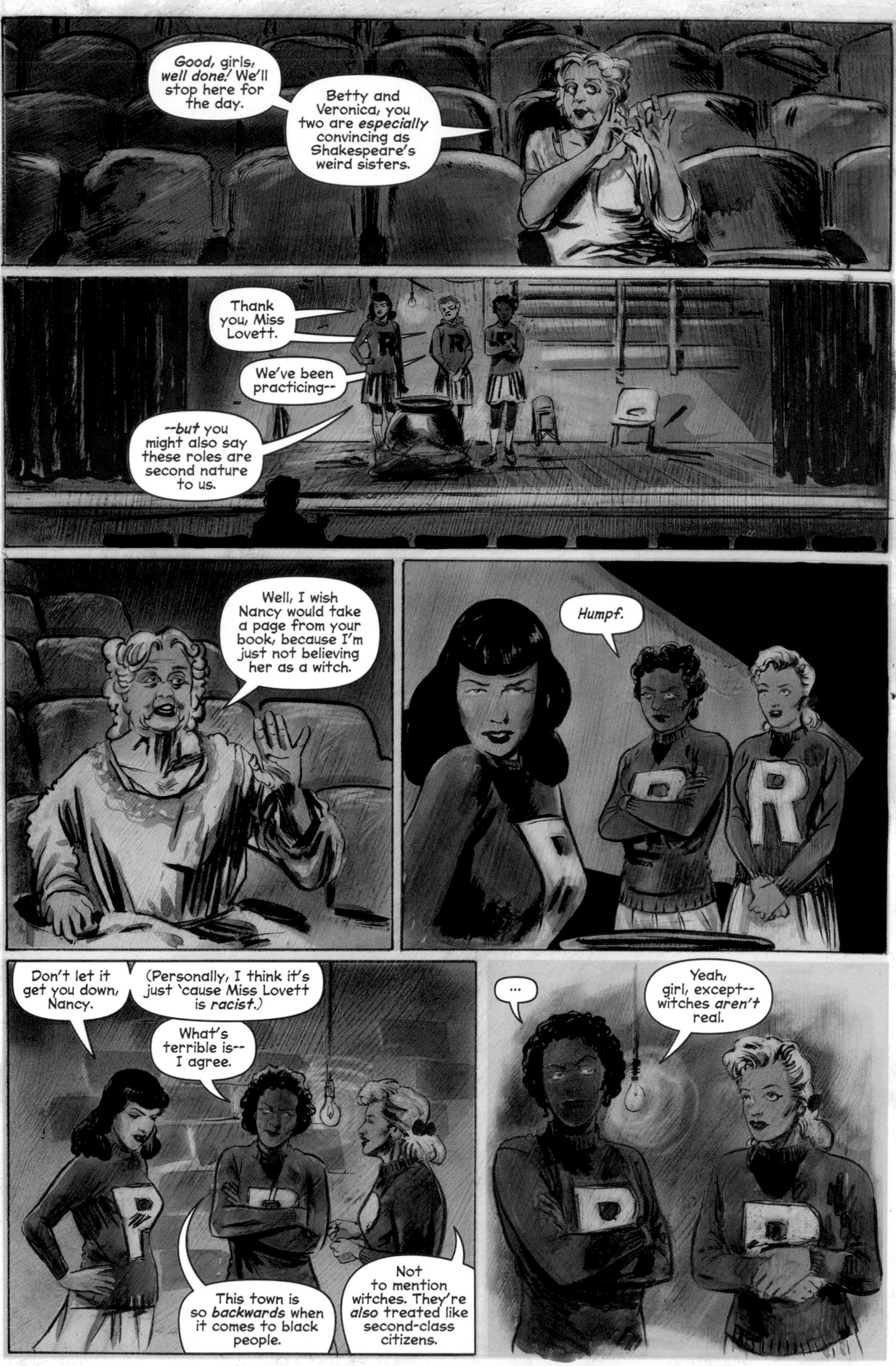
Good, girls, well done! We'll stop here for the day.
Betty and Veronica, you two are especially convincing as Shakespeare's weird sisters.
Thank you, Miss Lovett.
We've been practicing--
--but you might also say these roles are second nature to us.
Well, I wish Nancy would take a page from your book, because I'm just not believing her as a witch.
Humpf.
Don't let it get you down, Nancy.
(Personally, I think it's just 'cause Miss Lovett is racist.)
What's terrible is-- I agree.
This town is so backwards when it comes to black people.
Not to mention witches. They're also treated like second-class citizens.
...
Yeah, girl, except-- witches aren't real.

As a matter of fact, that's what we wanted to talk to you about, Nancy.

You know that after-school group Miss Grundy runs? Nature Appreciation Club?

The one that meets in Fox Forest?

That's the one.

Only... it's not *really* about nature.

Though *a lot* of studying is required, *a lot* of practicing.

For what? What are you two talking about?

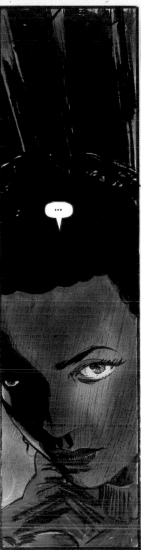

Power, Nancy. *True*, ancient power.

...

And sisterhood. Being a part of something... eternal.

Girls...

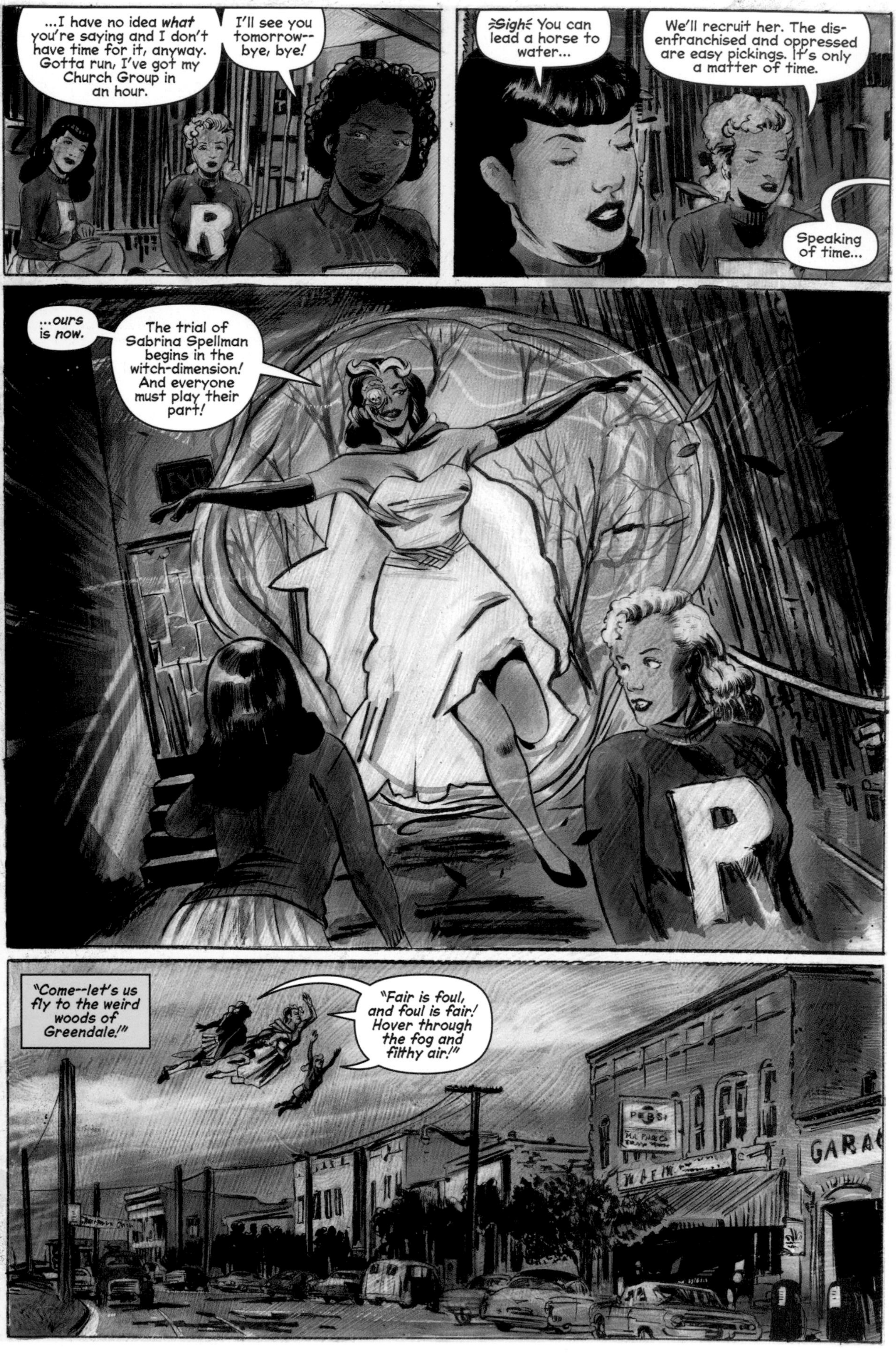
...I have no idea what you're saying and I don't have time for it, anyway. Gotta run, I've got my Church Group in an hour.
I'll see you tomorrow--bye, bye!
Sigh You can lead a horse to water...
We'll recruit her. The disenfranchised and oppressed are easy pickings. It's only a matter of time.
Speaking of time...
...ours is now.
The trial of Sabrina Spellman begins in the witch-dimension! And everyone must play their part!
"Come--let's us fly to the weird woods of Greendale!"
"Fair is foul, and foul is fair! Hover through the fog and filthy air!"
PEPSI
GARAG

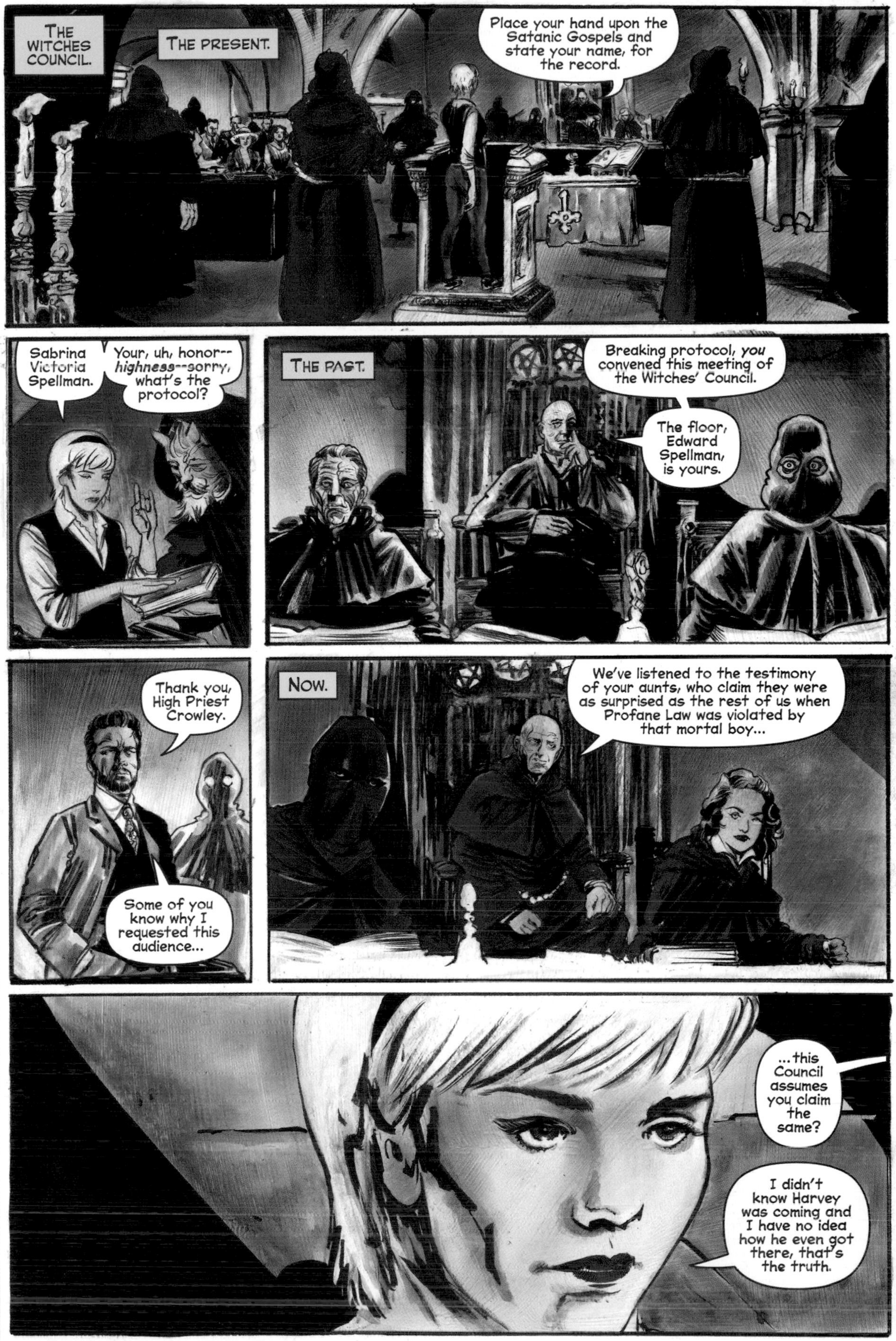
THE WITCHES COUNCIL.
THE PRESENT.
Place your hand upon the Satanic Gospels and state your name, for the record.
Sabrina Victoria Spellman.
Your, uh, honor--*highness*--sorry, what's the protocol?
THE PAST.
Breaking protocol, *you* convened this meeting of the Witches' Council.
The floor, Edward Spellman, is yours.
Thank you, High Priest Crowley.
Some of you know why I requested this audience...
NOW.
We've listened to the testimony of your aunts, who claim they were as surprised as the rest of us when Profane Law was violated by that mortal boy...
...this Council assumes you claim the same?
I didn't know Harvey was coming and I have no idea how he even got there, that's the truth.

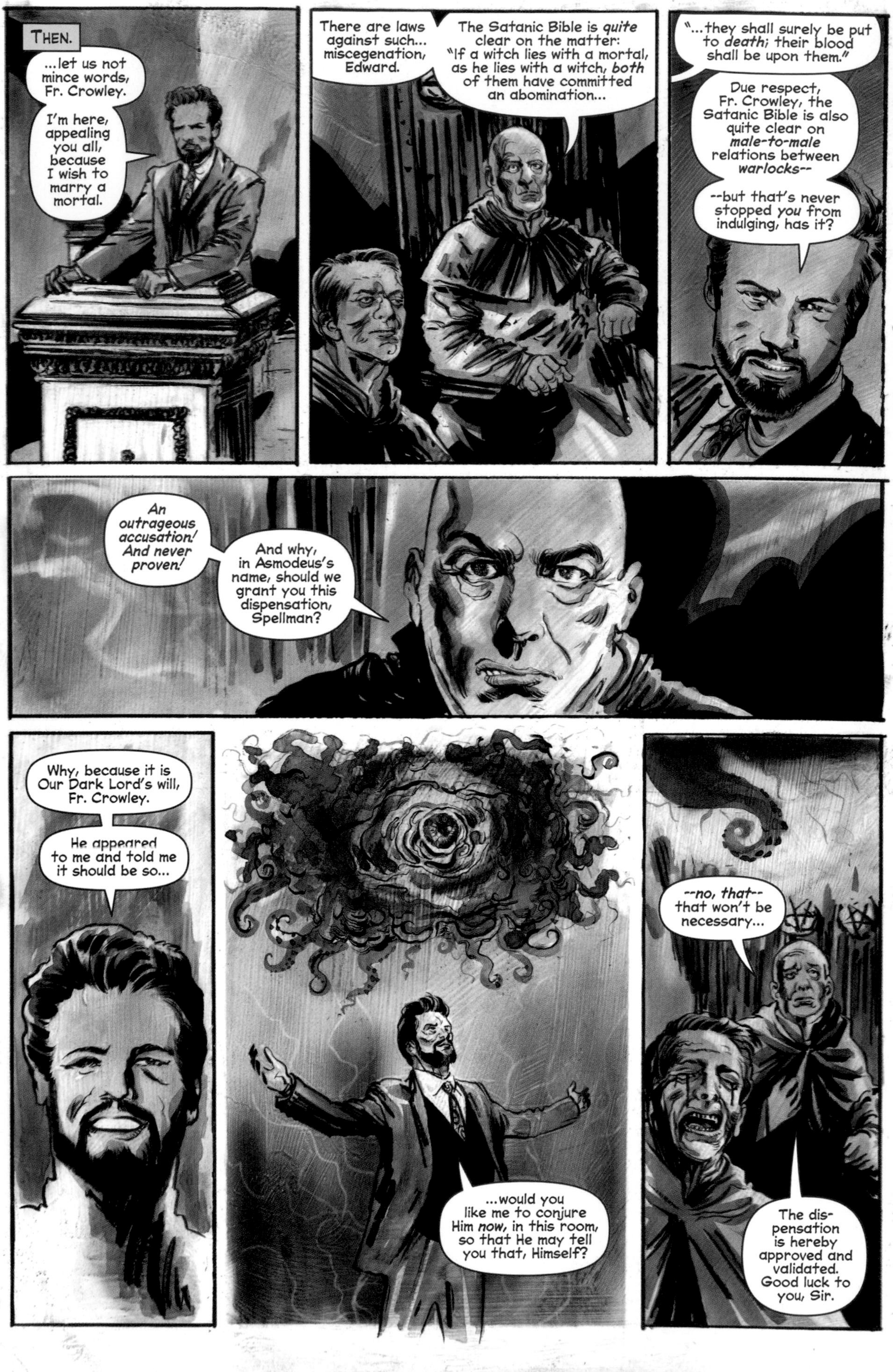
THEN.
...let us not mince words, Fr. Crowley.
I'm here, appealing you all, because I wish to marry a mortal.
There are laws against such... miscegenation, Edward.
The Satanic Bible is *quite* clear on the matter: "If a witch lies with a mortal, as he lies with a witch, *both* of them have committed an abomination...
"...they shall surely be put to *death*; their blood shall be upon them."
Due respect, Fr. Crowley, the Satanic Bible is also quite clear on ***male-to-male*** relations between ***warlocks***--
--but that's never stopped *you* from indulging, has it?
An outrageous accusation! And never proven!
And why, in Asmodeus's name, should we grant you this dispensation, Spellman?
Why, because it is Our Dark Lord's will, Fr. Crowley.
He appeared to me and told me it should be so...
...would you like me to conjure Him *now*, in this room, so that He may tell you that, Himself?
--no, that-- that won't be necessary...
The dis-pensation is hereby approved and validated. Good luck to you, Sir.

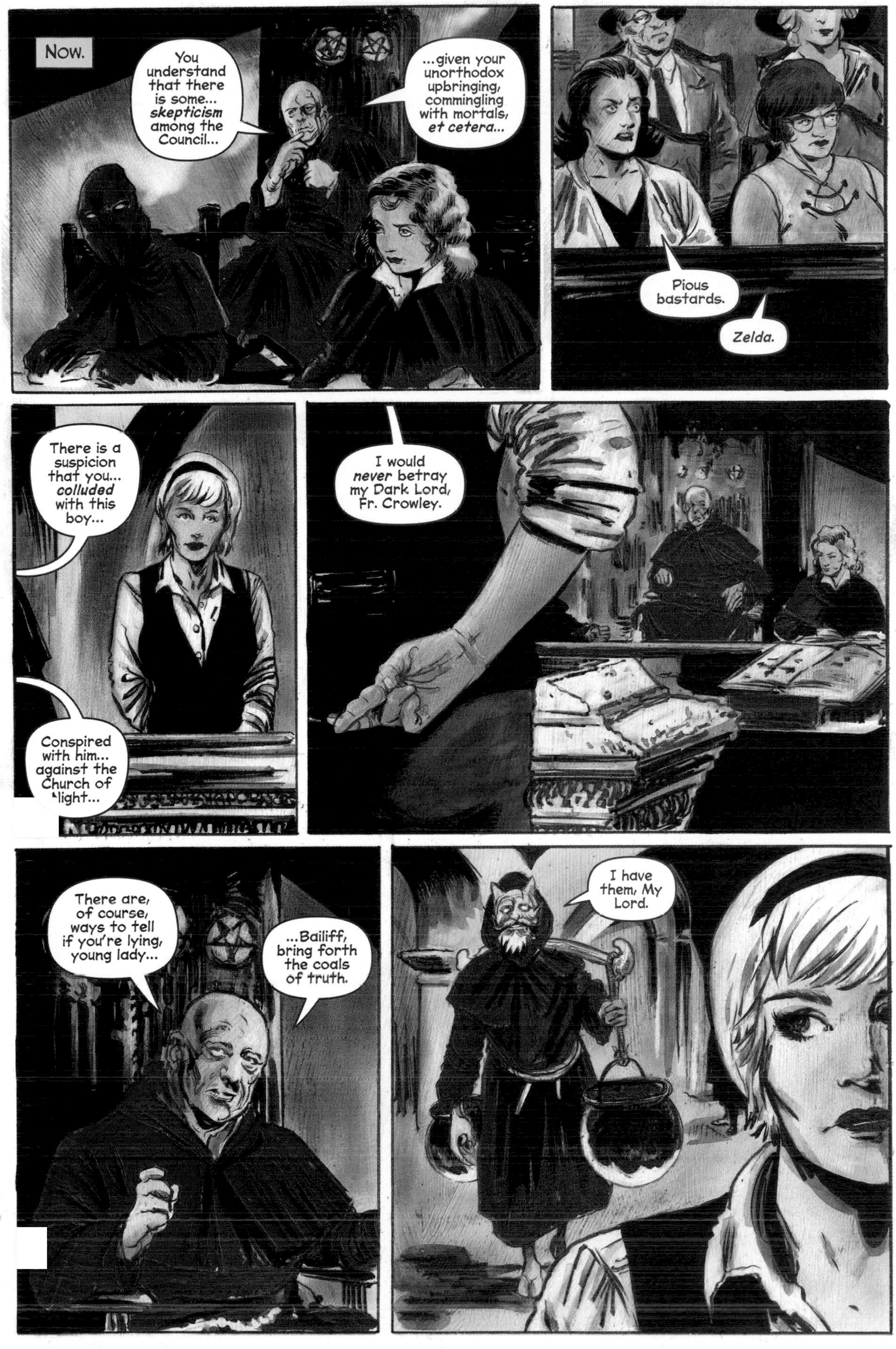

Now.
You understand that there is some... *skepticism* among the Council...
...given your unorthodox upbringing, commingling with mortals, *et cetera*...
Pious bastards.
Zelda.
There is a suspicion that you... *colluded* with this boy...
Conspired with him... against the Church of Night...
I would *never* betray my Dark Lord, Fr. Crowley.
There are, of course, ways to tell if you're lying, young lady...
...Bailiff, bring forth the coals of truth.
I have them, My Lord.

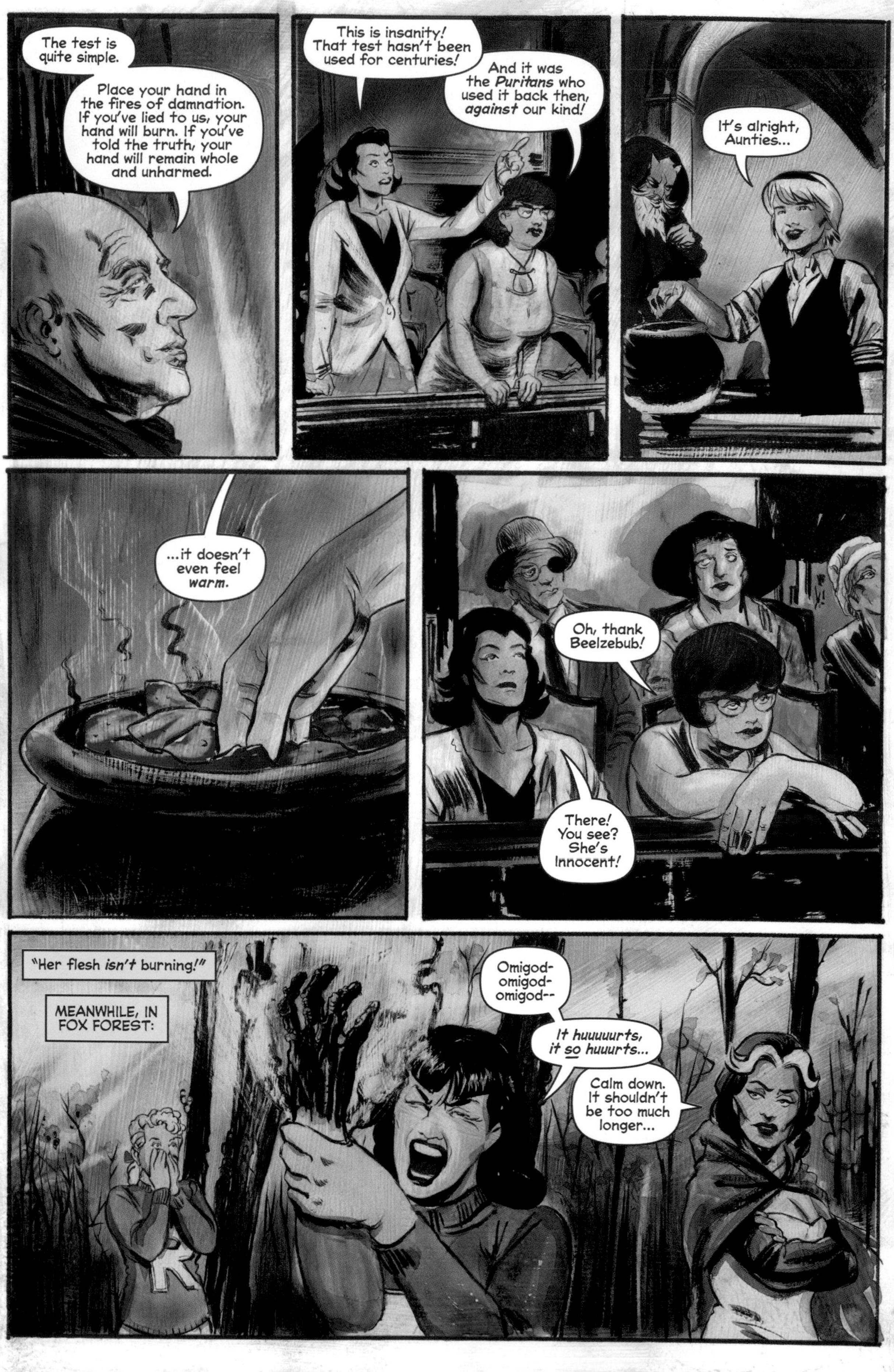
The test is quite simple.
Place your hand in the fires of damnation. If you've lied to us, your hand will burn. If you've told the truth, your hand will remain whole and unharmed.
This is insanity! That test hasn't been used for centuries!
And it was the *Puritans* who used it back then, *against* our kind!
It's alright, Aunties...
...it doesn't even feel *warm*.
Oh, thank Beelzebub!
There! You see? She's Innocent!
"Her flesh *isn't* burning!"
MEANWHILE, IN FOX FOREST:
Omigod-omigod-omigod--
It huuuuurts, it so huuurts...
Calm down. It shouldn't be too much longer...

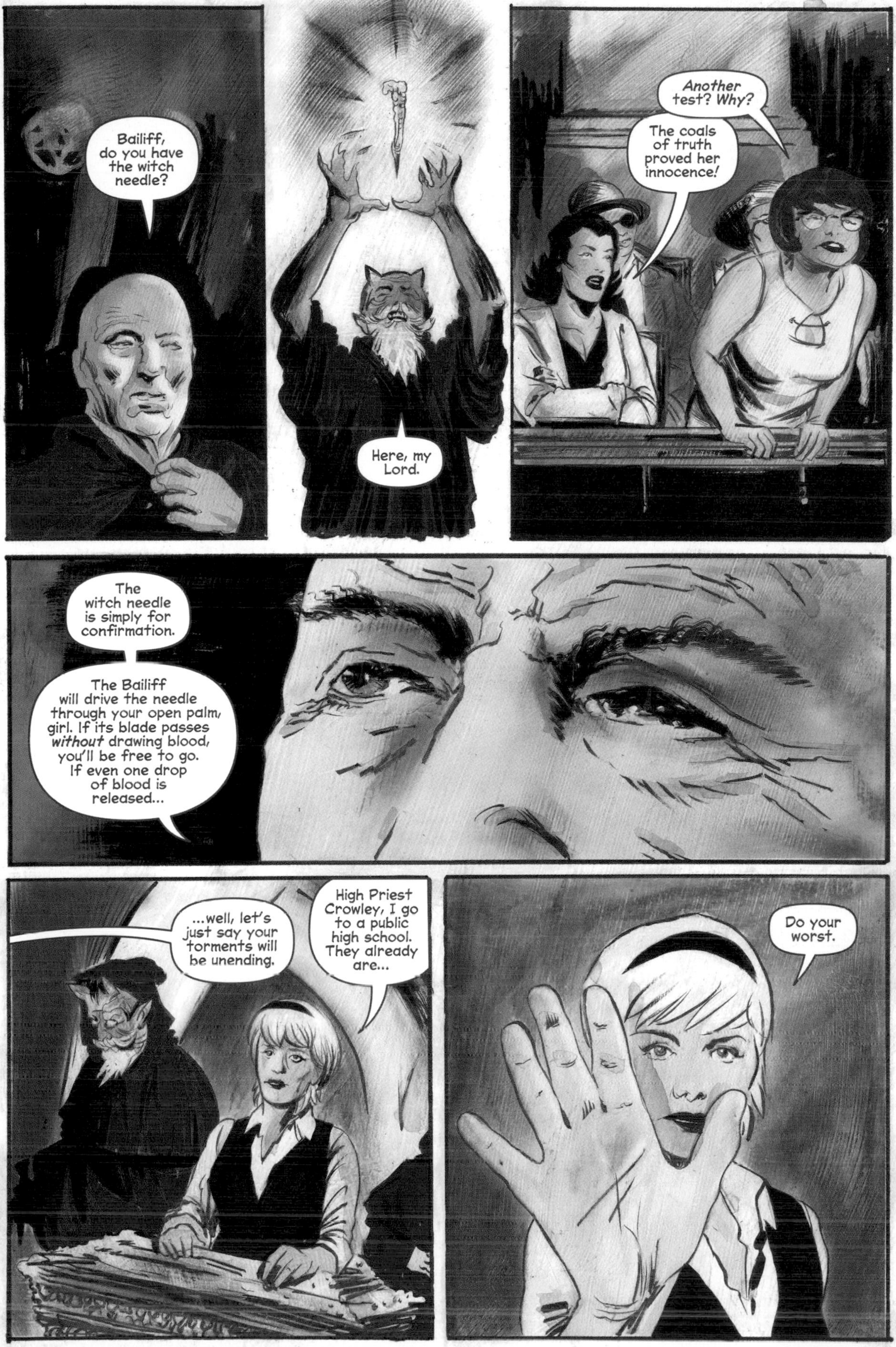
Bailiff, do you have the witch needle?
Here, my Lord.
Another test? Why?
The coals of truth proved her innocence!
The witch needle is simply for confirmation.
The Bailiff will drive the needle through your open palm, girl. If its blade passes *without* drawing blood, you'll be free to go. If even one drop of blood is released...
...well, let's just say your torments will be unending.
High Priest Crowley, I go to a public high school. They already are...
Do your worst.

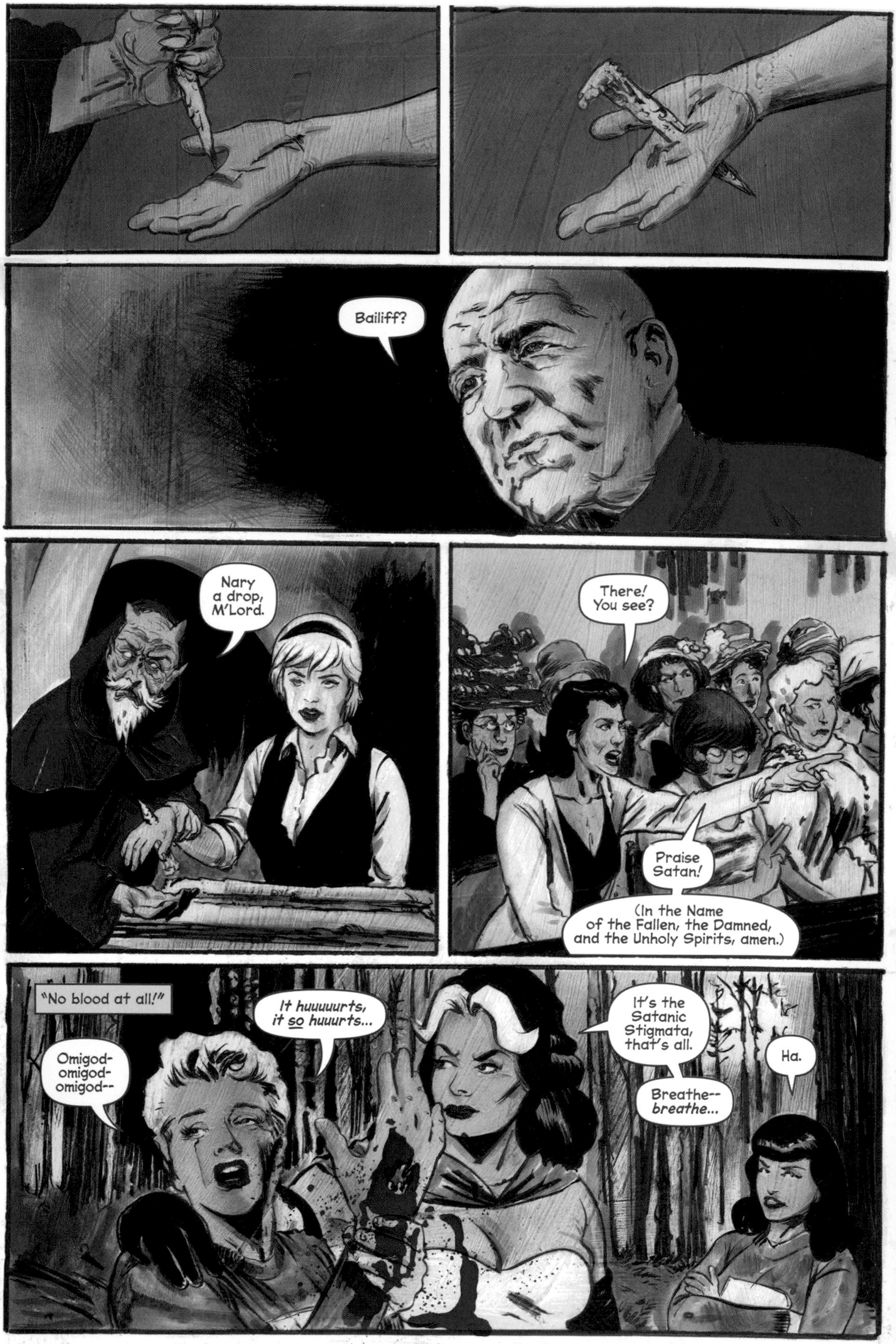
Bailiff?
Nary a drop, M'Lord.
There! You see?
Praise Satan!
(In the Name of the Fallen, the Damned, and the Unholy Spirits, amen.)
"No blood at all!"
Omigod-omigod-omigod--
It huuuuurts, it so huuurts...
It's the Satanic Stigmata, that's all.
Breathe-- breathe...
Ha.

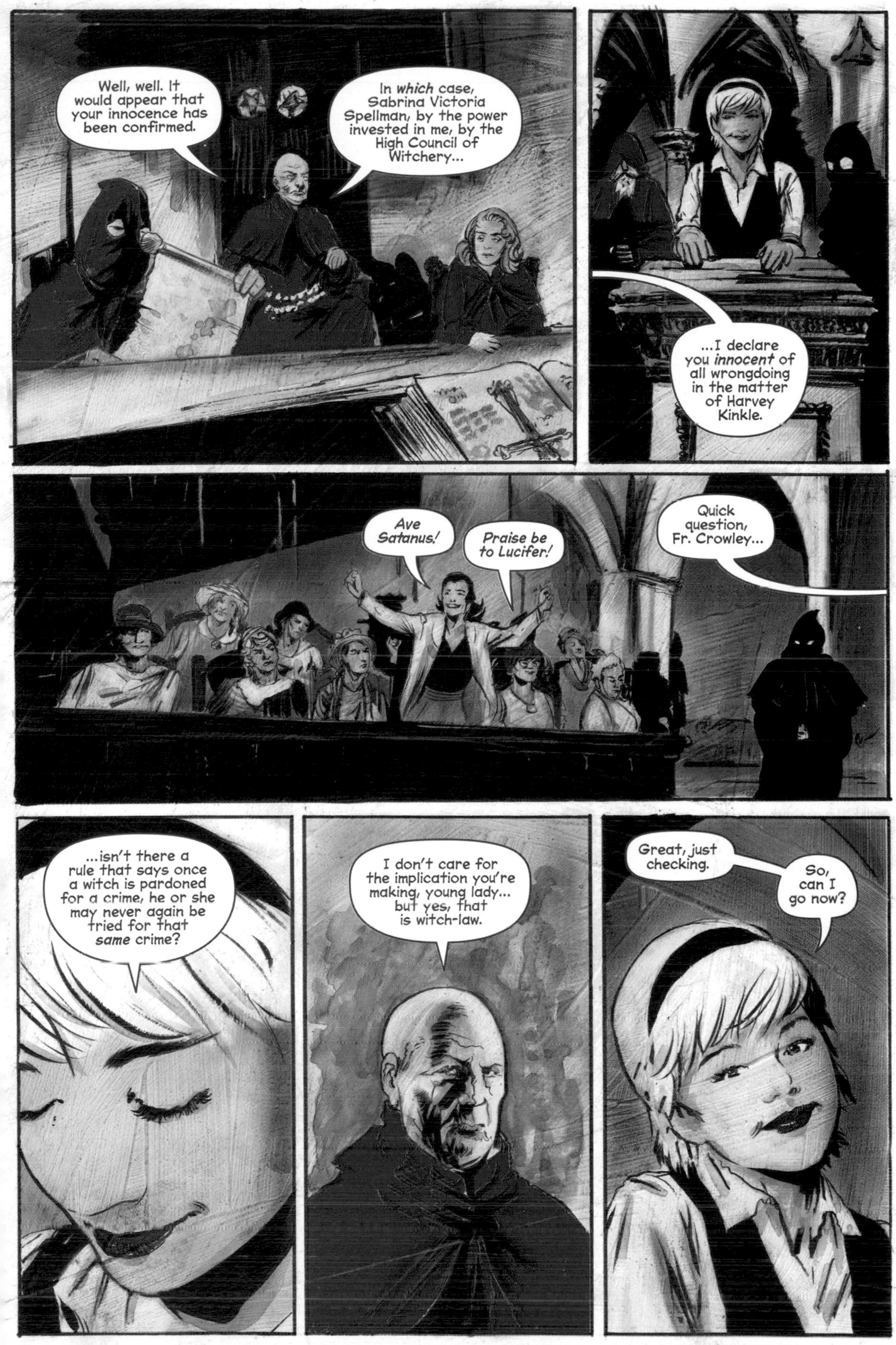
Well, well. It would appear that your innocence has been confirmed.
In *which* case, Sabrina Victoria Spellman, by the power invested in me, by the High Council of Witchery...
...I declare you *innocent* of all wrongdoing in the matter of Harvey Kinkle.
Ave Satanus!
Praise be to Lucifer!
Quick question, Fr. Crowley...
...isn't there a rule that says once a witch is pardoned for a crime, he or she may never again be tried for that *same* crime?
I don't care for the implication you're making, young lady... but yes, that is witch-law.
Great, just checking.
So, can I go now?

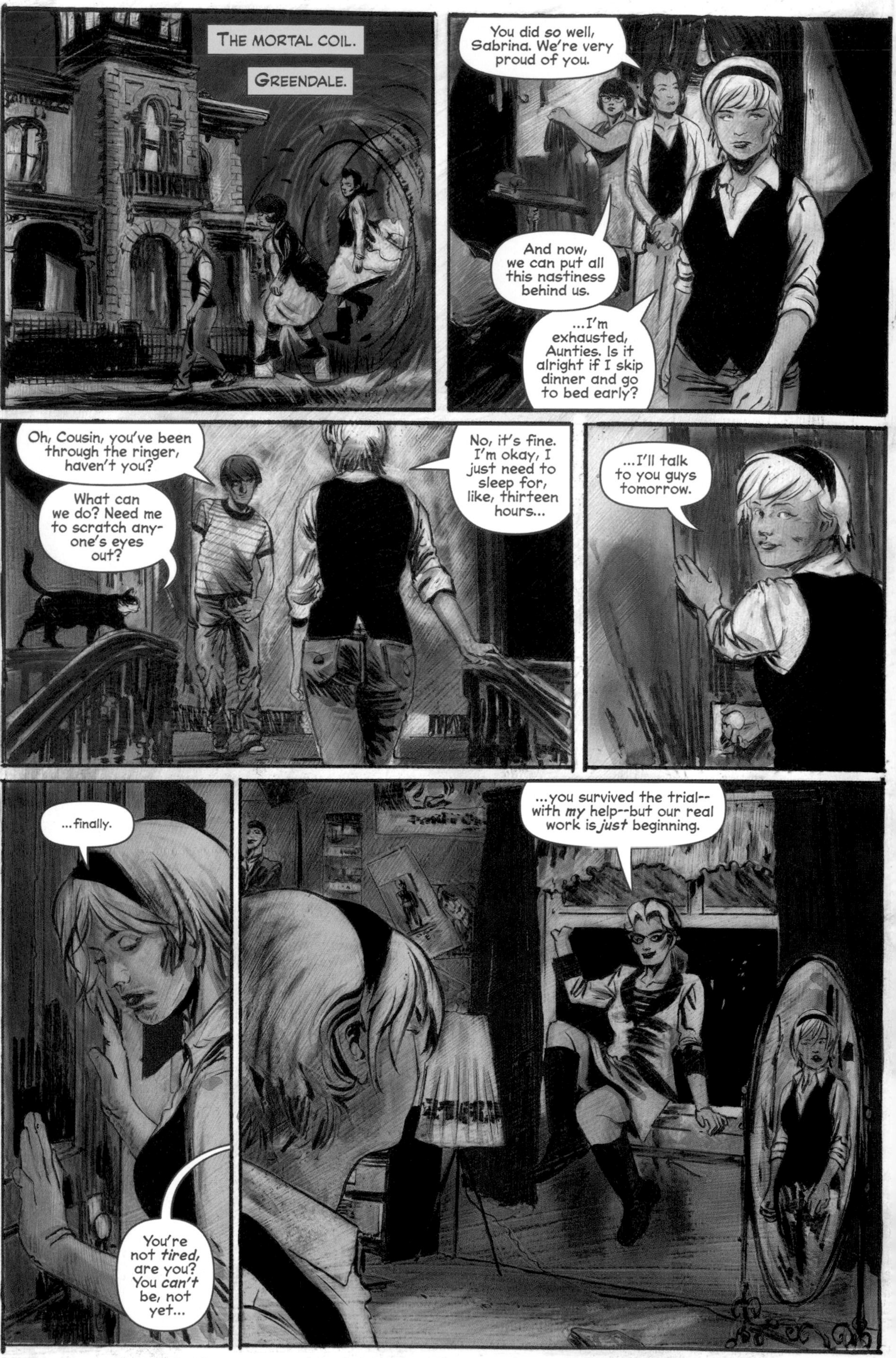
THE MORTAL COIL.
GREENDALE.
You did so well, Sabrina. We're very proud of you.
And now, we can put all this nastiness behind us.
...I'm exhausted, Aunties. Is it alright if I skip dinner and go to bed early?
Oh, Cousin, you've been through the ringer, haven't you?
What can we do? Need me to scratch any-one's eyes out?
No, it's fine. I'm okay, I just need to sleep for, like, thirteen hours...
...I'll talk to you guys tomorrow.
...finally.
You're not *tired*, are you? You *can't* be, not yet...
...you survived the trial--with *my* help--but our real work is *just* beginning.

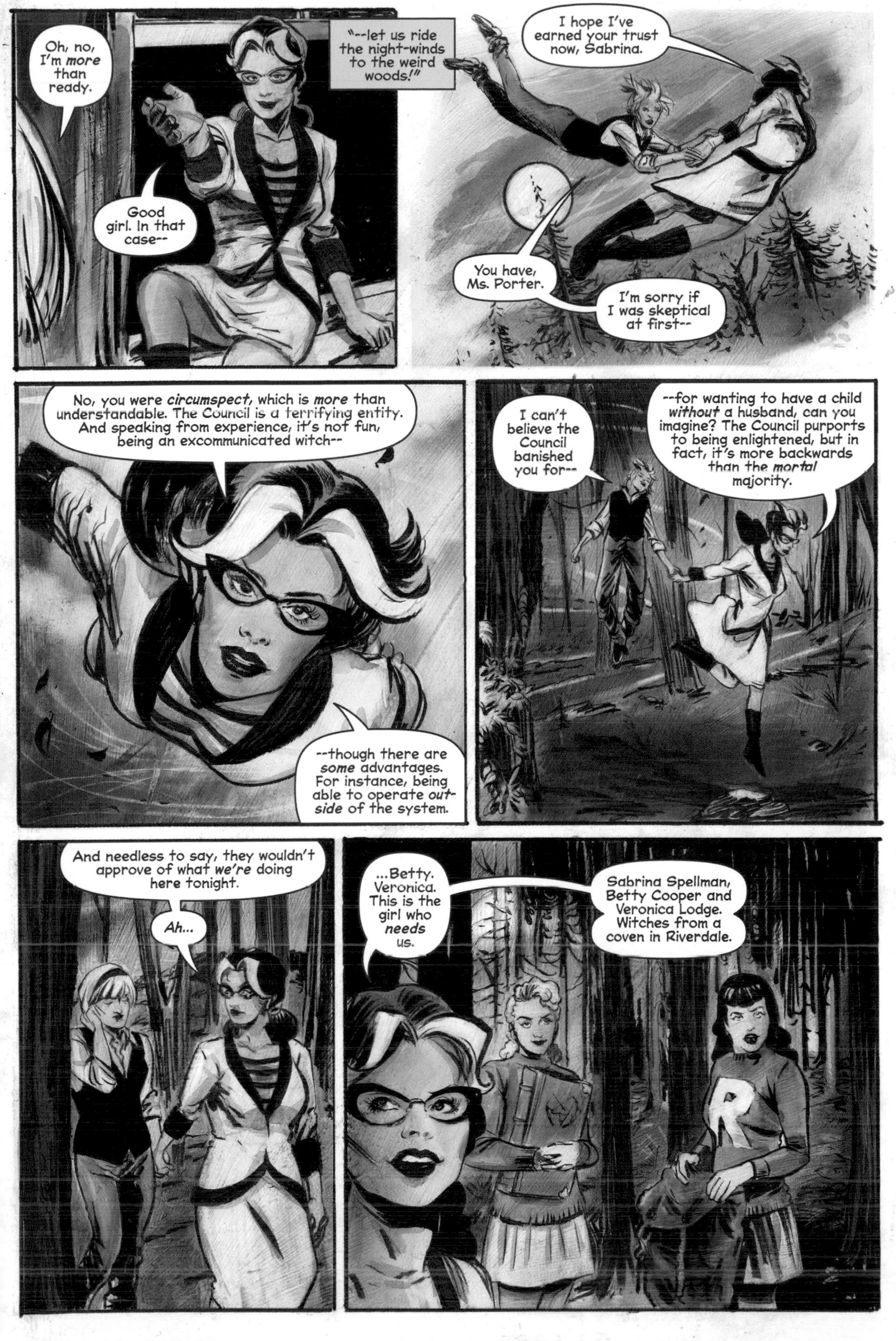
Oh, no, I'm *more* than ready.
Good girl. In that case--
"--let us ride the night-winds to the weird woods!"
I hope I've earned your trust now, Sabrina.
You have, Ms. Porter.
I'm sorry if I was skeptical at first--
No, you were *circumspect,* which is *more* than understandable. The Council is a terrifying entity. And speaking from experience, it's not fun, being an excommunicated witch--
--though there are *some* advantages. For instance, being able to operate *out-side* of the system.
I can't believe the Council banished you for--
--for wanting to have a child *without* a husband, can you imagine? The Council purports to being enlightened, but in fact, it's more backwards than the *mortal* majority.
And needless to say, they wouldn't approve of what *we're* doing here tonight.
Ah...
...Betty. Veronica. This is the girl who *needs* us.
Sabrina Spellman, Betty Cooper and Veronica Lodge. Witches from a coven in Riverdale.

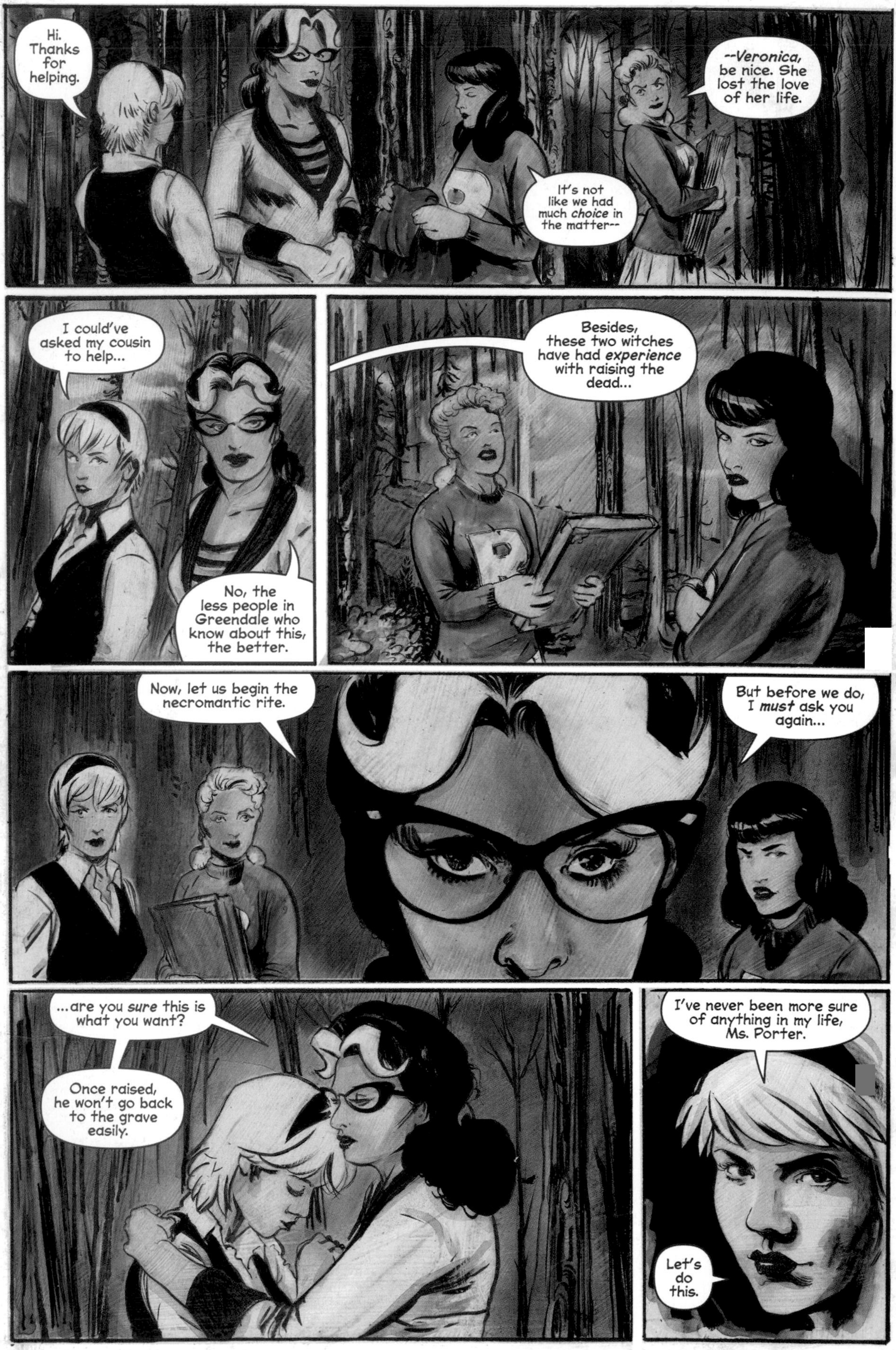
Hi. Thanks for helping.
It's not like we had much *choice* in the matter--
--*Veronica,* be nice. She lost the love of her life.
I could've asked my cousin to help...
No, the less people in Greendale who know about this, the better.
Besides, these two witches have had *experience* with raising the dead...
Now, let us begin the necromantic rite.
But before we do, I *must* ask you again...
...are you *sure* this is what you want?
Once raised, he won't go back to the grave easily.
I've never been more sure of anything in my life, Ms. Porter.
Let's do this.

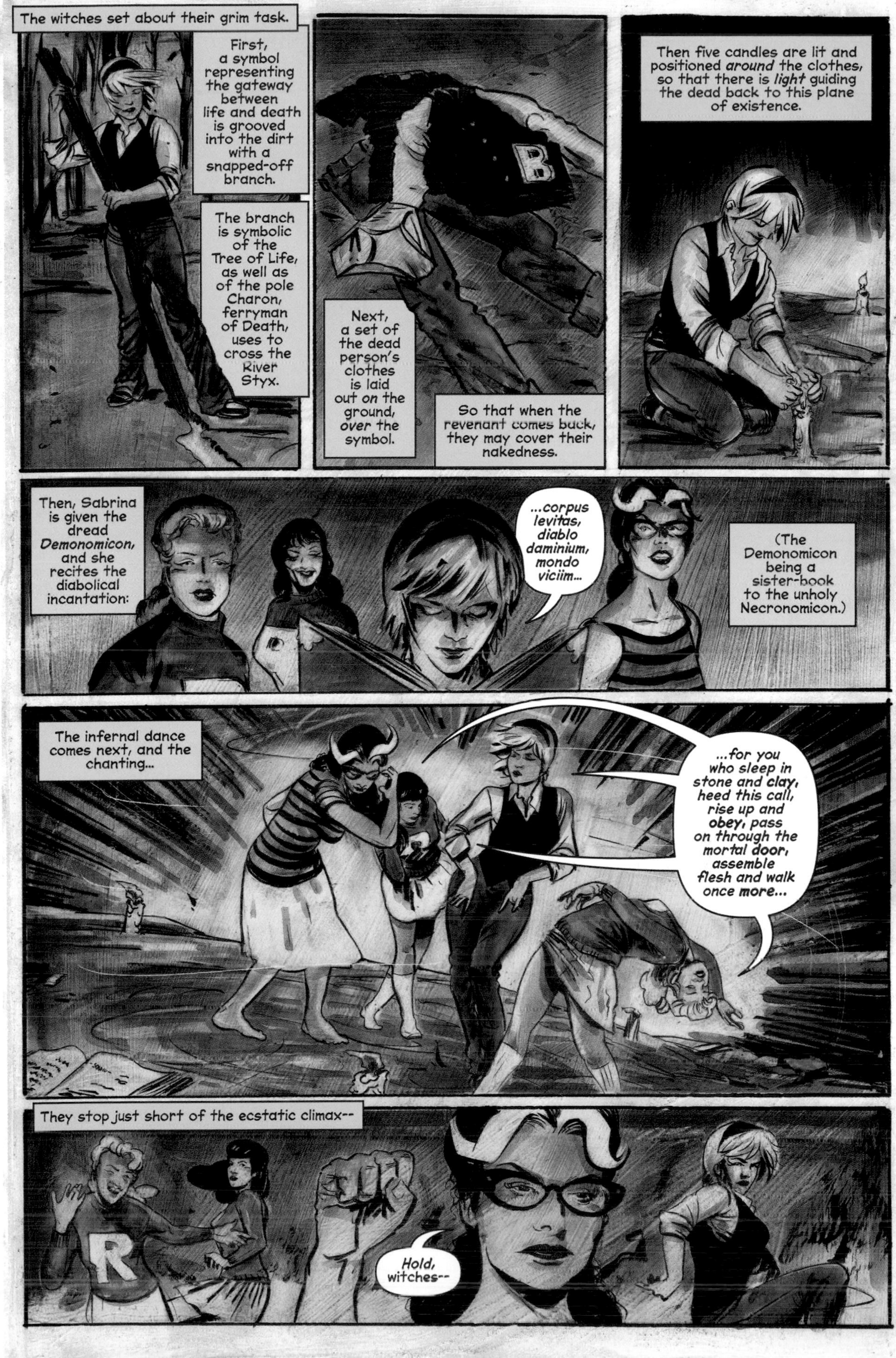
The witches set about their grim task.
First, a symbol representing the gateway between life and death is grooved into the dirt with a snapped-off branch.
The branch is symbolic of the Tree of Life, as well as of the pole Charon, ferryman of Death, uses to cross the River Styx.
Next, a set of the dead person's clothes is laid out *on* the ground, *over* the symbol.
So that when the revenant comes back, they may cover their nakedness.
Then five candles are lit and positioned *around* the clothes, so that there is *light* guiding the dead back to this plane of existence.
Then, Sabrina is given the dread *Demonomicon*, and she recites the diabolical incantation:
...corpus levitas, diablo daminium, mondo viciim...
(The Demonomicon being a sister-book to the unholy Necronomicon.)
The infernal dance comes next, and the chanting...
...for you who sleep in stone and **clay**, *heed this call, rise up and* **obey**, *pass on through the mortal* **door**, *assemble flesh and walk once* **more**...
They stop just short of the ecstatic climax--
Hold, witches--

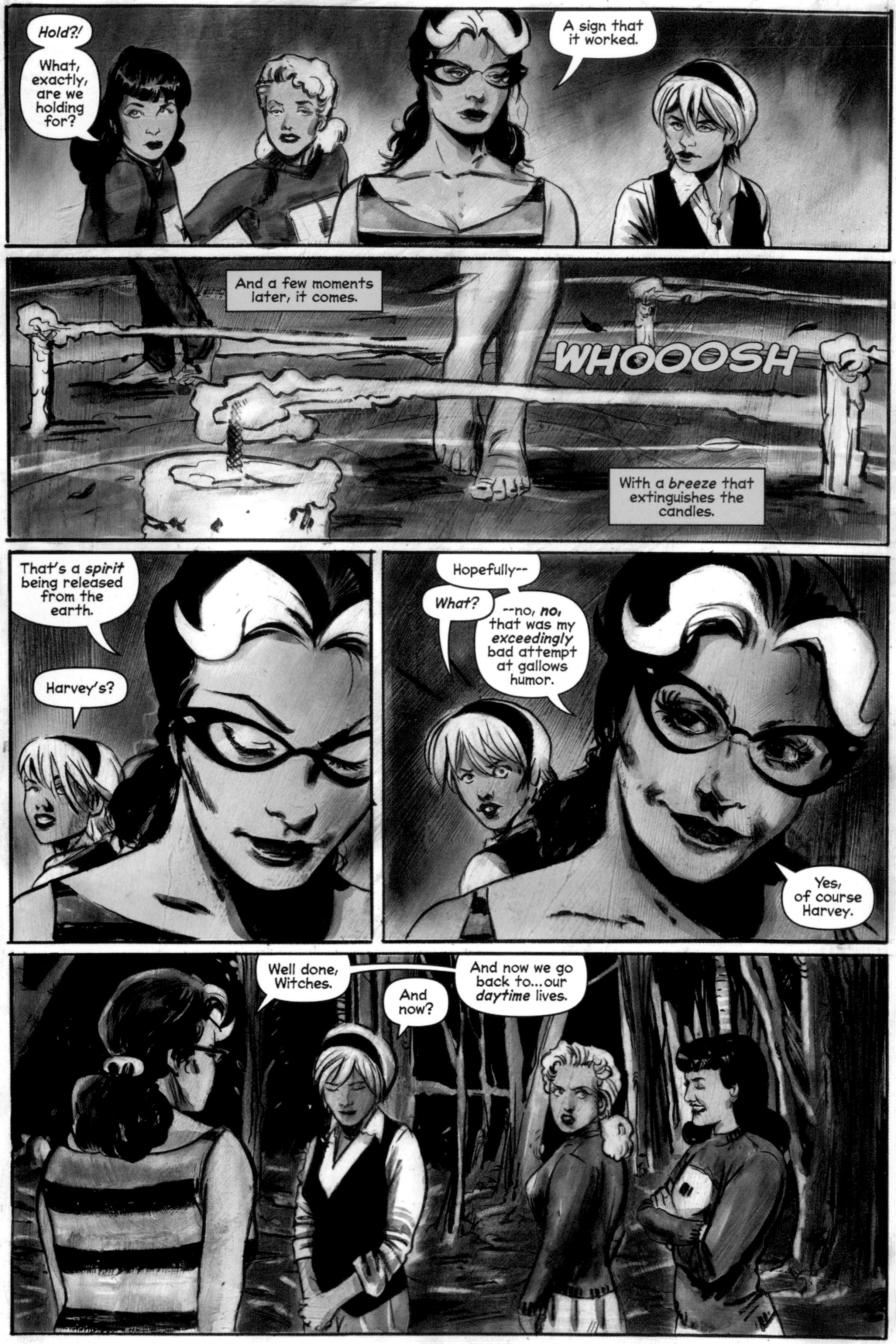
Hold?!
What, exactly, are we holding for?
A sign that it worked.
And a few moments later, it comes.
WHOOOSH
With a *breeze* that extinguishes the candles.
That's a *spirit* being released from the earth.
Harvey's?
Hopefully--
What?
--no, **no**, that was my *exceedingly* bad attempt at gallows humor.
Yes, of course Harvey.
Well done, Witches.
And now?
And now we go back to...our *daytime* lives.

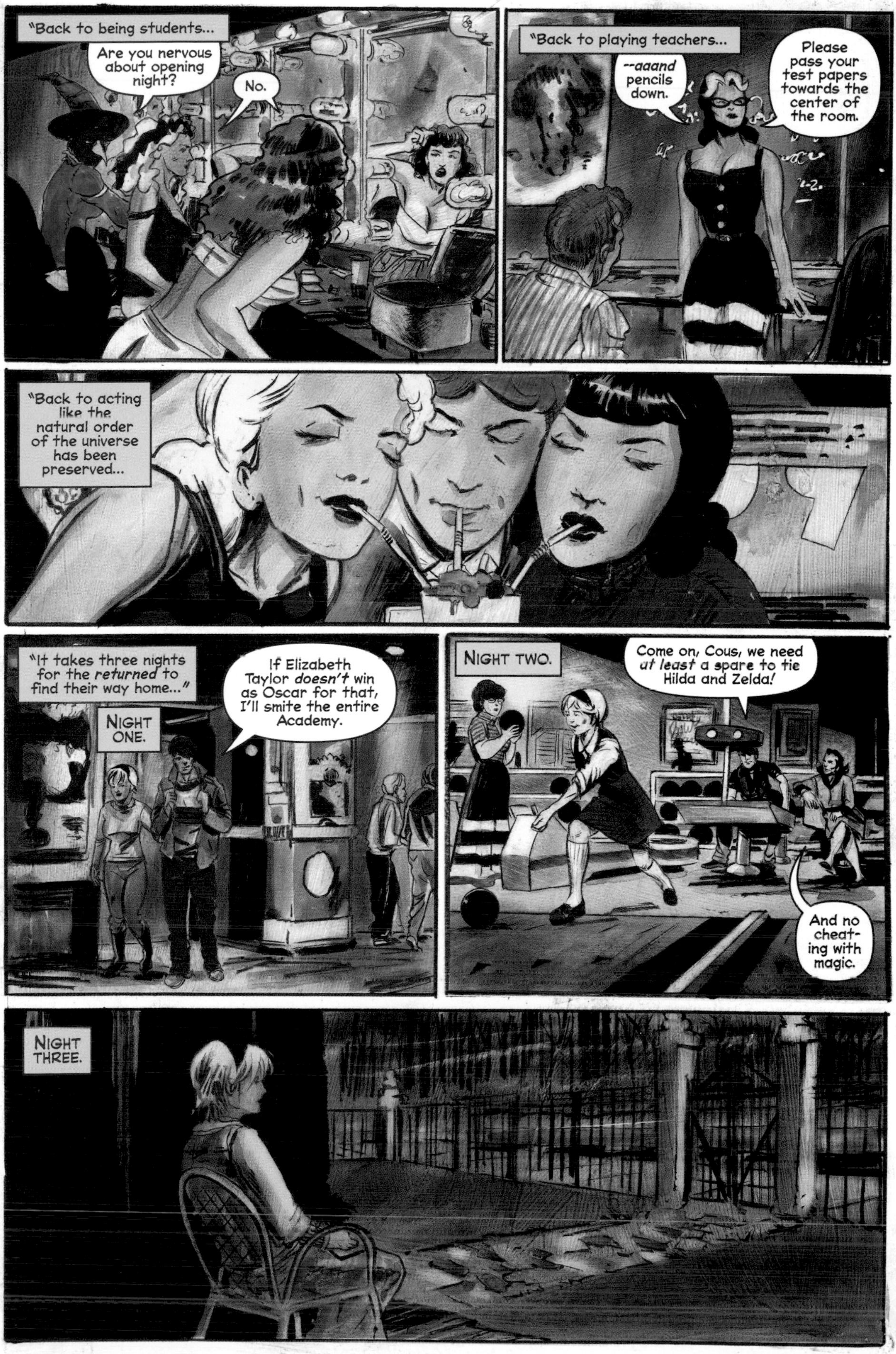
"Back to being students...
Are you nervous about opening night?
No.
"Back to playing teachers...
--aaand pencils down.
Please pass your test papers towards the center of the room.
"Back to acting like the natural order of the universe has been preserved...
"It takes three nights for the *returned* to find their way home..."
NIGHT ONE.
If Elizabeth Taylor *doesn't* win as Oscar for that, I'll smite the entire Academy.
NIGHT TWO.
Come on, Cous, we need *at least* a spare to tie Hilda and Zelda!
And no cheating with magic.
NIGHT THREE.

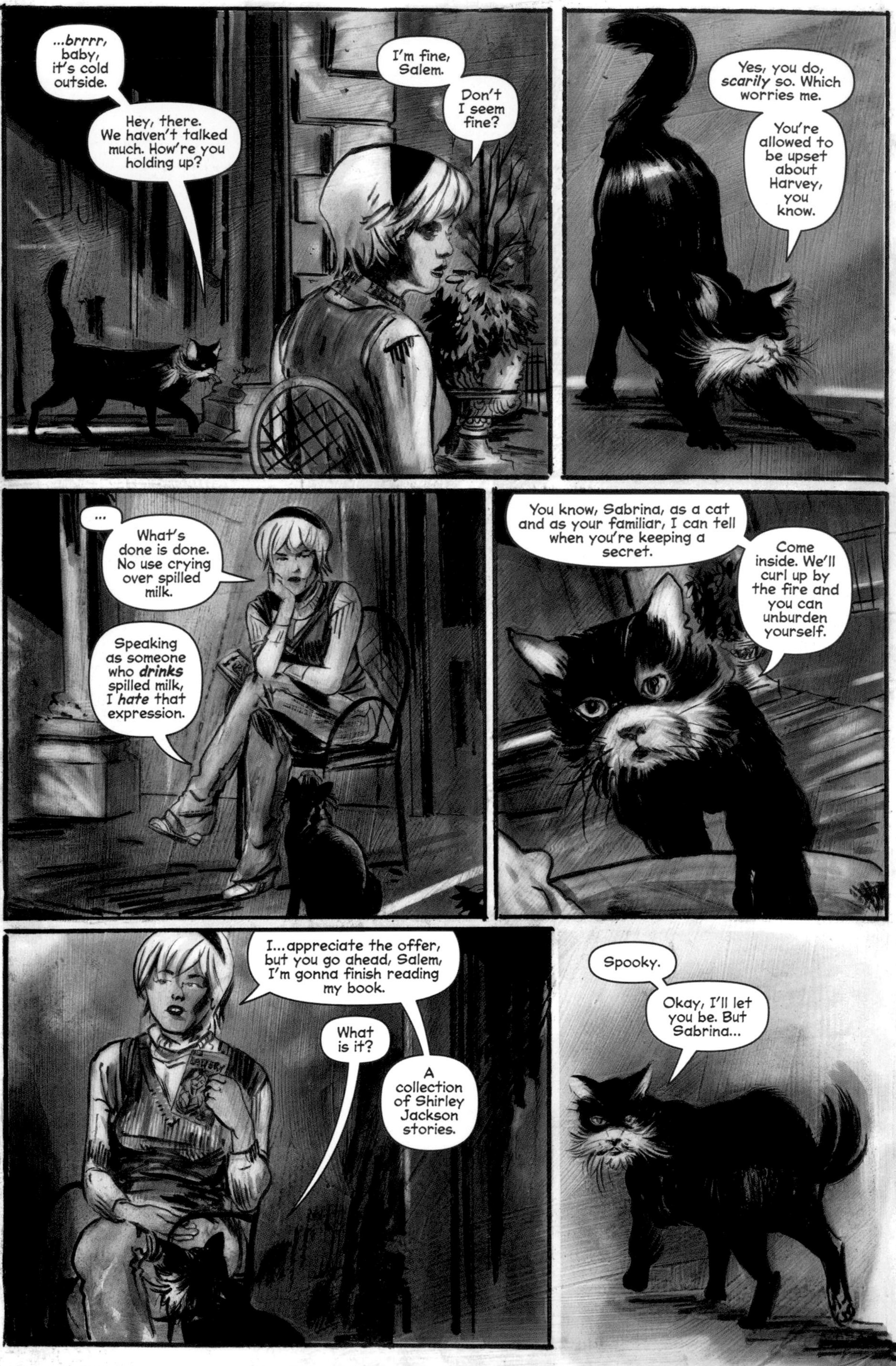

...*brrrr*, baby, it's cold outside.
Hey, there. We haven't talked much. How're you holding up?
I'm fine, Salem.
Don't I seem fine?
Yes, you do, *scarily* so. Which worries me.
You're allowed to be upset about Harvey, you know.
...
What's done is done. No use crying over spilled milk.
Speaking as someone who **drinks** spilled milk, I **hate** that expression.
You know, Sabrina, as a cat and as your familiar, I can tell when you're keeping a secret.
Come inside. We'll curl up by the fire and you can unburden yourself.
I...appreciate the offer, but you go ahead, Salem, I'm gonna finish reading my book.
What is it?
A collection of Shirley Jackson stories.
Spooky.
Okay, I'll let you be. But Sabrina...

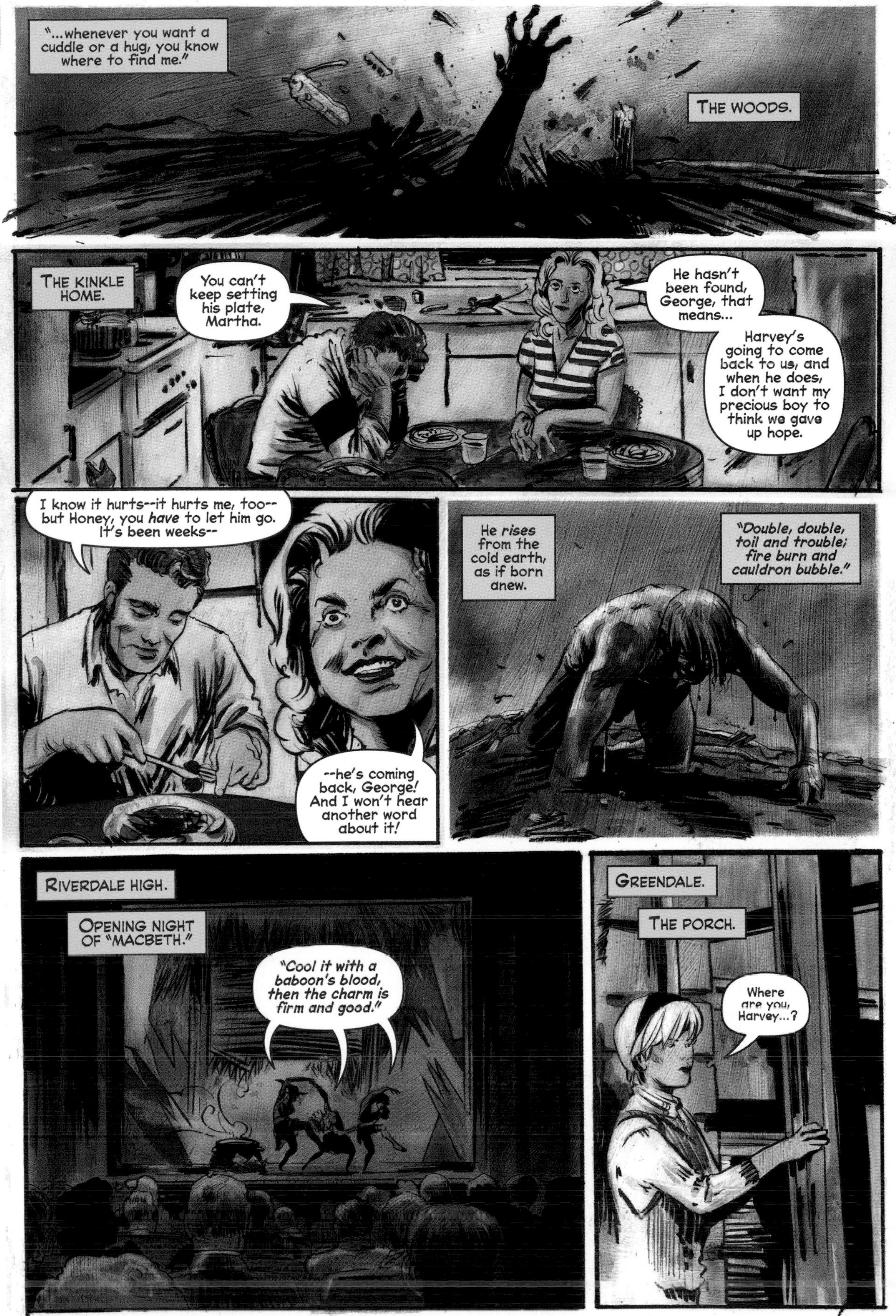
"...whenever you want a cuddle or a hug, you know where to find me."
THE WOODS.
THE KINKLE HOME.
You can't keep setting his plate, Martha.
He hasn't been found, George, that means...
Harvey's going to come back to us, and when he does, I don't want my precious boy to think we gave up hope.
I know it hurts--it hurts me, too--but Honey, you *have* to let him go. It's been weeks--
--he's coming back, George! And I won't hear another word about it!
He *rises* from the cold earth, as if born anew.
"Double, double, toil and trouble; fire burn and cauldron bubble."
RIVERDALE HIGH.
OPENING NIGHT OF "MACBETH."
"Cool it with a baboon's blood, then the charm is firm and good."
GREENDALE.
THE PORCH.
Where are you, Harvey...?

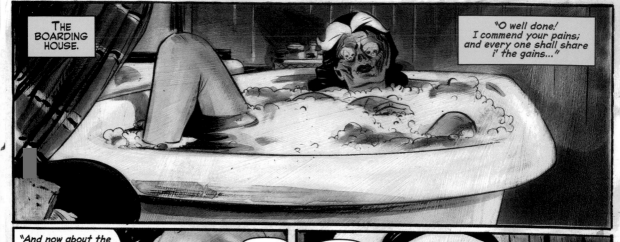

THE BOARDING HOUSE.

"O well done! I commend your pains; and every one shall share i' the gains..."

"And now about the cauldron sing, live elves and fairies in a ring, enchanting all that you put in."

--ouch.

--damn splinter.

"By the pricking of my thumbs..."

"...something wicked this way comes."

"Open, locks, whoever knocks!"

NOK NOK NOK

It's him.

"Sabrina?"

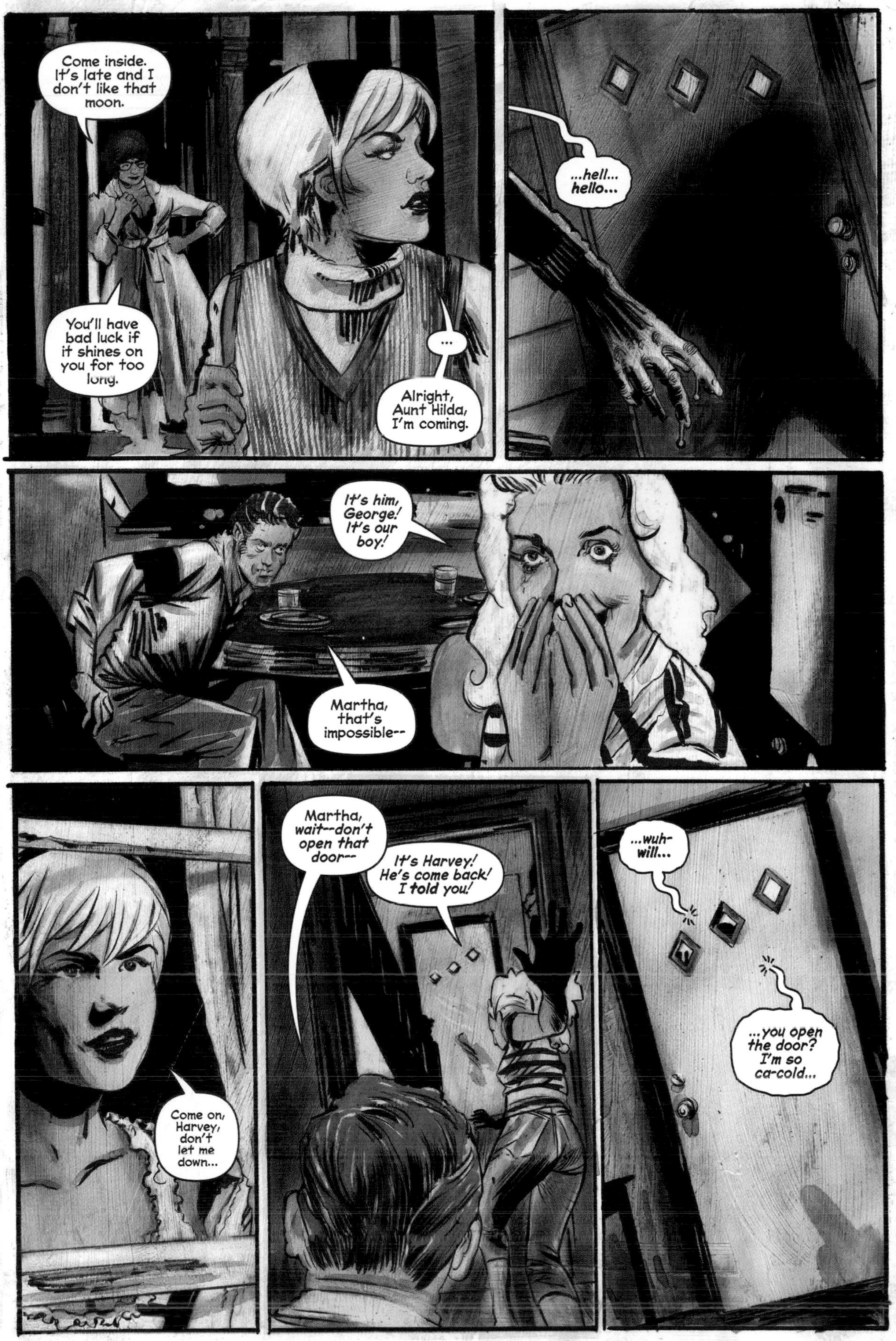
Come inside. It's late and I don't like that moon.
You'll have bad luck if it shines on you for too long.
...
Alright, Aunt Hilda, I'm coming.
...hell... hello...
It's him, George! It's our boy!
Martha, that's impossible--
Come on, Harvey, don't let me down...
Martha, wait--don't open that door--
It's Harvey! He's come back! I told you!
...wuh-will...
...you open the door? I'm so ca-cold...

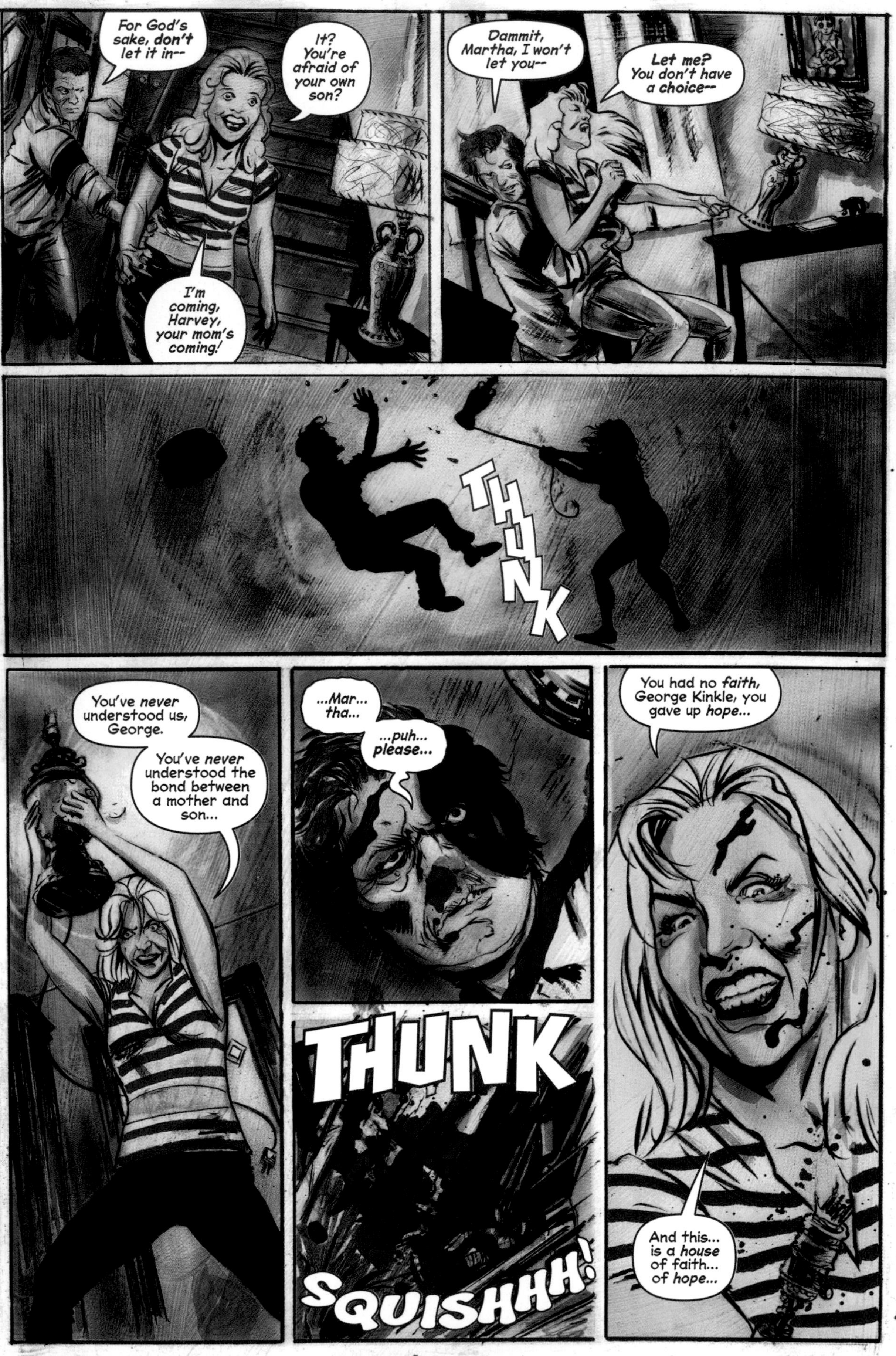
For God's sake, don't let it in--
It? You're afraid of your own son?
I'm coming, Harvey, your mom's coming!
Dammit, Martha, I won't let you--
Let me? You don't have a choice--
THUNK
You've never understood us, George.
You've never understood the bond between a mother and son...
...Mar... tha...
...puh... please...
THUNK
SQUISHHH!
You had no faith, George Kinkle, you gave up hope...
And this... is a house of faith... of hope...

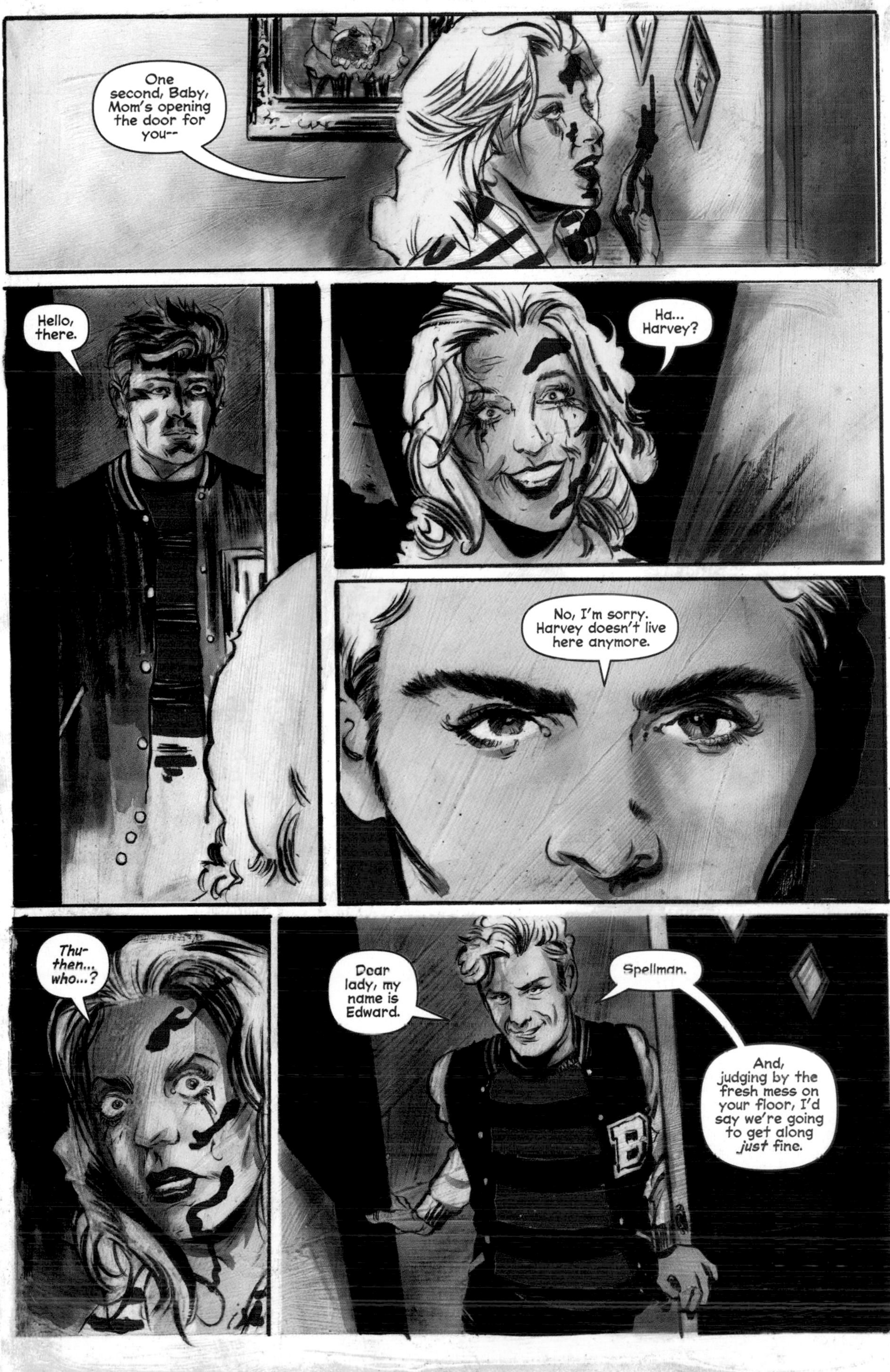
One second, Baby, Mom's opening the door for you--
Hello, there.
Ha... Harvey?
No, I'm sorry. Harvey doesn't live here anymore.
Thu- then... who...?
Dear lady, my name is Edward.
Spellman.
And, judging by the fresh mess on your floor, I'd say we're going to get along *just* fine.

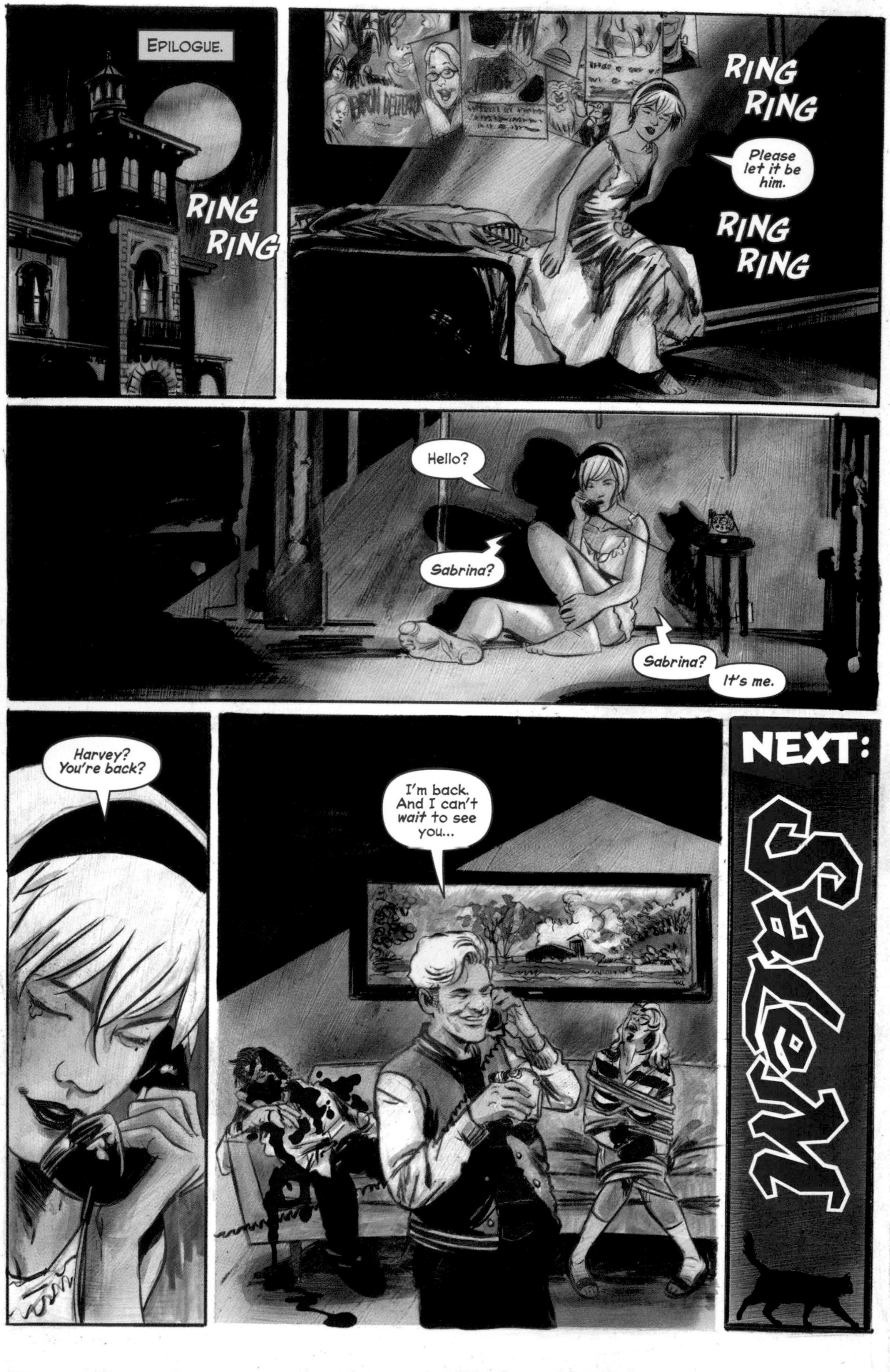

EPILOGUE.
RING RING
RING RING
Please let it be him.
RING RING
Hello?
Sabrina?
Sabrina?
It's me.
Harvey? You're back?
I'm back. And I can't wait to see you...
NEXT:
Salem

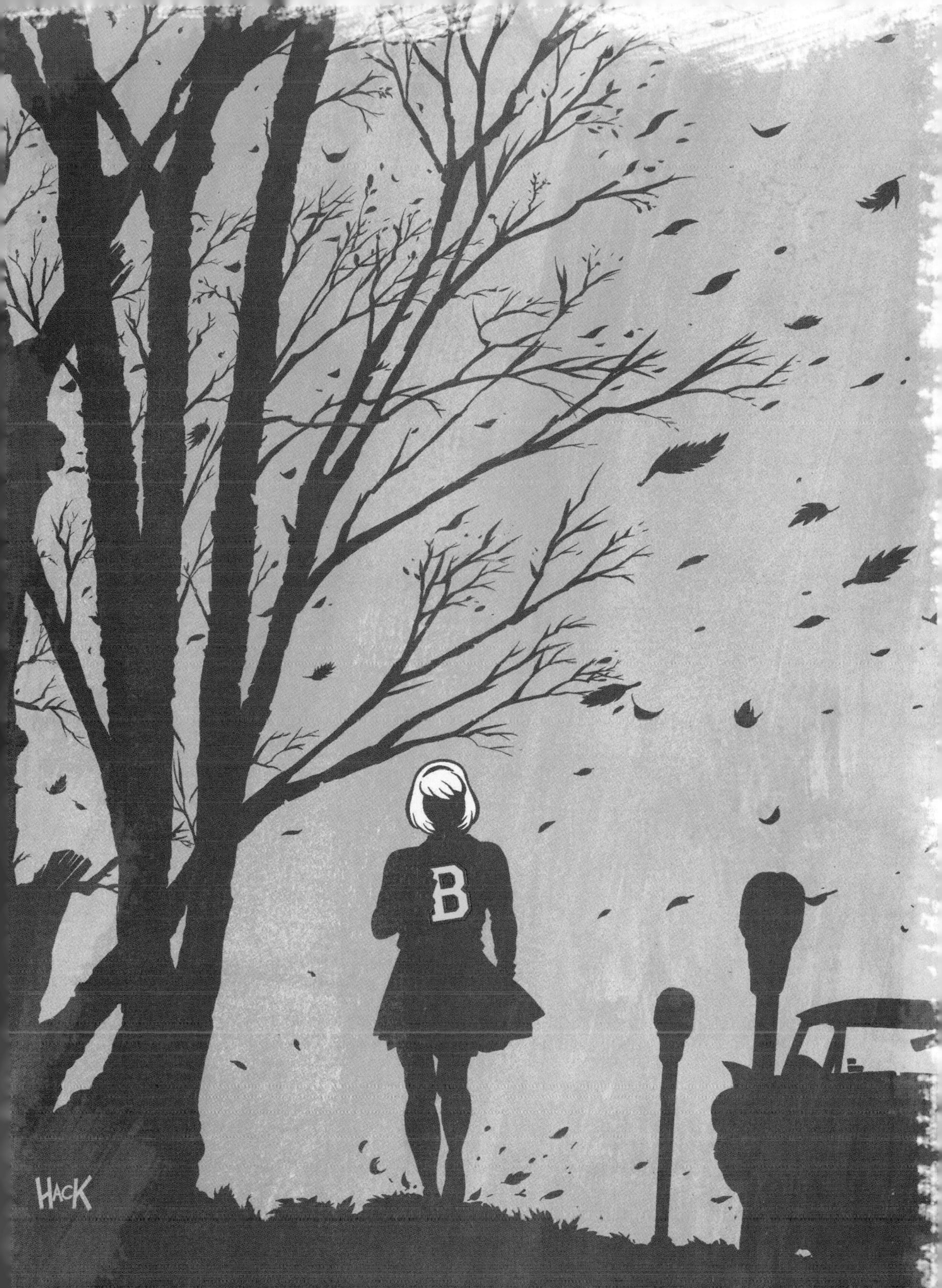
HACK
B

SPECIAL FEATURES

COVER GALLERY

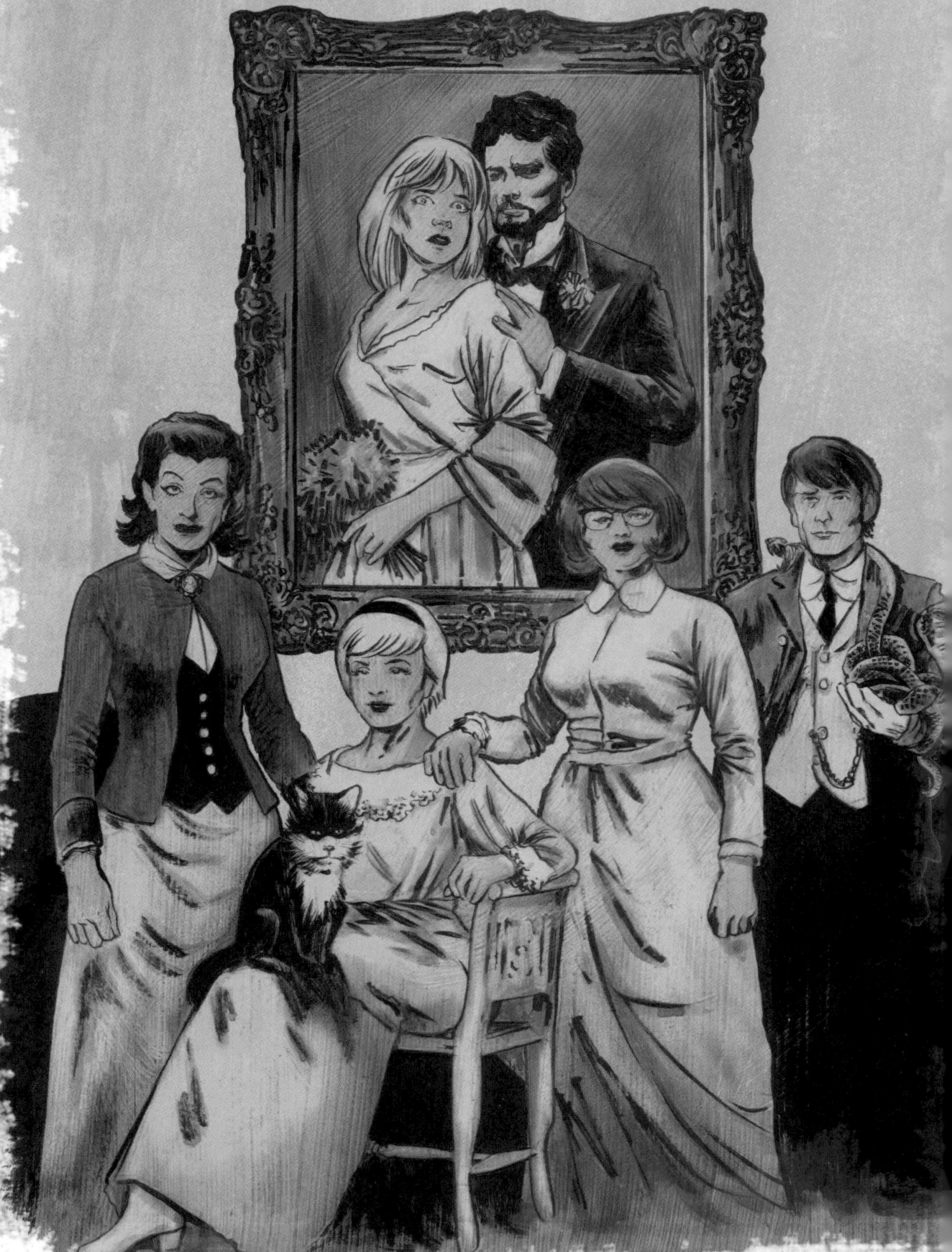

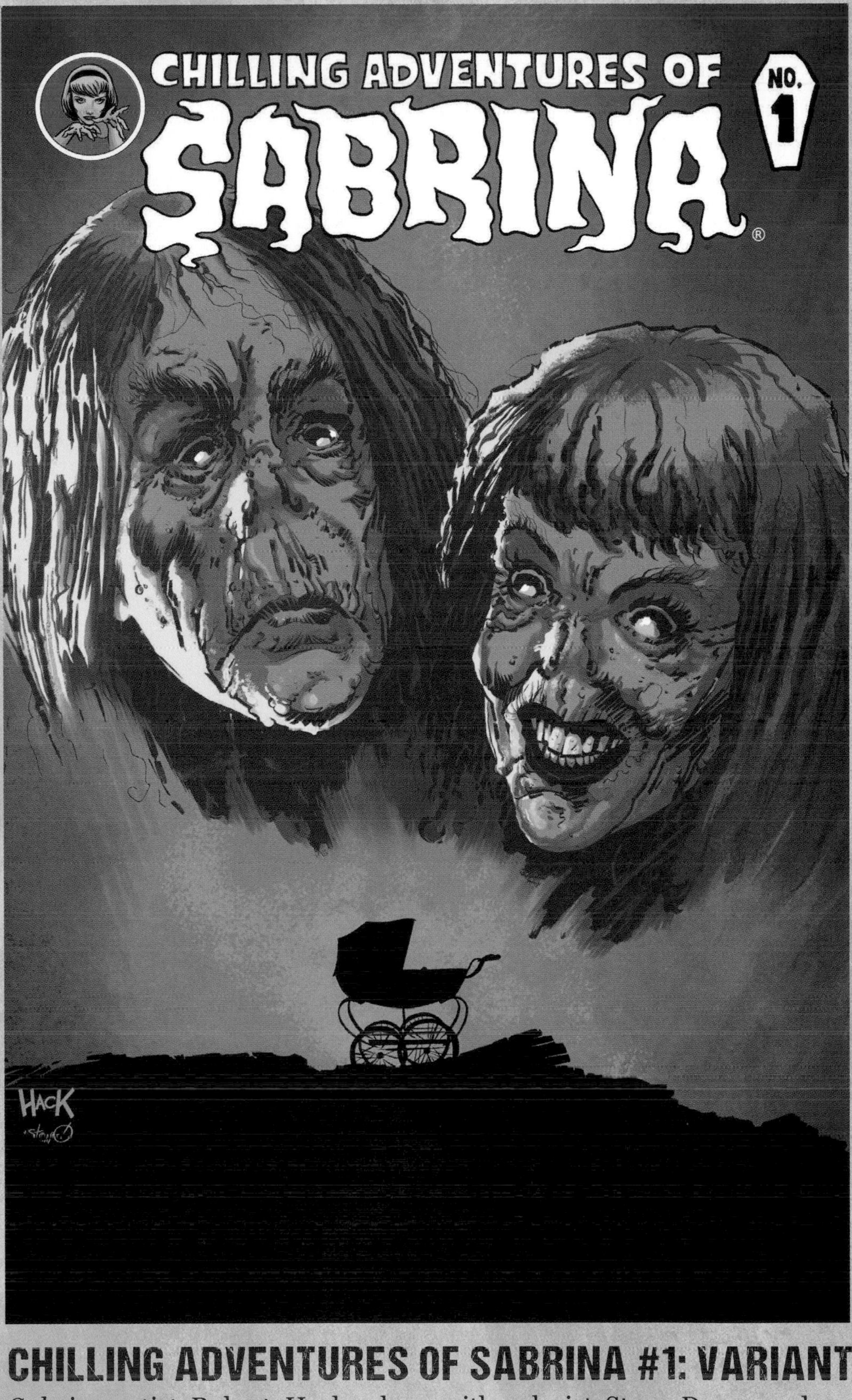
CHILLING ADVENTURES OF
SABRINA
NO. 1
HACK

CHILLING ADVENTURES OF SABRINA #1: VARIANT

Sabrina artist Robert Hack, along with colorist Steve Downer, drew inspiration from the classic 1968 movie *Rosemary's Baby* for this cover—the first in a series of horror movie-inspired variants.

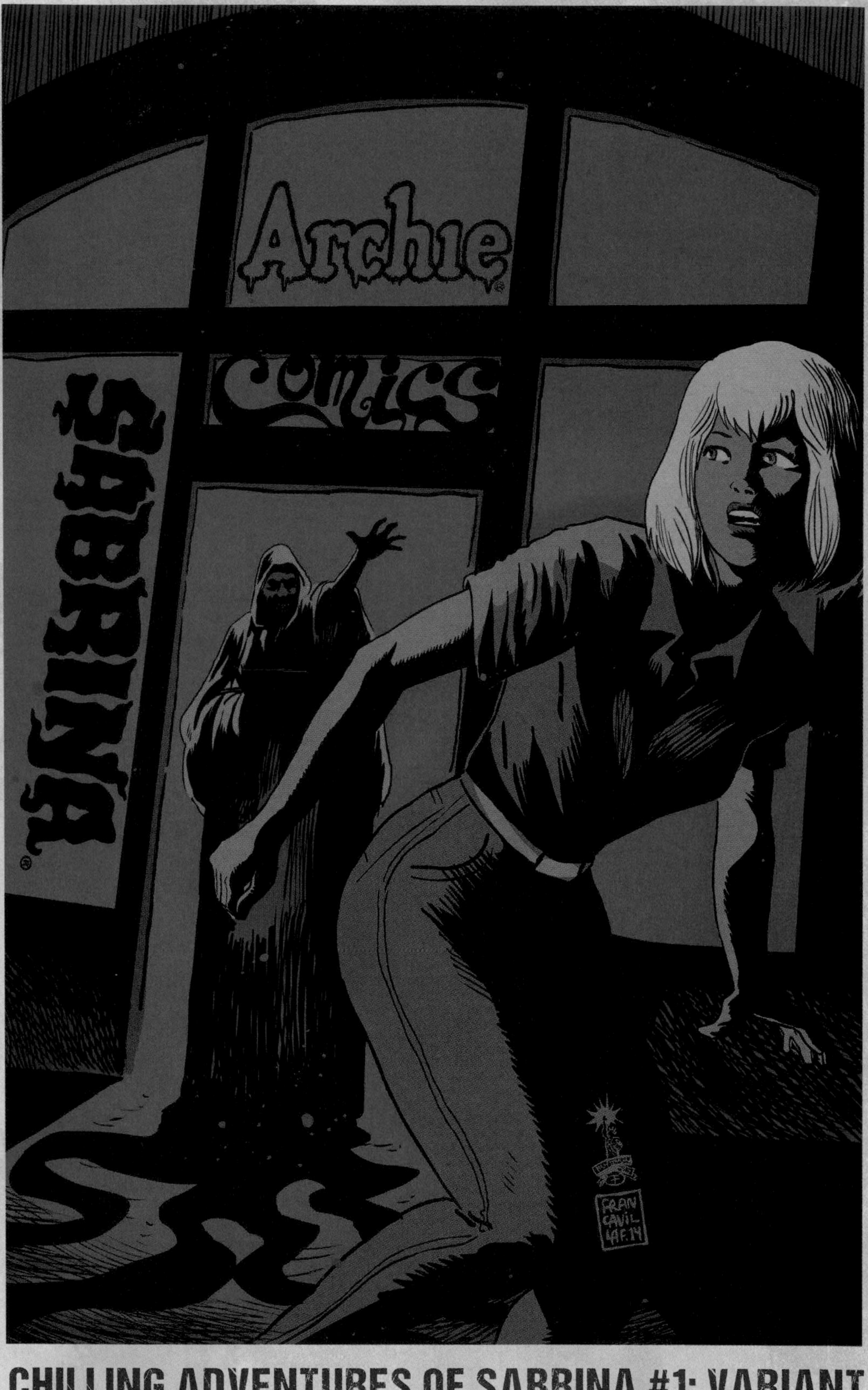
Archie
comics
SABRINA
FRANCAVILLA F.14

CHILLING ADVENTURES OF SABRINA #1: VARIANT

As part of a retailer incentive program, individual comic shops were able to have their own unique store logos placed on this cover by *Afterlife with Archie* artist Francesco Francavilla.

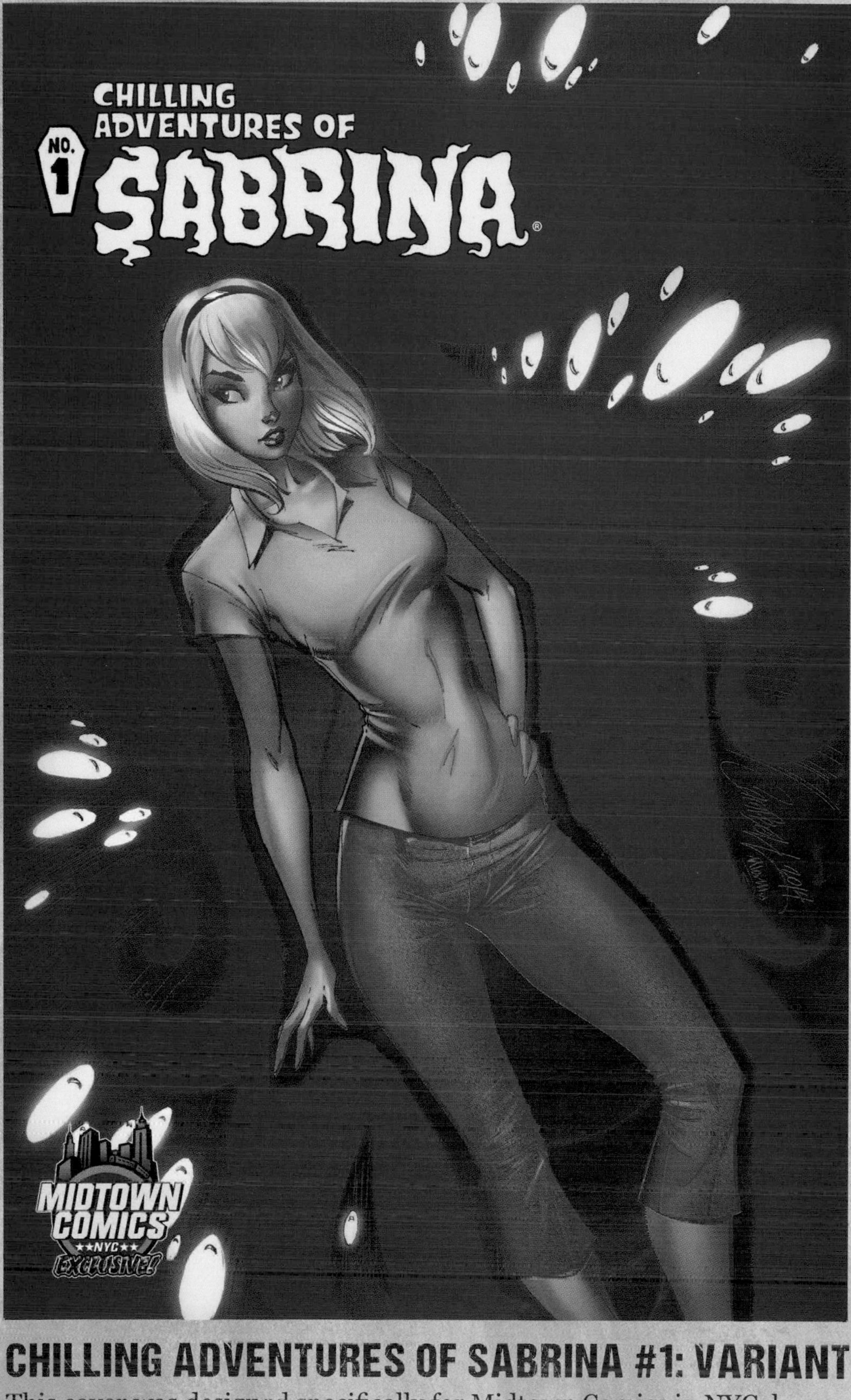
CHILLING
ADVENTURES OF
NO. 1
SABRINA
MIDTOWN
COMICS
NYC
EXCLUSIVE!

CHILLING ADVENTURES OF SABRINA #1: VARIANT

This cover was designed specifically for Midtown Comics in NYC, by J. Scott Campbell along with Ula Mos.

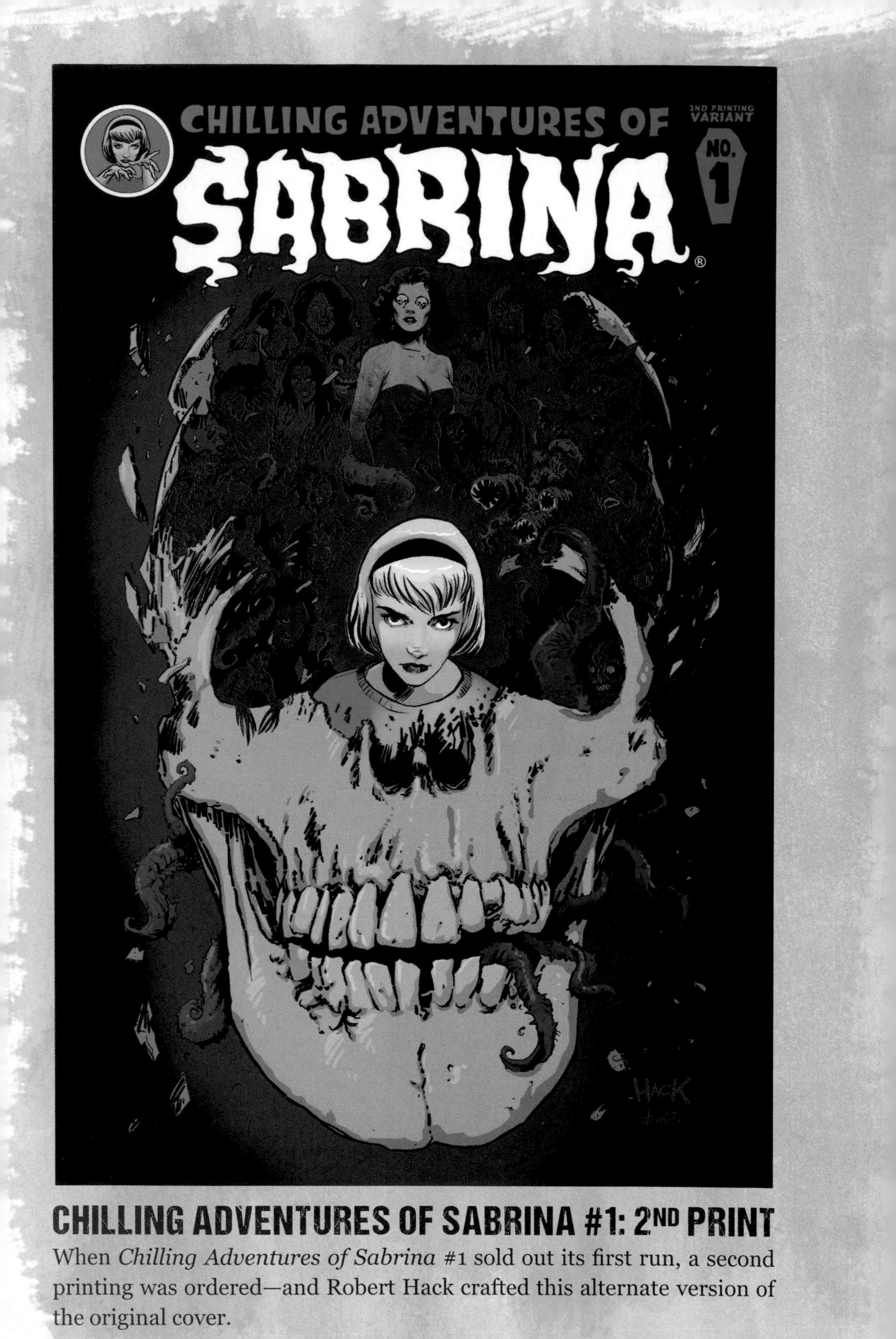
CHILLING ADVENTURES OF
SABRINA
2ND PRINTING VARIANT
NO. 1
HACK

CHILLING ADVENTURES OF SABRINA #1: 2ND PRINT

When *Chilling Adventures of Sabrina* #1 sold out its first run, a second printing was ordered—and Robert Hack crafted this alternate version of the original cover.

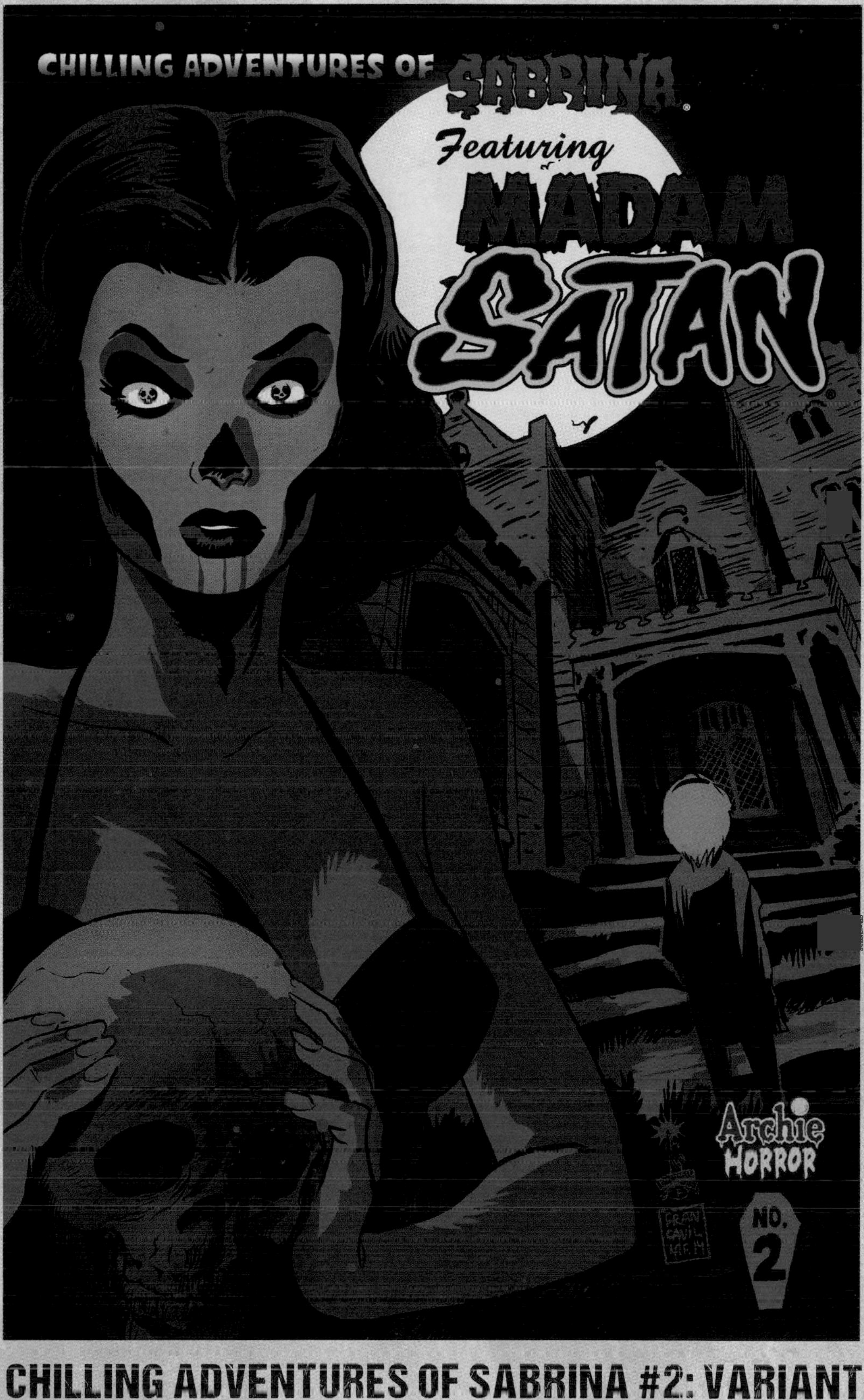
CHILLING ADVENTURES OF SABRINA
Featuring
MADAM
SATAN
Archie
HORROR
NO.
2

CHILLING ADVENTURES OF SABRINA #2: VARIANT

The introduction of the classic character Madam Satan into the world of *Chilling Adventures of Sabrina* was worthy of a variant cover for #2 by Francesco Francavilla.

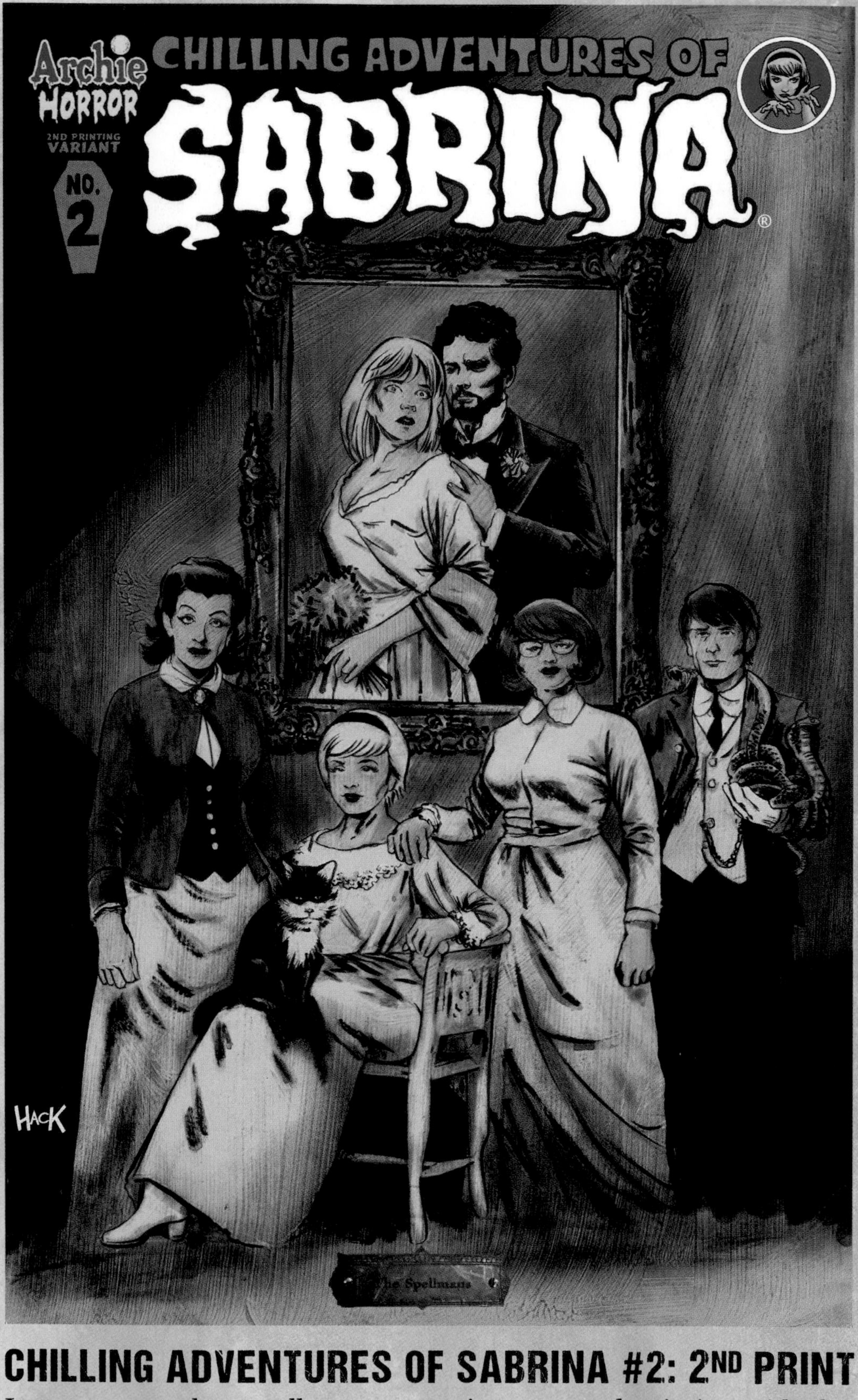
Archie
HORROR
2ND PRINTING
VARIANT
NO.
2
CHILLING ADVENTURES OF
SABRINA®
HACK
The Spellmans

CHILLING ADVENTURES OF SABRINA #2: 2ND PRINT

Issue #2 was also a sell-out, warranting a second printing with this Spellman Family Portrait cover by Robert Hack.

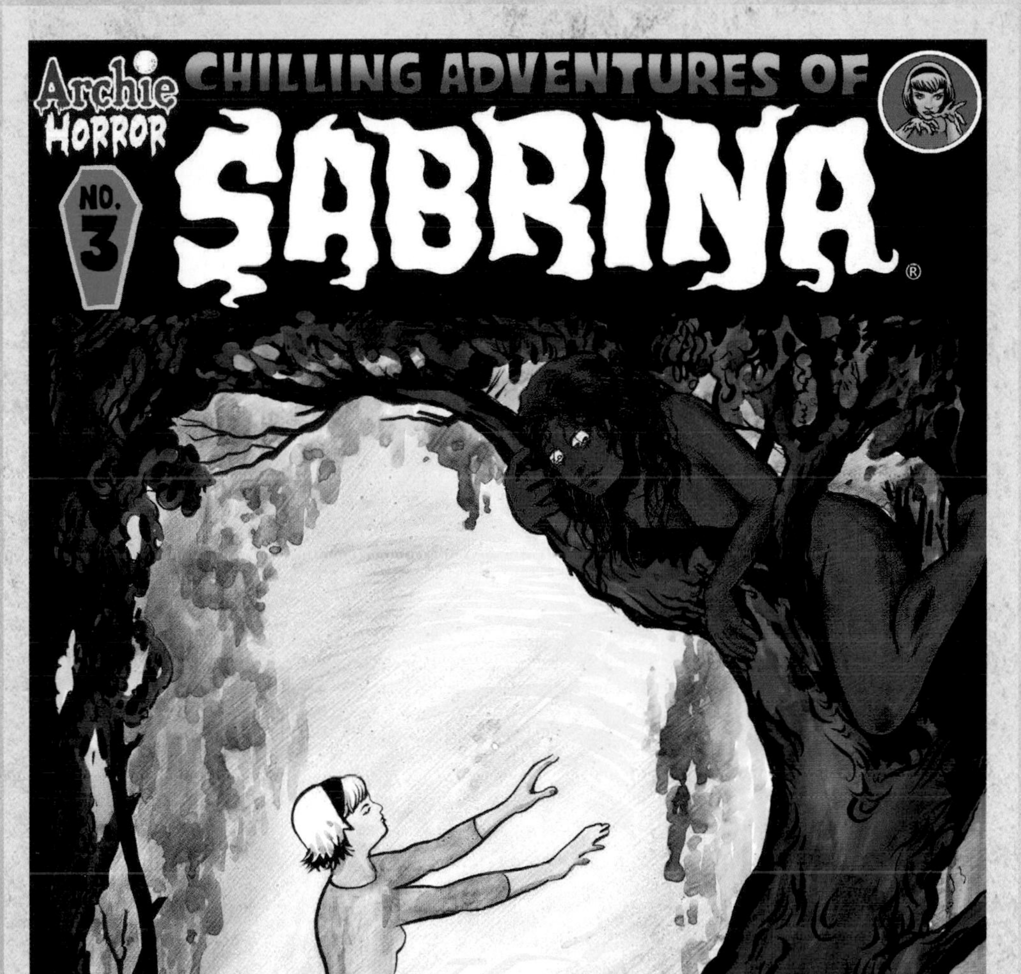
Archie HORROR
CHILLING ADVENTURES OF
SABRINA
NO. 3
ROBERTO AGUIRRE-SACASA
ROBERT HACK
ENSAMRATT: ARCHIE KOMISK, PELHAM
Hyllning till Häxan filmaffisch

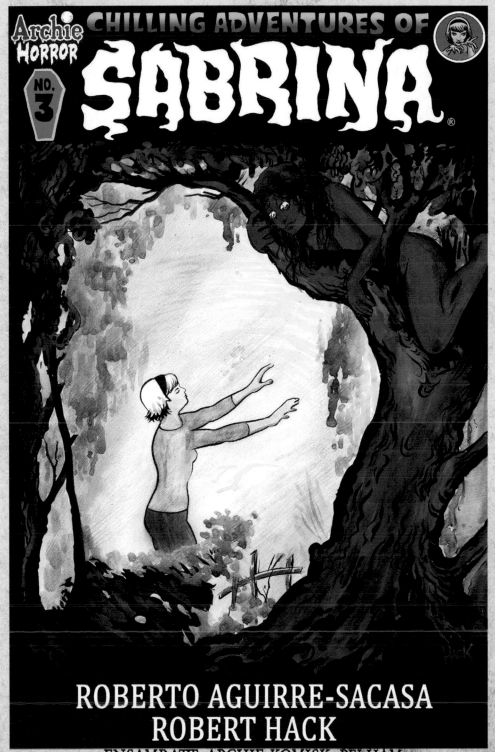

CHILLING ADVENTURES OF SABRINA #3: VARIANT

This cover by Robert Hack is his riff on a poster for the 1922 silent film *Häxan*, one of the first horror movies—all about witchcraft!

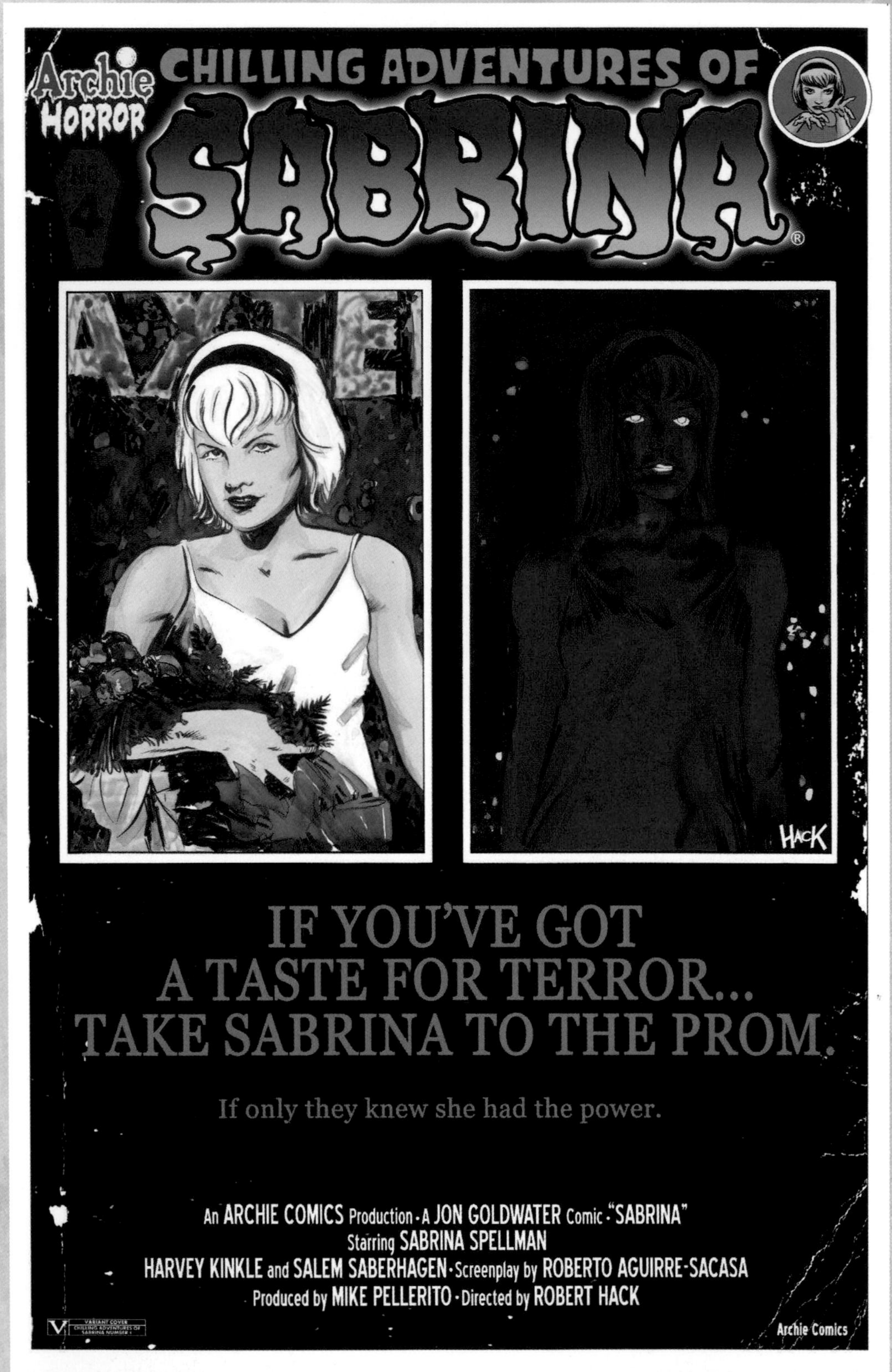
Archie HORROR
CHILLING ADVENTURES OF
SABRINA
HACK
IF YOU'VE GOT
A TASTE FOR TERROR...
TAKE SABRINA TO THE PROM.
If only they knew she had the power.
An ARCHIE COMICS Production · A JON GOLDWATER Comic · "SABRINA"
Starring SABRINA SPELLMAN
HARVEY KINKLE and SALEM SABERHAGEN · Screenplay by ROBERTO AGUIRRE-SACASA
Produced by MIKE PELLERITO · Directed by ROBERT HACK
Archie Comics

CHILLING ADVENTURES OF SABRINA #4: VARIANT

This variant by Robert Hack is based on the poster for the 1976 horror film *Carrie*. (The 2013 remake of *Carrie* was co-written by Roberto Aguirre-Sacasa.)

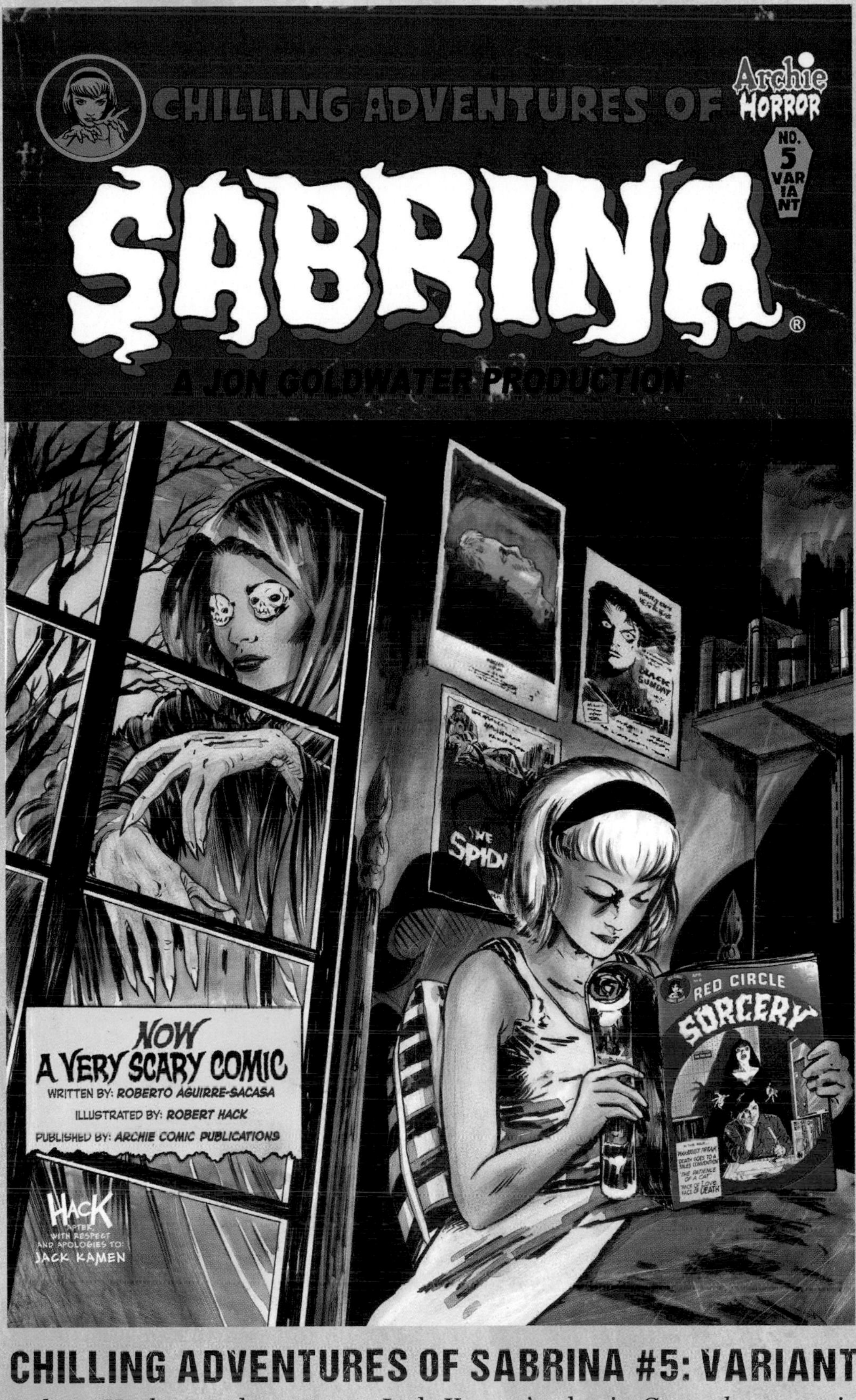
CHILLING ADVENTURES OF
Archie HORROR
NO. 5 VARIANT
SABRINA®
A JON GOLDWATER PRODUCTION
NOW
A VERY SCARY COMIC
WRITTEN BY: ROBERTO AGUIRRE-SACASA
ILLUSTRATED BY: ROBERT HACK
PUBLISHED BY: ARCHIE COMIC PUBLICATIONS
HACK
AFTER WITH RESPECT AND APOLOGIES TO: JACK KAMEN
RED CIRCLE
SORCERY

CHILLING ADVENTURES OF SABRINA #5: VARIANT

Robert Hack pays homage to Jack Kamen's classic *Creepshow* movie poster for the 1982 movie of the same name.

ORIGINAL SKETCH GALLERY

Take a behind-the-scenes look at some of Robert Hack's earliest sketches for Sabrina, Madam Satan, and the Spellman family home.

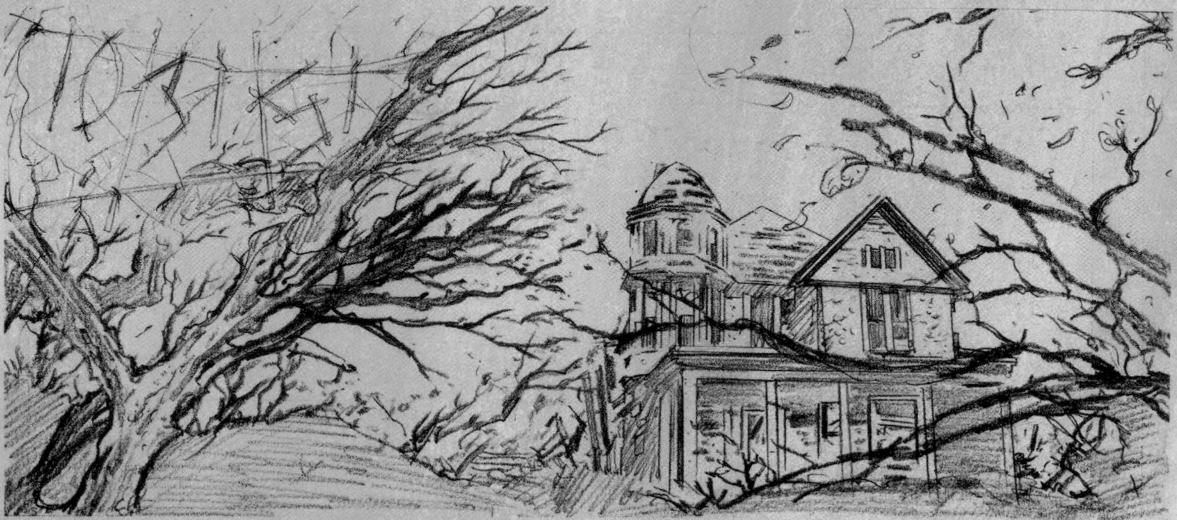

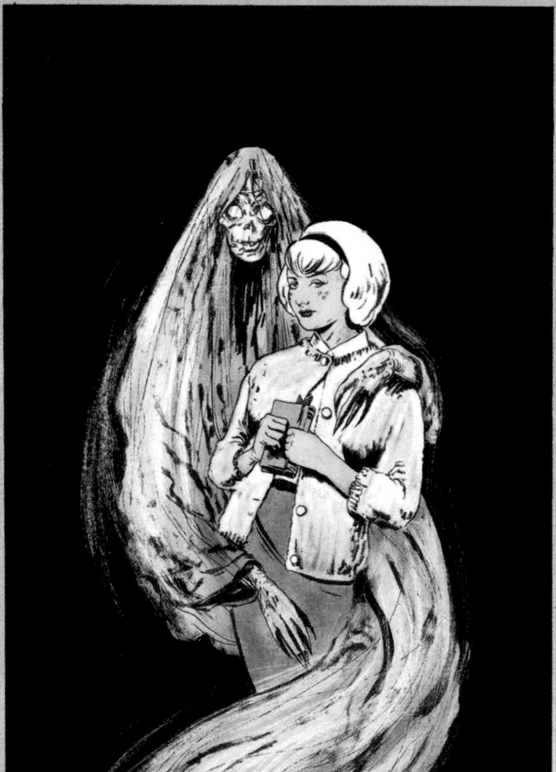
HACK

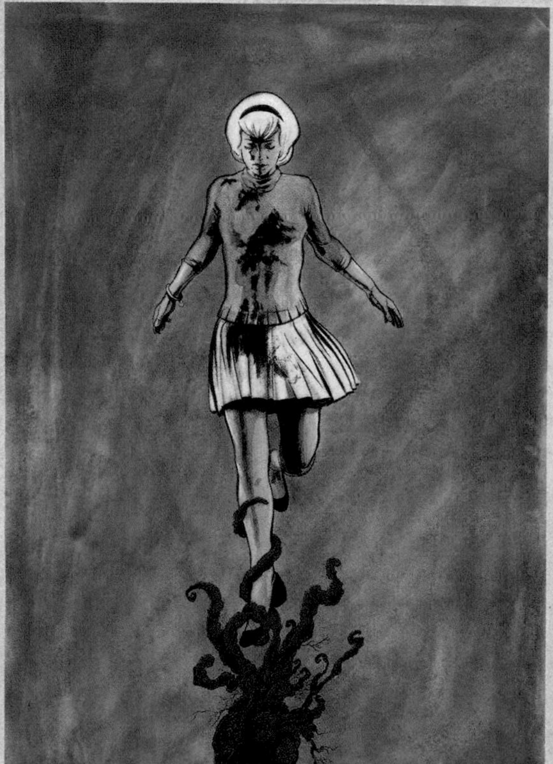
HACK

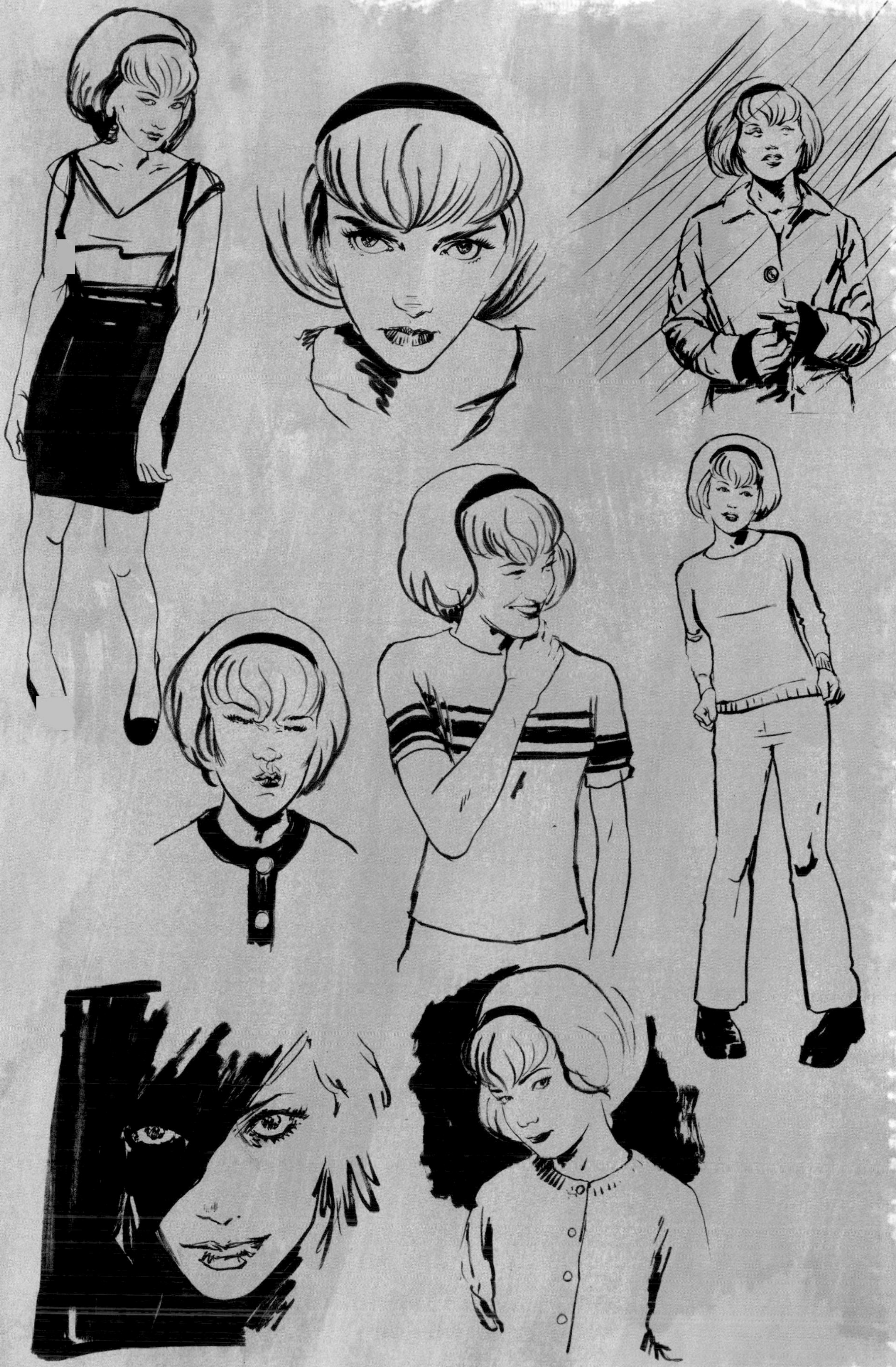

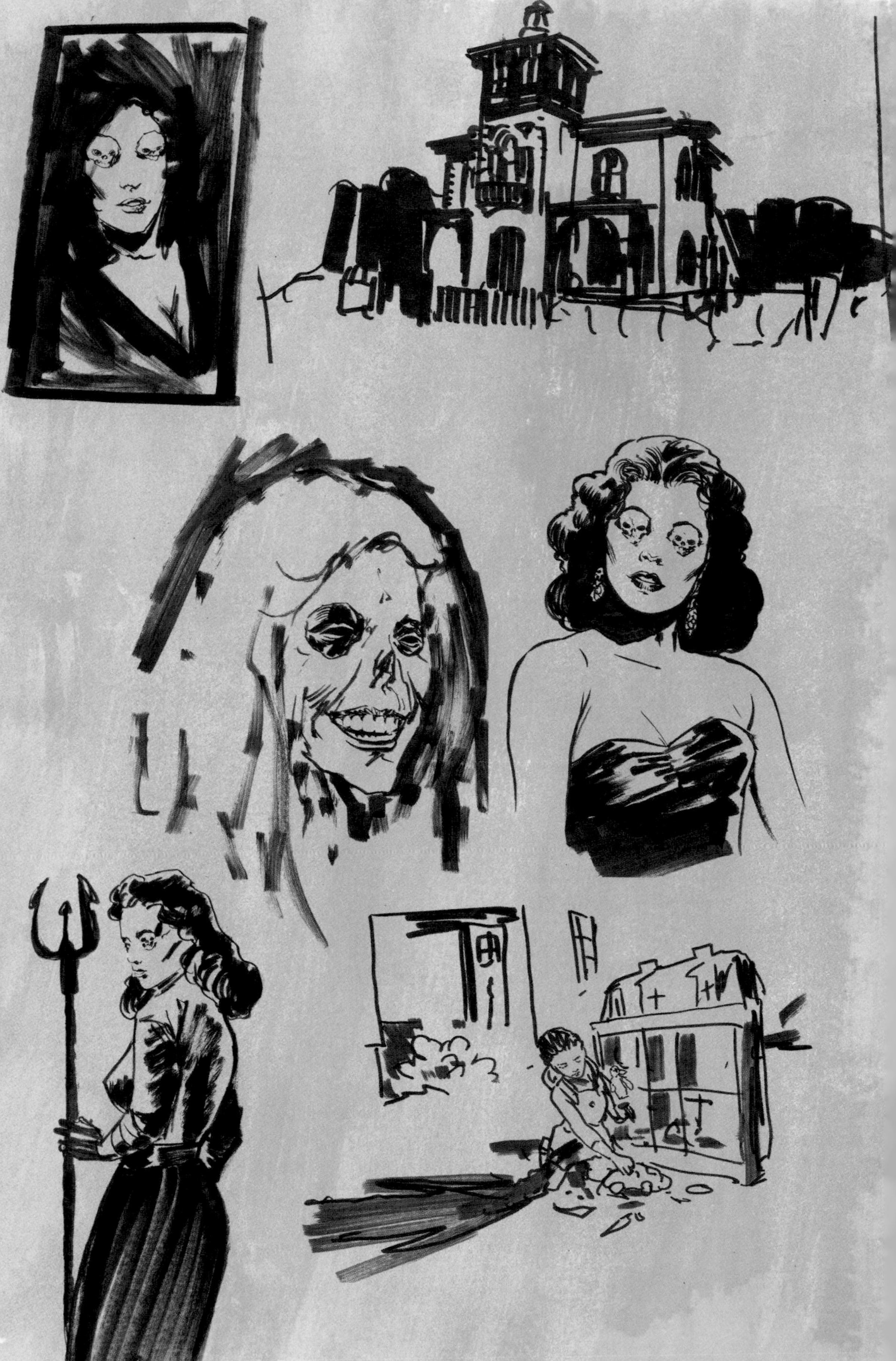

WHO IS MADAM SATAN?

Madam Satan made her first Archie Comics appearance in *Pep Comics #16* from 1941 (when the company still operated under the name MLJ Comics). Madam Satan was originally a woman named Tyra, who murdered her fiancé's parents after she discovered that they did not approve of their impending nuptials. After paying the ultimate price for her crime, she found herself in Hell, working under Satan. Her job was to seduce men into giving their souls to Satan, by using hypnotic control over them. Also, Madam Satan had the ability to kill men with a single kiss.

In this early appearance from *Pep Comics #17*, you will get a glimpse of her hypnotic and evil ways.

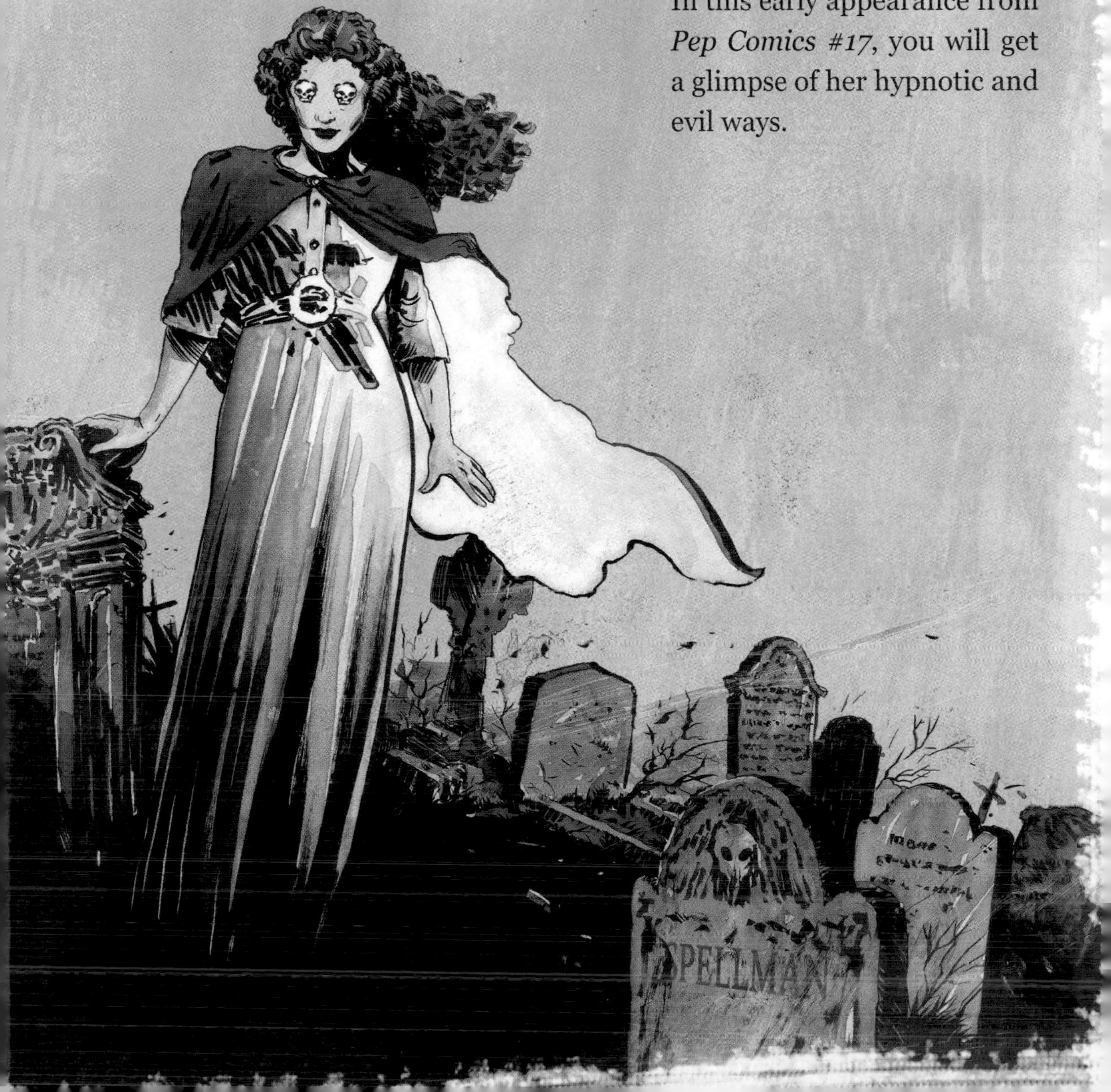

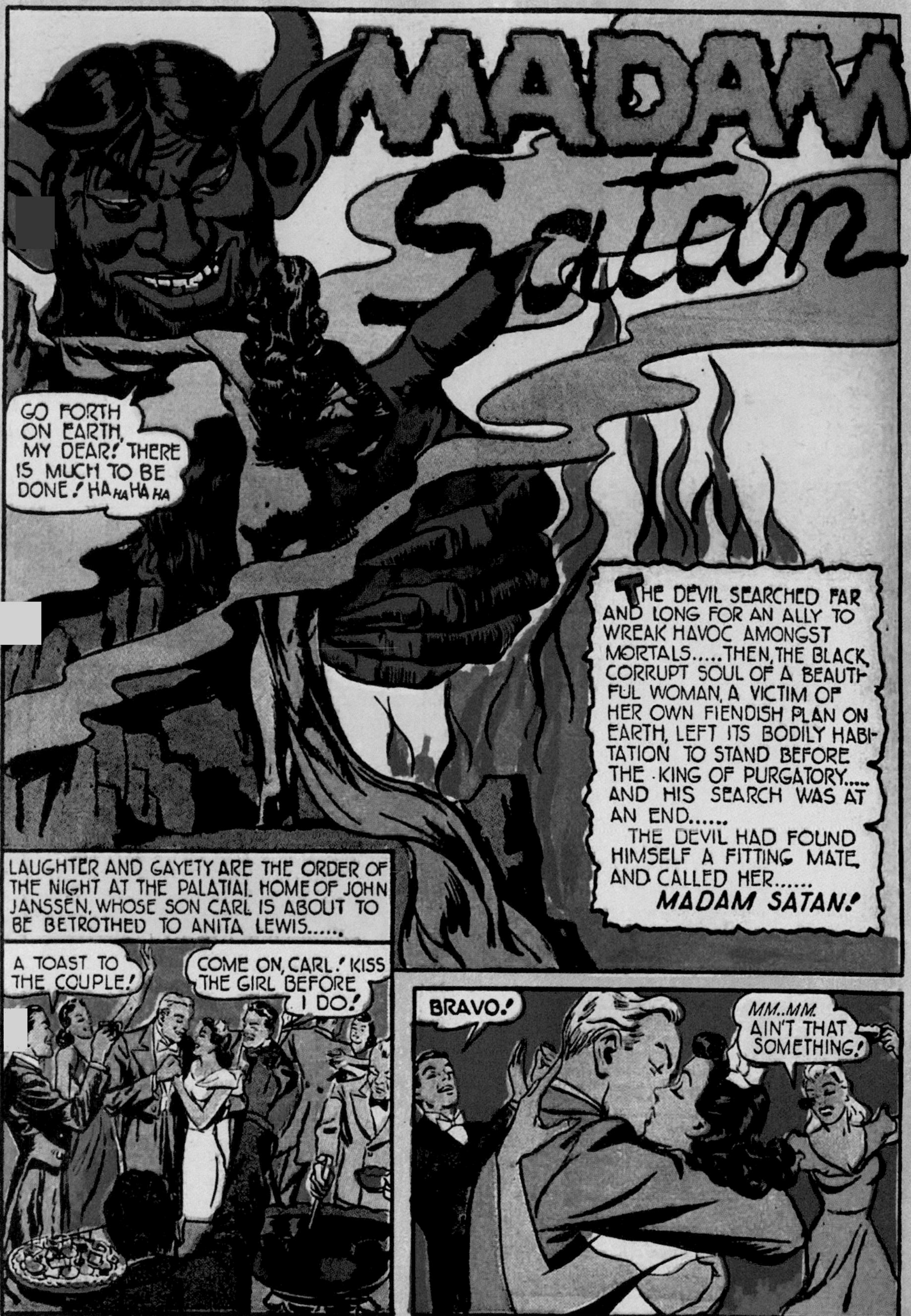
MADAM Satan
GO FORTH ON EARTH, MY DEAR! THERE IS MUCH TO BE DONE! HA HA HA HA
THE DEVIL SEARCHED FAR AND LONG FOR AN ALLY TO WREAK HAVOC AMONGST MORTALS.....THEN, THE BLACK, CORRUPT SOUL OF A BEAUTIFUL WOMAN, A VICTIM OF HER OWN FIENDISH PLAN ON EARTH, LEFT ITS BODILY HABITATION TO STAND BEFORE THE KING OF PURGATORY..... AND HIS SEARCH WAS AT AN END......
THE DEVIL HAD FOUND HIMSELF A FITTING MATE, AND CALLED HER...... MADAM SATAN!
LAUGHTER AND GAYETY ARE THE ORDER OF THE NIGHT AT THE PALATIAL HOME OF JOHN JANSSEN, WHOSE SON CARL IS ABOUT TO BE BETROTHED TO ANITA LEWIS.....
A TOAST TO THE COUPLE!
COME ON, CARL! KISS THE GIRL BEFORE I DO!
BRAVO!
MM..MM. AIN'T THAT SOMETHING!

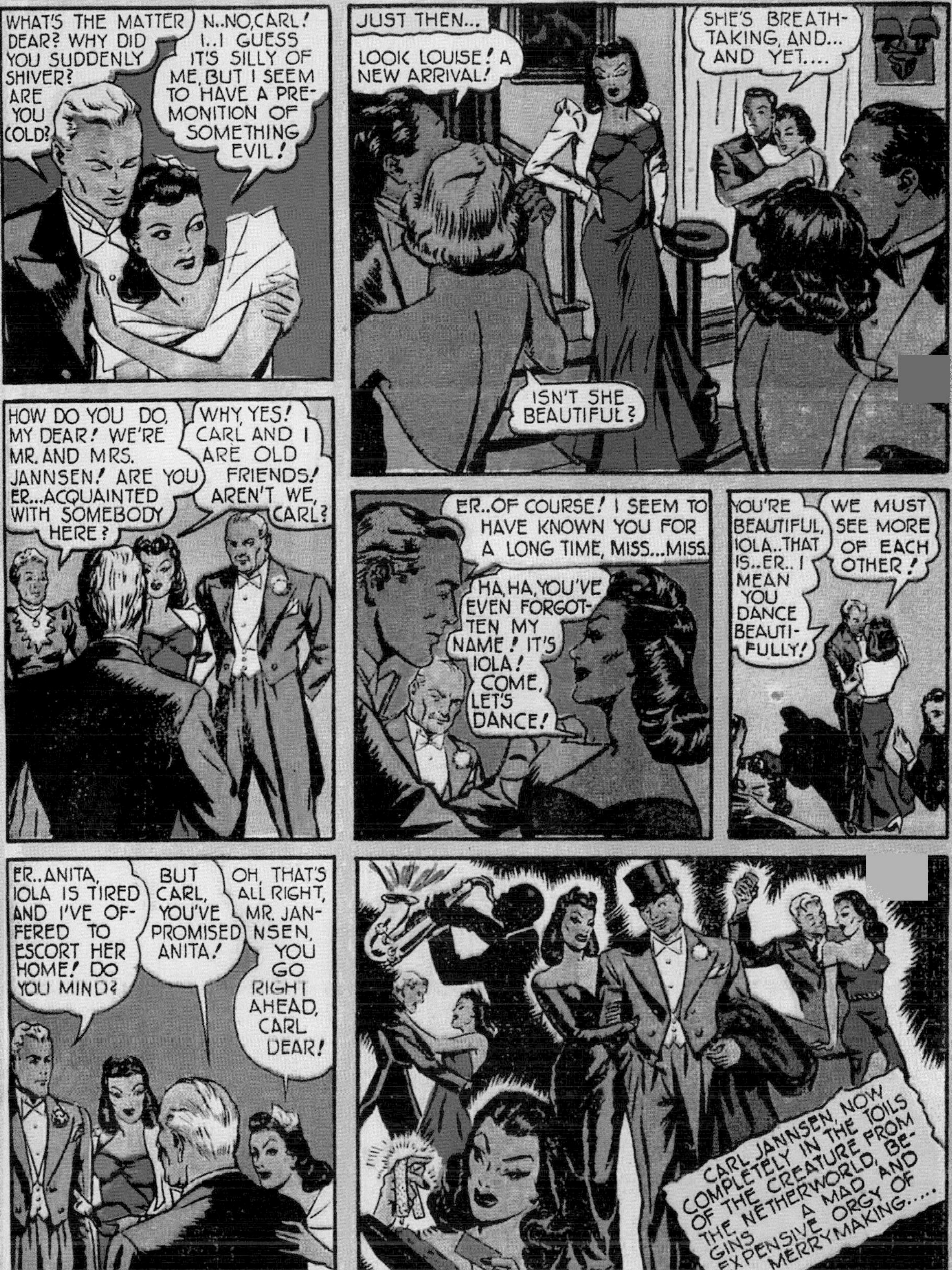

WHAT'S THE MATTER DEAR? WHY DID YOU SUDDENLY SHIVER? ARE YOU COLD?
N..NO, CARL! I..I GUESS IT'S SILLY OF ME, BUT I SEEM TO HAVE A PREMONITION OF SOMETHING EVIL!
JUST THEN...
LOOK LOUISE! A NEW ARRIVAL!
SHE'S BREATH-TAKING, AND... AND YET....
ISN'T SHE BEAUTIFUL?
HOW DO YOU DO, MY DEAR! WE'RE MR. AND MRS. JANNSEN! ARE YOU ER...ACQUAINTED WITH SOMEBODY HERE?
WHY, YES! CARL AND I ARE OLD FRIENDS! AREN'T WE, CARL?
ER..OF COURSE! I SEEM TO HAVE KNOWN YOU FOR A LONG TIME, MISS...MISS.
HA, HA, YOU'VE EVEN FORGOTTEN MY NAME! IT'S IOLA! COME, LET'S DANCE!
YOU'RE BEAUTIFUL, IOLA..THAT IS..ER..I MEAN YOU DANCE BEAUTIFULLY!
WE MUST SEE MORE OF EACH OTHER!
ER..ANITA, IOLA IS TIRED AND I'VE OFFERED TO ESCORT HER HOME! DO YOU MIND?
BUT CARL, YOU'VE PROMISED ANITA!
OH, THAT'S ALL RIGHT, MR. JANNSEN, YOU GO RIGHT AHEAD, CARL DEAR!
CARL JANNSEN, NOW COMPLETELY IN THE TOILS OF THE CREATURE FROM THE NETHERWORLD, BEGINS A MAD AND EXPENSIVE ORGY OF MERRYMAKING....
2

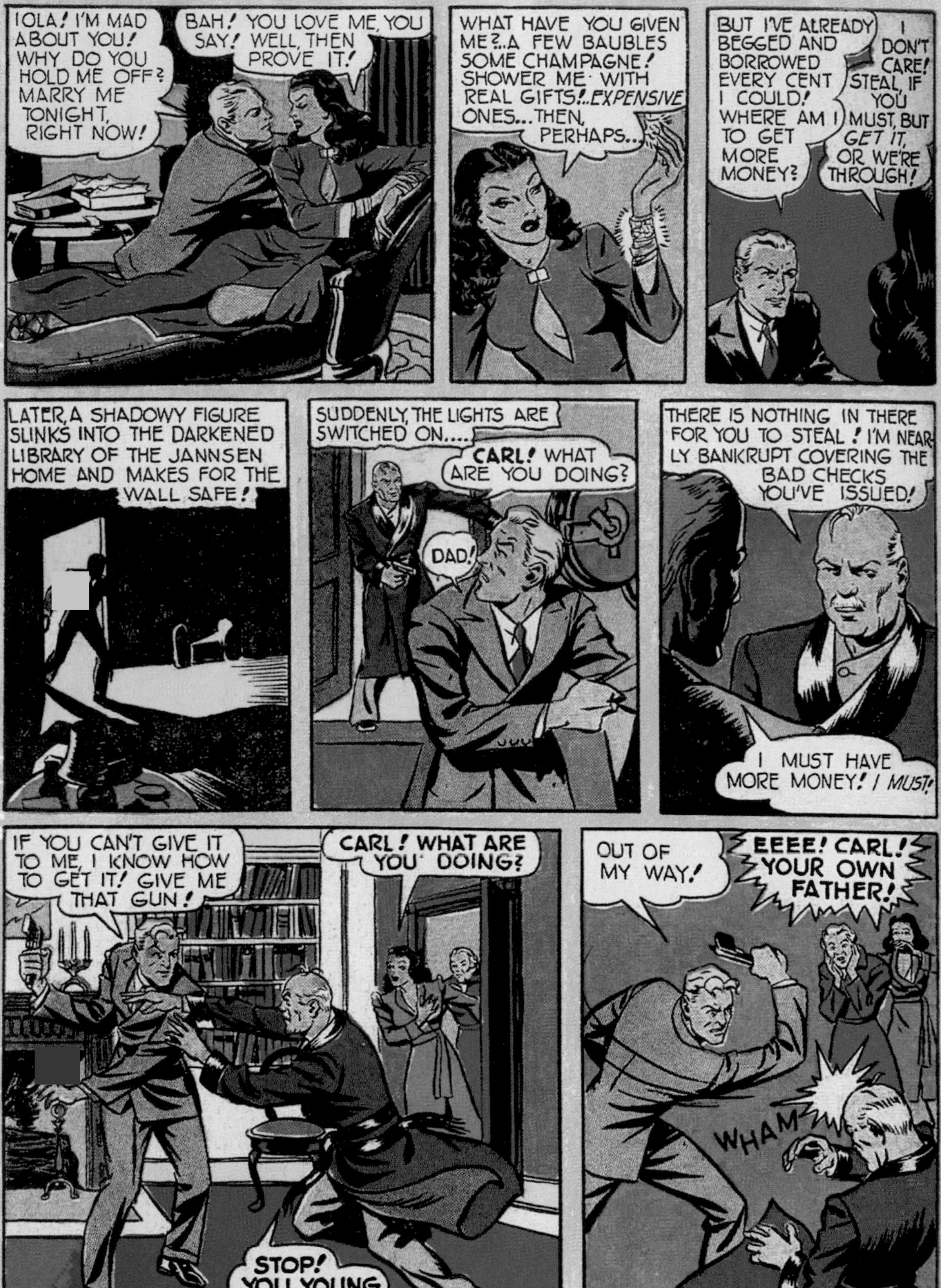
IOLA! I'M MAD ABOUT YOU! WHY DO YOU HOLD ME OFF? MARRY ME TONIGHT, RIGHT NOW!
BAH! YOU LOVE ME, YOU SAY! WELL, THEN PROVE IT!
WHAT HAVE YOU GIVEN ME?..A FEW BAUBLES SOME CHAMPAGNE! SHOWER ME WITH REAL GIFTS!..EXPENSIVE ONES...THEN, PERHAPS...
BUT I'VE ALREADY BEGGED AND BORROWED EVERY CENT I COULD! WHERE AM I TO GET MORE MONEY?
I DON'T CARE! STEAL, IF YOU MUST, BUT GET IT, OR WE'RE THROUGH!
LATER, A SHADOWY FIGURE SLINKS INTO THE DARKENED LIBRARY OF THE JANNSEN HOME AND MAKES FOR THE WALL SAFE!
SUDDENLY, THE LIGHTS ARE SWITCHED ON....
CARL! WHAT ARE YOU DOING?
DAD!
THERE IS NOTHING IN THERE FOR YOU TO STEAL! I'M NEARLY BANKRUPT COVERING THE BAD CHECKS YOU'VE ISSUED!
I MUST HAVE MORE MONEY! I MUST!
IF YOU CAN'T GIVE IT TO ME, I KNOW HOW TO GET IT! GIVE ME THAT GUN!
CARL! WHAT ARE YOU DOING?
STOP! YOU YOUNG FOOL!
OUT OF MY WAY!
EEEE! CARL! YOUR OWN FATHER!
WHAM
3

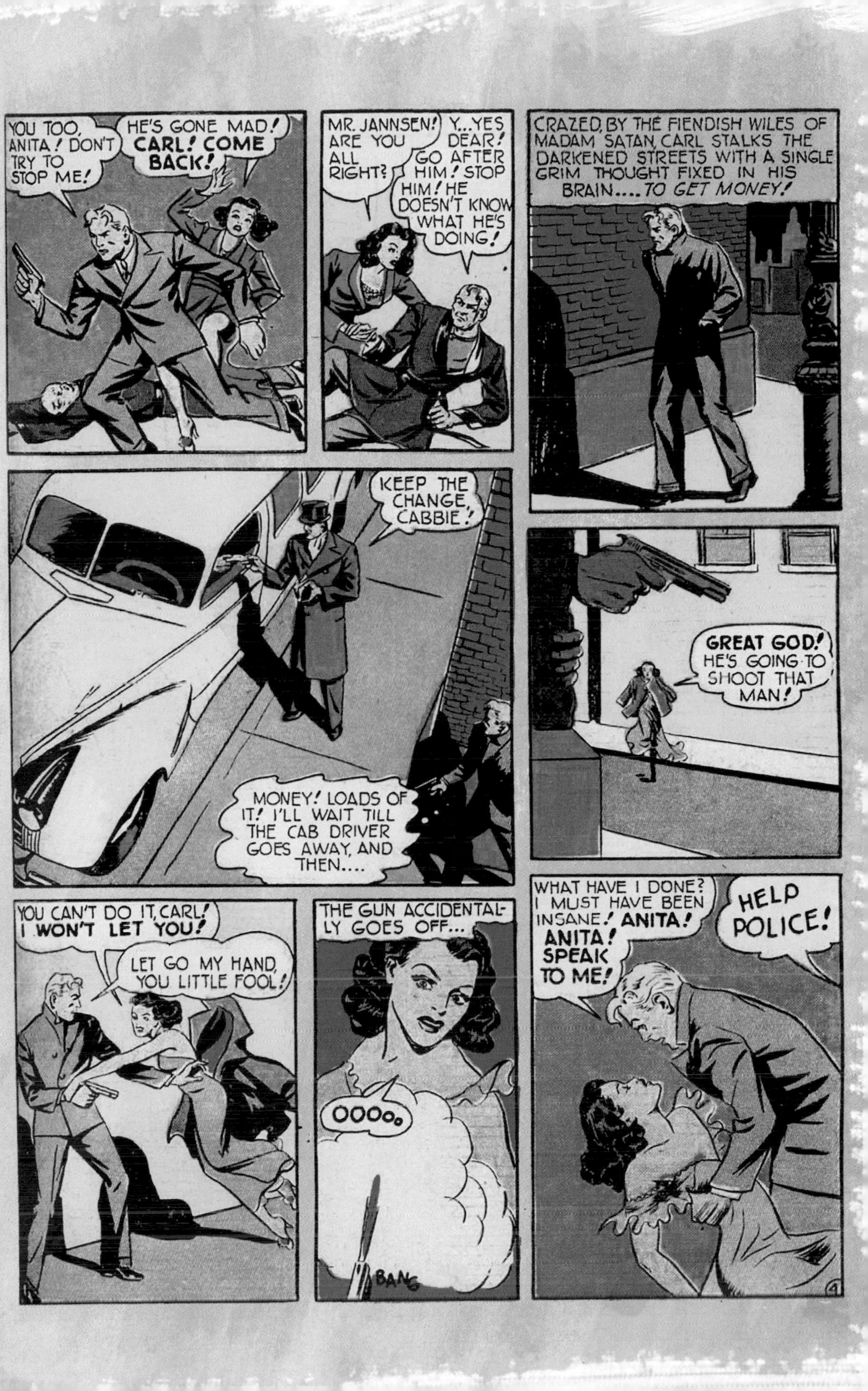
YOU TOO, ANITA! DON'T TRY TO STOP ME!
HE'S GONE MAD! CARL! COME BACK!
MR. JANNSEN! ARE YOU ALL RIGHT?
Y...YES DEAR! GO AFTER HIM! STOP HIM! HE DOESN'T KNOW WHAT HE'S DOING!
CRAZED, BY THE FIENDISH WILES OF MADAM SATAN, CARL STALKS THE DARKENED STREETS WITH A SINGLE GRIM THOUGHT FIXED IN HIS BRAIN.... TO GET MONEY!
KEEP THE CHANGE, CABBIE!
MONEY! LOADS OF IT! I'LL WAIT TILL THE CAB DRIVER GOES AWAY, AND THEN....
GREAT GOD! HE'S GOING TO SHOOT THAT MAN!
YOU CAN'T DO IT, CARL! I WON'T LET YOU!
LET GO MY HAND, YOU LITTLE FOOL!
THE GUN ACCIDENTALLY GOES OFF...
OOOOo
BANG
WHAT HAVE I DONE? I MUST HAVE BEEN INSANE! ANITA! ANITA! SPEAK TO ME!
HELP POLICE!
4

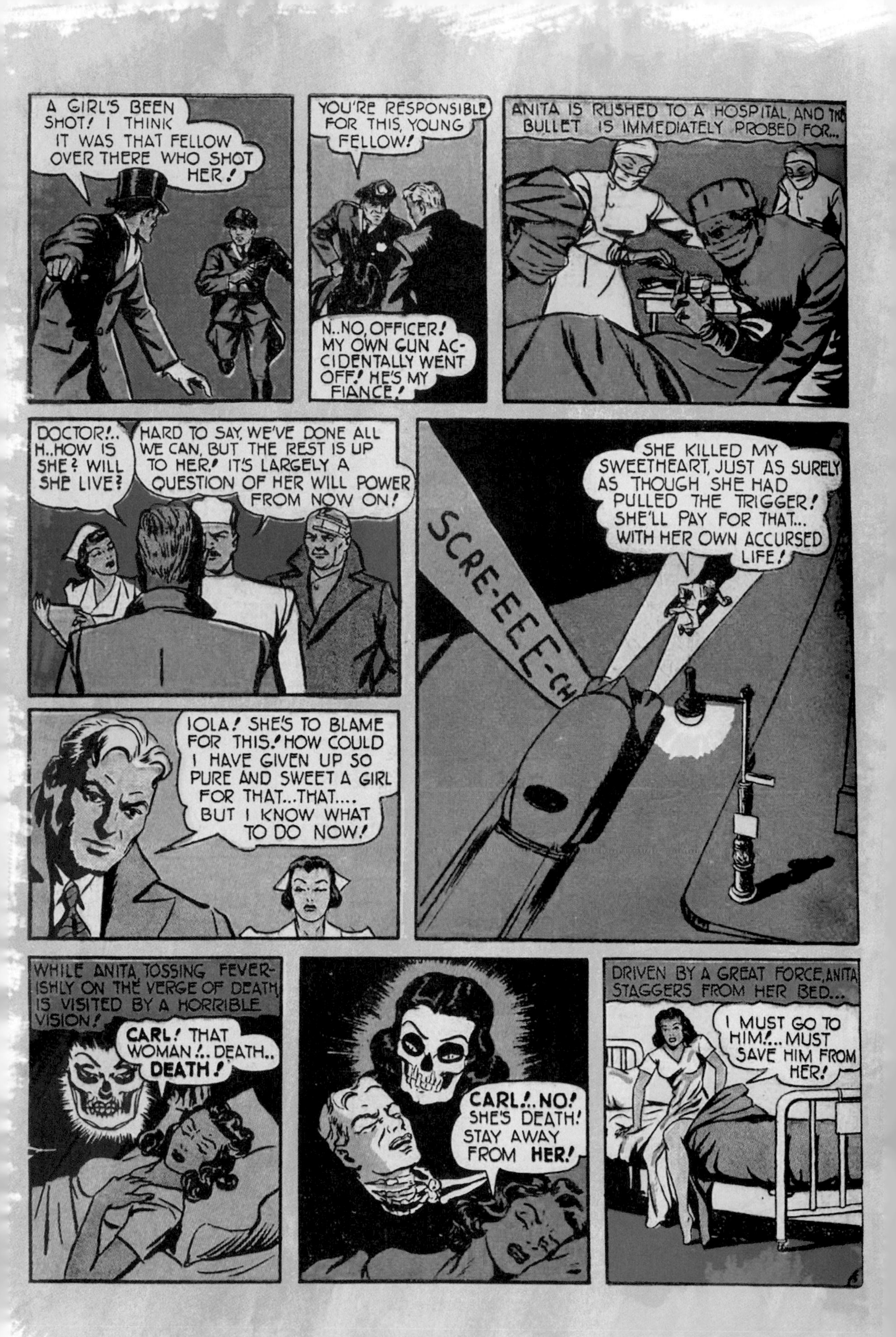
A GIRL'S BEEN SHOT! I THINK IT WAS THAT FELLOW OVER THERE WHO SHOT HER!
YOU'RE RESPONSIBLE FOR THIS, YOUNG FELLOW!
N..NO, OFFICER! MY OWN GUN ACCIDENTALLY WENT OFF! HE'S MY FIANCE!
ANITA IS RUSHED TO A HOSPITAL, AND THE BULLET IS IMMEDIATELY PROBED FOR...
DOCTOR!.. H..HOW IS SHE? WILL SHE LIVE?
HARD TO SAY. WE'VE DONE ALL WE CAN, BUT THE REST IS UP TO HER! IT'S LARGELY A QUESTION OF HER WILL POWER FROM NOW ON!
IOLA! SHE'S TO BLAME FOR THIS! HOW COULD I HAVE GIVEN UP SO PURE AND SWEET A GIRL FOR THAT...THAT.... BUT I KNOW WHAT TO DO NOW!
SCRE-EEEE-CH
SHE KILLED MY SWEETHEART, JUST AS SURELY AS THOUGH SHE HAD PULLED THE TRIGGER! SHE'LL PAY FOR THAT... WITH HER OWN ACCURSED LIFE!
WHILE ANITA, TOSSING FEVERISHLY ON THE VERGE OF DEATH, IS VISITED BY A HORRIBLE VISION!
CARL! THAT WOMAN!.. DEATH.. DEATH!
CARL!..NO! SHE'S DEATH! STAY AWAY FROM HER!
DRIVEN BY A GREAT FORCE, ANITA STAGGERS FROM HER BED...
I MUST GO TO HIM!...MUST SAVE HIM FROM HER!

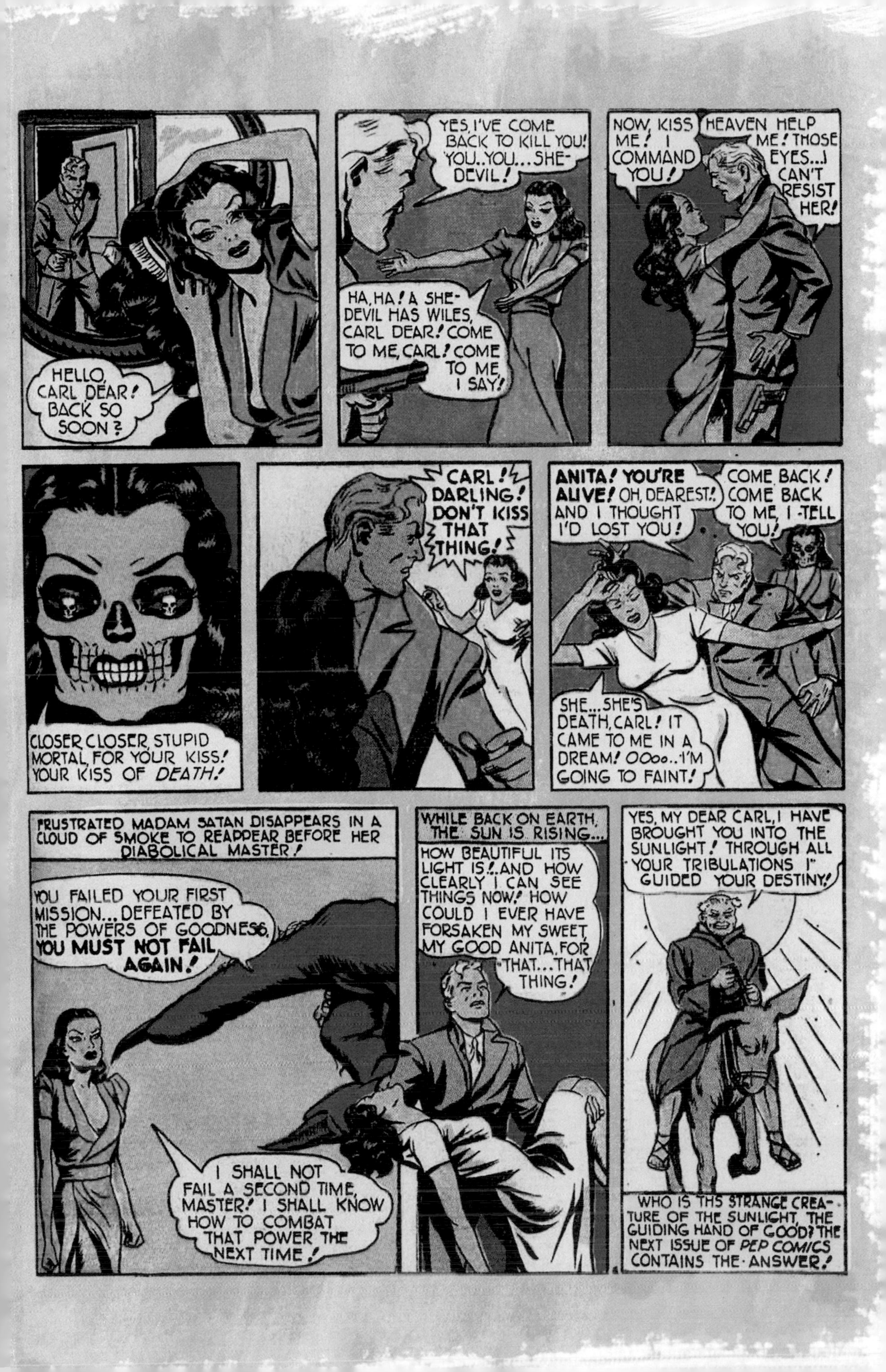
HELLO, CARL DEAR! BACK SO SOON?
YES, I'VE COME BACK TO KILL YOU! YOU..YOU...SHE-DEVIL!
HA, HA! A SHE-DEVIL HAS WILES, CARL DEAR! COME TO ME, CARL! COME TO ME, I SAY!
NOW, KISS ME! I COMMAND YOU!
HEAVEN HELP ME! THOSE EYES...I CAN'T RESIST HER!
CLOSER, CLOSER, STUPID MORTAL, FOR YOUR KISS! YOUR KISS OF DEATH!
CARL! DARLING! DON'T KISS THAT THING!
ANITA! YOU'RE ALIVE! OH, DEAREST! AND I THOUGHT I'D LOST YOU!
COME BACK! COME BACK TO ME, I TELL YOU!
SHE...SHE'S DEATH, CARL! IT CAME TO ME IN A DREAM! OOoo..I'M GOING TO FAINT!
FRUSTRATED MADAM SATAN DISAPPEARS IN A CLOUD OF SMOKE TO REAPPEAR BEFORE HER DIABOLICAL MASTER!
YOU FAILED YOUR FIRST MISSION... DEFEATED BY THE POWERS OF GOODNESS. YOU MUST NOT FAIL AGAIN!
I SHALL NOT FAIL A SECOND TIME, MASTER! I SHALL KNOW HOW TO COMBAT THAT POWER THE NEXT TIME!
WHILE BACK ON EARTH, THE SUN IS RISING...
HOW BEAUTIFUL ITS LIGHT IS!..AND HOW CLEARLY I CAN SEE THINGS NOW! HOW COULD I EVER HAVE FORSAKEN MY SWEET, MY GOOD ANITA, FOR THAT...THAT THING!
YES, MY DEAR CARL, I HAVE BROUGHT YOU INTO THE SUNLIGHT! THROUGH ALL YOUR TRIBULATIONS I'VE GUIDED YOUR DESTINY!
WHO IS THS STRANGE CREATURE OF THE SUNLIGHT, THE GUIDING HAND OF GOOD? THE NEXT ISSUE OF PEP COMICS CONTAINS THE ANSWER!

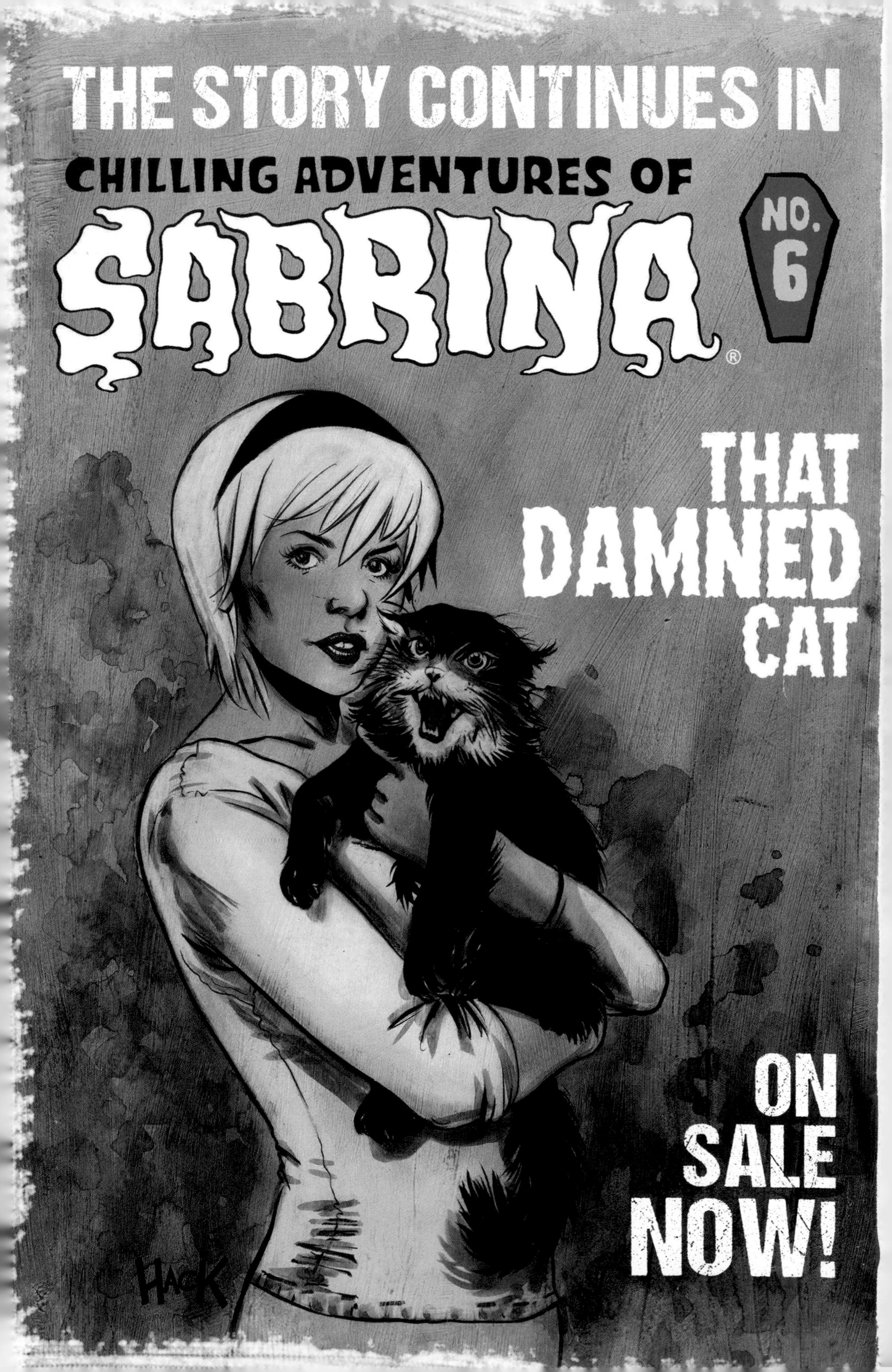
THE STORY CONTINUES IN
CHILLING ADVENTURES OF
SABRINA®
NO. 6
THAT DAMNED CAT
ON SALE NOW!
HACK